Arima's face was shrouded in shadow. Her wide eyes flickered over Melanion's face.

"Arima . . . I . . . ." the goldsmith began, as awkward as a schoolboy.

"I . . . I have waited so long . . . to be with you," she whispered. Melanion closed his fingers around hers. Life was brief enough, and tragic enough; love was all the sweetness it held. He drew her to him.

The taboos screamed "Stop!" but Arima did not stop. The first kiss brushed lightly, led to the next kiss, and the next, each harder, more frantic. Arima lifted her hands and buried them in the tangled curls behind his neck. The strength, the warmth and tenderness of a man overwhelmed her. There could be no wrongness. Melting her will to his, she cast her life and her heart to wherever the fates might take them . . .

Look for Nancy Harding's

The Silver Land

"A marvelous blend of magic, history and romance . . . magnificent."

—*Rave Reviews*

Available from POCKET BOOKS

Nancy Harding

POCKET BOOKS

New York   London   Toronto   Sydney   Tokyo   Singapore

An *Original* Publication of POCKET BOOKS

POCKET BOOKS, a division of Simon & Schuster Inc.
1230 Avenue of the Americas, New York, NY 10020

ISBN: 0-671-64619-2

First Pocket Books printing July 1990

10 9 8 7 6 5 4 3 2 1

POCKET and colophon are registered trademarks of
Simon & Schuster Inc.

Printed in the U.S.A.

dedicated to Arimas everywhere,
who, when faced with the unknown,
choose to plunge ahead

The Scythians have managed one thing better than any other nation on earth; they live in such a way that no one who invades their country can escape destruction.

—*Herodotus*

CONTENTS

PROLOGUE

SCYLAS SAT CROSS-LEGGED ON HIS FAVORITE FELT MAT, LISTENING to the night sounds around him. The thin cold air of winter gave them an insubstantial edge, like visions experienced in the shaman's smoking tent. He heard the wavering keenness of the wind soughing against the leather fence encircling his compound, the low murmur of bundled guards squatting by the campfire, a sudden interrupted snore from a nearby yurt. And he heard the peaceful sleep sounds of the shaggy horses—his horses, the comfort that had been his life for as long as he could remember—telling him that all was well.

He closed his eyes wearily, not wishing to see his encampment any longer, nor the awful immensity of the stars glittering down on him from horizon to horizon, like the all-knowing, unblinking eyes of the gods. No, tonight he would shut it all out; the sleeping men, the taunting wind, the women, even his beloved horses.

He resisted the impulse to flinch when a sudden, stifled

cry came muffled through the heavy felt walls of his yurt. Such a thing was shameful and not to be borne, but this time he would ignore it. Opoea was, after all, no longer young. The woman could be forgiven one small cry.

Fighting the need to stretch his cramped legs, Scylas remained immobile. Remember, he told himself, immobile is the great striped cat of the south, and the stallion, scenting the wind. In such there is strength, cunning, and wisdom. And success. Success for his woman, and for the birth of his child. All life energies must turn to that end this brittle, windswept night.

He opened his eyes slowly, studying the stars overhead. Another cry came, weak and broken like an old, tired mare, and he grunted low in satisfaction. She is a brave woman, worthy to be the wife of a Scyth chief.

Silence returned and he breathed deeply, sucking in the cold and feeling it cut in his throat. He did not turn his head when the gnarled old midwife lifted the decorated felt door of his home. In hasty, hushed words she informed him of the birth he had so long awaited, and at her news his disappointment flared, profound and never-ending.

The child was born a girl.

BOOK 1

ARIMA

But now outside my father's house I am nothing; Yes,
often I have looked on the nature of women thus,
that we are nothing . . .

—*Sophocles*

THE HORSES THUNDERED TOGETHER, TIGHT PACKED AND SNORTing. Their riders, cloaked in dust, cut them free, whirled and turned, guiding their mounts with their knees, their dirty bearded faces grinning fiercely.

"Faster, Bartatua!" old Scylas shouted, leaning forward eagerly over his gelding's close-cropped mane. Of course the horsemen could not hear him through the clamor of hooves and their own cries. No matter. The chief had wagered a good mare on his chief horseman; he did not want to lose it.

The knot of warriors passed sunward, nearly out of sight but for the dust cloud that followed them like locusts. Scylas straightened and stretched his back, his sharp eyes studying the target opposite him. He knew the red-feathered arrow of Bartatua; he could see it at the center of the deer hide. He might just keep his mare after all.

The riders had turned around a distant pillar and now wheeled back toward him. Scylas raised himself on his horse in anticipation. Out of the dust cloud horses emerged, and the individual faces of his men. He grunted. Bartatua was not in the lead.

They drew in front of him, the warriors so tightly packed they seemed to form one creature. One by one, war knives flew at the stuffed target as they passed—Phasus's, Oricus's, his young groom's . . .

Then Bartatua's, its gold-clad ivory handle glinting in the sun. Scylas settled back, satisfied. The mare would stay in his herd.

The knife of Bartatua had split his own red arrow in two.

Arima did not want to admit it, but the osier berry basket was heavy, and awkward, too. The hard willow rods that formed it dug into her hip, and its stiff shape jutted out uncomfortably. Perhaps carrying a child is like this, only frontward instead of to the side, she laughed to herself, refusing to let her mood be sullied by a little discomfort. Up on the sunbaked steppes the heat of late summer had yellowed the tall feather grasses and baked the rich black soil nearly to dust, but here by the wide river, shaded and sheltered by high banks and dense trees, she was cool, refreshed, and happy. And not too far ahead she spied more blackberries, plump and shining like dark jewels in the light.

Picking them was tedious and terribly slow, especially with the care she had to take to keep from snagging the long embroidered sleeves of her wool jacket. It seemed every thorn in the thicket was trying to catch her, and any pulls and tears she might wear home would be a clear indication of what she had been doing. The hands of Urgimas, her slave, flew when she picked berries, but here she was, taking as much time as a blind servant trying to sew! Exasperated, Arima turned the sleeves back to her elbows.

The sun was sliding behind the embankment when the young princess stopped. She'd put in a good afternoon's work. Work! The word had an exhilarating ring to it. Even a lowly osier basket brimming with plump, warm berries was an accomplishment to be proud of, a task successfully completed, a job. She preferred anything to just sitting around all day like most Scoloti women, indulging in gossip and needlework and chafing like tethered horses under the idleness their men forced on them.

Arima stretched her delightfully weary back and inhaled deeply. The coolness of the river could not dispel the sticky humidity of the evening and she suddenly realized her face was damp with sweat, her hands were purple with berry juice, and her arms . . . her arms were covered with tiny red scratches.

She almost didn't care, so buoyant was her mood, but she knew she should. Arima untied her red and black felt boots and laid them on a clean rock. Pulling up her long wool skirt, she knotted it in an awkward lump at one hip and walked toward the river. The late summer's grass, dry and harsh beneath her feet, felt free and wonderful. Near the banks the grass was greener, more supple, and the ground beneath it turned spongy and wet. She stepped into pure, raw mud and it squished between her toes. Arima laughed a sharp, clear peal of delight.

This is life! she smiled, wading into the shallows. The water was cool on her hot face, and it eased the burning scratches on her arms. The river beckoned her to throw off her clothes, to splash and swim, leap and dive like a playful otter or one of the silver fish that investigated her bare pink toes. It teased her, called her, and for a moment the urge was almost overwhelming to respond.

But she didn't dare. Too many uncertainties, too many fears. Suddenly weary, Arima stood ankle-deep in the river, her mood deflated by the heavy reality of her life. It will never be any different, she sighed. I will always be what I am, a slave to the menfolk as surely as Urgimas is a slave to me. Another horse in their herd, another sheep in their flock. Only the men are free.

Scylas handed his gilded skullcup to his groom and watched the distant riverbank. The race was long over, won by Bartatua, as he'd wagered. Not only would he not lose his good mare, he'd won two more, and a young gelding. The day was good.

He narrowed his eyes and steadied his horse in the shifting mass of riders. The young women of his tribe were coming back to camp as evening gathered, in twos and threes like busy geese, chatting happily about the day's business. He knew them all, by sight and by name, daughters and sisters of his fellow warriors. He did not know nor care what a good day for a woman might be, but they all looked content. He was pleased.

Until the last girl and her slave woman came up the path from the river, and no more followed. Scylas turned in sudden irritation to Bartatua. "Fetch her!" he snapped, and the chief horseman did not need to ask who his chief meant.

Arima, his daughter, had wandered again.

The other girls were gone, returned to the camp on the edge of the steppes, by the time Arima and her plump old slave made their way downriver, past the trampled grasses and overturned wooden stools where the wellborn girls had played at the water's edge, attended by dutiful slaves. Their silliness had long been a pleasure for Arima, but not today. Today she felt special, different from the other girls, and she was glad she had made an excuse to go upriver with Urgimas, berry hunting.

The sun was sinking fast and heavy blue shadows filled the low river valley. Looking up, she could see the black forms of two horsemen atop the bluff, their shaggy mounts as still as wood totems. Only the long hair of the men moved in the evening breeze. She knew they were looking for them.

"Hurry!" Urgimas gasped, breaking into as much of a run as her heavy body would allow. "We are late and your father has sent men for us!"

Arima knew she should run, but she didn't want to. "I'll try, Urgimas," she made excuses, "but I am tired."

One of the horses broke away and began descending the path, sinking into the heavy shadows below. "Oh dear Api . . ." Arima gulped, and for a brief instant the idea of running like the wind to appease her father crossed her mind. But no. She'd had a good day, had done a task well. She would take her chances.

Urgimas's frenzied flight stopped when the mounted warrior trotted up to them. His brightly colored felt trousers and long tunic were dirty from a hard day's riding, and the peaked leather cap of a Scoloti warrior was pulled behind his neck, too hot to be worn on a day such as this. He halted across their path, his dark eyes cutting through the slave to fall on a pale-faced Arima.

"Where have you been?" he growled, leaning forward over the horse's clipped mane menacingly. The waning sunlight glinted off the gold earring in his left ear. "Your father sent us to fetch you, and I do not like tending to women." He spat out the last word as if it were poisoned meat. Urgimas flinched, looking from the bearded warrior to Arima. The words of the man seemed to have the opposite effect on her charge, for color suddenly returned to Arima's blanched face and she drew her tall, slim body up to full height.

"I am a princess, Bartatua, a fact you'd best not forget!" she returned his challenge. He sat upright and a slow grin crossed his dusty face.

"A princess! Ha!" He laughed loudly. "A woman is all you are. A wealthy one to warm a wealthy bed, no more. Perhaps mine, eh, princess?" He leered at her, one hand dropping pointedly to his lap, and Arima's face reddened.

"I'd sooner sleep with the horses," she retorted, marching

around him with as much dignity as she could muster. She returned to camp at a leisurely stroll, forcing Bartatua to endure the indignity of accompanying two women as long as she possibly could.

The evening breeze was brisk up on the clifftop and Arima welcomed it. Hurrying her steps, she headed for the clustered round yurts and the large fire blazing in the center of camp like one great, all-seeing eye. The smell of boiling mutton came to her and her stomach rumbled in sudden hunger. Bartatua hailed Orontas, his companion, who waited at the edge of the encampment, impatient to join him. But he knew his duty, and the punishments if he failed to escort Arima back to camp.

He left the two women when they passed the outer tents of the herdsmen and laborers. Arima and Urgimas turned toward the large, gaily decorated yurt of the chief's wife, Opoea, sitting by itself away from the campfire. Already men were gathering around the great fire, drawn by food and drink and camaraderie. Arima, as she must, entered the low doorway of her mother's yurt, waiting for her eyes to adjust to the gloom and missing the brisk freshness of the evening outside.

"Arima! Are you alright?" Opoea called out, pushing a sleek grey cat from her lap and rising from the piled deer-hair cushions of her bed. She was an old woman, almost old enough to be Arima's grandmother; far too old, it seemed, to really be Arima's mother.

"I am fine," the girl answered softly. "Rest yourself, Mother. The men are eating, so dinner will be brought soon, when they are through. But see! Urgimas and I have a fine basket of blackberries, plump and sweet and still warm from the sun. Here, Mother, have some."

Arima crossed the circular room, her servant at her heels, and sat the osier basket on the thickly carpeted floor by Opoea's bed. Why must these dwellings be so padded, the girl wondered to herself, so stifling and cushioned, smokey and dark, when outside the air is fresh and sweet and clean? It is as if we women must live in wombs, close and warm, all our lives.

Opoea took a handfull of the berries and lay back on her embroidered cushions, savouring them. Her daughter sank to the bedding beside her. "Come!" the old woman said to Arima, waving to a slave squatting nearby, "wash before the meal arrives. Perhaps some clean clothes? You look tired and dusty."

"No, Mother, I am fine," Arima smiled, taking some berries to ease her hunger. She knew she would have to dress later, when the tent was dark and the scratches on her arms would be hidden. They watched the low hearth fire and listened to the laughter of the feasting men outside, feeling their hunger grow. It was night when a harried slave brought their food—a portion of the sheep's liver from the chief to his wife, and a small clay pot full of simmering meats and broth for the rest. Urgimas poured water over Arima's hands to clean them, ladled broth and meat into a shallow silver bowl, and handed it to her mistress. Arima had barely eaten when Bartatua stepped through the door, the smells of chill night air and maleness radiating from him into the warm yurt.

"Come," he motioned to Arima. "Scylas would speak to you."

The girl lowered her greasy fingers from her mouth and cast a quick glance at her mother. The old woman's pallor had increased. This was not right, this summoning of a woman at night, during mealtime. Something evil was afoot. Opoea handed her bowl to her slave and stood abruptly, her body nearly as slim and lithe as her daughter's.

"Alone, woman," the warrior shot a pointed glance at Opoea. "She is to come alone."

There was nothing the chief's wife could do. Her meal

sinking in her stomach, Opoea sat on the cushions and watched her daughter go.

Scylas was a tall man for a Scoloti, and his long greying hair still glinted copper in the flaring campfire light. He sat cross-legged on a fleecy sheepskin mat, the gold earring in his left ear and the gold disks and ornaments stitched to his clothes catching and reflecting the light as if he were a god. He barely glanced at his daughter when she appeared on the heels of his chief horseman, Bartatua. She was becoming a beauty, no question, and his keen eyes saw the looks of hunger on the faces of many of the men gathered there when they saw her. Yes, she was seventeen winters of age. Soon a good marriage, a good price, a good alliance would be made for her.

He grunted an angry greeting to the girl. She had inherited his height and was almost too tall for a woman, her deep blue eyes and raven hair a striking contrast to her fine ivory skin. Her mother had raised her well, but too indulgently.

"Where were you today?" he muttered, chewing a piece of mutton fat and refusing to look at her. "The other girls came back, and you were not with them. Where were you?"

"I walked upriver," she began, keeping her voice submissive.

"Alone?" Scylas snapped, favoring her with a brief, hostile glance.

"No, not alone. My slave was with me."

"That woman? That old Medean woman? That was not wise, girl. The Medes are not to be trusted. What were you doing upriver?"

"We walked. Urgimas collected berries. I waded in the water. That was all." She saw him motion to Bartatua and the guard took her arm, pulling it forward despite her struggles and weak protests. Scylas leaned closer and looked at her hand.

"Scratches, eh?" he mused. She could hear several of the

warriors chuckling, and her fear turned her stomach when her father suddenly ripped the sleeve upward on her arm.

"And more scratches!" he fumed. Arima slumped, feeling only the pain from Bartatua's grip squeezing her flesh.

"You lie!" Scylas barked, reaching up and striking her full across the face with the palm of his hand. Arima stumbled and the chief horseman pulled her upright. "Scoloti do not lie!" her father repeated, slapping her again. She waited for more punishment—a beating, curses, threats. Scylas settled to his fleece mat, picked up his bowl, and resumed eating. Bartatua released her and she sagged to her knees, her head spinning. The warrior, too, returned to his meal. Kneeling upright, the girl waited for a word from her father, some command, a dismissal, and with every silent moment that passed her hatred grew. Scylas never spoke another word, and the hatred gave way to vengeance. Yes, she was a woman, but she was also a Scoloti, and he would never get the better of her. Never.

Arima knelt in pain and silence as the night passed, her head hanging low, fighting the urge to cry, to flee, to kill him. She knelt while the warriors left the campfire one by one, guards positioned themselves around the encampment, and the horses were penned for the night. Curious camp dogs came up to investigate her and, bored, quickly left. She could feel her cheek swelling, stiffening beneath the bruises, and thought of the beating that awaited poor Urgimas in the morning.

And still she knelt, humiliation engulfing her revenge, the men going about their lives as if she didn't exist. Until finally, with the night half-turned above her, Arima's mother came and led her to her bed.

The cushions of her bed cradled Arima's throbbing cheek; the warm familiar smell of the lambswool felt soothed the humiliation in her soul.

"Here," Opoea said, rising from the hearth, a golden cup in hand. "Some broth left from the meal. It will calm you."

Arima turned her head away wordlessly, facing the darkness of the thick felt wall.

"Let me undress you," her mother persisted, intending to be kind but drawing only annoyance from her daughter. At the feel of one boot-tie being drawn, Arima whirled and twisted upright.

"No!" she hissed, trying to control the emotion in her voice. "Please, Mother. Leave me, I will do it myself." Urgimas looked up from her place near the doorway, fighting the fear in her own heart and surprised at her charge's sudden hostility. It has been a long day for her, she knew; first the unaccustomed physical labor and then her father's humiliation of her. The girl must be careful, she thought, or more disasters will surely follow.

Opoea drew back, startled, and Arima felt shame at her harshness. Her mother's life was drawing to a close, and her time had not been an easy one. She had also suffered long at the hands of Scylas the Chief.

"Just leave me, please," the girl muttered, her voice suddenly tired. Opoea withdrew to her own bed, seating herself and stretching out her arms for her slave to wash them before she retired. She did not cast another look at her daughter.

Arima slumped and drew a hand across her swollen face, nursing her rage as if it were a balm that could somehow heal her. Nothing to do about it now, she thought. Nothing to do about it ever, really; this she knew, deep in her heart, but she avoided facing it. She gazed around the darkened yurt. Not until everyone else was asleep did she allow herself the peace of slumber. . . .

. . . The world was a misty wonder of soft green and warm yellow, the steppes carpeted with small red tulips and low iris, yellow, blue, and violet. An innocent springtime, with the wind a happy whisper far removed from her cares and woes. Arima awoke to this magic, her eyes seeing mosses and grasses and a patch of newly opened clover by her nose. Puzzled, she sat up. The sky shimmered pale gold, like the foil adorning Scylas's royal bed. Standing, she gazed around; as far as she could see there was only vast, empty steppes, splashes of bright flowers, and the sky.

At a sudden sound, a sound she knew well, Arima turned. Hoofbeats pounded into the soft black loam and echoed through the heavens above. Galloping wild and fierce and free, a tattoo as endless as a heartbeat, and the beast was coming toward her.

She gasped aloud at the wonder of it, the sheer awesome beauty. A great grey stallion, its coat soft and gleaming like a river's morning fog, raced in her direction, mane and tail unclipped, flying free of any hindering Scoloti adornments. It rushed past her so closely that the wind in its wake blew her hair aside, and only the gleam of fire in its large dark eye as it looked at her in passing gave any hint the creature knew she was there.

Arima held her breath and turned to watch the beast. Away it pounded, vanishing from sight like a puff of smoke and leaving behind only the mighty echo of its hoof-beats.

On and on . . . Or was it her heart, beating wildly? Or was it . . . ?

Arima opened her eyes to grey morning light and the sound of rhythmic, repeated pounding, almost in time to the throbbing of her swollen cheek, and she knew there was no horse at all. It was only a dream, a dream brought on by her aching bruise and the morning beat of slave women, pounding animal hair into new felt for winter.

There was no horse. The thought drove into her with each incessant thud and a sudden despair gripped her. So that was what it was like, freedom, and only in dreams would she ever know such power, such wonder.

Sighing, she summoned Urgimas and rose to dress herself.

A yurt was a beautiful thing, a marvel of design and utility, and the royal yurts especially were bright jewels on the vast empty reaches of the steppes. With thick walls of heavy felt padding lashed down over circular frames of birch and willow, the tents shimmered color, from the wide woven straps that held down the walls to the brilliant felt cutouts of fantastic beasts, griffons and eagles, antlered stags and wild cats that decorated the walls. Outside, above the juncture of roof and wall, were swirled and interlaced felt designs of red and blue, yellow, black, and green to confuse the evil spirits that inhabited the dark nights and harsh winds and to keep them from entering the safety of the family's dwelling. Above and around the rolled felt doorway of Scylas's yurt plaques of gold glittered in the sunlight and long tufts of dyed horse's tails fluttered in the wind. They were a symbol of his wealth in herds and a badge of his rank as chief of the Auchatae, one of four branches of the fierce nomadic Scoloti. They were not of the Royal tribe, but like them, the Auchatae were descended from the sons of Targitaus, the god who was the progenitor of all the Scoloti peoples, called Scythian by the Greeks. Long ago the god gave his people four sacred objects with which to survive and conquer their harsh domain: the plow, yoke, battle-ax, and golden drinking cup. But it was the Scythians themselves who came upon the real source of their power over their neighbors—the horse. Without the horse, the Scyth was no more than a small, poor farmer, tied to the land and to his crops. With it, he was all-powerful, roaming, conquering, demanding and receiving tribute from the traders passing through his lands from the far north to the Greek trading posts on the shores of the great Northern Sea below them. The horse was freedom, power, life, and the Scyth tribes wandered wherever it was necessary to keep their herds healthy and well-fed.

This day the yurts of Scylas's people were being dismantled under a heavy autumn sky. Arima sat on a carved and painted wooden chest, waiting for the packing to end. Every tent, from the humble grey dwellings of the laborers and slaves to the splendid homes of her father and mother, lay on the ground, a jumble of rolled mats and carpets and felt hangings, wicker frameworks lashed together so cunningly that the entire circle of a yurt's wall could be folded in on itself until it was no more than a large bundle of sticks. In the distance the livestock was moving; horses, mostly, for Scylas considered anything else to be a woman's keeping. Still, he kept a small flock of sheep for wool and hides and meat, and oxen for transportation.

Arima could see why the horses were her father's first love. Her eyes roamed from the wagons being loaded to the milling, moving herd of animals. Warriors galloped beside them, their leather caps thrown behind their necks to let their hair stream free. Camp dogs ran alongside, silent and eager, and black ravens rose and wheeled at the din, tossed on the wind with the gusting autumn leaves. How she envied the men their freedom, the never-ending new experiences in their lives, the fierce pleasure they seemed to take in everything . . . and no one to answer to but Scylas. What must such a life be like!

"Arima!"

A sharp call from her mother roused the girl. Their wagons were loaded, except for the chest upon which she sat. Arima stood and two slaves removed it.

Opoea rested comfortably atop piled cushions in a large four-wheeled wagon. Its top was covered with bent willow rods supporting light felt pads, forming a secluded home on wheels. The old woman's long grey hair was pinned up beneath an embroidered circular cap, and her body concealed by a red silk cloak. Conscious of her position as Scylas's wife, she wore many dangling gold earrings and bracelets that jingled cheerily when she moved. She motioned Arima to come and join her. Wishing instead for the horseback freedom of the men, the girl climbed into the wagon; women were never allowed on horses.

"Why so sad?" Opoea asked, seeing the downcast look on Arima's face. Her daughter picked up their grey cat and settled herself on the cushions, gazing pensively through the front of the wagon, toward the distant, moving herds.

"Why can't women ride horses, Mother?" she whispered, stroking the cat absently.

Opoea's face grew grim. This was a side of her daughter that she did not like to see. "Hush, girl!" she scolded. "We are forbidden, and it has been that way since the time of Targitaus. You must accept it; like a tamed horse or hunting dog by the fire, a woman must let the men decide what's best for her."

Arima shot her mother an angry glance. "But we are not animals, Mother!" she spat. "We are people. We think and feel as the men do, yet we are less in their eyes than their horses. They at least have the freedom to run, to feel the sun when it shines, the cleansing rain, the moon and stars above them."

"And our freedom is submitting to our husbands and sons and fathers. They have knowledge of the world we know nothing of, and we must trust and accept their judgements for us." Adding emphasis to her words, Opoea pulled Arima's long green travelling cloak over the girl's lap and bared ankles. She must, somehow, make her daughter understand, but she could see by the glint in Arima's blue eyes that she remained unswayed. She feared for her daughter's future.

"I will never submit . . ." she heard the girl breathe, and for a brief instant her troubled eyes took on the fire of an untamed stallion. Opoea turned away, sick at heart, as the wagon began to move.

They were headed for their wintering grounds, a journey of many days, leaving behind them the vast summer pastures of the north. To the south the yurts and herds could be sheltered on the broad plains beside the river, protected from the intensity of winter on the open steppes.

With nightfall the wind grew cold, blowing away the heavy clouds and chilling the tribe with a bitter foretaste of winter. A large, plain yurt was hastily erected for the seclusion of the women, who enjoyed the chance to chat and socialize; the men, even Scylas, slept under the stars, rolled in thick sheepskins.

Scylas listened to the crude talk of his warriors and watched a spitted sheep over the fire drip sizzling fat into the flames. He was old—too old, perhaps—and this current journey and the night's cold made him only too aware of it. His thoughts turned to his own eventual death, a subject he preferred to avoid, while he waited for the meat to cook. The time had come for him to make provisions for his future, and the future of the Auchatae people he led. Yet he had no son, no heir to pass his rank to. Only Arima.

He spat noisily to the ground and the warriors fell silent, looking at him with puzzled glances. The old chief lifted his head and gazed defiantly around the campfire, and his men returned to their talk.

A lifetime of trying, he brooded, returning his stare to the sheep, and only Arima to show for it. Many women, one wife, and his only offspring was—has Tabiti of the Hearth cursed me?—a girl. The only recourse left to him was to marry her off to a suitable heir. Someone capable, trusted.

His eyes shifted immediately to Bartatua, his chief warrior, laughing loudly at a tale just told to him. He was capable, honest, quick-witted, born of the Auchatae by both his mother and father. Perhaps ten years older than Arima, he was old enough, experienced enough, to be able to handle her. He already had a wife, only one. But that would be no problem, Scylas shrugged to himself. She could be made subordinate to Arima. And Bartatua would be made his heir.

Scylas called the man's name and the chief warrior looked in his direction with surprise. He had a clean, open face and it was hard for the man to hide his emotions well; and this fact, too, Scylas liked about him. He could be read like the weather signs in the clouds. Scylas motioned with one hand and Bartatua rose, his trim body as supple as a great cat's. The old chief, too, was on his feet and together they walked toward the hastily penned horses and away from prying ears.

Bartatua was puzzled, his fingers absently toying with the sheathed arrows and bow at his left side. Scylas turned, his fierce brown eyes suddenly boring into him. "Have you any complaints with your life?" the chief blurted unceremoniously. Bartatua was taken aback by the question and gave no answer.

"Your position as my chief warrior? Your horses? Your wife and hearth? Is it all well with you, then?" the old man continued. The warrior tried to suppress a frown as he pondered an answer. What such questions might mean.

"My life is good, Scylas," Bartatua began. Perhaps his chief was unhappy with his performance? "And my wife is well.

"But the horses seem restive," the warrior continued. "They know winter approaches, and they do not look forward to their long confinement. Your herd increased greatly with the last foaling, Scylas." He laughed in what he hoped was a good-natured gesture. The chief's guarded expression never changed. "More than the number of your warriors and slaves increased. The beasts are harder to handle."

"And what of your future?" Scylas interrupted him. His dark piercing eyes seemed to be probing Bartatua's soul.

"My future?" The question caught the warrior off-guard. "I am a warrior, and will amass a small herd of my own, sire some children, and die warm and dry in my own bed, if I'm lucky."

"Children?" Scylas perked up. "Have you any now?"

Bartatua shook his head.

"And how long has she been your woman?" Scylas pressed.

"Eight winters."

"And no children?" The chief seemed dismayed. "Perhaps you should put her aside and take another woman to wife."

Bartatua hesitated. He was genuinely fond of his woman. She was a comfort to him when he needed comfort, she knew his tastes and his quirks like a rider knows his horse. Another woman?

"But, Scylas," the warrior began, "your own wife was married many times eight winters before she gave you a child. Some women are odd that way. There is time . . ."

Scylas looked at him icily, and Bartatua suddenly realized the old man had a plan in mind for him. If he was wise he would go along with it.

"I will give you another wife, man," the chief said levelly, seeming to dare defiance, "and a new position. But first, fetch some wine."

Bartatua obeyed. Either the old man was suddenly thirsty, or there was an oath in the offing. He returned shortly, carrying Scylas's gold skull-cup full of undiluted Greek wine.

"My offer," the chief announced, taking the cup. "Wed my daughter, and become my heir."

Bartatua was glad for the shadows of evening, for they hid the paleness of his face when the blood drained from it. Arima? Heir? The words seemed scarcely real. And yet they were real, for Scylas was reaching for the long iron dagger strapped to his right thigh. Following his lead, the warrior

21

drew his own knife. It was to be a blood oath, binding and eternal.

"Do you agree to my proposal?" Scylas hissed fiercely through the gathering darkness. Wordlessly, Bartatua nodded. The two men knelt, long knives in hand, and Scylas placed the gilded skull on the ground between them.

"It is sworn, then," Scylas muttered, slashing his left palm with the knife.

"It is sworn," Bartatua agreed, doing the same. Each dripped blood into the wine and Scylas stirred it with his knife point. Raising the cup, he drank a long draught and handed it to the warrior. No more words were spoken; nothing needed to be said.

The oath was sealed.

"In spring?"

The words eased from Arima's mouth like blood seeping from a wound. The dreaded day, the dreaded fate, at last approached. "To Bartatua . . ." The sentence died, too horrid to be completed.

The tribe had arrived at its wintering grounds the day before, and only when they were settled had Scylas announced the news to his daughter.

"Spring." the girl repeated, wanting to turn away, to flee the suddenly oppressive confines of her father's spacious yurt, but not daring such disobedience. Scylas sat cross-legged near his hearth, sternly erect and refusing the comfort of the cushions piled behind him. He had ordered the tent emptied; only his old blind cook remained, stirring a kettle of boiled rabbit and millet and ignoring the scene before him.

Arima didn't know what to do. Her father obviously expected a reply, though she knew it was only a formality. The oath between Scylas and Bartatua was sealed. The man who owned her now had bargained her away to a new owner, and there was no answer she could give.

"Please . . ." she sobbed aloud, tears filling her eyes. Scylas stared stonily at the small dung fire before him, refusing to see his daughter's anguish.

"Father, please!" Arima repeated. In sudden desperation she stepped across the carpets and threw herself at the chief's feet. "I beg you, Father, don't do this terrible thing! I wish to marry no one, least of all Bartatua. Please, Father!" She buried her face in the bright wool and gold ornaments of his trousers and reached imploringly for his hands. Feeling his callused fingers, she closed her own soft hands tightly around them. His hands remained as unmoving as if they had been carved of wood. An abrupt, real terror rose at the certainty of her fate, and the girl broke into a muffled wail.

"Please," she begged. "I will remain unmarried. I will care for you and mother in your old age. I will see to your herds and—"

"Bah!" Scylas spat at the improbability of this last statement. His patience had worn out with this filly he had sired. With a mighty shove of his hands, he flung Arima backward and stood.

"Enough, girl!" he fumed, stalking toward the door. "It is sworn. A blood oath. You will marry, you will give me heirs to inherit my wealth, you will do as you are told. An unmarried woman is as useless a burden as a horse with no feet. What place has Api the Earth Mother for either of them, eh?"

"No! Father. No!" Arima screamed, pulling herself to her knees. "Not Bartatua! Anyone else but him."

"Old father time, then?" Scylas laughed aloud, pointing to the blind, toothless ancient placidly stirring his kettle.

"Yes! Anyone, Father, but not—"

"Marry him and be a slave, too, eh?" Scylas shouted back, his rage breaking. In two swift strides he was on the sobbing girl, seizing her long black hair in one hand and an upraised forearm in the other. Savagely he jerked her to her feet. "Then see how it is to be a slave, girl, and learn a little obedience as you do. May the gods help Bartatua in breaking you, for I have had little enough luck at it."

His old muscles were still powerful, and he dragged the struggling girl from his yurt, past snickering warriors and a red-faced Bartatua, drawn to the sounds of the fighting. Past the two plain tents of the enaree he went, the half-men standing outside their dwellings, dismayed at the discord. He carried her to the herd of penned sheep. "A slave is it?" he shouted, lifting her into the air. Arima flailed at him, screaming her defiance.

"I will not, Father, never, never!"

"Sheep are a woman's work," he barked, and heaved her over the wicker fence. "Then clean them!"

Arima sprawled across the muddy, manured ground as the sheep bolted in fright. She lay still, her face hidden in one arm, nurturing her defiance.

"And stay there till the fold is spotless!" Scylas shouted. His booted feet were silent in the crushed tall grasses as he turned and strode away. She knew it was an endless task he had assigned to her, and that she would stay with the sheep, live with the sheep, until he chose to free her.

For three days Arima dwelt in the sheepfold, her red and blue and gold skirt soiled with mud and dung, her hair matted, her embroidered felt jacket offering scant protection from the abrupt chill of the autumn nights. Then she would huddle with the dozing ewes, seeking warmth from the dense wool on their bodies. They adjusted to her presence, almost accepted her as one of them, and she wondered if she might sooner become a sheep than a docile married woman. The only visitor she had during those three lonely days, the only person in camp who dared to cross Scylas's wrath was Lipos, the younger of the two enaree residing with the Auchatae Scyths.

He strode up to the wicker fence deliberately that first dawn, daring anyone to stop him. Three of Scylas's warriors at first seemed ready to do just that, but paused and withdrew. Lipos was left to go about his business unchallenged.

Arima squatted on the far side of the pen, leaning against the lashed saplings of the fence, hoping the milling sheep would hide her from curious eyes. When she saw Lipos approach, her first instinct was to ignore him. She didn't like the half-men. They seemed an aberration of the natural order of things, as if hares could suddenly fly or fish walk about on land. The gods made the world as it was supposed to be, and one did not tamper with that.

"Here," the enaree said quietly, extending a leather sack over the fence. To her the half-men had always been fearsome figures, secluded and unsocial, seen in some smokey tent where illness dwelt, working their cures, or around a bonfire in the darkness of night, summoning up their magics for the good of the tribe: a bountiful foaling season, a good hunt, defeat of an enemy. But here, in the soft golden light of dawn, a morning breeze stirring his long yellow hair, Lipos looked neither fearsome nor unnatural, only kind. Arima stood and walked toward him, slouching to diminish her height among the sheep.

"Food." The enaree smiled, watching the hungry girl open the sack. He had best prepare the women's purification tent, he mused, and the mashed herbs and spices to be used, for this poor, smelly creature would need a good cleaning when Scylas relented.

Arima's deep blue eyes studied him, wary yet grateful, as she tore a piece of flat wheat cake with her teeth.

"Good?" Lipos smiled. Arima smiled slightly and nodded a reply. In the dawning light, with his reddened cheeks and lips and dangling gold earrings, Arima could almost take him to be a woman.

"Are you injured?" the enaree asked gently.

"No," the girl muttered between mouthfuls. "Only my pride."

"Ah!" He wagged a slim finger at her. "That is the cause of all your woes, Arima! Women should have little pride in themselves, more in their husbands and their children."

Her gaze hardened at hearing the same tired words she'd heard so many times before. From mother, from grandmother, from Urgimas. Words of advice, all wasted.

"Is that why you are enaree?" she hissed sarcastically. "Your pride is more than a woman's, not quite that of a man?"

His kind expression didn't falter. He'd been challenged by better wits than hers and won every time.

"No. I am enaree because my good sense is greater than either's. By being both, I am neither, and save myself a lot of grief in the process."

Arima relented. She liked his answer and could even see the logic behind it. It was plain Lipos was not at all as she'd imagined an enaree to be. "Then what's to be done with me, Lipos," she whispered, "for I, too, have good sense. Shall I be enaree, too?"

Lipos leaned against the fence and laughed at her question, and his laugh had that open, robust quality men's laughter often showed. "Women cannot be enaree," his grey eyes twinkled merrily. "Women can only be what they were born to be."

"Brood mares." Arima spat out the words. "Ridden by men and dropping their foals for them."

"An inelegant but apt way to phrase it," Lipos said, nodding. "But have you given any thought, child, any thought at all other than stark rebellion, to this future your father has decreed?"

Arima returned his gaze and shook her head mutely. She was a blunt person, she knew, and would never be able to hold her tongue. What subtleties could she see in her future?

"When Bartatua takes you to wife, what will he do?" the enaree prodded.

"Any fool knows that," she snapped, annoyed and slightly embarrassed at the question. "He will use me, take his pleasure of me, and I—"

"No, no!" Lipos shook his head, spreading his slim hands apart. "Before that, when he catches you, literally takes you . . ."

Arima blinked at him, a sudden ray of light entering her dark life. "I will be given a horse, and if I can outrace him, elude him, I am free of the bond!" She gasped at this blunt awakening. A hope!

"But women cannot ride horses. It is forbidden. Any bride put on a horse will be caught, because the warrior has ridden all his life, and the woman, never. I am no different in that, Lipos," she said, downcast.

He reached across the fence and closed his hand around her mud-stained fingers. "But you can be." He winked at her, retrieved the empty sack, and departed.

"Leave!" Lipos barked to Urgimas, entering the women's purification tent. The old slave rose to her knees clumsily, brushing the straggling, sweaty brown hair from her face. She was torn between the authority of an enaree and her duty to Arima and, without thinking, she threw a brightly dyed wool cloth over the young girl's naked body. Lipos's mouth turned back wryly at her gesture.

"Do you think I care one bit to see her?" He snorted in derision. Poor Urgimas faltered, unsure what to do.

"I said leave!" the enaree repeated, and the sternness of his voice convinced her. Urgimas lowered the cloth to the clean, sweet rushes of the floor, bent into a crouch, and exited the tiny tent.

Arima cringed instinctively, her hands covered with a paste of powdered cedar, frankincense and herbs awkwardly covering her body. Only women had ever seen her before unclothed. Men had never even been close; they were scornful, ever about their business, looking but not caring to approach her, except in violence, as her father did.

"Arima," the enaree said quietly, seeing her fear, "put yourself at ease. I am only half a man, remember? Your body concerns me little, except perhaps for the time I may one day have to heal it, drive away evil spirits, aid you in childbirth."

Lipos untied the front of his colorful felt jacket and removed it. Cleansing oneself was a woman's social ritual, and so, to be social, he must participate. Concentrating on his own body, he took a handful of the paste from a painted wooden jar in front of Arima and spread it across his chest, over his abdomen, along his arms. He much preferred the women's method of cleansing to the steamy, intoxicating tents of the men.

Arima sat still, her face turned away, watching him from the corner of one eye while pretending not to see. "Why are you here?" she breathed, lowering her arms haltingly and resuming her cleaning. He was an enaree, she knew, and his presence there was natural, acceptable, yet she still felt uncomfortable.

"It was the only place where I could speak to you privately," he responded, never once looking at her. Despite his womanly ways, he very much had the chest and arms of a man, and Arima shifted slightly, trying to turn her back to him without offending him.

"I will see you before your marriage, you know," he interrupted her, still busy with his cleansing, "to be sure you are a virgin for Bartatua. I, or old Catoris. You'd just as well get used to men now, Arima, although I think we can assume that you are untouched . . ."

Arima blushed violently and continued to smooth the paste down one forearm.

"Enough," Lipos muttered, "and keep it that way . . ."

His words seemed absurd. She had lived all her life with

the same small band of people, knew everyone by name, and their family histories. Her life was a cycle of seasons and wanderings, migrating with the wild geese and herds of steppe antelope. She would die here, too, she knew. What man of her tribe would dare take her, knowing she was Bartatua's woman?

"I must take you on a journey," the enaree suddenly blurted and Arima paused, one hand suspended over the paste bowl.

"You must be prepared for your marriage, you see." He reached out, clasping her hand kindly in his. "The women will tell you a woman's things, and there is much you already know, but my task will be a different one. You are the daughter of a chief. There are higher matters you must know, deeper things than ordinary women, but not so much as a man."

Understanding, she raised her eyes to meet his. "And you ride?" she whispered, terror rising at the sudden implication of his words. Lipos nodded.

"There will be little time," he replied. "You must learn quickly, and be unafraid."

Arima was blunt, and rebellious, but she was also trusting. His next words took her by surprise.

"And in exchange—"

"Exchange?" She was puzzled and drew back from him. It had never occurred to her that there might be a motive behind Lipos's sudden concern for her.

"Exchange," he repeated bluntly. "A simple thing. Merely tell me what you can about your father, that is all. How it is with him. What he says, what he does, his health, who visits him, where he goes. A small matter."

The sweetness of the cedar in the close space of the tent suddenly became overpowering, and Arima's stomach turned. She pulled her hand free of the enaree's grasp and slumped away from him, wishing desperately for fresh air, wind, sun. A simple thing. Yet, somehow, wrong. But it was her only hope, her only chance for freedom from Bartatua. The decision loomed before her, one of those moments, rare in life, when the choice would be of great import, a pivot around which the future would turn.

"Yes," she nodded, and the word choked her when it left her throat.

"I am in the power of an enaree," Arima brooded, the greasy chunk of mutton in her fingers turning repulsively tasteless. "A half-man, yet more powerful than a whole man. And nothing now to do, for I have given my word. A lie would be as wicked and dangerous a thing as crossing an enaree. Has my rebelliousness finally brought me the trouble Mother always said it would? Why does he want me to spy on my own father? What benefit is it to him what my father does and who he sees?"

Sighing, the girl dropped the mutton into her silver bowl and placed it on the patterned carpet before her.

"Are you ill?" Opoea asked, aware of her daughter's odd mood and the pallor of her face. Old though she was, she would give Scylas a piece of her mind if his dumping Arima in the sheepfold had caused her to get sick.

"No, Mother," Arima rose from the hearthside, "I am just tired. I want to lie down."

Opoea did not reply. Arima crossed to her sleeping-couch, Urgimas at her heels, and arranged the pillows to her satisfaction. One pillow, her favorite, sewn by her grandmother's mother with prancing felt stags and stallions, she placed under her head. Arima lay quietly, staring at the comfort of the low central fire while Urgimas removed her horsehide winter boots. Sick at heart, the girl drifted into a light, troubled sleep.

The horse went thundering past again, hooves pounding, mane flying, its breath coming in sharp, ragged gasps that spread in the luminous air, pressing onward the urgency of the creature's flight.

Battle—yes! For in the distance, atop a long, low rill of land, Arima saw warriors cloaked in black, as still as stones against the evening sky.

The pound and thud of the stallion's heart as her own, the fear in the horse became fear within Arima, till she found herself gulping for air along with the great grey beast. . . .

"Arima!"

She fought the insistence of her mother's voice, the fresh smell of a newly kindled beech fire, the hand shaking her arm.

The horse! The horse was freedom, and the black-clad warriors were . . .

"Perhaps we'd better fetch Catoris."

It was Urgimas's voice, tinged with fear, a puzzling fear until Arima's mind cleared and she realized she was gasping for breath. "No!" the girl said, pushing the hands away and struggling to sit. "I am alright. It was just a bad dream. Not the enarees, Mother!" She looked around the dark morning light of the tent and saw Opoea, her silver hair unbraided and hanging around her shoulders, as fine and straight as flax. Urgimas, brown eyes wide and puzzled, looked on while behind her a cluster of frightened slaves gaped. Arima suddenly felt foolish.

"A little broth, Mother," she said, trying to sound reasonable. "My stomach seems to have caught a chill." Appease them, soothe their fears, and let the yurt of Opoea return once more to sleep.

She sipped the warm, greasy liquid listlessly and handed the golden cup to Urgimas. Horses indeed! she snorted inwardly, reclining on her couch and turning to face the felt wall. I do not believe in such dream creatures, nor in freedom, nor in life. Only in the evil of this world, and the wickedness in men's hearts.

And the inescapability of either. That, truly, is the only world there is.

Lipos sat across the hearth fire from Scylas, while beyond the heavy walls of the Royal Yurt a moaning autumn storm gathered force. The old chief was eyeing him skeptically.

"In two days, you say?" He raised his thick dark brows quizzically.

"Yes," the enaree answered, his voice low and husky. Lipos leaned forward gracefully, the gold griffons adorning his woman's cap glinting in the firelight, and folded his hands lightly atop his knees. "Though merely a girl, it is true, Arima is still your offspring and of royal Auchatae blood. She must be taught what there is for her to know, in order to be a proper vessel to bring children—your grandchildren—into the world. And more so since her husband is not royal."

Scylas shifted his body to one side and motioned for a goblet of Greek wine to be brought. He seemed unconvinced by the arguments, and Lipos began to fear for his plan. The young enaree waited for Scylas's blind slave to bring the wine, the ancient moving as unerringly around the tent as a cat on a dark night. The chief took a great long gulp of drink and waited for the enaree to continue.

"It is true there is much she cannot be taught, but still there are things, women's things, that she should learn," Lipos added.

"Such as?"

"Spells to ward demons from her family's tent. Simple cures for children's ailments. Guarding the health and well-being of her husband."

"Obedience?" Scylas suddenly interjected a loud laugh. "That would be the best magic of all, you half-man! Teaching that one obedience!"

Lipos found himself annoyed by the old man's remarks. He speaks of his own flesh as if she were an animal to be trained. A flare of pity moved him; how well he knew the pain of being measured by the body, not the spirit!

"She will learn," Lipos said smoothly. "She has the will of an unbroken horse, made worse because she feels so power-less. Like a young horse, show it what it is capable of and it will begin to settle down. A few charms, some magic words—such things will ease her mind, and domesticity will follow with daily chores, the needs of a husband, children to bear."

"And how many days will this take?" Scylas cut him off. The duties of women were a boredom he could not abide, as was the polished speech of an enaree.

"Ten days. Past the full moon," the half-man stated. Scylas drew back momentarily, startled by the length of time needed. His own teaching on the eve of his marriage had taken only four days. Why should a woman need all of ten?

"The full moon is needed for the spells," Lipos hastily added, seeing the old chief's doubts.

"That I understand." Scylas nodded at the hearth fire. "But ten days is too long. She must be here, in a tent, and protected from the weather. Hear the wind and rain outside! Winter is fast approaching!" He paused and raised his brown eyes to the young enaree. "Five days."

"There is too much to teach!" Lipos protested, seeing his plans crumble. "Five days will scarcely be time."

"And what good will a daughter be to me if she is dead of a fever? What of my grandchildren then, eh?" Scylas de-manded, his dark eyes sparking anger. It was plain he was not used to being crossed. Lipos reined in his annoyance.

"Very well," the enaree soothed, trying to calm the situation. "I will do what I can in five days."

One who did not know could not have guessed that Lipos was an enaree. When the day came for their departure, the young half-man turned out by the Royal Yurt dressed as nothing more than a Scoloti warrior going on a hunt. He wore the loose, brightly patterned trousers of a man, tucked into ankle-high heelless leather boots. Beneath a heavy quilted felt jacket was a long red wool tunic, belted at the waist. On his left hip hung a gorytas, the trademark of Scythian warriors, a tooled leather case holding both bow and lethal three-edged arrows. A sheath and long hunting knife were tied to his right thigh. And in his left ear he wore an elaborate gold earring of Greek craftsmanship, as most Scyth men did.

His unusual appearance added to Arima's discomfort. She sat atop a small pile of folded felts and furs in the back of a tiny two-wheeled wagon, a blue and yellow wool hood clenched beneath her chin against the gusting winds driving between the yurts. She looked at the enaree apprehensively. Five days alone with him and to learn what? Charms and magics, and to ride the stolid dun mare harnessed to the cart. Five days to master what a man learns in a lifetime. And not on some fine prancing war gelding, swift as the wind, but on an old, shaggy brood mare. And even if she did learn to ride the creature, would it prepare her for riding a horse of her own choosing from her father's herds, when the time came to elude Bartatua? Scoloti war-horses were keenly trained animals, responding to the pressure of the rider's knees when he needed both hands free to fire arrows. What would such an animal do, ridden clumsily by a woman?

Arima tried not to think of it. Scylas had emerged from his yurt and was listening to some message from Lipos, the words driven by the wind so that the girl could not understand them. In the name of Papaeus, the great father god, she hoped the weather would improve! Lipos would take her to some isolated, inaccessible spot on the steppes, away from the shelter of trees and river valleys, and the wind already smelled of the sharp cold of winter. Five days of it, without even a yurt for shelter? Arima shook her head.

Lipos's address was done and Scylas uttered a few curt words in reply. Almost angry words, she judged by the look on his leathery old face. Arima straightened, trying to look womanly and dignified when Lipos turned toward the wagon, hoping for a parting word from her father, a handclasp, some small acknowledgement of the importance of the step she was about to take. Scylas merely returned to the warmth of his tent, and the girl turned her face away, sudden tears of pain smarting her eyes.

Lipos could see the hurt on Arima's face when he approached the wagon, the harsh words of Scylas still jarring in his ears. Despite his training, his professed detachment, he could not help but feel pity for the girl. Nor could he help but wonder at the old chief's attitude. True, she was not a son, and a tragedy it was that she was his only offspring; but she was intelligent, spirited as a royal child should be, far above the common herd. With a hand of loving discipline to guide her, rather than the outright scorn shown by her father, the young princess could turn out to be a credit to any man.

Perhaps Bartatua would prove to be such a man, and find himself luckier than he now could foresee.

Lipos nodded to himself as he mounted the shaggy mare and guided her from the compound. Yes, perhaps with my guidance the future will not be so bleak for the betrothed couple. From the corner of his eye, he saw old Opoea peering from behind the felt flap covering her yurt's door. A gnarled hand rose in farewell, and he hoped Arima had seen it, and was pleased.

"The circle is protective."

Lipos studied Arima through the gathering twilight. Though she was well-swaddled in furs, her face was pinched and drawn from the cold.

"That is why our yurts are circular, our hearths are circular, even our sheepfolds and horse pens have no sharp corners. In such places evil can hide, bringing sickness or bad luck to all who dwell there."

Arima seemed bored, trying to focus on his face while her gaze repeatedly wandered away. It was only natural, the enaree supposed. Women were unsuited to such rigid learning and besides, she had seen little of the world around her, hidden away as she had been in yurts and wagons for most of her life. He could see where the beauties of sunset below a low cloudbank could hold more interest than his words.

"You must listen, Arima!" he chided her sharply. Perhaps here, now, her training in obedience was to begin. "We have only five days. Tomorrow you ride, but in the evenings when the light goes we must have our teachings. You will be so busy, so pressed these five days, girl, that your stomach will cry out for food and your eyes for sleep. Now pay attention to me!"

Arima shifted her back to the wind and toyed with a frayed edge of the wool hood draped around her face. The tiny campfire Lipos had built, sheltered behind a windbreak of leather, was enough to cook a sparse meal but afforded hardly any warmth at all.

"I heard you. The circle is protective," she muttered stiffly through cold lips. "My ears can hear you while my eyes are elsewhere."

"You will remember it better if both are on me," the enaree retorted. Arima slouched beneath the foxskin robe she wore and turned her attention to Lipos. On and on it went, into the night; the stability the hearthstones bring to a dwelling and the importance of picking them carefully; healing in streams, washing away the ills that inhabit a body; the fierceness of Scoloti art, to frighten away the demons that dwell all around; the power in trees, and the charms to protect a yurt from lightning thrown down from the skies. She could barely keep herself awake when Lipos finally stopped the teachings, far, far into a clear starlit night. Arima huddled between the windbreak and the campfire and lay down, snuggling into the furs. The strangeness of her first day in the open world did not disturb her sleep. The great black sky above her, the boundless steppes around, gave a peace to her soul she had never felt before. Unbound, unfettered, she felt free.

Horses in herds, beneath warriors, even yoked to the front of a wagon, had seemed to be ordinary things, of a manageable size and an understandable temperament. Approaching the large brown beast she was to ride, placid in the blue morning light, Arima felt suddenly uneasy. It was impossibly large, its back to her chest, as broad and sturdy as a bale of felt. The old mare sensed the girl's apprehension. She lifted her head and tossed it on the leather reins Lipos held.

"How do I get on it?" Arima asked the enaree. Lipos rubbed the mare's nose to calm it and smiled at the girl.

"Pull yourself up. You've seen how the men do it."

Indeed Arima had, but with them it looked natural and effortless. She felt anything but natural, standing by the patient creature, smelling its warmth and the dirt in its thick hair. Could the men be right, that women were not meant to ride such a beast?

Pulling her mouth back in determination, Arima extended her arms and leaped toward the mare. She landed with a solid thud against its side and nearly fell back. But resolve held her, and she pulled herself over its back, hitching her long skirts up to let her legs hang free down either side of the mare. The old horse shifted on her feet at the odd scramblings going on atop her, and Arima clenched reflexively at the mare's thick mane, the world beneath her moving in sways and lurches that sent her heart into her mouth.

"Lipos, I . . ." she blurted, fear quavering in her voice. The enaree ignored her, stepping in front of the mare and leading her forward. Arima stifled a gasp at the movement and hung on for her life.

"You ride as though you were perched on a sword's edge!" The half-man studied her from the corner of his eye. "Relax! Your rear end will be sore enough from this, even if you don't sit there like a stiffened corpse!"

Arima didn't understand what he meant. How could one relax, when the sway threatened to toss one to the ground at any moment? Relaxation seemed the last thing she needed now.

They had gone fifty paces when Lipos halted and turned to Arima in exasperation. "Have you ever seen a warrior sit on a horse like that?" he barked, annoyance flashing in his eyes. "I am trying to help you, girl, but you must listen to my advice, and heed it." He dropped the reins to trail on the ground and walked back to Arima. Roughly he grabbed her arm and jerked her from side to side. "Loosen up! Loosen up!" he ordered. Arima twined her fingers into the mare's mane and bit her lips, trying not to cry out, to let him see her fear.

For some reason Lipos seemed satisfied, for he released her, took the reins, and began to trot the horse forward briskly. Arima's head had barely cleared when the beast lurched away, faster, the flat expanse of windblown yellow grass jarring disconcertingly in the corners of her eyes. Suddenly the world was not so stable a place. . . .

"Stop!" she gasped, turning her face down to study the mare's back and fighting a swift nausea that gripped her. "Lipos, stop!"

He acted as if he hadn't heard her. On he trotted, the waving grass seed heads at her knees adding to the swirl of movement around her, the chaos of a world gone mad. In desperation she slumped forward, her forehead itchy in the dirty stiff hair of the horse's neck, and moaned aloud.

"Are you just a woman, or something more?" Lipos taunted over his shoulder as he ran. Her weakness irritated him, but he could also understand it. Such an experience as this was as alien to her as if she had suddenly sprouted wings and could fly.

"Retch if you must, and then get on with the lesson," he went on. "Or do you admit defeat? Are you just a woman, too, like all the rest?"

"No," Arima gasped. With a glance he could see her face pale against the dun mare, all the rose bloom gone from her cheeks, her long fingers clinging to the mare's tangled mane as if it preserved her very life.

"Tell me to stop! Admit this is not for you!" the enaree prodded. She must fight back, or give in. He knew it, and she must realize it, too. This was her crossroads. He was getting winded himself, but he dared not stop. Fight, Arima! Fight!

It was a beast, like any of the thousand others in her father's herd. She had seen them born, and seen them die; in a torment of disease, or slain for the cooking pot, or, for the favored war-horses, quietly, when life and vigor left them with old age or a bitter winter. Like anyone in her tribe she knew their heart, their blood and bones, their spirit.

Swallowing stiffly, Arima lifted her head away from the ceaseless pull and throb of the mare's well-muscled neck. Its rhythmic movements were suddenly not alien at all, but as familiar as her own heartbeat.

Granted, it was only an old, tired mare, but it was a horse nonetheless. Generations of Scyth blood in her veins, blood born and dying on horses so relentlessly that the Greeks to the south called them centaurs, half-man, half-horse. This blood beating in her heart cried out to the blood of the horse beneath her and drew strength from it. Arima forced herself to sit upright, and relax her clenching fingers, and take a great, fortifying gulp of the winter air.

Yes, I am a woman, and I am afraid, she sighed shakily, closing her eyes and concentrating on the feel of the animal she rode. But I am also Scoloti, and I will learn.

* * *

The mare became her freedom, a reason for living such as she had never known before. The nights that remained of her lessons were a boredom, words and concepts she cared little for, details that smothered her imagination like a down-filled pillow. Time and again Lipos had to chide her, drawing her wandering mind back to the subject at hand; which herbs could heal which children's illnesses, the remedy for a burned finger, what to give a husband whose stomach ached from eating bad mutton. And, since she was a royal child soon to be wed to her tribe's heir, she was taught the responsibilities of such a position, the protocol for visiting chiefs, her duties at royal funerals, her standing in relation to that of the women of the Royal Scoloti. It was a tedium to Arima, but she knew the nights were for learning. It was a chore to be done with, then to sleep for a few precious hours to awaken before dawn, her heart racing with eagerness for the horse. She had not known it was possible to feel so alive, to have each morning a new adventure. The feel of the horse, the smell and sound of it—that was all she cared to live for.

This day, the fifth day, Arima could scarcely await her final ride. Impatiently she tramped back and forth across the broken grasses of their campsite, waiting for Lipos to unhobble the old mare. It was plain to her that the enaree was not pleased by her poor showing as a pupil, and by her increasing obsession with the horse. Perhaps he had second thoughts about teaching her to ride? She really didn't care. If he wanted his information from her about her father, he had to teach her to ride, try to save her from her fate with Bartatua. They had agreed. And for the joy of riding, she felt she would betray even her own soul.

Lipos stood and turned toward her, the leather hobbles in his hand. "Ride a short time," he instructed, "and then we must do more teaching."

"More?" Arima pouted, reaching to pat the mare's shoulder.

"Yes." The enaree was emphatic. "We had only half the time we needed to teach you, remember? Lessons through midday, and a final ride before night." He caught the distant look in her blue eyes and knew she was, as always, only half-hearing him. "Arima . . ." he cautioned.

The girl looked at him, her fingers twining the braided reins. "I hear you," she muttered coldly. She didn't want to dwell on the last words he had uttered.

Abruptly Arima turned away, reaching up to boost herself onto the mare's back. By now the animal was used to her awkward attempts and stood patiently, unflinching, waiting for the girl to settle herself. Lipos stepped closer and placed a hand on Arima's bare knee, jutting from beneath her bunched skirt.

"Remember, Arima," he repeated, looking up at the girl, "return before the sun is high. We still have much to do."

She suddenly didn't want to be near the enaree, or feel his hand on her skin, or hear his lecturing voice. He had introduced her to such freedom, and now he was about to take it away. Pressing her booted heels into the mare's shaggy ribs, she turned it away from the half-man. Without a parting word she trotted away, toward the lavender sky of dawn. Inhaling the light morning breeze, smelling the sweet dry dustiness of the grass, she felt at peace. So this is what it feels like to be a man! she marvelled. Mount your horse and go where you please. Not a bad life! No wonder men guarded their privileges so jealously.

The mare plodded on, her old tired head rising and falling as she moved. Arima shifted her bottom on the horse's bony back; she'd already got used to the bruises and blisters of the first few days. Riding in men's trousers and on thick saddle pads must be so much more comfortable. She laughed aloud. It would be many days after they returned to camp before she allowed anyone to see her naked in the cleansing tent, not till her backsides were healed.

The sun rose higher, the sky fading to the soft blue sky of

winter. To her right a tawny grey crake rose abruptly from the ground, its wings fanning the grass aside in its haste to flee. The mare's steps slowed and she lifted her head, eyeing the bird's departure. Arima leaned forward and patted the horse's neck, whispering reassurances into her ear. It's alright, it's only a bird.

With a shock she realized what had happened. She had identified so strongly with the horse, felt its uncertainty— she and her horse had become one!

Throwing back her head, Arima laughed joyously at the cloudless sky. If her heart could take wing and soar like the crake, then surely it would have at that moment.

We are one!

With an exultant whoop that startled a small flock of sparrows from their hiding places, Arima put her heels to the mare and together they galloped toward the climbing sun, the vanishing birds. She was free!

Lipos paced the campsite, listening through the sighing winds for the slow, steady thump of the mare's hooves on the black soil. He heard nothing.

He turned, pausing at the wagon to stare absently at the goods he had piled there. Tomorrow they were to return to camp. Today was to be their final lesson, and here it was well past midday, and still the girl had not returned. Frustrated, he thumped a clenched fist against the painted side of the wagon.

Curse her! he fumed. He had thought she was different; he saw things in her worth cultivating. Obviously he had been wrong. Here, today, it was clear. She was as fickle, as flighty and untrustworthy as any other woman.

Turning from the wagon, he ran his eyes around the circle of the horizon, scanning the grasstops for a sudden flight of birds, rising in swift agitation, that might signal Arima's return. Only the monotony of brilliant winter sky and dancing grass met his gaze.

The sun was crawling down the sky in a motion so slow it seemed the day must be twice as long as other days, when a sudden alarm of late-migrating buntings made Lipos whirl toward the east. The small flock rose, wheeled noisily, and scattered into the distance. The enaree froze, his ears strained in their direction. Out from the rustling grasses, so faint he barely heard it, came his name.

Arima was disoriented when he found her, a large bruise swelling her forehead, her eyes glazed with panic. She seemed barely able to stand and the enaree ran forward, folding his arms around her protectively.

"The horse," she mumbled, dimly recognizing Lipos, the campsite, the parked wagon. The enaree cast a quick glance behind her as he led her to their fire. The beast was nowhere in sight.

"Tell me later," he tried to soothe. "We must see to your wounds first."

Arima dragged herself to a halt and turned on him, her slim fingers gripping the front of his felt jacket fiercely. "They killed it!" she gulped, tears welling in horror. "By the gods," she broke down, collapsing against him, "they killed it."

"Who?" he muttered, pulling her toward the fire. "The mare is dead. Who killed it?"

"Wolves." Her voice died. "Five wolves. In the name of Api, may I never live to see such a thing again."

A chill ran down Lipos's spine. Wolves, already hungry and searching the steppes for food. And now the two of them were alone, no horse, their only protection his bow, a knife, and the campfire.

With the violet dusk Scylas became worried, but only slightly. This was the sixth day, the day the enaree was to return to camp with Arima, yet they had not come back. His concern nagged at him fitfully, flitting about the edge of his thoughts like a darting swallow. This chill evening, dissolving into black shadows and an odd, still mist that crept around the edges of camp, the old chief's attention was elsewhere; on the laden trading caravan that was passing through his territories from the savage wastes of the north, and on the willowy young woman the trader hoped to sell to a rich Greek merchant.

She moved through the shadows, ghostlike beyond the campfire, her skin as white and fine as fresh milk. Long hair, white-blonde, drifted behind her shoulders. Scylas watched the unmatched grace with which she moved, bringing her master a platter of horsemeat, dried berries, a skin bag full of kumiss, fermented mare's milk. She rose and knelt as effortlessly as a deer, eyes kept properly to the ground, her figure firm, well-rounded, and healthy.

Scylas felt an aching, a longing for this wraithlike foreign creature such as he had not known in years. His relations with Opoea had all but stopped after the birth of Arima. It was a disaster foreordained, his wife's attentions focused solely on her long-awaited baby, and himself suddenly finding her old, sagging figure to be unappealing. The occasional war captive amused him, women either cold and hostile or stiff with terror. And there were always female slaves, as familiar as the camp dogs roaming about.

But this pale northern woman, well, even now she seemed to sense his interest, for she lifted her large pale eyes, rimmed with golden lashes, and cast him a quick glance as she passed the firelight. The rich warm meat broth in Scylas's mouth suddenly turned tasteless and he swallowed it stiffly, his mind whirling with thoughts of that delicate face devoured by his lips, her white skin soft beneath his hands.

Bartatua ended his reverie, kneeling at his side with a proffered gift from the merchant. Scylas looked at the short string of golden amber beads in obvious disinterest.

"Is that all?" Scylas spat out, casting a heated glance

across the campfire to his guest, his rival. The merchant was dark, his olive skin nearly as smooth as the girl's, his long hair hanging in thick oily curls to his shoulders. He was steady, too, from years of dealing with the unpredictable tribesmen of the north. He didn't blink an eye at the old chief's outburst.

"You come here with eight wagonloads of goods!" Scylas growled at him. "To pass through my lands, drink from my wells, devour my grasses, requires more than a paltry string of beads in payment!"

The merchant had been expecting this. The amber had merely been an opening wager. "Hides, then?" he asked soothingly. "Most of my cargo is hides. Sealskin, otter, very fine. Wolf and bearskins, a few of each?"

Scylas fingered the string of amber, watching the firelight plumb the yellow depths of the beads. It was of exceptional quality, clear and pure.

"And amber?" he inquired. Furs he had aplenty, but good amber always fetched a nice price from the Greeks to the south. He studied the merchant, seeing him shift slightly in discomfort. Force could be used if necessary; for now, he would try tact.

"What of your amber?" the old chief repeated, holding the strand of beads swinging in the air. The dark man's gaze went from Scylas to the beads and flew briefly around the circle of assembled warriors, all curious, serious, and well-armed. "A small chest," he muttered, his heavily accented voice low and bitter. Whatever he lost to this Scyth chief, he had no choice. Here, the Scyth dictated who passed, and at what price.

"Twenty strands such as this." Scylas said flatly. The merchant's jaw dropped.

"Just the amber. Keep your gold." Scylas knew the man had gold from the north hidden away. Merchants always had gold. What did it matter? Scoloti riches would put this fool's sum to shame. He waited for the man to answer.

"Twenty strands!" the merchant protested. "I don't have much more than—"

"Bah!" Scylas stood, handing the beads to Bartatua. "A small chest holds fifty or more such as that. You still have your furs, your gold, the rest of your amber."

The old chief's head turned at soft footsteps approaching. The northern slave girl passed by, the warm scent of her fur-clad body wafting to him on the night air.

"And her . . ." Scylas growled, jerking his head toward the woman. She obviously didn't understand their tongue, for her steps never faltered as she carried more kumiss to her master. The merchant looked at her and shrugged. There were always more women to be had. The old man drove a hard bargain, but the merchant knew he could not escape it.

"Agreed." The man sighed, standing and downing the thick pungent drink with what he hoped was an air of bravado.

Bartatua was furious. He paced the circle of yurts like a trapped bull. All around him was still and silent, the tribesmen long since asleep. All but one.

Time and again as he stalked past Scylas's large tent he could hear the two of them—his chief and the slave girl—grunting, panting, small high-pitched squeals of feminine excitement, half fearful and half in pleasure. For an old man, Scylas certainly had stamina. Or was it just the little foreign mare that so inspired him?

The chief horseman paced beyond Scylas's yurt, trying to ignore the muffled gasps he heard within it. His own wife waited for him, and listening to the antics of the old man, he felt the need to take her as soon as he could. And yet there was this other matter that held him back, that raced his heart, that caused anger to well in his throat like vomit.

Arima.

She and Lipos were a day late, and normally Scylas would be enraged, if not worried, that the two would so violate his stated will. But now it seemed to barely concern the old man, so taken was he with his new plaything.

Bartatua fingered the carved ivory hilt of the dagger strapped to his thigh. Turning, he kicked the dry, crushed grass in futility. Arima alone he could see being late to return, but not the enaree. They were highly trained men, learned and responsible. Something must have happened.

A sobbing moan from the girl caused him to look up at the tent of Scylas, his brown eyes filled with sudden hatred for the old man. To ignore the plight of his own daughter and one of his enaree is not right, he fumed. A man must be a man, it is true, but not at the expense of his duties. A low snickering from the warriors guarding the perimeter of camp came as a sudden insult to Bartatua's ears and he whirled, walking with long angry strides toward the penned horses. He could take no more of this humiliation.

Other ears also heard the shrieks and moans, in a tent across the clearing from Scylas's. Opoea's withered eyes squeezed out the first tears she had cried in many years, and with desperate hands she clenched a cushion over her ears, to shut out the sound.

Arima and Lipos had decided on their best course of action. The wolves would be busy the rest of the night with the mare's carcass, and such a meal would satisfy them for the next several days. In that time Arima and Lipos could walk back to camp, but the journey would leave them exposed to both the weather and any other creatures that might happen on them when they left the safety of the wagon and campfire. And in those days, the two would be missed by Scylas, who would send out a rescue party. His warriors would have no trouble following the trail made by the clumsy wagon and old mare. The safest thing, they agreed, was to remain where they were and wait.

They rolled the wagon close to the campfire and upwind of it, to shelter the flames. The fire was their main protection, and they could not risk it being put out by the weather. Lipos had no medicine for the girl's bruised head, but he made her lie down in the wagon, warmly covered, and put a wet cloth over the injury. He carried the furs and sheepskins well away from camp and discarded them, for fear a predator might be attracted to their smell.

Lipos sat guard by the fire as the night passed. While the girl slept restlessly, he listened to the sounds of the moaning winds and small grey owls and the occasional distant howl of a sated wolf. It prickled the back of his neck, to hear it, and to remember what Arima had told him.

She had ridden the mare through a fine winter's morning, the luxury of freedom wrapped around her like a fine robe, when suddenly a thin yellow wolf had appeared out of the grasses, its jaws working methodically as it slathered on the scent of the old horse. The mare spied it at once, and despite her age and tiredness she reared mightily, striking out at the beast with flying hooves. The action was futile, but it saved Arima's life. Thrown from the horse, the girl lay dazed and half-concealed in the tall grass while the wolf, joined by its pack, chased the panicked horse. She wanted to go after them, to rescue the old mare, but she had no weapon, and it would have been her death, too. Crawling on her hands and knees, the girl stumbled along the crushed grass track where she had come. Behind her the wolves were strangely silent; all she could hear was thudding hooves, weaker, more unsteady, and the occasional gasping pant of an eager wolf. Finally came a high-pitched scream from the horse, then silence. In terror, Arima had forced herself to stand and run, an ominous hush fueling her flight.

And so she had come back, half-crazed from the ordeal and the sickening death of the mare, her first horse.

Lipos stood and restlessly paced the small circle of their camp, his ears attuned to the night while his mind churned with worry. Here they had no brands for light to fend off the wolves, only dead grass, and what remained of the sack of dried dung he'd brought for fuel. He didn't like to admit it, but he doubted it would last one more day. And then what?

An exuberant yowl cascaded through the night air and the enaree shuddered and returned to the security of the wagon. A wolf bragging to the world the way a hunter would with a fine red stag or a fierce boar to his credit? Shouting his prowess to the heavens.

Lipos lowered himself cross-legged to the ground, his back to the wagon. Checking his weapons, the enaree slowly turned his head, scanning the black, endless horizon, scenting the air for dawn.

Scylas felt so invigorated the next morning he decided on a rabbit hunt. Except for a few men left to guard the camp, all his warriors were forced to participate.

Bartatua nearly choked at the news, bantered about the camp by grinning guards and horsemen. Ah! the little northern vixen had got the old man's blood flowing again. Now better times would return to camp: hunts, raids, trading parties. Warriors young and old went about their morning tasks anticipating the day's hunt, and the promise of more adventures to come.

But what of the enaree and his own daughter? Bartatua fumed, fetching a scarlet leather bridle, sewn felt cheek pieces, and gaudy saddle pad from his yurt. Tabiti, his wife, had prepared a morning gruel, wondering in silence why he had slept the night by the campfire and not in his own tent. Bartatua was so enraged he overlooked her dutiful gesture. Two Auchatae missing and what does their chief do? Spends the night riding his woman and the day riding his horse.

He left the yurt without a word to his puzzled wife. Perhaps they will return this day, he tried to reassure himself. He strode toward the horse pens, equipage in hand. Young boys scurried among the milling animals, guiding chosen horses out for their owners. Dust rose in a low cloud above them and Bartatua ran a hand through his tangled hair, shaking the dirt loose and cursing the sun that had ever risen on this bizarre day.

A boy of about seven, as agile as a squirrel, scampered up the fence of lashed saplings and appeared in Bartatua's face. "Which one?" he shouted over the din of thudding hooves, startled neighs, and eager, laughing men. His young face was streaked with dirt and bits of straw dangled from his hair. Bartatua smiled wryly at him.

"You know my favorite," he called back, "the black gelding with one white leg." The boy nodded and slipped down the fence, disappearing into the mass of horseflesh. Trying to summon some enthusiasm for the day's hunt, Bartatua left the fence and walked past knots of chatting warriors, men already harnessing their mounts. He arrived at the gate to the paddock just as the young boy led his horse out, calling it forward with a low whistle.

"Here," Bartatua snapped, tossing the bridle to the surprised boy and feeling little enthusiasm for the day to come, "can you do it yourself?"

"Oh, yes!" the delighted boy gasped, nearly choking on the pride that engulfed him. For such a youth as himself to be entrusted with a warrior's prized mount was nothing to be taken lightly. Perhaps Bartatua himself, chief warrior of Scylas and betrothed to the chief's daughter, would be the one to teach him the skills of war. If, that is, he could prove himself worthy.

He knew how to put the bridle on so as not to startle or hurt the horse, how to adjust the ornate felt cheek pieces properly. He fitted the horse carefully under Bartatua's gaze, brushing dirt from its back before strapping on the padded saddle seat, picking bits of straw from its sides. Proudly he put the reins in the warrior's scarred hand.

"Good," Bartatua grunted, checking the fit of the saddle pad. With a slight smile at the boy he pulled a few bits of hay from the youth's hair before mounting his war-horse. No other praise seemed forthcoming, nor any offer, so the boy turned and vaulted back into the horse pen, hoping to curry more favor elsewhere.

Bartatua dreaded the start of the hunt. Old Scylas emerged from his yurt, his skin an odd grey, sickly-looking despite the grin on his face and a sudden new light in his brown eyes. Bartatua wondered at it; he had not seen his chief look so ill before. It seemed to bother the old man little, though, for when a slave brought up his favorite war-horse Scylas leaped astride it like a man in his prime. He wore his gold-plated gorytas and hunting knife, and the morning sun glinted off the plaques of gold sewn to his thick felt jacket. Without formality or ritual, this gleaming apparition gave a shout, put heels to his horse, and vanished into the dissipating morning mists, a retinue of brightly clad horsemen thundering behind him.

With his long, keen hunting knife Lipos sawed at the edge of the wagon, trying to loosen enough of a strip of wood so that he and Arima could pull it free. He couldn't understand why, two days overdue, no one had come for them, but he had to do more now than wait and wonder. The sky was already violet with the approach of dusk, but the supply of dried dung might not last the night. Nearby, the wolves still prowled. The wagon offered protection, but he and the girl had agreed that some bits of it must be sacrificed in order to keep the fire burning.

The heavy wooden wheels were beyond them without a mallet or stout rock to knock their pins loose and free them. Bare-handed, it was hopeless. At Arima's suggestion they decided to pull off one side of the wagon, to burn, and turn the remnants of it upright on one side, as shelter. It seemed a sensible plan, and Lipos was surprised that a woman should have thought of it.

But was the task possible? The old, dry painted birch

wood was hard and he feared he would dull his knife if he kept hacking at the cart side with it. Which did they need more—his knife or the fire?

"I have it!" Arima muttered, her fingers grasping at the sliver of wood the knife had pried loose. Dropping the knife to the ground, the enaree grabbed at the slit, adding his strength to hers. Slowly they pulled and pulled, heard the wood creak and groan and then, with a loud snap, split clean along the wagon top, nearly toppling them backward when it gave.

Despite her throbbing head and scraped fingers, Arima clenched the precious strip of wood in both hands and held it over her head like a triumphant warrior brandishing his first scalp. "We have it! We have it!" She laughed, doing a quick little dance in the dirt to confirm her joy.

Grinning, Lipos picked up his knife and began cutting another notch in the wagon. With enough wood cut to last the night, a fire to protect them from the cold and wolves, their rescue might come the next morning. Who could say what had delayed Scylas's help? An envoy from the Royal Scyth, the Paralatae? An illness, perhaps of old Opoea? Maybe Scylas himself was sick. But if so, the people would be in Bartatua's hands, and he would not wait long and risk losing a future wife and title to the tribe.

The first faint stars were twinkling in the charcoal sky when the two finished dismantling the side of the wagon. They heaved the cart into the air on one wheel, and it crashed onto its now-demolished side. Husbanding the precious wood, Lipos insisted that the girl crawl under the shelter of the upturned wagon to sleep while he kept watch. The enaree fed the fire sparingly, only enough to keep it alive, while his eyes scanned the darkness, his ears probing the night for the sound of prowling feet.

Morning came too soon for Bartatua, sleeping bone weary and cold on his saddle pad beside his horse and beneath a canopy of stars. With dawn the light was sheer and grey, like fine smoke, and the sky was covered with a silver blanket of clouds. Muttering under his breath, the warrior stood and pulled the saddle pad from the ground. He picked the dirt and grass from it and pulled his horse close on its tether line. Around him the other warriors of Scylas were stirring, relieving themselves at the edge of camp, saddling their geldings and casting uneasy glances at the thick sky. The unspoken concern of most of them, Bartatua knew, was that this hunting expedition of Scylas's was madness. No herds of saiga, the tiny steppe antelope, had been spotted. Hares would be scarce this close to winter, and most large game— deer, boar, wild oxen—would have travelled to more sheltered river bottoms. A flock of low-flying grey geese, scouting from one feeding ground to another and calling raggedly in the thin cold air, flew overhead and Bartatua looked up. It was the most promising thing he'd seen since they left the settlement. Five hares and a small fox was the whole of what they had caught the previous day—a pitiful count indeed!

Bartatua was disgusted with the whole venture, and with Scylas as well. What had been admiration for the old man had turned to scorn, openness had become suspicion. It was true all men used women and enjoyed them, but for some old fool to take leave of his senses over a pale northern wench was a shameful thing. A pointless winter hunt, neglect of his duties to the tribe, and the risk that his only offspring and a highly valued enaree might be dead or dying as well! More than one Scoloti chief had been killed for consorting too devotedly with a woman of the foreigners.

Bartatua walked his black war-horse away from the rousing men and stood beyond camp to relieve himself. The wind was rising in force and the warrior could smell the sharpness of a coming storm in it. He studied his horse keenly. Rather than standing placidly or taking a few morning mouthfuls of grass, the shaggy beast had its head up, its nostrils working the wind. Bartatua was convinced of the imminence of snow.

He walked back to the slowly rousing Scylas. The old chief sat on his ornate saddle pad, downing kumiss from a goatskin bag. A two-day stubble of beard darkened his leathery face and his eyes were as red as if he had barely slept. Bartatua did not like his appearance. The man was obviously ill, and if he was to die with Arima gone, the succession would be open to decision by the enarees. Or to warfare within the tribe.

"We must return," Bartatua said bluntly to the old man. Scylas looked up, a sudden light of lust in his eyes the only sign of health on his face, and Bartatua found himself hating his chief for it.

"Yes," Scylas croaked, burping on the heavy fermented drink. "My little ivory trinket awaits." He stood and laughed loudly, clapping his chief warrior on the shoulder as he waited for his horse to be fitted for the ride to camp. The kumiss must have been particularly potent, for he found his legs to be considerably less sturdy than they were the night before.

"Arima . . ." Bartatua began. Scylas waved him away impatiently with one hand. When he now had a woman, willing, obedient, delectable as women should be, the last thing he wanted to hear about was one who was the exact opposite—his willful, unbroken daughter. "Lipos has her. He is a highly skilled enaree. They will return safely," Scylas snapped, wishing to end the conversation. Bartatua tried a different approach.

"But to disobey you so, sire, two days late, in defiance of your orders."

Scylas leaped unsteadily astride his powerful bay gelding. Dismissing Bartatua without another word, he walked his mount into the milling throng of horsemen. Bartatua glared after him sullenly, chewing his lip to silence himself, and sprang onto his war-horse.

Perhaps they are, even now, returning to camp, he consoled himself. He urged his horse into a gallop to catch up with the retreating figure of Scylas.

With the ashen dawn Arima and Lipos ate a meager meal and huddled together by the wagon, watching a lone sparrow brave the wind to hunt for food in the crushed grasses of their campsite. The enaree had not intended to teach her this, but facing the very real possibility of his death, he wanted to leave the girl with a lesson of more value than the mental tricks he had given her thus far.

"A final lesson," Lipos muttered stiffly. He looked at Arima; her gaze never shifted from the foraging sparrow. "A wisdom all enaree know but seldom tell others. Arima, what do you know of creation?"

"Papaeus created the world, and the Scoloti were created by Targitaus, in a past so long ago that even the grandfathers cannot remember it," the girl stated simply.

"Mankind is like sweat from the brow of Papaeus, created from his efforts; of him, yet apart. Brought forth from his essence, but so much less than he is."

Arima lowered her eyes so far that it seemed she had closed them altogether. He knew she was listening intently to his words, a lesson that finally caught her interest.

"And because we come from his urge to create, we possess a similar need. Women as well as men, all are alike in this."

Arima turned her head sideways and gave him a brief, fleeting smile of appreciation. "Women, too?" she confirmed. Lipos nodded.

"Women the most, Arima, for they are intimately bound up in the cycle of creation, of birth and death. A man's role is different. Some sow their seed far and wide. Others merely remove life. They go to war, they hunt. A warrior shows off his first scalp with as much pride as a mother displays her infant; hunters stand and observe a fresh-killed boar with the same awe and admiration as women gather to wonder at a newborn babe."

"And enaree?" The girl smiled, teasing him.

For Lipos it was no joke. "Music, art, our magics and medicines; this is how we enaree fill our urge to copy the creatings of Papaeus. Everyone strives to be little gods. No matter where your life leads you, Arima, the role you were fashioned for will not elude you."

She shifted her eyes back to the brown sparrow, digesting his words as Scylas would digest a fine meal.

"Always remember this. Women are comfortable with living and dying, not with killing and destruction. But men, Arima," the enaree paused, reflecting on some hidden anger in his voice. "You will never find a man who is at peace with his own mortality."

There was no more to be said. In silence he returned his eyes to the lone sparrow. It searched a few moments more, nibbling some stray seeds, and darted away over the swaying grasses.

When midday arrived with still no rescue, Lipos knew something would have to be done. For whatever reason, it looked like they had been forgotten, and with the sky promising snow the enaree had to make some decisions.

Arima huddled in the shelter of the overturned wagon, picking at a scrap of coarse millet bread. She had always been so vibrant, quick-witted, defiant, but now all that seemed to have left her. Her skin was grey and pinched in the unrelenting cold and her startling blue eyes were nearly as pale and colorless as the sky above them. Crouching low against the bite of the wind, Lipos circled the tiny campfire and knelt at the girl's side, grateful for the shelter of the wagon. Hope is the spark that gives life, he knew. Without it any creature, man or animal, dies. He must infuse the girl with hope.

"I will return to camp," he said confidently, as if he were

discussing a trip to a nearby wheat field. Arima looked at him in shock.

"But the wolves, the snow—you cannot!" she protested. More color drained from her face at the idea. The enaree placed a reassuring hand on the thick felt covering her shoulders.

"If I hurry, I can reach Scylas by nightfall." He smiled. "I will leave you the knife, and take the bow for myself. You have the fire and food. You will be alright until I return."

"But, Lipos, no!" Arima repeated, rising to her knees and facing him. "If we are separated, our chances of surviving will be halved. I, here alone, am all but defenseless, while you make your way equally alone across the steppes through snow and wind and darkness. Please, Lipos. No."

The enaree tightened his hand on her shoulder, touched by her concern for him. He had always thought she cared for no one but herself. "I must, Arima. If you wish to be independent, capable of thinking and acting on your own, then you must accept that there will be many hard decisions in your life, painful and difficult ones. It is part of growing up. I can stay here and protect you as a weak woman unable to care for herself, and we will probably both die in the end. Or you can be strong and brave, and gamble as men so often do. It would be our only hope for survival. If it works or not is in the hands of the gods, but we must at least try."

He studied her pallid face and was relieved to see resolve enter her eyes. Their old sparkle returned, and she nodded. "Here," she said, handing him the remains of her bread. "You will need strength to make your trek."

Lipos took it and gulped it down against the empty knot in his stomach. He had scarcely eaten all day. Unsheathing the long knife at his thigh, he handed it to Arima.

"Keep this at hand, always," he said. "If a wolf attacks, go for the head, the heart, the throat."

Arima winced at the images in her mind and nodded at

his instructions. She closed her scabbed, dirty hands reverently around the gold-inlaid hilt of the heavy dagger. A warrior's long knife and she, a woman, was holding it!

Lipos understood the emotion of the moment for the girl, and he let her savour it briefly before he continued. "Keep the fire burning, low and small to conserve wood. You must never let it go out. You must stay awake, though the night and the cold lull you to sleep. You must guard the fire with your life, for it is your life; do you understand?"

Arima lifted her eyes from the knife to his face and nodded. "Yes," she whispered stiffly. Lipos patted her arm confidently and stood.

"Good." He smiled. "Now I must go."

"We will meet again," the girl said, her voice full of resolve. Again and again, she always seemed to surprise him. "If not in this world, then in the next," she concluded. Lipos smiled and turned, with more fear in his heart than he dared to show, and trotted away into the tall dry grass. Arima listened to his footsteps fade. For the first time in her life, she was truly alone. No mother, no girlfriends, no slaves. She clenched the knife angrily. I am no longer a mere woman, she spoke aloud. I have ridden a horse, and now I hold a warrior's knife. I will face this fear and loneliness, I will master it, and I will survive.

It was not a heavy snowfall, but it was enough to coat the landscape and weight down the dry grasses and cover the yurts of Scylas's people with a layer of warm insulation. It was the cold, not the snow, that threatened, so pervading and brittle that the felt walls of the tents froze, cracking and snapping like thin pottery when the wind broke them. Bartatua stood at the doorway of his yurt, listening to the eerie sound of yurt-cries in the darkness. Scylas was warm, he knew; exhausted on the soft white breast of his latest plaything, and caring little about the fate of Arima and Lipos. But the rest of his camp cared, and slept uneasily for it. The hollow, haunted eyes of Opoea were especially unsettling as she invented some excuse to leave her tent and bustle by him on business, throwing him a pleading look while not daring to speak with him, to go behind her husband's back. But Bartatua saw the desperation in her heart, and he could not forget it.

A series of cracks rent the night like the dry, sharp rattling of arrows in a gorytas, and the urgency of the sound moved Bartatua to act. He lowered the heavy tent flap of his yurt and turned into his home. Flipping open a large wooden chest that held his clothes, he pulled on first a padded wool coat, then an outer wrap of wolfskin that came nearly to his ankles. His winter boots were of horsehide, lined with bearskin. So bundled he could barely move beneath his clothing, the warrior pulled a peaked leather cap down tightly over his ears and tied it beneath his chin. He took two folded bearskins from the pile where they were stored and settled a long look on Tabiti, his wife. She slept soundly on her couch, her tiny, girlish face nearly hidden beneath a pile of goose down quilts. He did not wake her, but turned and left the tent.

The two horses he selected seemed reluctant to leave the warmth of the herd and the sheltered paddock, and when he led them out past the unquestioning guards the animals moved stiffly, protesting their midnight foray. Huddled low over the neck of one horse, Bartatua jabbed it fiercely with his heels, cursing into the wind as he tried to urge it forward faster than it wished to go. He did not dare risk his best mount in such a storm, and these two did not seem to want to go anywhere but back to the herd. Angrily he fumbled beneath his coats for his bow, using it to give a smart whack to the horse's shaggy rump. Bartatua replaced the bow in his gorytas as the startled horse trotted out into the swirling flakes and stinging wind.

It was near dawn when he found the enaree, partly shrouded in snow and barely alive, and Bartatua knew his fears had been well-founded. Lipos roused at the taste of undiluted Greek wine and through swollen blue lips he directed the chief warrior to the missing girl.

Soon after Lipos left, Arima heard a distant, wavering wolf howl and a visceral panic seized her. Her impulse was to abandon the fire and the wagon and run after the enaree, but she forced her fear into submission, clenching the knife tightly. The snowfall proved to be a blessing as well as a curse, for it drove the lone wolf away in search of shelter, and the rest of the night was spent with only the fall of snow on grass for companionship.

The cold threatened where the snow did not, seizing first Arima's hands and feet, creeping up her arms and legs, until the drowsiness Lipos had warned her of came. Rather than fighting it, she welcomed it, a friend promising escape from the shivering, the hunger, the fear. It beckoned her warmly and Arima, in relief, ran to it.

Ran to it across warm, sunny meadows speckled with wild peonies, a wide green heaven fired with red stars. And there, in the distance, grazed her mare. She ran to it, threw her arms around its neck, hugging it, welcoming the feel of the shaggy coat, the sweaty warm smell of its body. No incense here or sweet flowers; just dirt and sweat and the smell of an animal's power, and she loved it.

But the old horse turned away, rejecting her. Arima caught a sob in her throat and tried to cling to the mare's neck. Angered, the horse reared, struck out, and galloped free, leaving a sobbing Arima lying curled on her side in the sweet, sun-washed grass.

I let the horse die! she dreamed. But she didn't care what happened. The mare, her only freedom, was dead and she had let it die.

The soft, reassuring throb of hoofbeats came to her, radiating up through the dark loam and into her ear. Arima raised her head, relief flooding her heart. A warm nose pushed forcefully against her cheek, trying to rouse her. The mare had returned! Smiling, she opened her eyes.

The eyes that met hers were fierce and dark, the head sleek and grey. It was the stallion looming above her, its breath hot against her face. Weariness overcame Arima and she fell back to the ground, one dirty hand reaching for the great horse.

Bartatua found her at dawn, huddled on her side, about twenty paces from the overturned wagon and dead camp-fire, one arm stretched forlornly into the snow-laden grass. And around her—if he lived to the age of the gods, he would never understand it—trampled in the scant snowfall, the large, clear hoofprints of a horse.

BOOK 2

MELANION

I sacrifice to no god but to myself,
and to my belly here, to this great god.
—*Euripides*

HORSES! THEY ALWAYS GAVE HIM TROUBLE. HE COULD NEVER GET their legs exactly right. Oh, it seemed to matter little to the barbarians who bought his works; they were happy with most anything. But it mattered to him. He, Melanion, was a goldsmith like his father and his father before him. Every time he did an inferior piece, he could hear the shades of his ancestors questioning his abilities.

The horses' legs never quite suited him.

The small, high window in his shop was covered with a translucent piece of greased sheepskin, the cold dawning light that filtered through barely adequate for his needs. Melanion turned the minute wax carving he was working on, trying to determine precisely what was wrong. Winter work suited him better when he was melting the gold or polishing a finished piece of jewelry. Then, at least, the heat from the fire kept his fingers warm. But this wax carving in the cold was not to his liking. The wax grew too brittle, and delicate sculpting such as he favored was nearly impossible unless he warmed the tiny figure repeatedly in his hands to keep it pliable.

Drawing a quick, deep breath, he lay the carving on a napped piece of calfskin and stretched, straightening his back to relieve the knots in it. There was little trading to be done here on the shores of the landlocked Northern Sea in winter, but it was the time to replenish his stocks, to prepare the gold ornaments and trinkets so beloved of the Scyth chiefs and noblemen who would come trading with the spring, the melting of the snows, and the breaking of the ice-bound rivers.

Melanion shook his head and stood, casting another dissatisfied glance at the wax carving. A rearing stallion, held fast by two Scyth warriors whose leads to the animal were scarcely bigger than a horsehair. He liked such challenges, creating delicate new designs like this, and his customers did, too. His prices were high, his wares sold well, and he lived comfortably. Life was good.

Walking across the cramped second-floor room Melanion called home, the goldsmith bent and peered into a clay oven built into one corner. The embers from dinner's fire still glowed and he poked at them with a charred stick, stirring the coals to life. He pushed in several small chunks of dry wood, waited for the fire to catch, and began to fix himself a morning meal. Cold roast duck, he thought hungrily, taking the remains of the previous day's dinner from a shelf over the oven. A little brown wheat bread and some thick ale, it will be enough. And once the oven warms the room, I can get back to work on the wax carving.

A rattle came at the wooden door and he knew by the sound who it was. A slab of duck meat in hand, he crossed the room and lifted the bolt.

"Praxis," he stated, as if declaring the sky was blue or the sun was round.

"You work too much!" the tall, dark-haired young man

announced, stepping unbidden into his friend's room. Melanion exhaled in mild annoyance and closed the door. His friend had already spied the wood platter with the breakfast of leftover duck and bread and veered toward the plank table eagerly.

"Don't touch that!" the goldsmith snapped, racing his friend for the food. "Eat at your own place if you are hungry, or at the ale shop or the brothel."

Praxis laughed loudly, his steps never faltering. "Just came from there, my friend!" he hooted. "The cathouse! Come with me tonight; you should see what they've got! Three girls from Egypt, fine and dark and sleek as lionesses. Oh, Melanion, I tell you truly, they . . ."

He rolled his eyes dramatically and gestured with one hand in a motion that would do a tragic actor proud, while reaching for the duck meat with the other. Melanion appeared to be listening while he slid the plate out of reach.

"They what?" he asked, smiling in mild amusement. His friend could be annoying, always interrupting him and staying to drink too much, but still he was his friend, and Melanion enjoyed his antics.

Praxis's face fell and his head jerked sideways when his probing fingers found only the rough-planed wood of the table instead of plump, succulent roasted bird.

"They what?" Melanion repeated, halfway interested in the three Egyptian slave girls. Egyptian was one race he'd never had before, though he'd heard tales. He waited, eyeing Praxis carefully. It was obvious his friend had been out all night. His eyes were bloodshot, his attention span briefer than the flight of a housefly, and a stain of red wine spilled down the front of his woolly goatskin cloak.

"Sit down!" Melanion commanded, removing the soiled cloak from Praxis's shoulders and pushing a wooden stool toward him with one foot. "A little cold water will clear your head, and a little food will help your stomach." He tossed half of his last round loaf of bread to the table and pushed the duck meat back toward his friend. "Now tell me about the Egyptians!" The goldsmith grinned, settling himself amiably on a stool beside the bleary Praxis, all thoughts of work gone from his mind. But Egyptian charms suddenly seemed the last thing on Praxis's mind, for he lifted his sagging head and looked at Melanion in abrupt intensity.

"Persians," he blurted. Melanion straightened in surprise at the word.

"What?" he shot back. "What in the name of Pan are you on about now? Here, have more water. Don't tell me you paid for Persian women as well as Egyptian, all in one night!"

"No, no." Praxis shook his head, trying to clear his thoughts and remember what it was he had to say. "Persian noblemen are coming to town."

Melanion's amusement swiftly turned to interest. Persians in this godforsaken trading post were a rarity but they were rich enough, and paid well enough, that when they did come, everyone scrambled to take advantage of them. "When? Where?" he asked.

"Toward spring, they say," Praxis muttered between mouthfuls of food. "But no one knows why. There will be many, though, noblemen, and buyers for noblemen. We will be rich!" He grinned, poking a strand of meat into his mouth with one forefinger.

"But why so many?" Melanion slumped back, leaning against the mud-plastered log wall behind him. Money excited him, naturally, but as a Greek he had an inbred mistrust of the Persians.

Praxis shrugged, lifted a large clay cup, and downed the water in two swallows. "Who can say?" He thumped the cup to the table. "Maybe they heard of the excellence of your goldwork and my gem cutting and came to see for themselves!"

Melanion grimaced mockingly at his friend's jest and stood. "I do know, Praxis," he muttered, his mind suddenly alive with ideas and anxious to get back to work, "that you'd better get home and get some sleep, stop your all-night escapades, and do some work yourself, if you expect to take advantage of this windfall." He reached the door and turned, hoping that Praxis had taken the hint. He hadn't.

Melanion shook his head and returned to the wax carving he'd been working on. Praxis was slumped forward over the table, snoring loudly in a drunken sleep, his cheek resting on the bread loaf like a pillow.

Olbia was a frontier town, a trading colony established by the Greeks of Ionia where the river Borysthenes emptied into the Northern Sea. Because of its remoteness from the civilized Mediterranean lands to the south and its proximity to the savage, raiding nomads of the northern steppes, Olbia, like its sister colonies, was fortified with walls built of the plentiful timber that forested the river valley, with a garrison of soldiers from Greece to defend it. The vast wealth from the northern trade routes that entered its gates and left on ships from all over the known world made the burden of extra precaution worth the effort to Ionia, and to those of her citizens who endured the harsh frontier existence in order to reap a profit.

After having paid a fee to the Scyth chieftans whose lands they passed through, great caravans from the north sold their goods in the trading colonies lining the Northern Sea: furs of every description, cowhides and sheepskins, salt and honey, wheat from Scythian fields and amber from the Baltic, gold and slaves from Keltic lands, and copper and iron from the western mountains. Even timber went out from the fertile river valleys, sent to the wood-starved lands of the Mediterranean. In exchange the Greek traders sold olive oil and Greek wine to the Scyth tribesmen, also finished cloth and art objects, fine jewelry and metalwork. Like any frontier existence, life in the colonies was not easy, the climate was harsh, and amenities were absent. Yet it was where a man could grow wealthy, and that made up for any hardships he had to endure.

An exciting life, too; and that, as much as the wealth, was what attracted the Greek goldsmith Melanion, who had ventured across the rough Northern Sea in an open trading ship four years earlier, near his twentieth birthday. How well he would remember that day, a milestone in his life; lying seasick, cold, and wet amidst bales of fine linen cloth, the greased, waterproof oilskins covering them raising such a stench in his face that his stomach found little peace. His only escape was to imagine he was at home for his birthday, on the rocky coast of Ionia, with his old mother poaching fish for his birthday meal, his little sisters running squealing through the windswept house, and the sweet, full fragrance of a platterful of autumn fruit perfuming the room.

But today was not a day for such remembrances. This was a feast day, honoring the local harvest gods, and Melanion and Praxis had decided to celebrate in style.

In exactly what style, the goldsmith couldn't be sure. He fretted as he pulled a coarse wool tunic down over his chest, wincing at the itches that followed. Scarcely a day went by that he didn't miss fair and sunny Greece, its air as clear and luminous as a glowing jewel, its houses open and fresh and clean.

Melanion grimaced, twisting the tunic around from under his left arm. The cloth was coarse, and the manufacture was cruder. Give me a Greek chiton any day, he reflected; loose and draped and of wool so fine it carried a sheen, not these awkward, itchy barbarian clothes. Heavy shirts and thick trousers and boots on the feet, instead of sandals! A bulky fur coat beneath which a man could scarcely move, and in the depths of winter two, or three. And the worse abomination of all, a leather cap, tight and uncomfortable. But without all this, a man stood to freeze to death in winter.

Bah! he spat to the matted floor in exasperation, buckling

a heavy leather belt around his waist. As soon as I've made my fortune, I'm out of here and back to fair Greece. Leave this barbarian land to the barbarians.

Praxis entered unannounced and threw himself down into the only proper Greek chair in the room. "You're not ready, I see," he observed caustically. Melanion cast him a look of irritation and pulled up his new wool trousers, embroidered in the Scyth manner. He'd never understand how his friend managed to do it, but no matter where they were or what the circumstances, Praxis was always well turned out, at ease, as proper-looking as a native no matter what costume he was wearing, whether Scyth trousers or Egyptian kilt or Persian greatcoat.

"What's the news from the brothel?" Melanion muttered, trying to turn his mind to something other than the awful itch of the trousers on his backsides.

"The Egyptians are gone," Praxis sighed tragically, "but in their place are four new girls—two Medes, a Thracian, and a Cimmerian."

Melanion's ears perked up at the latter. The first two he'd heard of, but not the last. "A Cimmerian? What is that?" he asked. Plopping to a stool, he pulled a soft leather Scythian boot over his bare foot.

"A barbarian woman," Praxis answered, leaning back in the chair and stretching his long legs toward the meager warmth of the cook-oven. "Once they were a powerful people, so I hear, but now there is little left of them. Similar to the Scyth, with whom they warred, but different. For where Scyth women are meek and docile, Cimmerian women fight and hunt as well as the men. This one is a wildcat." He winked at Melanion and grinned.

"You've had her, then?" the goldsmith said, pulling on the second boot.

"No," the gem cutter shook his head. "Just tales, that's all, but tales are usually well-attached to the dog that wags them." He arched his brows and looked at his friend. Melanion was finished with his boots and grinning broadly at the pun.

"You spent too many years in Egypt, my friend." Melanion stood. "Now you even jest like them!" He clapped a hand to Praxis's extended leg so violently the gem cutter bolted upright at the sting. "I'll take the Cimmerian wildcat, Praxis; you tame the two Medes."

Melanion wondered what the life of a wealthy man might be like, though he had little doubt he'd get there eventually himself. Ah, to be a man who could afford a hetaera, a high-priced courtesan, beautiful, educated, intelligent. He and Praxis's booted feet thudded dully on the log streets as they walked toward the waterfront, the harbor, where all the nightlife was. Not that he complained about his life, mind you. He lived more comfortably than most in such a remote spot. But he couldn't help but wonder what a rich life must be like, where a man could take his pleasures in clean surroundings, with gracious company. . . .

As if to illustrate his thoughts, loud shouts suddenly emanated from a wineshop they were passing, and in the flickering dollop of light shining across the muddy logs the dark figure of a man suddenly erupted.

"Curse you to Hades," a voice called out from the tavern, followed by raucous female laughter. The ejected drunk landed on all fours, shook his head like a dazed animal, and vomited all over the log street and nearly atop Melanion's foot.

"Hey!" the goldsmith shouted, springing sideways to avoid the mess and colliding roughly with Praxis. Further comment was pointless. The drunk, a Greek sailor, had sagged to the street and lay unconscious, his mouth sagging open, one cheek resting in his own stale wine.

The wineshop had settled back to its usual level of noise, and patrons were stepping around the sailor as they entered and left it. Off in the darkness, a flute and an Egyptian sistrum began playing, a thin discordant tune of celebration.

Yes, what must the life of a rich man be like, Melanion thought wistfully as the music wavered through the night; to go for his pleasure without having to dodge drunks and vomit and horse dung in the process.

The brothel was an incongruously new building of hemlock logs and fragrant with the fresh, clean smell of raw wood, even over the staleness of sweat and ale and the feeble flower waters the girls used to scent themselves. Set on a roadway scarcely a hare's jump from the cavernous warehouses of the harbor, it was new only because the former building had fallen apart from age and neglect, collapsing onto the street and spilling its contents of frightened girls and rutting sailors onto the dusty road early one warm spring morning.

The bony old harridan who ran it welcomed the two artisans inside. Melanion always thought of her as Medusa, similarly thin, intense, and unpleasant as the pictures of the Gorgon his mother had created in his mind when he was a boy. All the old woman needed was snakes on her head. Still, she welcomed them familiarly and with more enthusiasm than she showed the staggering, shouting sailors and foreign traders. Business was business, but even a Gorgon had her limits.

"Evening, men." She forced a smile, glancing up at the two handsome young Greeks. If only she were twenty years younger . . . well, maybe thirty years.

She ran a tight ship, Melanion had to give her that. He ran his eyes around the low-ceilinged room, hazy from the smoke of dancing oil lamps on tall iron stands. Her girls sat on thin cushions on a bench along the far wall, all naked or nearly so, some lounging seductively, their eyes leaving no questions in a man's mind, others huddled as fearful as trapped rabbits or sitting like rigid marble statues. Two burly red-haired men stood at either end of the room, arms folded across their broad chests, their flint grey eyes scanning the crowd, ready to deal swiftly with any rowdy customers. An attendant, a withered old man, patrolled the girls, poking the timid ones with a hazel rod to force them to act more enticing. His efforts usually failed, and Melanion could see behind their eyes the look of someone's young wife, a bewildered daughter, a frightened child. Still, for a brothel in a frontier town, the place was clean and well run.

Praxis, forgetting the Medean women, had spied a morsel to his liking, a young girl with dark, cascading hair and a face so sweet it turned Melanion's heart to see it.

"Two drachmas for the night." The Medusa seemed adamant, unmoved by Praxis's attempts to haggle.

"I don't want her for the night, woman, just for a few minutes," the gem cutter protested. "One obol; that's still a good price. How about it? At that rate you could get many times two drachmas for a night with her."

Medusa shook her head, losing interest when a group of merchants entered behind them.

"A bit of lapis, then," Praxis gave in. The old woman knew his occupation, and what she could get out of him. He drew the string on a leather pouch at his waist and fished out a lump of deep blue stone, round and polished and nearly as big as his thumbnail. Melanion stifled a gasp when he saw it; Praxis must really want the lovely creature who'd taken his fancy.

The old woman, too, could not conceal her surprise.

"From far-off Armenia, land of rugged mountains and fierce horsemen." Praxis held the gem out on his open palm. Medusa snatched it away like a swooping eagle.

"I could use a fierce horseman myself," she growled, granting the gem cutter admission with a nod of her head. "One hour," she called after him. His back to her, Praxis motioned a reply with one hand as he strode toward his quarry. The girl saw his look and rose to meet him, a diaphanous linen gown hiding none of her charms. Melanion was disappointed to see a hardness appear on her cherubic face; inside, she was no different from the others.

"And you?" Medusa snapped, pocketing the piece of lapis and interrupting the goldsmith's musings. "I haven't got all night, you know. Others are waiting. What will it be for you?"

Melanion scanned his eyes over the assembled women. The idea of a wild little Cimmerian intrigued him but, having never seen one, he wasn't sure what a Cimmerian looked like. Was she pale, like the willowy northern beauty eyeing him from the far corner; or dark, like the two Medean women sitting together, rubbing oils onto their sleek bodies? He paused, watching them, before his eyes roamed on.

"You have a Cimmerian . . ." he began. The old lady drew herself up full-height and exhaled loudly.

"You, too?" she spat. "Ten more Cimmerian girls and I will be a rich woman."

"You have her, then?" Melanion prodded. "Where is she?"

"Not here!" the woman laughed. "Too wild! Everyone wants her—few have had her. What is your offer?" She knew his line of work, too, and that he could pay well if he so desired.

Melanion's mind whirled through a hurried parade of thought. Was it really so necessary that he have this barbarian girl? She would obviously be more expensive, and he saw many wenches here to his liking. Why not leave her to the rich merchants and traders and have a more reasonably priced bit of fun? He was, after all, here to enjoy himself and not to outbid the wealthy.

His hand went into his leather money pouch and he withdrew a tiny nugget of gold. Medusa's eyes sparked interest but she was wise. Where there was one nugget, there would be more. "Huh!" she snorted. "You must be some stallion. For that much gold you can have her for the space of two cries of an eagle. Do you perform that well, then?"

Melanion felt his ears redden and he heard snorts of derision from the men waiting behind him. Normally he would let it pass. He had no doubts about his abilities in bed. But she had challenged him in front of everyone and his manhood must not be questioned. He brought out another nugget, slightly larger than the first.

"This is my final offer, woman." He lowered his voice menacingly. "For this much gold I could walk out of this pigsty and find myself two streetwalkers to keep me company for the night."

She moved to snatch the nuggets away but he was quicker, closing his hand around them. "I see her first . . ." he said flatly.

Medusa was too eager for the gold. "Ars!" she bellowed. One of the red-haired giants stepped away from his post by the wall. "Show this gentleman the Cimmerian," she barked. The guard grunted and turned, motioning Melanion to follow. Trying to act as confident as the rich men he'd seen, the goldsmith threaded his way through the crowded room.

She wasn't exactly beautiful, his Cimmerian whore, but she did have an interesting face, and the artist in him appreciated it. The nose was too long, the chin a bit too pointed; by classic Greek standards she might almost be called ugly. But her cheekbones were high and fine, and, coupled with her odd grey almond eyes, they gave her a regal dignity the other girls seemed to lack. She sat in a locked storeroom that had been hastily brightened with dyed cloths thrown over a pile of old furs and nailed to the bare log walls. She didn't slouch as the timid girls did, nor invite provocatively. She sat upright, draped in a piece of white linen, her chin thrust out defiantly, her shoulders back as if daring any man to touch her.

But one did. Ars the guard leaned into the tiny room and snatched away the cloth that covered her. The girl never flinched, her eyes didn't blink as they stared back at the goldsmith, and Melanion wondered fleetingly if he would be able to handle her. The stories plainly were true.

"Nice, eh?" Ars grinned conspiratorially. Melanion thrust the gold at him and turned, suddenly wanting to shield the barbarian girl from his leers.

"Go," he mumbled, pushing the giant away and reaching for the rope door handle.

"Eh, good eh?" the guard roared lustily at Melanion's seeming eagerness. "An hour, then. Good luck!"

Melanion slammed the door against the guard's loud laughter and turned. The girl had not moved. Roaming his eyes down her naked body, he found pure male fire replacing his previous concern. And yet he knew to merely grab her would result in a fight. He could see it in her eyes. He was here to enjoy himself, not to fight.

Her eyes shifted as wary as a lioness's when he moved closer. To her surprise, he sat down beside her on the makeshift bed, his hands resting in his lap. If she had ever thought to admire a soft, comfort-ridden Greek man, she supposed she could admire him. He was tall, well built, and his face had a kind, intelligent look she had not seen on any of the other men at the brothel. His hair was the color of ripe wheat, pale gold and rippling, and his blue eyes, though filled with lust, seemed as gentle as a pup's. "Name? Your name?" he spoke into the closeness of the room. She knew the Scyth word; she did not care to reply.

The Greek tried again. "Melanion . . ." He pointed to his chest. The finger shifted to her. "And you?"

"Sela," the girl whispered, turning her face away and showing at last some of the fear he knew she must be feeling.

Assuming she would not know Greek, he tried a few more Scyth words on her.

"You are from . . ." he urged, trying to win her trust.

"Far away," she blurted. It was obvious she knew the Scyth tongue.

"And you came here?" His eyes kept drifting down to watch the slow rise and fall of her small breasts, and the fire growing inside him made attempts at conversation harder and harder. The girl sensed this. Her posture grew tense and her breathing became rapid and shallow. But still she did not try to cover herself or turn away from his hungry gaze, as if to do so would be to admit defeat.

"Stolen like a chief's prized mare," she said dully. Melanion found himself amused by the quaintness of the expression. Forcing his eyes from her body to her face, he found her staring at him openly, daring him to touch her. It was enough. He was a man, and he'd paid good gold for this time. If he wanted to chat, he could visit the ailing bake shop owner. Standing abruptly, he pulled off his heavy fur cloak and threw it aside. There was not time enough to undress, much as he liked the feel of a woman's skin next to his. Nakedness was natural to a Greek, but now he had to take her while he was clothed, like a barbarian man. Untying the waist of his trousers, he dropped them to the floor.

"Lie down," he ordered. The girl sat unmoved, as if suddenly unable to understand Scyth words. Her stubbornness infuriated him. He was ready for her; any fool could see that. Throwing himself atop her, he forced her back onto the piled furs.

"Sela is it?" he muttered, closing a hand around her breast. "You must learn to do what you are told . . ."

He began biting her neck hungrily, but she remained cold and lifeless. Where was the fight in her? What had happened to the Cimmerian wildcat? He raised his head and looked at her. She was staring at him, hatred and defiance in her eyes.

"You are no tigress," he mocked her. For this he had paid a month's wages in gold? He'd just as well make love to the spitted calf out in the whorehouse. He thrust hard into her, a move that always elicited some type of reaction from a woman. The girl blinked briefly and did nothing. Puzzled and angry, he rode her as hard as he could. He had always prided himself on his lovemaking abilities, but he drew no response from her at all.

He finished and stood, giving a final bit of attention to her breasts to try and feel like he'd got something for his money. Sela lay still and silent, looking at him with her odd, high-cheeked gaze. "By Aphrodite, you are as cold as ice," he muttered, pulling up his trousers. He didn't know the time, but he hoped his hour was nearly up. Her presence was suddenly unbearable to him.

"I am a chief's daughter," she spat in flawless Scyth. "I make love as well as any woman. But only with *men . . .*" She sat up, snatched the linen cloth from the floor, and draped it around her body. Her eyes returned blankly to the door as if he weren't there, and Melanion suddenly saw the truth to it all.

In name only was she a wildcat, the little Cimmerian slave girl. And wise old Medusa made the most of it, trading on the novelty of Cimmerian women, keeping her in a locked room, charging a high price. Intrigued, a procession of rich men had paid handsomely for her, been puzzled and then humiliated by her coldness, and had been too proud to admit it. Wasn't she, after all, a tigress? Everyone said so. Failure by failure, tales of her wildness grew, told by men boasting to overcome their shame. And none of it was true . . .

"I'll be back," Melanion growled, thankful for the return of Ars. He was no quitter. Somewhere in that aloof white body beat the heart of a woman, and he was determined to find it.

* * *

The sun had warmed the day nicely; a rarity, Melanion thought tiredly, in this cold, windswept land. He felt foolish, prowling the nearly empty agora, hoping to find some trinket that a woman would like. Even had the shops been open and the tradesmen bustling about, buying women's things was not his habit. What do married men do? he wondered. Send out a slave woman? Let the wife buy her own things? He was glad for the heat of the sun radiating from the log road and stone walls, warming him as the violet shadows of evening crept between the shuttered buildings.

The wineshop owner's wife had mentioned a place, open even in winter, where women could purchase such frills as they needed. He saw it ahead, just where she'd said it was; a tiny shop tucked between a vast shuttered building and the far wall of a grey stone temple to Baal. He knew the temple was open by the two stone pillars, head-high, upon which incense burned defiantly in the gathering gloom. The priests fed them continuously with fragrant lumps of frankincense, giving the street a pungent-sweet smell that seemed to have permeated the very mud beneath his feet. A welcome change from dung and garbage, he sighed, pausing before the old planed door of the women's shop, summoning his courage. If he had not been told, he would not have guessed it hid any sort of business. Squaring his shoulders, he went in.

The narrow shop was darker than the dusk outside, and the smell of incense outside the temple paled before the scent of unguents and perfumes that assaulted his nose. Surely every fragrance known to woman mingled around him! Involuntarily he took a step backward, toward the safety of the door and the freedom of fresh air. Past torches flickering on the wall, shadows danced and light flared, women's garments hung still and deathlike, a glint of silver chain beckoned, far down the narrow room.

"Melanion the goldsmith!"

He started at the sound, and at the sight of a graceful

woman who materialized from beyond the hanging dresses. Melanion squinted, wondering who she might be, and why she should know him.

"You don't remember?" There was merriment in her voice. The woman drew closer, her face growing clearer, and he remembered. "The Feast of the New Year!" he blurted. Her face was nearly eye-to-eye with him and he scanned it briefly. The skin had lost its tone—even in the poor light he could see that—and she was far too made-up, but old memories came flooding back. His first year at Olbia, unsure of himself, longing for home, wandering aimlessly through the revelers who celebrated the holiday, he'd stopped to help a woman whose cloak had snagged on a nail. They chatted, bought more wine, and ended up in each other's embrace, nestled in a pile of straw by the stables. The night was so hazy he scarcely remembered it, but he did remember her, the first real woman he'd ever had.

"I, ah . . ." he muttered, finding his task all the harder now. He couldn't even recall the woman's name.

"You need something?" she prodded, still smiling. Melanion ran his eyes down her embroidered gown, lavish in the Persian manner. Yes, he did remember a bit of it, chiefly her regal body, a body such as no young girl could dream of. He toyed briefly with the idea of forgetting about Sela and taking advantage of the opportunity that had suddenly presented itself. The warm smell of her as she stood before him was beginning to affect him.

"A gift," he blurted, returning his eyes to her face. "I need a gift for . . . a friend."

"What type of gift?" She knew he could pay well. "A robe, perhaps, or a fine gown of sheer Egyptian linen?" She turned toward the hanging clothes but Melanion stopped her. Clothes would be no good. A fine robe or sheer gown would be the last thing Sela needed.

"Something small, easy to conceal. It is a surprise, you see."

The black kohl around her eyes wrinkled merriment. "Some ointment!" she declared and marched off into the shadows. Melanion had no desire to follow her and so he waited, shifting restlessly from foot to foot. Why was he even going through all this for some plain-looking slave girl?

The woman returned with a jar of creamy white alabaster, small and round and fitting neatly into the palm of her hand. Lifting the lid, she thrust it under his nose. Melanion inhaled, lightly at first, then more deeply. It was nice, he had to admit. Sweet, full, rich.

"From Egypt," she explained. "Scented with their sacred blue lotus flowers. The odor is so fragile, it does not last long. Any woman would love it."

He did not know what "any woman" would love. It smelled good to him. "Yes," he said nodding, anxious to leave. "How much?"

Sela lay still, waiting for the rough, callused hands of the merchant to be done with her. He'd been unceremonious in his attentions. Marching in the door, he'd flung off his rich sable cloak, dropped his breeches, and in one swift move had both stripped and mounted her. His need was so overwhelming he neither needed any arousal nor noticed her lack of fire. The one blessing in such men, Sela mused dully, is that they are soon done and gone. *I feel sorry for his wife, or has the fool ever been clever enough to find one?* That always lifted her spirits a bit; imagining these dirty, frantic, sex-mad men in their own homes, with babies wetting their knees and wives nagging in their ears. *What kind of husbands were they, what kind of fathers?*

Her back was chafed raw against the rough cover of the bed as the man forced her back and forth, back and forth, and she flinched and resisted the impulse to hit him when his fingers dug too harshly into her breast. Some men might consider that exciting, and she would give him none of that. He bit her neck hungrily, his dirty hair falling into her face, and she held her breath against the smell of it. I could cry at the thought of freedom, she choked, but I will not. They will never defeat me.

By the merciful gods, is he finished? Sela closed her eyes tiredly. The merchant was standing, pulling his breeches up from his ankles, grabbing his cloak from the floor. He seems perfectly satisfied, she thought scornfully, peering at him through a scant slit in her lids. What a lump he is! Why doesn't he save his money and go mount a sheep somewhere; he'd get just as much pleasure.

Her heart fell when the wooden door opened, the merchant left, and another customer entered. Her weary eyes, sagging closed, flew open at the sound of a Greek accent.

"Sela?" it said.

She sat up abruptly, for some reason feeling the need to cover herself. It was the Greek goldsmith, wooly goatskin cloak in hand, eyeing her openly. She slumped forward, trying to hide herself from him as he stepped toward the bed.

"I brought you something," he muttered, his voice husky with what she had learned was male passion. Curious, she lifted her head. A gift? For her? She was a harlot, not a woman to be courted.

He held out a round white object that seemed dwarfed in his large male hand. Reaching out to take it, she slouched back in awkward shame. The Greek laughed at her, friendly and open, and thrust the gift closer.

"See if you like it," he urged, tossing his cloak aside. They both knew his time was limited. Puzzled, Sela took the little white globe from his hand. The top lifted off and when she opened it a scent almost intoxicating in its sweetness filled the musty room.

"From Egypt," he explained, sitting beside her. The girl immediately tensed. Men had many tricks, many ways of seduction. Gifts, she knew, were one of them. "No." She shook her head and thrust the perfume at him.

"It's yours," he insisted, pushing it back to her. "I have no use for it. Would you have me going around smelling like an Egyptian princess?"

Sela smiled slightly at the idea and cradled the beautiful jar in her hands. Such a lovely thing for one who had had only ugliness in her life lately. Despite her caution she held it close, lifted the lid, and sniffed again, closing her eyes in pleasure. No sweaty men and dirty furs and stale, smokey rooms—just the pure sweetness of a flower. Wiping a finger through the thick, oily pomade, she held it up and cast a puzzled look at Melanion.

"Just wipe it on," he urged. "It isn't like the cheap flower waters the other girls use. It will last much longer. It should! It cost me half a month's wages!"

Sela took her forefinger and wiped the unguent slowly down the side of her neck and Melanion stared at her, swallowing at the sensuousness of it. Did she do that deliberately? he wondered. Has one small gift won her approval?

"Take it." She snapped the lid in place, as if suddenly aware of his thoughts. "You will not buy me with one jar of perfume, no matter how fine it is."

Melanion grew irritated. Why? He wasn't sure. Her words were true—that was his motive. But was that why they annoyed him so? "I could force you, girl," he snapped, taking the jar from her angrily. "Twenty times a day I could pay the old hag who owns you, and come in here and force you, and be spending my gold for my pleasure, not yours. I could get ten friends and we could all use you, and not have to treat you like any kind of person at all. You are too contrary, fine princess. I try to treat you like a woman, and you insult me. I'm sure one of the other harlots would welcome so fine a gift."

The force of his words surprised him; his anger came as a shock. Why was he determined to waste his time and money to thaw her woman's heart, when there were fifty girls outside the door who could pretend well enough, and cheaply enough, to suit any man. Why?

Suddenly subdued, Sela lowered her face into one hand. Damn her, Melanion thought, staring not at her naked body but at the downcast face. Without looking up, she took her free hand and removed the lid of the jar he held. "You do it," she whispered, inviting him. Sitting straight, she closed her eyes and thrust her poor, battered body to view. Melanion couldn't help but pity her. Somehow, a woman's nakedness was not so exciting when raw red finger marks marred her breasts, and scrapes from men's teeth scarred her slim neck. Wiping a forefinger through the ointment, he touched it to the hollow beneath her jaw and swept it down, over the curve of her neck, the dip at her throat, between her breasts, to her stomach. The sweetness of the perfume, the softness of her skin, overwhelmed him. Closing his hand over the jar, he leaned forward and clamped his mouth to hers.

"You old satyrs!"

The ale shop stank from the smell of unwashed bodies, sour beer, and filth. In the gloom of the low wooden roof, a darkness punctuated by horn lanterns spaced along the log walls, Melanion saw a bench upon which lounged several drunken soldiers. He hailed them as he entered, and their captain raised a hand in response.

"Another Greek! We should throw a party!" the man shouted amiably. Nothing better than a cheerful drunk, the goldsmith grinned, buying a small clay jug of ale at the door and threading his way between the sagging bodies and sprawled legs of the drinkers. Smelly it might be, but the ale shop offered a welcome, warm and sociable spot amidst the winter barrenness around them.

The captain pushed roughly at a soldier sitting next to him. Melanion pulled the twisted rope stopper from his ale jug and took a long, slow swallow as he waited for a space to be cleared on the bench. The captain was having difficulty with his man; the soldier had toppled sideways, a limp arm nearly knocking the captain's high-crested bronze helmet to the filthy floor.

"By Hades!" the captain muttered, trying to juggle ale, helmet, and soldier with two hands. The soldier sagged further, belched loudly, and settled into a contented snooze.

"Here," Melanion offered, grinning at the man's predicament. He took the captain's ale jug, and the man looked up at him in surprise.

"Drink that, goldsmith, and I'll make you a eunuch," he snapped, standing and flinging the snoring soldier, armour and all, in a clattering heap on the floor.

"A eunuch, eh?" Melanion retorted. "Need someone to keep you company?" The men around them broke into loud hoots of laughter.

"It could only improve your love life, goldsmith," the captain shot back, retrieving his jug of ale.

"Oh, I don't know," Melanion settled back on the bare wood bench and took another gulp of ale, "that Cimmerian seems to enjoy me well enough."

"So I've heard," the captain belched. "Lucky the man who can afford her. You don't make a soldier's pay, and thank the gods for that, my friend. With what I earn, I'm lucky to afford two jugs of cheap ale, one for me and one for some horny housemaid I've lucked upon. You goldsmith," he snorted and wiped his nose with the back of one hand.

"I'll buy you more ale tonight." Melanion tried to sound amiable. "It has been a hard day. My back is sore, my eyes are burning. At least a soldier is out in the fresh air, and not stuck away in some smokey room, squinting over goldwork in light so poor a cat could barely see."

"You make your money, friend," the captain retorted, shrugging. The soldier in the floor shifted, rolling against their legs, and the man kicked him away roughly. "Mongrel!" He spat down at the soldier. "What kind of men do they send me out here? Mongrels!"

He certainly seemed to be in a sour mood. Melanion roamed his eyes over the crowded room, looking for some other opportunity. Gossip had it that Persians were coming to trade, and he'd hoped his friend the captain, commander of the Greek garrison in Olbia, could give him an introduction to one or two of them. But the man was plainly in no mood to talk. A group of Thracian seamen huddled in one corner, rolling dice, with an excited crowd gathered to watch. Perhaps he'd stand a better chance of getting rich with some heavy betting. But Thracians, he sighed and gave up the idea. Their dice were probably weighted. He watched one of them snatch his soft peaked cap from his head and throw it to the floor in exasperation while the onlookers laughed. An honest Thracian, poor fool, he smiled to himself; they are the only kind of Thracians who lose.

"Dice, eh?" the captain muttered, tipping his jug up, finding it empty, and peering into it as if to see where the ale went. Melanion shook his head and took another drink.

"Too risky. I only like to gamble when I know I'll win."

"Like the Persians," the man answered, placing the empty jug with ridiculous precision on the bench by his helmet. If it dropped and shattered, he'd have to pay for it. Carefully he fumbled in the purse at his belt, his face falling when his fingers found nothing.

"Here, take this." Melanion pressed a tiny bronze obol into the man's hand. "Buy another and come tell me about the Persians."

The captain turned back into a cheerful drunk, stood unsteadily, and picked up the empty jug. "Watch that for me, will you?" he motioned to his helmet. In Olbia, anything not watched was soon stolen. Melanion gave a brief nod and watched the long red cloak thrown behind the captain's shoulders sway in time to his staggering gait as he made his way back to the shopkeeper. He soon returned, settling down with a sigh and pulling the rope stopper from a fresh jug of ale.

"The Persians," he began, dropping the twisted rope to the floor. The new drink seemed to refresh him. "Ah, yes, a handful of noblemen due any day."

"Noblemen?" Melanion's interest rose.

The captain nodded and paused to collect his thoughts. "Yes, noblemen, on business, so they say. They secured permission to come here, and I saw the reports. Kinsmen of the king, I believe. I did not like it. Who can trust a Persian? And we, being Greek, and wealthy."

Melanion nodded grave agreement as he waited for the man's rambling story to continue. What kind of business were they on? Might it include goldsmiths?

"They claim they want to buy some goods. Well, why not? We are a rich colony," the captain went on.

Melanion could wait no longer. "What about gold?" he blurted. The soldier on the floor suddenly groaned and rose to his hands and knees, but a shove from the captain's foot sent him toppling sideways and back into oblivion. The captain's dark eyes creased in amusement at Melanion's words.

"Ah, I thought so, my good friend!" He laughed loudly. "Spend some time with the old captain, eh? Buy me more ale, too. You're only courting business, aren't you? I should have guessed. I, too, am Greek. I know your methods, Melanion."

"A woman," Melanion blurted, anxious to shut him up before the whole shop knew of the Persian visit. The man paused in midword, his mouth hanging open.

"A woman," Melanion repeated. "Put in a word for me, get me some business with the Persians, and I will give you money for a woman at the brothel."

The captain's eyes squinted disbelief and he ran a hand

through his sweaty brown hair. "Any woman?" he muttered. May as well make it worth his while.

Melanion nodded.

"Even the Cimmerian? Wouldn't mind sharing her, would you?" He clapped a hand on the goldsmith's broad shoulder. What could he say? She wasn't his. Almost angrily, Melanion nodded.

"Agreed, then!" the captain boomed, finishing off the new ale. "Some Persian noblemen for you, the Cimmerian wildcat for me."

Melanion didn't want to think of it. The thought of this stocky, muscular captain doing who-knows-what with Sela angered him. He'd been forced to it, he tried to convince himself; cornered like a stray dog, and tricked into his undoing. He stood abruptly.

"I'll stop by to collect my money in a few days," the captain said, grinning. Melanion stepped over the sprawled body of the soldier and silently strode away.

Melanion admired the Persians, despite the deep-seated animosity his people held for them. Holding dear the ideals of individuality and love of freedom, Greeks took an intense dislike to the strong central authority of the Persian government, the absolute power of their kings, and their expansionist ways.

But they were rich.

To Melanion that fact alone excused a multitude of Persian defects. Through his friendship with the garrison leader in Olbia and a few well-chosen words over a good meal, now two resplendent Persian noblemen stood in his shop, fingering the most delicate gold jewelry he had to show them. Their dark beards and long hair, oiled and curled into neat ringlets, swung ridiculously back and forth as they muttered to each other, and the goldsmith found he had to occupy himself with other tasks to keep from bursting out laughing. For a great civilization, he reflected, its people certainly dressed in a barbarian manner, the garish colors and designs of their trousers and coats nearly as jarring as the costumes of the most unlettered Scyth chieftain or Keltic warlord.

"How much for this?" The taller Persian nobleman interrupted his musings. Melanion looked up from the armlet he was pretending to buff and saw the man's dark, slim fingers dangling a heavy gold collar. The goldsmith's breath caught when he saw it, for it was one of his most expensive pieces.

"Three hundred Attic drachmas," he said, judging the man's reaction in his swarthy face. Three hundred drachmas!

The nobleman didn't flinch. Even the pomaded curls of his beard were still. "Too much," he exhaled, lowering the fine piece of goldwork as if it hurt him to let it go.

"But feel it!" Melanion lifted it away from the man, hefting the heaviness of the gold for emphasis. "Fine Nubian gold, pure, a grand investment just for the metal alone, and that does not even include the workmanship I put into it! Look!"

The goldsmith held the collar into the light from the high shop window, filtering in a fine glow through the oiled skin that covered it. The glow was artfully calculated, for it highlighted the raised lotus blossoms of Egyptian design that encircled the piece. He'd deliberately used that motif, knowing it was more appealing to Persian buyers than the garish designs he produced for the local Scyth chiefs.

"And what are you, little man, that your workmanship is so highly valued?" sniffed the shorter nobleman. Ah, these Persians! Melanion stifled his annoyance. The measure of a man was not the man, but his wealth, his rank, his proximity to the king himself.

"I come from a long line of skilled goldsmiths," Melanion bragged coolly. "My grandfather made gold chains and vessels for the Temple of Apollo at Delphi. His father was employed by a pharaoh of Egypt."

"And why do you not work for a pharaoh, eh?" The taller one grinned. He slid his fingers lovingly over the necklet in Melanion's hands, and the Greek could tell he had a powerful hunger for the piece.

"The world is a more crowded place today." Melanion withdrew the collar as if to return it to its locked box. "Where once a Greek craftsman was considered a prize, today he must compete with Medes, Thracians, even the sons of Egyptians his grandfather's father helped train!"

The tall nobleman chuckled. "Too true, Greek!" He turned and spoke rapidly to his companion. Melanion lowered the collar to its box, visions of sudden wealth vanishing like sand between his fingers.

"Wait!" The tall Persian halted him. "We will take the piece if you come down a bit on the price. Two hundred."

"No. The gold alone is worth—"

"And a commission."

Melanion's ears perked up at the alluring phrase. The nobleman didn't bandy words about.

"An armlet, but of Persian design. Can you do that, Greek?" the Persian asked.

"An armlet, that's all? Cut the price for the collar by a third, in exchange for doing an armlet? Why don't you just rob me and be done with it?" Melanion growled. He turned away angrily. They must think they are dealing with a fool, the arrogant Persian bastards.

"It will be a test, you see," the man said, soothing him. "We must know if you can do a Persian design. Your work is very fine, but all we see here is Greek, Egyptian, Scyth."

"A test for what?" Melanion was suddenly annoyed by their presence, by the oppressive odor of rose water and oily pomade that hung around them, by their dark eyes and dark skin and immaculate hands and garish clothes. He almost didn't care to hear their answer.

"We cannot give you details, only tell you this: it is a test for another commission that will make you a wealthy man. To become so, you must do only two things—finish the armlet by spring and bring it to us at a place you will be told of later. If it is satisfactory, then the second thing you must do is relocate your business."

"Relocate?" Melanion fumbled at the word. This whole transaction was taking on the odd, unreal quality of a dream. "Where?"

"To the east. Join up as a goldsmith to the nobles marching with the army of the Great King, King of Kings, Darius the Great of Persia."

Melanion went first to the Temple of Apollo, a small crude structure but the best the frontier town could offer, to deposit for safekeeping his gold jewelry and the small sack of Attic drachmas the Persians had paid him. By the Fates, who could have foretold—not even the great Oracle of Apollo herself—how this day, when it began, would be ending! Had all his years of study and practice, of wandering, planning, and scheming, suddenly paid off? There, in the person of two dandified Persian noblemen, had his fortune been made, his future assured?

He rounded a corner of the frozen, rutted street and glanced ahead to what passed for the agora, the marketplace, in Olbia. Empty market stalls, shuttered against the gusting wind, stood as forlorn as ailing friends. A smattering of temples to deities both Greek and barbarian lined one side of the open area. Different gods and goddesses, yet all alike in the spare unnaturalness of their makeshift dwellings. In a bow to their status, most of the temples were at least partly of stone—a facade, a foundation—rather than the crude wood dwellings of their human worshippers, but even at their best the temples were a long way from the splendid edifices of Greece, of Egypt, of Mesopotamia.

Melanion deposited his precious goods with the priest on

duty at Apollo's temple and left, taking with him just a few of the drachmas he'd received for the collar and yet-to-be made armlet. Such a day as this deserved a celebration. A good hearty drink and a hot gruel of beans at an ale shop, and then . . . He jingled the tiny coins merrily. Another visit to Sela, the dark Cimmerian princess.

It was his seventh visit to her, and by now they were friends of a sort. Sela knew the ruse old Medusa was using her for, and when it came to Melanion she went along with it. He was the only man who treated her decently, who brought her good ale, fresh bread, a vial of perfumed ointment. She responded by playing her part for him, screeching and sobbing, moaning, begging, making all the world beyond the locked storeroom door listen, awed and admiring of the Greek stallion who'd finally subdued her. All, that is, except the other men who'd been fooled. They listened, they puzzled, and silently they wondered to themselves just what magic this blonde Greek possessed, to so inflame this girl who had all the passions of a pine board. It was a great game, and Melanion and Sela loved to play it.

But this night, when Medusa opened the brothel door to him, her leathery old face showed a certain discomfort at his presence. That is odd, Melanion thought, she knows my needs, I pay well, I cause no trouble. Usually she is glad to see me. Yet there is no mistaking the unease in her eyes.

"Sela is not well tonight," the woman hissed beneath her breath. "Another girl will do for now, and perhaps in the future when Sela is better you can . . ."

Melanion waved away the short, dark-haired girl, Praxis's favorite, who advanced toward him. It was plain they had planned it before he got there.

"How about two, then?" Medusa tried to bargain. "For the price of one Cimmerian, you can have two of my other girls."

"No!" the Greek declared. "If Sela is unwell, I will be

brief with her. What are these little girls to me, compared with the Cimmerian wildcat? Give me three or four for the price; they still will not be equal!" Medusa seemed baffled by his attitude, in light of what she knew about the girl, but when Melanion pulled out a drachma, glinting yellow by the torches, the old woman flinched visibly.

"Well, no. The girl is ill," she protested, plainly waiting to see if he'd produce another coin to go with the first. Melanion's suspicions were high, and he held firm to the one he'd offered.

"Just a few minutes," he said, tempting her, turning the coin to catch the light. It glistened like a cat's eye in the shadows. "I will not be rough with her or aggravate her condition. A few minutes, no more."

He didn't know what to expect when he entered the cramped room. A bad cold, a rash, some Eastern plague? He never expected what he found.

Sela had been beaten. She lay curled on her side, her back to the door, the piece of linen cloth scarcely covering her bruised legs. He couldn't see her face, but he could tell by her ragged breathing in the silent room that she was in pain.

"Sela! What happened?" He rushed forward, nearly stepping into a shallow wooden bowl of clear water sitting by the makeshift bed. Sela's slim hand moved halfheartedly at his voice, her fingers attempting to cover the bruises on her face.

"It is over," she whispered, her almond eyes looking at him through the shadows.

"What is over? What happened to you?" He removed his goatskin cloak and threw it behind her. Sitting beside the girl, he was afraid to touch her for fear of hurting her more.

"The ruse, it's over." Sela choked, an edge of hysteria rising in her voice.

"Here now . . ." Melanion patted her bare shoulder awk-

wardly. "I brought you a little jug of ale and some bread."
He fumbled in the leather pouch at his waist while the girl
tried to regain her composure. He found the food and thrust
it at her. "You need food. Have you eaten today? The ale will
clear your head." He wasn't sure what to say or do. Treating
the injured was not a man's work. But he did know that he
was puzzled, and angry.

Sela reached blindly for the ale, and he pushed the little
clay jug into her hand. Rising on one elbow, she tilted her
head back so cautiously he could feel her pain. Downing the
ale in three desperate gulps, she sagged back to the bed.

"I don't have much time. It's all the old woman would
allow," the Greek whispered urgently. "Tell me what happened. Why is the ruse over?"

"A soldier, a big powerful Greek," Sela muttered,
". . . drunk. He paid a fortune for me."

Melanion drew in a sharp gasp of air. The captain! And
he'd paid the whole bribe for Sela! He was a fool to have
offered so much, and Medusa was a fool to have taken it.

"When I did nothing, he hit me. Said all women liked it.
Three times he hit me, and I still did nothing. He was
enraged, Melanion."

Her almond eyes clouded and tears gathered along her
lashes.

"He said it was all a trick, and the fourth time he hit me,
I'd had enough. Cimmerian women are not beaten."

She exhaled shakily.

"I hit him back. We fought fiercely."

Melanion looked at his hands, curled helplessly in his lap.
He knew it was all his doing. His greed had brought it on
her. When he looked up, to his surprise, Sela was smiling.

"He did not get the better of me. He will not hit a
Cimmerian woman again." Reaching out, her right hand
probed beneath the topmost fur of her bed and she pulled
out a stiff, greyish piece of flesh, dark with encrusted blood.

"My first battle trophy!" She laughed lightly, and Melanion saw it was a human ear.

He drank ale, but could not sleep. A little stale bread and sheep's-cheese did no better. A walk in the frigid night air gave him little relief, nor did hot tea made from an herb that brings sleep. That night all he saw before him were those two sultry, defiant almond eyes. All he could hear in his mind was not the peaceful oblivion of sleep but the quiver in her voice, the challenge in her tone, the fear and the fight all combined in one slim, battered body.

Melanion brushed the curling yellow hair from his forehead and stared into the black depths of the ceiling above his cot. Somehow the whole bloom of promise had been plucked from the vine of his life, in the space of only a few moments. The happy future, the promised wealth, the lifelong dreams, all were gone and all because of him. . . .

He sat up; sleep was hopeless. Peace of mind was hopeless. Working on the Persian armband was hopeless, not while his mind churned so.

In the last few moments before Ars rushed him from the storeroom, Sela had tucked away her "trophy" and whispered the hurried truth to him. Old Medusa planned to sell her, as soon as her bruises healed. Many men had suggested it to the woman, but the princess had been too lucrative a property to sell. Now the secret was out. Men all over town, newly emboldened by the captain's loud drunken demands for the return of his coins, told one another how they, too, had been duped by the old woman and how the celebrated Cimmerian tigress was only a lifeless stuffed kitten. Feeling was running high against her, customers were going elsewhere, it was bad for business.

The girl had to go. For a good price, of course, made better when her bruises were healed. Then she would be as good as new and bring good money to her owner. Then, old Medusa felt sure, a captain of Thracian archers who'd seen Sela briefly while he was engaged with two other girls could be convinced of what a bargain he'd get. Especially since he was away at the moment, and by the time he returned all the talk would have died away. He'd never know what a mule's foal he was really buying—until it was too late.

The thought turned Melanion's blood nearly as cold as the silently falling snow outside. The thought that this Thracian archer could, in a rage at his deception, beat Sela, kill her, sell her to someone else, on and on until her life was swiftly over, was too much to bear. And not just that nightmare. There was also the simple fact that she was a princess, beautiful, intelligent, fierce of heart, and did not deserve a life of slavery and abuse. Why, if he was the marrying sort, he might even want her for himself. He was not, but even so, to subject Sela to such a fate would be like chaining a wild eagle to a rock. It was not meant to be.

He knew, before he had formed it clearly in his mind, the path his ideas were taking. He had nearly two hundred drachmas secreted away at the Apollonian Temple. He did not know the asking price for Sela, but perhaps it would be enough.

"Three hundred drachmas . . ."

The words fell like doom on Melanion's ears. He knew he could talk the old woman down a bit, but he would still be nearly a hundred short. He didn't have money like that. He was just a goldsmith. He wouldn't receive more on his commission from the Persians till spring, when he was to deliver the armband and join with the army of the Great King. And that would be too late to save Sela.

"Two-fifty," he found himself saying. No matter that his lips were working independently of his brain. Old Medusa did not like the offer anyway.

"Three hundred," she repeated. "Didn't you hear me, or do you have a nugget of gold hidden in each ear?"

"I have almost two hundred," Melanion tried to reason

with her. "Next spring I'll get more from the Persian noblemen."

"Next spring!" Medusa fumed, rising from the low round table in a corner where the two sat, dickering over a heavy, dark ale. "What is that to me? Next spring could see us all dead. I am running a business. Three hundred it is, like it or no‘ If you don't have the price, someone else will."

"Two-eighty?" He tried one last time, looking up at her imploringly.

"You really want her then?" The woman gave him a crooked smile. "She must really rattle your spear, eh?"

Melanion forced a laugh at her pun, trying to see hope in her statement. He didn't have eighty more drachmas. He didn't know where he could get them, either. Praxis, maybe. He'd worry about that later, if the old harridan relented.

"Done!" She slapped the palm of her hand to the wooden table so soundly that the noise made Melanion jump and silenced the business going on in the room. The Greek looked into her face suspiciously. Surely it could not be so easy.

"You've been a good customer," she said, seeing his surprise. "I hope to see more of you, along with your gemsmith friend. And any rich Persians with fat money pouches you may make the acquaintance of," she hinted.

Ah! So that was it! "Of course," he agreed, rising. "You can be sure I will recommend you highly to them." The words sounded hollow, distant, scarcely his own. He walked woodenly to the door. His body acted on instinct while his mind churned with worry. He'd done it, made the deal, and Sela was his.

As soon as he could find the money.

Praxis buffed a large cabochon of amber with fine wet wood ash till it glowed. He was in the middle of a working day, with much yet to be done, when Melanion burst in on him, as free with his time as if it were a festival day. Praxis listened to his friend's tale of woe with rising skepticism.

"I knew you fancied the girl, but for the love of Eros, Melanion, will you turn over your entire fortune on her account?" Praxis lowered the amber and stared at his friend in disbelief. "No woman is worth that much! To barter away your wealth, your dreams, your future, for some little barbarian princess! Forget her, Melanion. Take my advice and forget her. Take a different wench every night for a month and by the time you're done, you won't even remember her name, and you'll still have most of your money, too!"

Spitting on his forefinger, Praxis worked more ash into a paste and returned his attentions to the piece of amber. He didn't notice the clouded anger that crossed his friend's face.

"Then I'll get no help from you?" Melanion snapped. Praxis looked up in surprise.

"Don't rouse your ire with me, Melanion!" he protested. "I think you're being a fool, but even so, I haven't got it. Some amber, a piece of lapis, a small vein of fine Persian turquoise, that's all. In the winter there are few merchants coming through, you know. You picked a bad time of the year to go slave buying."

"I'm not slave buying!" Melanion grumbled, rising from the painted Greek chair where he'd sat to tell his tale and watch his friend work. What was the use? Praxis didn't understand, and even if he did, he just didn't have the funds. "Thanks anyway." Melanion turned to the door, dreading a return to the biting cold outside but knowing he had to try every road open to him before he'd admit defeat.

"Wait," Praxis stood, wiping his messy hands on a leather apron. "A bit of something here might help you . . ." He opened the upright doors on a heavy cedar cabinet where he kept his supply of stones. Melanion couldn't see what he was doing, but the gem cutter soon turned, a lump the color of dried blood and the size of a small apple in his hand. "Here . . ." He thrust it out to Melanion proudly. The goldsmith looked at it in astonishment. It was a garnet, fine and dark and nearly the largest he'd ever seen. Suddenly he felt guilty at the idea of taking the treasures of his friend.

"No," he said, backing away from the proffered stone. "I can't take that! Such a gem—you must have been saving it."

Praxis waved it in the air in front of Melanion. "Take it! I can get another. Or you can buy me another when your Persian money starts piling up. Go on! I'll trust you for it!"

Melanion slowly closed his fingers around the cold scaly roughness of the garnet. "Thirty drachmas here," he tallied to himself as he muttered a thanks and left the room.

In three days he could only scrape up forty more drachmas; twenty-five for the garnet, which he sold to an Egyptian sea captain fleeing the harbor before it became iced in for the winter, and fifteen for a simple gold bracelet bought by the owner of the ale shop. That left him forty drachmas short, **a huge** sum when one considered that the wage for a hoplite, the heavily armed Greek foot soldier, was only twenty-five drachmas a month. His goal was still as remote as if Sela were held captive atop Mount Olympus. And in ten days the Thracian captain would arrive, to settle some personal accounts and move on before winter brought to a halt all trade and travel till spring. Ten days to come up with more money than most men see in ten months.

Perhaps Praxis is right, Melanion mused, tallying up his meager possessions by the light of a small oil lamp. Two hundred drachmas would buy a lot of things. Clothes. Women. New gold-working tools, a better furnace, an assistant perhaps. Money breeds money, as sure as mice beget more mice. With better equipment and an assistant I could expand, draw in more customers, move to a larger, more civilized city somewhere near the Great Sea, which would bring in still more business, and more money, and . . .

Melanion blew on his cold-numbed fingers and rubbed them together briskly to warm them. His wax tablet was so hardened in the chill room that attempts to scratch out a tally on it were futile. It didn't really matter. He knew exactly what he had, and what it was worth, and what he must do with it. Pulling his wooly goatskin cloak around his chin, Melanion rose from the table, extinguished the stone lamp, and fumbled his way through the darkened room to his cot, and sleep.

Praxis had not seen his friend for four days, so it did not surprise him when the familiar loud thump came on his door early one morning and he opened it to find a very cold, shivering Greek goldsmith standing on the log walkway outside. Praxis welcomed him in, but not until his friend dragged two large leather sacks in with him did the gemsmith realize what had happened. In his desperation for the Cimmerian girl he had sold nearly everything he owned and now came to stay with his best friend. But the girl?

Praxis stuck his head out into the frigid air, looking up the empty street and down. There was no girl to be seen.

"Where is she?" he gasped against the cold, slamming the wooden door and bolting it. Melanion lowered the two heavy sacks, stretched his aching back, and turned sheepishly to his friend.

"I let her go," he said flatly.

Praxis thought the floor would swallow him, so complete was his astonishment at what he'd just heard. "You let her go!" he fumed, suddenly angry at his friend's irrationality. He begs from his friends, squanders his fortune, sells all he owns, and all to buy a girl he then lets go. "You're a fool, Melanion. Everyone will be thinking it, but I will say it. By the gods, you're a fool. Just what did you hope to gain by all this? A 'commission' from some barbarian king, perhaps?

You'll get enough of those anyway, come spring. But why, Melanion, why?"

Praxis was an easygoing fellow, and there was not much in life he took that seriously. But money was one thing he understood, and valued. Without it, very few of the other charms in life were attainable. And his insane friend had just squandered a fortune on a girl he didn't even care enough about to keep!

"She was a princess." Melanion began to explain. "There was something about her; it's hard to explain. Regal and fierce, like a tiger cub, but also waiflike, helpless."

"A princess is all the better. She could have borne you some healthy, intelligent children. Let's hope more helpless women don't strike your fancy, or we'll all end up selling ourselves into slavery to help you out!"

Melanion seemed unconcerned. "I am not interested in children, not even by a slave," he muttered. He dragged his packs into a corner and decided it was time Praxis paid him back for all the unexpected visits and unplanned meals he'd given his gem cutter friend. "What do you have to eat?" he announced grandly. "I'm hungry!"

Praxis's annoyance dissipated at the breezy confidence of the goldsmith. Melanion showed all the carefree sureness of a man who knew he'd done the right thing, that it sat right with the gods, and he was at peace with himself. Praxis had to admire his courage and his conviction.

"Let me fix some food," Praxis sighed. It was no use to argue with Melanion. A man who believes he is right plugs up his ears to logic. And besides, the girl was gone. He couldn't get her back. What use were wasted words?

The gem cutter rummaged on the shelf over his clay oven. Only the usual, in small supply. Beans, barley, cheese, a bit of smoked goose—yes, that would be good. He had a few treasured dates, too, bought from a passing Egyptian trader. He had no ale, but some wine, sour and harsh. Melanion had come at a bad time.

At a hurried tap on the door Melanion rose to answer it. Praxis put the food aside when he recognized an Armenian trader, swathed in a long felt coat, his dark hair dusted with snow. He often bought lapis and turquoise from the man and could not afford to ignore him.

"Greetings!" the man began formally. "I am on my way from town and thought I'd see if you need more stones before I go. I have a few nice ones to sell." His rough hand pointedly toyed with a small leather sack tied to his belt.

"Sorry, friend," Praxis crossed the room, "you come at a bad time. I have no funds right now to buy much of anything."

The Armenian shrugged and groomed his beard absently. "Some ale, perhaps?" he suggested. Praxis shook his head. "I have none," he said.

"No." The man's dark face broke into a grin. "I see you only have poor wine. The ale is mine." He pulled a wooden flask from beneath his coat. "I'll gladly share it if it buys me a little time to warm myself."

Praxis laughed and motioned the trader to his one good Greek chair. "Sit, my friend. The meal will be sparse but you can share it with us." Eager for a diversion from Melanion and his woes, Praxis began pulling the food from the shelf.

"I have it all worked out," Melanion explained while cutting a slab of cheese from the last of a mold-encrusted wheel. The Armenian had just left, after a long and sociable, if meager, meal.

"Oh, you do, eh?" Praxis joked, pouring them both a cup of watery wine warmed near the clay oven.

"You heard the trader. A Scyth princess is to wed in spring. I can't let a chance like that pass me by. I won't stay here long, you see, and when I return from the steppes I will be a rich man. In the meantime I can sell a piece or two that I have left to support myself."

"A rich man?" Praxis was doubtful.

"Yes. I can make this money last until I go to work for the Persians next year. The winter has just begun. A trip north shouldn't be too difficult."

"A trip in winter?" Praxis protested. "Even the greediest merchants aren't that foolish."

"I must. The girl's father will need gold jewelry to buy, to ornament her properly for her marriage and to show off his wealth. You know the pride of these barbarians. In winter they will not travel here to buy it, so I will go to them! It will be some of the easiest money I ever made."

"I doubt that, my friend." Praxis raised his cup of wine. "Nonetheless, here's to you, your success, to the wealthy Scyth papa, and to the happy bride."

BOOK 3

LIPOS

Power is a slippery thing, and has never lacked lovers
to woo it.

—*Solon*

"ALL SHE MUMBLES ABOUT IS A HORSE."

Urgimas cast a worried look at Catoris. The old enaree squatted outside Opoea's yurt, sheltered from the incessant north wind, absently chewing a hazel twig. Time and again he had attended the feverish Arima, and time and again he had failed to restore her health or to drive away the evil spirits that tormented her. And what was almost as bad, the enaree insisted on doing his musings outdoors, in the increasing bitterness of winter, with Urgimas of necessity shivering at his side.

"The old mare?" Catoris cast his steely eyes a sidelong glance at the slave woman's pinched face. Urgimas shrugged.

"I don't know. I would guess so. The wolves killed it, you know, and the poor girl was witness to it."

"I know what happened, woman," Catoris snapped, returning his gaze to the gathering ice along the sluggish river. Lipos still recovered in the yurt of the enaree, and he told his elder everything that had happened. Everything. The attack of the wolves. The desperate attempt to sate their hunger by using the old mare as bait, the ensuing nights of fear as the beasts lurked nearby . . .

Still, something bothered Catoris about it. But until he questioned the girl, he could never know. "Bartatua saw horse tracks?" he muttered into the wind. Urgimas nodded once, slouching lower against the cold. If he was not an enaree she would curse him, she thought angrily, for making her old bones suffer so in the cruel bite of winter.

"Of the mare?" the enaree continued, as much to himself as to her. Urgimas shrugged and waited.

But how could that be? Catoris pondered silently. The old horse had been dead several days. There had been wind, snow, and prowling wolves to obliterate its tracks. How then could the hoofprints be so fresh, so near at hand? And what was Arima reaching for? She was in no condition to tell Bartatua when he rescued her, and all she has said since rousing is to call for the horse, the horse.

A sudden unexpected chill shook his lean frame and he stood, a troubling thought flitting about his mind. A spirit horse, he realized. The restless ghost of the dead mare, venturing back to the security of their campsite, now tormenting the feverish girl. Ignoring the huddled slave woman, Catoris stepped out into the gale and returned to his yurt.

Lipos was so hoarse from a sore throat that he could barely speak, and full feeling had not yet returned to his fingers. He had stayed in the enarees' yurt since he was brought back by Bartatua, except for one brief visit to Arima. She was alive, but beyond that he couldn't say much. Burning with fever, she varied between delusive rantings and deep, exhausted sleep. The entire camp knew she cried out for "the horse" and it sickened him to think that, in her delirium, their deception might be discovered.

He lay near the hearth fire, reclined on a pile of deer-hair pillows while he methodically crushed dried herbs and stoppered them in small horn vials. It was a boring task, made more so by the awkwardness of his numb fingers. When Catoris entered the sparsely furnished tent Lipos was glad for the company, until he studied the look on the old man's face. Its intensity disturbed him.

"Don't rouse yourself," Catoris snapped, his mind preoccupied with some grave matter. The very instructions caused Lipos to drag himself upright in concern.

"What has happened?" he croaked, forcing the words painfully from his throat. "Is it Arima?" He watched the old man intently for some clue to what was afoot. The yurt was lined with carved and painted chests of cedar wood, their designs magical symbols to protect their precious contents. It was to one of these that Catoris went, and Lipos groaned inwardly when the enaree opened it. In the name of Papaeus, he slumped, the old man is on to us. He watched Catoris lift from the chest a fine, thick wolfskin, the pelt unmarred by spear or arrow wound, the savagely grinning head still intact, large paws dangling from lifeless legs. The shell of a wolf. All it needed was a spirit to inhabit it, Catoris's spirit.

Lipos flung aside the bearskin robe that covered him and moved to stand. He must go with Catoris. He knew what was to happen.

"Stay!" the old man barked, as if commanding a dog. Lipos froze, looked up through the flickering light at his mentor, and their eyes locked. He knew defiance was useless. Saving his burning throat, he fell back to the pile of cushions and looked away bitterly. Satisfied, Catoris lifted his power-stick from the pole where it hung in the center of the yurt, draped the wolfskin over one arm, and left the tent.

Lipos gave him a few moments, to be well-gone, before he stood. He was forbidden to follow, but there was still something he could do. He took down his power-stick from the tent pole, went to his own cedar chest, threw hemp seeds on the hearthstones and, sitting cross-legged by the fire, he began to dream.

Catoris entered Opoea's yurt decked in his sacred wolfskin and the eyes of the women gathered there rounded like owls' when they saw him. "Leave!" he snapped, waving them aside. Wordlessly they scurried from the tent, seizing furs, robes, and felt blankets to wrap themselves in as they fled. Only Opoea faced the fearsome enaree, still half-man, but now half-wolf as well.

"I will stay," she said flatly. Catoris studied her, looking for some light of fear in her eyes, uncertainty, a weakness he could exploit and play on like a wolf worrying an injured deer.

He saw none. Despite the frailty of her appearance, the greyness of her face, the woman's spirit was strong. He relented.

"Sit there." He pointed to neatly folded furs on the far side of the tent, his voice nearly a growl in the darkness. Picking up a bound bunch of straw by the hearth, he flailed at the fire till it was nearly out. His eyes adjusted quickly to the dim light, and reaching up with a long pole, he pushed and prodded at the vent-hole in the center of the roof until he had closed it and near-total darkness descended on the yurt. Dropping the pole to the carpets, he sat cross-legged by the sleeping girl's couch, pressed the carved and painted tip of his power-stick to the center of his forehead, beneath the jutting wolf head, closed his eyes and began to chant.

Opoea started at the sound of the guttural singsong that suddenly filled the tent. Its power was almost a tangible thing, flowing outward like smoke from the wolf-man, rising and falling, swirling and probing into every crevice of her home, weighting down her head, filling her nostrils, pressing on her chest till it ached from the effort of breathing. Allowing her to stay was an indulgence on his part, she knew, or was it a punishment? She tried to control the growing panic she felt at the rawness of his power. Perhaps she had been wrong. Perhaps she should have fled with the other women. The darkness moved, swirled, melded before her watering eyes. The drone filled her ears, her lungs, her very heart, till it was not a man sitting before her, it was a wolf, hunched down, facing her daughter, its head drifting hypnotically back and forth, back and forth, until with a heart-stopping scream, Arima cried out in the false night of the enaree.

The evil yellow wolf sprang out before her. In terror the mare flailed at it. Arima could smell the overpowering vastness of the steppes, and the bite of the wind, and the horse's fear.

She was falling, tumbling, the grass rushing up to meet her, the mare trying to flee the yellow wolf, the yellow wolf which saw her, its eyes menacing, death dealing. The wolf knew. . . .

The girl cried out again and Opoea fought the stupor holding her down like a spider's web. What was the wolf-man doing to her child? Her anger rose, the chanting grew louder, and she slumped to one side on the wool carpets, eyes staring wide, as helpless as an animal with an arrow through its spine. Arima! she cried. Her mouth fell open, but no sound would come.

The old mare fought. Catoris could see that, feel it, as his fangs tore into tough sinew and throbbing muscle. Curse the mare, he thought savagely. Where is Arima? He heard her screaming, but he could not see. Could not tear himself away from consuming the horse, trapped in the wolfskin of his own creation. His companions had joined the kill, chasing the tottering mare through the grasses, spattering heaven and earth with the intoxicating warm red blood, till he coughed it from his throat and blew it from his nose. He could not escape it, not for all his powers as half-man, this animal lust for the kill. It held him in thrall.

Arima, where is she? Rage for the kill became rage at the girl. He knew how the mare had died. Arima must have been there. If only he could see her.

An earsplitting scream rent the sky, and through a haze of blood the yellow wolf that was Catoris looked up and saw a hawk attacking, diving straight for his face, talons extended to strike.

With a screech the hawk hit him, driving into the eyes of the wolf. A yowl of agony erupted from the creature's throat as the world went black before it.

Feeling returned to Opoea, bringing sense and control with the unearthly howl that suddenly filled her home. Scrambling to right herself, she crawled on all fours to the collapsed figure of the wolf-man. He was alive but unconscious, the thick spit and blood where he'd chewed his lower lip drizzling from his slack mouth and making him look, in the dark tent, scarcely human. She didn't dare to touch him, nor the power-stick that lay cast aside on her carpets. Pulling herself shakily to her feet, she ran to her daughter's bed. Arima was awake, and struggling valiantly to sit.

Lipos threw several black lumps of pine tar onto the hearth fire, to cover the smell of the burned hemp. Pine tar was an old remedy for throat disease; Catoris would be none the wiser. A stiff drink of kumiss was what he needed now. Rising on fever-weakened legs, he returned his power-stick to its place on the center pole. He was satisfied with his efforts. Arima had been protected; their secret was safe.

A sudden fit of coughing assailed him and he doubled over, inhaling the burning tar in an effort to clear his lungs. Gasping, Lipos made his way to the cedar trunk that held his belongings. Quickly, before Catoris returned, he replaced the dried hawk wings that he had used in his incantations.

Arima had awakened from one nightmare into another. After the vast, open freedom she had discovered on the mare, the close confines of Opoea's yurt entombed her. Like a horse, her nostrils ached for the wind.

Instead, her mother tossed more dried dung and twigs on the dying hearth fire, throwing the tent into sudden illumination. And then Arima saw the old enaree sprawled, a dead wolf . . .

The girl recoiled at the sight of him, the wolf's head cast backward at a grotesque angle, its dead eyes reflecting sightlessly the flaring firelight. If ever a vision came from the domain of demons, this was it.

"Mother," she whispered, her eyes searching the yurt for the familiar comfort of Opoea. What had happened to Catoris? How had she returned to the settlement of Scylas? Mother was at the tent door, summoning help. In a moment Bartatua and his friend Oricus entered.

"There," Opoea muttered, her voice hard. "By the fire."

Cold radiating from their heavy fur cloaks, the two men approached the unconscious enaree. Arima shrank back from them, grasping instinctively to pull a blanket in front of herself. It was forbidden for a man not of her family to enter a woman's yurt and see her in her bed. Oricus was careful to keep his eyes averted, almost comical in his attempts to study the floor, the tent poles, the hearth, the enaree. It was plain he was as uncomfortable with the situation as Arima was.

Bartatua cast a quick, mocking glance down at Catoris, stepped over his sprawled figure, and faced Arima. His brown eyes bore down on her with such intensity that the girl turned her face away, to the patterned swirls on her felt blanket, her cheeks burning red in confusion. "Are you well?" Bartatua asked, and despite the fierceness of his gaze, his voice held genuine concern. Arima nodded, awkward. Satisfied with her response, the warrior turned and bent over, taking Catoris under the arms. Oricus lifted the enaree's feet and the men shuffled from the tent, Catoris slumped between them, the wolf's head dangling backward beneath his neck, its stiff dry snout dragging across the carpets and into the dirt as they returned the enaree to his yurt.

Opoea watched them go, grateful that the unearthly presence of the half-man was removed from her home. His power-stick lay where it had fallen; no one would dare to touch it. It must remain there until one of the enarees returned for it.

But no matter. The inconvenience was a small price to pay for the restoration of her daughter's health. Opoea walked to Arima's bed while the other women timidly reentered the yurt. Their fearful eyes openly studied Arima, Opoea, the fallen power-stick, while they tried to return to their routines. Opoea sat beside Arima and took her hand. The girl was pale, her face bruised, but otherwise she seemed well. "Did Lipos teach you many things?" she asked, smoothing her daughter's thick dark hair affectionately. A good thing to forget wolves, dead horses, enarees, and all other such disturbing matters. Routine was always best.

"Some. There was so little time. I could have learned much more, Mother," Arima whispered, knowing it was an absolute truth. She could have learned to ride more expertly, if only the wolves had not intervened. "Did Catoris heal

me, Mother? Is Lipos well? And who saved us?" So many
questions crowded her mind, awakening as she was from a
long journey in the dreamworld.

Opoea smiled good-naturedly. A curious Arima was a
healthy Arima. "Lipos is fine; it was Bartatua who took it on
himself to save you." The old woman's voice died away,
leaving an aura of bitterness behind. "But no matter!" she
finished brightly. "You will be very fortunate to have a man
such as Bartatua for a husband. He will take good care of
you and your children. We must begin to think of your
wedding, Arima, the goods you will need to set up a
household, the finery for your marriage. The dowry will be
your father's concern, but we women have only the winter to
do our part. We must keep busy sewing and clipping and
embroidering, dying felts and . . ."

Arima shut out her mother's well-meant words. The
stuffiness of the tent, the boring mundaneness of the winter
that faced her, the unending marriage preparations, the life
she was fated to live. How could she endure it? "Mother, I
am tired. I would like to sleep," she interrupted the domestic litany. She felt that if she heard much more, she would
burst into tears.

"Of course," Opoea nodded, patting Arima's hand and
rising from the couch. "Would you like some broth first, or
tea?"

"No, Mother; I am fine." Arima curled on her side,
toward the dancing hearth fire. "We can finish our planning
tomorrow."

Opoea smiled slightly, stepped over the power-stick of
Catoris, and walked to her bed. Arima raised her head in
surprise when her mother settled down, not on her bed in its
usual place of honor opposite the door, but to one side, as if
she were just one more woman in the family of Scylas.
Rising on one elbow, the girl looked to the place where
Opoea had slept for nearly fifty years. There was a couch

there, but sitting on it, having her hair dressed by an old slave, was a pale blonde girl young enough to be Arima's sister. Puzzled and angry at this desecration of her mother's position as chief wife of Scylas, Arima lay down. Her gaze caught her mother's, staring across the dim tent, and Opoea looked away quickly, her old eyes brimming with hurt and shame.

The days quickly became maddening in the riverside winter camp of Scylas. The warriors were unhappy with their chief, who neglected his men and his duties for the young northern girl he had acquired. His chief wife spent her time in barely suppressed rage at the insult her husband had dealt her. Arima forced herself through the daily chores of living, dreading her future, dwelling in the brief freedom of the past. Even the two enarees seemed angry with each other. Lipos's voice took days to return, and old Catoris was afflicted with an eye disease that resisted all efforts to cure it. Normally the chief would hear of all this unhappiness and take steps to restore harmony to his people, but not old Scylas. His interests clearly lay elsewhere. It was plain, the people said; demons had taken up residence among the Auchatae Scyth. Evil times had come. Was worse to follow?

Only Tabiti, Bartatua's wife, seemed to be at peace. Arima found herself spending many days at Bartatua's yurt, talking with the quiet, slim young woman while she sewed her bridal goods, just to be away from the strained hostility in her own tent. Tabiti was that rarity on earth, sweet and with a heart which held no malice and a mind content with the life the gods had handed her. Named for the goddess of the hearth, it was fitting, for she seemed to have no greater pleasure than bustling about it, tending her household, caring for Bartatua. Arima felt like a traitor, intruding on such a happy life.

"How is your mother?" Tabiti asked quietly, not looking

at Arima when she spoke. Her attention was riveted on the feltwork cutout she was snipping into a tunic for her husband. Arima flexed her fingers and glanced at the childlike face of Tabiti, her fine brown hair braided around her head. If only she could find a small portion of the young wife's gentle nature! She envied her.

"Her health is suffering," Arima muttered, laying her own feltwork pillow across her folded knees. "She is so old, and to be treated so, at the closing of her life, is hard to bear."

Tabiti looked up, her luminous blue eyes shining sympathy at the worry in Arima's voice. Her own mother had died years ago in a plague; she knew the suffering it caused a daughter. "Bring her here with you tomorrow, Arima," she suggested. "We will make room for her, and she will be cheered by all the silly girl-talk. Bring her!"

Arima half-smiled at the childish enthusiasm in Tabiti's voice. If only the world was so simple, its problems so easily solved. A different yurt, a day of girl-talk. "I have tried, Tabiti. She refuses to leave. It is her yurt, she says; a dowry from her parents when she wed my . . . when she wed Scylas." She would not call him father anymore. Tabiti nodded understanding and motioned a slave to fetch some refreshments.

"Yes," the young wife whispered. "I can see her thinking. We women have little enough that is truly ours in this world."

Arima looked at her in surprise. She would never have imagined such an observation from kindly, domestic Tabiti. The girl cast a sidelong glance at Arima and laughed at her amazed expression.

"It should not surprise you, Arima," she said, her blue eyes crinkled in merriment, "that while I love my husband, my home, and my life, were I given the choice there would be more I would take for myself. But we are women. We are given no more choice, and so I am content."

And Arima could see from the open honesty on Tabiti's face that her words were true ones. She was content.

"Children, perhaps," Tabiti muttered as an afterthought, and this time it was Arima who detected the pain in the words. "But maybe you will give Bartatua children!" The girl brightened. "Then I will care for them as my own! Think of it, Arima! Bartatua's children."

Arima tried to share her friend's enthusiasm and hope, but the very idea turned her blood cold. As much as she admired Tabiti, she could never be Tabiti. The gods had made her Arima, and Arima she would remain.

Rhea dressed like the queen she was not, yet because of Scylas's infatuation with her, the favors he showered on her, no one dared to speak against her. She wore long black skirts and jackets of the finest wool, which she knew set off her white-blonde hair like threads of gold on sable. Her embroidered cap dangled with charms of gold and from her ears swung earrings set with bright beads of amber and turquoise. Such finery was acceptable for special occasions, but Rhea wore it everywhere, every day, showing off her beauty and wealth and favored position to all she passed.

Arima hated her, hated her for what she was doing to her mother, for the strains she brought to the yurt that had been the girl's lifelong home, for the attentions Scylas showed her, such as he had never shown his own daughter. Even hated her for her beauty, as delicate as a fragile spring flower, with fine pale skin and blonde hair such as had intrigued the dark-haired Arima since she was a child. She would sit with her mother when evening gathered and watch Rhea prepare herself for her nightly romps with Scylas. The Northwoman seemed to take special delight in flaunting her body before the two of them, Arima and Opoea; sitting nearly naked on her couch, caressing her own slim curves as she smoothed scented oils into her skin, wordlessly taunting the two women with what they knew Scylas would soon be doing to that body.

Arima hated her. She was a demon.

A gentle, silent snow had been falling all day and drifts were beginning to pile up against the warm yurts clustered by the riverside. With dusk the snowfall did not increase or abate, but kept on with the same gentle monotony as it had all day.

Rhea seemed concerned. Arima watched her with malicious delight, dressing herself for her nightly bedding, keeping an anxious eye on the weather, sending one of her slaves repeatedly to the yurt door to check on the snowfall, waiting to hear the footfalls of the guards Scylas unfailingly sent to escort her to his tent. None came. The young woman's arrogant expression faded to concern and Arima was pleased to see little lines of worry furrow the delicate skin of her face.

The daylong twilight of the snowfall was fading to darkness when a familiar sound came from outside. The heavy tread of male feet, stopping at the door to kick off an accumulation of snow. Rhea's ears were as alert as a watchdog's and she rose from her bed, her expression returning to its usual sensual beauty. Scylas had not forgotten her; the escort had come.

Arima flinched when the heavy felt door of the yurt jerked open and Scylas entered, trailed by two warriors. He was so swathed in furs against the cold and his own increasingly poor health that he was barely recognizable, and the startling redness of his face showed that he had been drinking. A quick glance to her mother showed that Opoea understood immediately what was afoot. Rhea took a bit longer to comprehend but it came to her soon enough and the puzzled look in her eyes gave way to a well-practised seductiveness. How could she know the odd ways of these Scythians? She could only learn them as she lived them; but Scylas was a man, that she did know, and his intent was plain in the hungry way he looked at her.

The slaves and serving women scurried to the far side of the tent, away from Rhea's couch, and Arima groaned aloud. He couldn't! Not here in front of his own daughter, his chief wife! But he was besotted, both with the Greek wine he'd drunk and the foreign woman he'd bought. Convention and decency meant nothing to him any longer. Scylas waited for his two men to take the heavy bearskin cloak from his shoulders. Beneath it he sported a dirty tunic and, as if to contrast with them, ludicrously new and lavish trousers of red and yellow wool. He wore no weapons, no jewelry except one dangling gold earring in his left ear. Bearing the cloak, the two warriors crossed the floor and squatted on either side of the door, guarding their chief.

Arima looked frantically to her mother, hoping she would, could, put a stop to this spectacle. Opoea seemed determined not to return her gaze. The old woman sat bravely, cross-legged on her couch, staring straight ahead as if to unseen vistas, her slaves clustered on the carpeting around her. Only the tight knots in her jaws showed her tension. The guards, too, were in the same peculiar state of not-seeing, not-hearing, what their chief required. Arima cast a frantic, furious glance around the room. The slaves were settling down to their pallets as if this were just another night. The girl's eyes went back to the man she must call father, and the woman she hated above all others. His tunic was off, and his burly shoulders in the low light were still as powerful as a bear's. Rhea's small hands were white against the skin of his back as she frantically caressed him, and when he moved she could see that the foreign woman was naked.

Arima wanted to scream aloud at this outrage, to pick up a burning brand and strike them, to seize a long, heavy dagger from one of the warriors and kill them both. But it was useless. There was no recourse for any of them but to endure it all. A drunken chief, a demon woman. Choking on her anger, Arima lay down and moved her face as close to the heavy wool wall of the yurt as she could. She pulled a cushion over her ears to shut out the sounds of their dalliance. Rhea used it to great benefit and that night her moans and shrieks of ecstasy were especially graphic. Once, between fits of broken sleep, Arima peered from beneath the cushion over her head. They were still at it, her father riding the demon woman with outstanding vigor, biting her neck as if he meant to suck the blood from her body. Arima felt like retching at the sight and she burrowed back under the cushion, wondering if soon Bartatua would be doing the same to her. In the darkness Urgimas reached up from her pallet by Arima's bed and gave her charge's hand a fierce, reassuring squeeze.

When sleep finally came to the yurt, a silent figure rose, crept past the slumbering guards, and into the night's snow.

She could not help but think back to her youth, when her hair was thick, the burnished brown color of a nutshell, and her body was firm and supple. How handsome Scylas had been, the best archer of the Auchatae, his bow arm powerful, his eye keen as an eagle's. She could ride as well as Scylas, could easily have escaped him on her father's war-horse, but she'd turned the beast awkwardly, let him race to her side and take her in his arms. Then came their first lying together, in the close warmth of the wedding yurt, and her body strained to his.

Opoea blinked rapidly against the tears she felt rising. Sitting cross-legged in the snow outside her yurt, the wind seemed to die, the world stood strangely still. At the stiff rustle of a wool skirt nearby, Opoea looked up. Standing before her was a woman, her clothes lavish with gold threads, a headpiece across her forehead so heavy with ornament that it seemed to sparkle with its own light. She recognized her at once. It could be no other than the goddess she had prayed to every day of her married life, Tabiti of the Hearth.

"You have done well," the Lady nodded, "as well as any woman could."

Opoea could not take her eyes from the beautiful face, embodying in its radiance all the arts and skills of home-making, the peace and harmony of a contented yurt.

"Leave men to their mannish things," Tabiti smiled, extending a hand to Opoea. "Come," the Lady whispered, "a better hearth awaits you."

Arima awoke when the slaves began to stir, and she saw the two guards by the door rouse with a jerk, casting quick glances to Scylas to be sure he had not seen their transgression. The old chief snored drunkenly, one arm thrown across the naked white stomach of Rhea. Arima lay with her ears still buried beneath the pillow, unsure of what she should do now, what the custom was in such a situation. Follow mother's lead, she supposed. She looked across to Opoea's couch, to see if she was rousing. The bed was empty.

"Mother!" Arima screamed in dark foreboding, shattering the morning silence of the tent. She flung aside the heavy blankets covering her and jumped from the bed, nearly colliding with a startled Urgimas, rising from her pallet on the floor.

"Where is Mother!" Arima cried, looking around the yurt. The guards had risen to their feet, Rhea sat upright behind Scylas, and the old man was rolling over, propping up on one arm, trying to clear his head. Wearing only a white wool shift, Arima pushed past the confused guards and jerked the door flap aside. If Opoea left, went to another yurt to escape the humiliation, there would be footprints, something.

A choking cry from Arima tore the snow-smothered silence of the winter's morning, and all the slumbering yurts jarred to life.

"Mother, no!" the girl sobbed, running unprotected into the frigid air. Scylas ran after her, shirtless and fumbling with his trousers as he tried to catch her. But Arima was gone, kneeling in the drifts beside the yurt, brushing snow from the stiff, frozen face of Opoea, who sat cross-legged outside the tent that had once been hers.

Arima no longer cared. She felt inwardly free, a bond suddenly snapping as she wept over her mother's lifeless form. Rising to her feet, the girl ignored the clusters of people who spilled from yurt doors all over camp, ignored the frightened guards who realized that their negligence had allowed this to happen. She ignored the hand of Scylas, reaching lamely for her arm. She stalked into the yurt of Opoea—yes, the yurt of Opoea, not the yurt of Rhea—with destruction in her eyes, Scylas on her heels.

"Arima, come here!" Scylas barked at her from the hearthside. For the first time in her life, she ignored him, striding toward the barely clad Rhea, who stood by her couch.

"She was old . . ." the foreign woman began. Scylas, angry and alarmed, sent the guards after his daughter but they reached her too late. With a wild cry, the cry of a wounded animal, of a stallion defending his herd, of a hawk about to strike, Arima grabbed the slim white neck of Rhea and bore her to the ground. The rest was maelstrom, madness, the screams of the demon-woman, coarse shouts from Scylas, large hands grabbing at her. But Arima would not let go. The wolf seized its prey and refused to release it, and so would she. Lipos was wrong; women could kill. She wanted to feel that fine white neck snap beneath her fingers. She wanted death.

A blow struck the side of her head, and she felt the

demon's neck slide from her sagging grip, felt herself slipping away, saw herself in one last vision riding like the wind on a tall yellow gelding, sitting behind Opoea, whose hair streamed thick and dark in the wind. A youthful Opoea turned and smiled to her, as if to say, "I am happy."

"Leave her alone!"

The small voice cut through the chaos, and Scylas looked up to see the girlish form of Tabiti, wife of Bartatua, her long hair undone, standing inside the doorway with two burly male slaves behind her. She had hastily wrapped herself in a long horsehair cloak and the wet snow clung in clumps around the bottom of it. The little figure advanced unhesitatingly across the disheveled carpets, the slaves on her heels. Scylas's men, supporting the inert form of Arima, looked to him for instruction. Rhea slid from beneath the girl, choking and gasping dramatically while clenching an ugly red bruise on her neck. Scylas nodded to the guards, and they let his daughter fall to the floor. Tabiti rushed forward, anger on her gentle face, when she saw this.

"What have you done to her?" she demanded, facing Scylas squarely, sparks in her eyes.

"Where is your husband, girl?" the old man retorted. "What manner of man lets his wife roam the camp alone and order chiefs about?"

"You know where he is," she said, putting as much force as she could in her voice. She could say more, but didn't; had the old fool forgotten where he'd sent him? Had he forgotten the mission altogether? Was his mind that far gone?

"Yes, ah, yes," Scylas blustered, trying to act as if he knew where he'd sent his chief warrior. A jarring note of reality suddenly intruded on his revels of the past days. His wife was dead, his daughter lay unconscious by his own command, and his heir had gone he knew not where on an order he could no longer remember. He looked down at the floor.

Tabiti was patting Arima's face, trying to rouse her. Remorse and shame gripped him at the sight.

"Fetch Catoris," he ordered a guard.

Arima awoke in an unfamiliar tent, the side of her head throbbing. Through a haze of pain she studied the yurt, fitting the pieces together. An upright loom stood to one side, Greek in style and most unusual on the steppes. A hide-covered shield, several daggers, and two gorytas were suspended from the tent's central poles. A man slept on a couch opposite the door, his back to her.

Shakily Arima sat. A man? A second glance at the weapons told the story. They were Bartatua's. She was in the yurt of Bartatua. But he had been gone, off to trade a pair of wagon-trained oxen for a fine Persian stallion for the herds of Scylas. Why was he here now? How long had she slept?

Tabiti appeared, gliding soundlessly on slippered feet across the tent and to the sleeping man. She shook his shoulder, and when he turned Arima saw that it was not Bartatua. It was Lipos, the enaree. He looked, saw that she was awake, and sprang from the couch, raking the long yellow hair from his eyes. "Fix the tea I gave you," he instructed Tabiti as he strode to Arima's bed.

"Why am I here?" the girl demanded. "What has happened? What did they do with Mother?"

"Stay calm," the enaree instructed her, examining a scabbed wound above her ear. "Scylas ordered you brought here, to your future home, where Tabiti could look after you better than, well . . ."

"Better than the slaves could, now that my mother is dead," she spat, pulling her head away from him. "And the demon?"

"Demon?" He sat back on his heels and studied her curiously.

"That Northwoman. She is a demon, you know. There has been nothing but bad luck ever since she came here."

Lipos nodded agreement but said nothing. His plans had indeed taken a turn for the worse. He knew there was misfortune in the camp; he suspected Rhea was involved. The bits of information Arima had halfheartedly provided him had been useless. Childish things and petty details. Scylas had boiled mutton for his meal. Rhea used herbal poultices on the old chief's weary back. The Northwoman had a scar on one leg—was that significant? She nightly went to Scylas's tent—did she never suffer with the women's affliction? That was the only bit of Arima's information that really interested him, for if Scylas was lying with an unclean woman, one who should be confined to her yurt, that might explain the bad luck plaguing the camp. No man would knowingly do so. Rhea must have put a spell on him.

Tabiti knelt on the carpets beside them and handed Arima a silver cup of medicinal tea. "Drink it all," the enaree instructed, pushing the worries from his mind.

"What of Rhea?" Arima repeated, downing the bitter drink as quickly as she could.

"She still lives in the other yurt," Tabiti said. "You can return there when you are well, or you can remain here, and I'll have your things brought. Scylas and the enarees agree that it will be alright, since you are already sworn to Bartatua. The choice is yours to make."

Arima returned the cup to Tabiti, and her brows rose in amazement. A choice that was hers to make? Not just another order from Scylas? Whatever remorse he felt, whatever tricks he tried, nothing would bring back Opoea's life or cause Arima to forgive him. And besides—she cast a brief glance at Lipos's pensive face—if she stayed in Bartatua's tent, she could do no more spying for the enaree.

"I only hope that I hurt the demon," Arima declared, gingerly feeling her wounded head.

"Oh, you did." Lipos laughed low, as if he were afraid of being overheard. "You must have quite a grip. Her throat was so crushed she can hardly speak. Catoris is seeing to her now."

The irony of the head enaree seeing to the foreign woman while she, the chief's daughter, was sent his apprentice, was not lost on Arima. So much for Scylas's remorse, she thought bitterly. His heart is still with the whore.

Tabiti interrupted her angry musings. "Catoris?" she breathed. "I thought his eyes were, I mean . . ." She knew little of such matters, only women's gossip, and the fact that few had seen the old enaree since he had driven the demon horse from poor Arima.

"It is true," Lipos said flatly, looking at the curious gazes of the two young women. "He must have picked up a poison from the old carpets in Opoea's yurt, or from the dry wolfskin, or perhaps the horse-demon afflicted him. His vision is now impaired by an oozing white mass in each eye, and he cannot seem to heal it. Most puzzling."

The stallion Bartatua had acquired was a masterpiece, a beauty that even the finest Greek artisan couldn't duplicate. Sleek and strong, its coat so black it seemed nearly blue in the brittle white light of winter, the creature was bred for speed and agility and intelligence, for fighting enemies and for mounting mares. The puffs of icy air that blew from its flaring nostrils nearly choked the hardened warrior with emotion. Such things spoke of sheer, raw power such as man could only dream of, and envy, power that only horses could possess.

They walked slowly along the edge of the frozen river, a thick lambswool blanket covering the precious animal, napped leather tied around its feet to keep it from slipping on the ice. Bartatua rode one of his own geldings and Oricus rode at his side, leading their two packhorses loaded with supplies. The cold was fierce and Bartatua was eager to return to camp, but he dared not hurry for fear of injuring Scylas's prize. The two old Armenian traders who accepted a pair of oxen for this magnificent beast were surely the losers, for the horse was worth far more.

But who was he to complain? Perhaps he could get one of its first colts as part of his dowry for Arima, or have a few of his best mares in foal to it? If he bargained carefully, played the old chief just right, he could end up with one of the finest herds in the tribe.

Oricus pulled to a halt and Bartatua stopped beside him, puzzled when his friend pointed silently to the bushes ahead, where the riverbank jutted into the frozen river. Bartatua narrowed his eyes and studied them. Yes! He too saw it! A definite movement, more jerky and exaggerated than any animal would make. He handed the reins of his mount and the stallion to Oricus and wordlessly dismounted. By the time he had gone two steps across the snow-dusted ice his hand was beneath the heavy bearskin cloak he wore, withdrawing his long war knife. In a crouch he ran across the ice, more silent than the wind.

A bundled figure knelt on the snowy riverbank, a small knife in hand, and hacked futilely at the thick ice covering the water. Fool! Bartatua thought contemptuously. Doesn't he know he will only damage his blade and never get any water that way? What manner of man knowingly damages his weapon. . . .

Whatever manner of man he was, he was obviously no warrior, nor a Scoloti, though he wore a Scythian peaked leather cap with its sides pulled down warm over his ears. The rest of his clothing was a motley collection of Persian, Greek, Thracian. A bulging sack beside the man aroused the warrior's interest, too. Well, whoever this foreigner was, Bartatua had best find out. Dagger in hand, he sprang forward like a cat.

The stranger put up almost no fight, save a bit of initial struggle from the surprise of his capture. Bartatua pulled the man's head back against his chest while pressing the knife to the man's throat. "Speak!" he growled, jerking the head again for emphasis. The stranger looked up at him. His eyes were nearly as blue as Tabiti's. With another jerk the Scythian cap slid from his head. A mass of yellow Greek curls spilled out.

"I am Melanion," the stranger said. "I seek the camp of Scylas."

It was early in the day when Bartatua arrived at the Auchatae camp. He led the stallion up a path rising from the river's edge, hacked out of the frozen soil and kept cleared of snow. Such a tiny intrusion of human life into the vast wastes he had just travelled seemed to say "welcome," and the friendliness of the pathway warmed him like good wine. Behind him he could hear Oricus's horses laboring up the slope and the foreigner, his hands tied before him, gasping when the packhorse on which he rode lurched precariously. The scent of smoke from the yurts grew unmistakable when he neared the camp, and the sounds of barking dogs, crying geese, milling sheep clustered against the cold came on the breeze. Then the sight of them through the bare white tangle of birch trees, like jewels cast against the grey-white land-scape, the yurts of his people. Home.

Bartatua's joy was short-lived. Clearing the path through the forest, he emerged to a camp that was different from the one he'd left. He immediately spotted two tall stakes placed near the central fire. Mounted atop them were the sagging, frozen heads of two of his companions, fellow warriors of Scylas, their dead faces almost delicate in the cold, blue-white like the fine stone the Greeks used to carve their statues.

A keen, quick glance around the clustered yurts yielded another mystery. Beside the tent of the enaree a high platform of saplings had been erected, and atop it lay a corpse, prepared and wrapped and laid out of reach of wolves until spring thawed the ground enough for burial. There must be some connection between the executed warriors and this body, but what? And who was it who had died? Old, sick Scylas?

Oricus trotted to his side, and the worry on his weathered face was plain. "The old man has died," he muttered to Bartatua through a frost-encrusted beard.

"I fear so, too," the chief warrior replied. "But perhaps, from the look of things, he was murdered." He motioned toward the posted heads with a shrug.

"Well," Oricus commented, "you are his heir. We'd best look into whatever happened in our absence."

Two lone guards stood by the campfire, so bundled in furs they could be mistaken for bears invading camp. Bartatua gave them a silent nod as he rode toward them. Their eyes cut briefly to the huddled figure of the Greek behind him.

"Who has died?" Bartatua asked, "and what happened to those two?"

"Opoea," one of the guards huffed into the wind. "And they were responsible."

"But how? Did they murder an old woman? Where is Scylas?" Bartatua asked quickly.

"The old man is the same," the second guard said, turning toward the fire. "As to your questions, go to your yurt. The answers will be found there."

The matter seemed over as far as the guards were concerned. An old woman's death, a proper execution—what more was there to say? Perplexed, Bartatua trotted his weary mount across the clearing, whistling for someone to come and see to the animals. Three bundled slaves emerged from his tent, helped their master and his bound guest dismount, and admired the splendid new stallion as they removed the animals' packs.

"Shelter him well," Bartatua barked, motioning toward the new horse. "Put him in a yurt if necessary. He is unused to the cold here, and Scylas will have you flayed alive if the creature dies. Do you understand me?" The glare in his brown eyes was fierce enough to drive home the point, and the oldest of the slaves took immediate command of the stallion, leading it away as reverently as if he held a god on the tether.

Melanion was glad to be down from the horse and walking again, for the activity warmed his body and staved off the biting cold. When he first touched ground after such a slow, precarious journey, his legs felt odd and heavy, as if he'd borrowed them from someone else. But feeling soon returned, and he stumbled his way behind his captor, mulling over the few words of conversation he'd been able to pick out. Someone had died—well, that was obvious from the body-platform erected by the plainer of the festive tents around him. But the two staked heads? An unease settled into his stomach at his predicament. He'd expected a more triumphant welcome, ushered in to see their king, grand sales of golden wares. Instead he was a warrior's bound prisoner, in a village plainly in the midst of some sort of crisis.

A heavy padded flap over the tent door ahead was pulled aside by a woman's hand, and his eye did not miss the gold rings that ornamented it. The Scyth warrior stepped in, and Melanion followed, ducking his head through the low doorway.

The tent's interior was only slightly less cold than the outside; scarcely warm at all. The entire household was clustered around the hearth fire in the center of the floor, women servants and male slaves, three blue-grey cats the color of dark quartz, two long-haired brown dogs of average size, and two well-dressed young women, one placing a jug of frozen wine by the fire to warm, her eyes downcast in modesty. On the hand that reached out to stir a kettle over the flames Melanion recognized the same rings he'd seen at the doorway. A wife, obviously, and a pretty one at that. And the other woman, wife as well?

She sat cross-legged across the hearth from him, her long

skirt and padded felt jacket a riot of colors, as if a rainbow had fallen to earth in her garments. Even the soles of her soft felt boots were ornamented, he could see from the way she crossed her legs. She had been sewing, for a large embroidered felt lay stiffly across her knees, and the artist in him looked curiously at the animals that writhed across it, wondering at their meaning. The young woman lowered her piecework and looked up, not shyly, with eyes averted as the other woman did, but directly, confidently, almost in challenge. Almost the same way Sela first looked at him.

"Arima!" the warrior blurted, and the seated young woman looked at the Scyth man. Melanion studied her; thick long hair, dark and lush, tossed behind her shoulders and spilling out from beneath a little cap hung with gold ornaments. They caught the firelight when she turned her head and spoke to the man, and the gold threads across her well-rounded bodice caught the firelight, too, and the large gold earrings she wore, and the fine even sheen of her skin, like old ivory, and the blue lights in her eyes.

The warrior thrust him roughly forward, interrupting his reverie. The seated woman was looking at him again, and the standing woman, and the slaves and servants. Even the dogs sat up, watching him, ears pricked forward curiously. Only the cats seemed unconcerned.

"Name?" the man was asking him. Melanion's command of their language was better than that; he didn't have to be spoken to like a child.

"I am Melanion," he said as flawlessly as he could, and enjoyed the look of surprise on their faces.

"You speak our language?" the warrior asked, shrugging off his heavy fur coats. Uneasily Melanion noticed a wicked knife strapped against the man's right thigh.

"Yes. I have traded with your people before," the Greek said, as smoothly as he could. At Olbia all the Scyth he'd seen had been clannish, hostile, shrewd traders, and rich.

Here, on their own lands, it was plain they were also as bloody as the tales had it. He'd have to tread carefully.

"A trader." The warrior spat. He seemed to have no love for traders.

"No! I only trade what I have made. I am a craftsman, a goldsmith."

"A goldsmith!" The man's tone brightened considerably. "And you come to buy Scoloti gold?" The subject was obviously dear to the man's heart.

"To show you what I have made," Melanion corrected him. "I have some of my finest pieces, for the wedding of . . ."

The dark-haired young woman rose at his words, and she was taller than Melanion had imagined. Slim, well-built, her attractive figure showing even through the heavy wool clothes she wore. He found himself envying the man beside him, her husband.

"Arima!" the warrior snapped. The girl paused briefly and shot him a look of defiance with her intense blue eyes, the deep, rich blue of fine lapis, of a summer cornflower.

Without a parting word she turned and walked away to a shadowed bed well off the cold floor. Its arching ends of painted wood curved high like the ends of a ship, and its center was piled with gaily decorated cushions. A plump older woman, grey haired and stiff in movement, trailed behind her.

"Come," the warrior said, trying to hide the irritation in his voice. "Some kumiss, and then we will see the chief." In one swift admirable sweep he withdrew his dagger, sliced off the thong that bound Melanion's wrists, and returned it to its sheath. Hostility suddenly replaced by nomad hospitality, he motioned the Greek to his hearthside.

Melanion tried to suppress his irritation at what he saw spread out before him when he was admitted to the chief's tent. The entire contents of his trading sack had been pulled out, clothes tossed to one side, his bronze razor and small round mirror and tweezers were being examined by several warriors, and his entire precious stock of gold ornaments were cast across the brightly patterned carpets on the floor, arching in a curve around the kneeling form of a girl with silken blonde hair, who toyed with them as excitedly as a child. She cooed and made silly noises while she held them up and tried them on, one after another. He would have noticed how lovely she was were he not so damnably annoyed.

He shot a heated glance at his captor, and to his surprise saw the man's face just as angry as his own. Not till the warrior turned aside did Melanion see the chief, an older man, vigorous in body but somehow weak in spirit, reclining on one of their oddly shaped beds, a well-made goblet of gold in one hand.

"Scylas!" the warrior beside him stated, not as a greeting but as if he were emoting a known fact that needed no explanation. Tree! Rock! Scylas! The old man looked toward them.

"Is this how you treat a guest, a highly skilled craftsman from distant lands?" The warrior swept an arm over the mess strewn about the tent. "He has come to sell jewelry for Arima's wedding. And this is how the Auchatae welcome him?"

The simpering idiocy of the blonde girl on the floor ceased at the words and the look she turned toward them was anything but childlike. The hardness and coldness of it startled Melanion. It was plain the little she-cat was not all she seemed.

"Very well," the old man muttered drunkenly. "I have the right to inspect everything brought into my lands, you know, but very well; have your way. Rhea, gather the man's things and return them to him."

The girl rose on her knees, pouting prettily, and began

pulling the precious objects toward her like a fish-girl at the shore raking in clams. For Melanion, it was the final insult.

"Here!" he snapped, charging forward like a guard dog at the desecration being done to his fine labors. The nearby guards dropped the shaving tools they were examining and their hands went to their daggers. Bartatua was just as quick, his knife swiftly drawn and held down in warning.

"Peace! No bloodshed in my yurt!" Scylas at last took action. Waving his guards aside, he rose from the couch. "Rhea, here." He held out the wine cup, a two-handled Greek design, and the girl obediently stood and took it from him. She knew better than to beg for the gold trinkets, but she knew how to use him well.

"Arima chooses first," the chief fondled the girl's slim white neck affectionately, "and then you may have some. After all, it is her marriage."

Melanion breathed a sigh of relief as the tension in the yurt eased. But the words of the old man set his mind awhirl. Arima, the defiant raven in the warrior's tent—she was the bride for whom he had come.

Next morning the Auchatae camp was abuzz. Not with the Greek's arrival, or the beauty of his wares, or the welcome return of Scylas's heir, hale and hearty and in his right mind, as Scylas seemed to be no longer. In the harsh morning light of winter, with the sky a cloudless blue and the wind gusting erratically, the camp came alive at the news of the wondrous Persian stallion Bartatua had brought back with him, a beast so fine it exceeded not only the other horses in Scylas's herds, but even the mounts of the High King of the Royal Scyth himself. Never had such a magnificent beast been seen.

Warriors entered and left the old yurt erected for the stallion, muttering their envy and admiration. Three of the best grooms in camp had been assigned solely to groom, feed, and water the horse, and to keep it safe and well exercised. Two shaggy old ponies, gentle and reliable, were brought in to keep it company and help to warm it. Blankets of lambswool were placed over it, its legs wrapped against the cold. Nothing was held back to provide comfort and health and security for Scylas's prize.

When the women, their curiosity aroused by the talk of the men, began to scurry to the horse's yurt and peek in through the doorway at the amazing creature, Arima could stand it no longer. She had tried to behave herself; she had tried to be obedient and respectful toward Bartatua, in return for his generosity in allowing her to stay in his yurt. But this was too much. Her interest burned higher with each whispering group of women she heard pass by, groping for words to describe the beauty of the beast they'd just seen.

She had been working dutifully on her dowry, bed coverings, wall hangings, and marriage clothes, more to honor her mother than in anticipation of her wedding. But when a woman of many summers, who probably wouldn't live to see the next one, passed by with her slave, cackling excitedly about the Persian horse, Arima put aside the felt cutouts she was making and rose.

"Urgimas, fetch my otterskin cloak," she said. "I must see this wondrous creature for myself." The serving woman came promptly and draped the dense grey fur around Arima's shoulders.

Four archers guarded the stallion's yurt. What a silly idea! Arima mused when she approached them. A horse dwelling in a tent like a man! The guards recognized her and guessed why she was there, but still they barred her way. "I want to see the Persian horse!" She tried to sound firm, royal, without angering them.

"Only those with permission can enter," recited one of the men, a litany he'd said many times before.

"But it is my father's horse!" Arima protested. "Surely I am allowed." Urgimas shifted behind her, uneasy at the confrontation.

The archer shook his head firmly. "No one is allowed to enter without—"

"I give her permission," a voice cut him off. The two women turned to see Bartatua standing behind them, trimly attired in a close-fitting felt tunic, blue trousers, and a long jacket of spangled yellow wildcat skin. The guards moved away without question and Arima, lowering her eyes from Bartatua's, lifted the heavy felt door aside.

It was as if she had entered a dreamworld. The spacious yurt was dimly lit by two small campfires, ringed with stone and obsessively tended. Between them, toward the rear of the tent, a fence of saplings had been erected and behind it, ghostlike in the gloom, moved the two old ponies, one a dusty grey, the other the color of dried grass. Behind them, drawn away as if afraid of its odd surroundings, moved another presence, a black shadow in the gloom.

Arima walked to the fence, her eyes fastened on the dark form.

"Do you see him?" Bartatua was at her side, his eyes, like hers, on the animal.

"Barely," she whispered, unused to being addressed so directly and familiarly by a man. The whole scene was unreal; she, with permission to see the precious horse, accompanied by Bartatua, who was treating her not with scorn and contempt, but with respect.

He gave a sharp high whistle and she heard the horse's hooves thud against the earth floor as it turned to the sound. Again Bartatua whistled and the stallion walked forward out of the darkness, neck extended, its fine large nostrils scenting the air as it approached the extended hand of the only human it knew in the camp. Arima was entranced and felt a little of her contempt for Bartatua being replaced by admiration.

"Ho, boy," Bartatua muttered soothingly to the creature. It whiffled his hand and lifted its elegant head to survey the man's face. "Unhappy in here, are you?" the chief warrior sympathized. "A dark, stuffy tent is no place for a war-horse, is it?"

Arima was studying the horse, its great size, the fine shape of its head, the well-muscled body, and rich black coat. She knew little about horses but even she could see the difference between this Persian mount and their own smaller, more compact horses. And when she compared this vision of power to the poor decrepit mare she had ridden, the difference was so great it made her head spin. The warrior who rode this horse could not be beaten, or run down if pursued.

Warm breath suddenly tickled her face, and she looked up, startled. It was the stallion, gazing at her with its large dark eyes. Arima gasped and retreated a few paces.

"He approves of you!" Bartatua laughed at her reaction. "You should be honored. Not many here he has approved of!"

Arima felt Urgimas behind her, her gnarled hands holding her arms protectively. Her eyes took in the beast again; it seemed to have lost interest in her and had turned away, munching beech mast from a leather bucket pegged to the fence.

"Touch him!" Bartatua suddenly blurted. Arima looked up at the chief warrior. His leather riding cap had been pulled down behind his neck and his brown hair, sweaty despite the cold, hung in damp tendrils over his forehead. She was suddenly very aware of his closeness, and the aura of maleness that surrounded him.

"Go on, touch him!" he repeated.

"No, I . . ." Arima drew away in fear. Much as she would like to, a woman must not touch a warrior's horse. It was forbidden. Her weakness might contaminate the horse, bringing disaster to its rider in some future battle. Touch the fine Persian horse of Scylas?

"The horse will not be ridden in battle, Arima. If it was, it would be gelded, and that would end its life as a sire. It has approved of you," Bartatua explained, understanding the girl's fears. "The nature of most women disturbs a war-horse, but you must be different. See, he accepts you."

The horse looked her way again, tossed its head, and resumed eating. Hesitantly Arima stepped back to the fence, raised herself on tiptoe, and stretched her arm out. Lipos had taught her to ride, in secret, but this was no secret at all. The stallion accepted her, Bartatua accepted her.

Her fingertips touched the sleek, powerful shoulder of the horse, and his skin quivered at the feel of it. Arima gasped and withdrew her hand; she didn't know a horse's skin could move in such a fashion. She stepped in front of Bartatua and reached out again, but this time she slid her hand over the horse with more ease and confidence. How mighty it felt! How full of life and vigor! An ache, a burning rose in her hand and tingled up to her body. Oh, to embrace the beast! To speak to it, ride it, know its every mood! The yearning was as powerful as a woman in love, a mother for her babe.

"Enough," Bartatua muttered, seizing her wrist and pull-ing her hand back. Could he read her thoughts the way he could read the weather signs, the trail of an animal? Arima looked away, frightened, wishing he would release her arm. He didn't. Poised in midair, he held it up till the discomfort of it forced her to turn toward him.

"My woman," he said simply, and his callused fingers closed tight around her wrist. He was hurting her. He must have realized it, but she knew she would not tell him. Through the stallion she had suddenly been made aware of power—of men, of horses, powers which she, as a woman, had no access to. This is what Opoea had tried to convey to her. The only safety for a woman was to submit. She hated the answer when she gave it, and she hated herself for saying it.

"Yes," she said meekly, and he let her go.

* * *

The Greek goldsmith was brought to Scylas's tent for the evening meal, and at its completion Arima was summoned. She came, dressed in dark, mossy green, eyes downcast, suitably demure.

Her manner has changed, Melanion noted curiously. The defiant raven seems tamed.

"Father." She bowed politely to the old chief who sat cross-legged on a deerskin cushion. He nursed a goblet of warm wine the entire evening, Melanion observed, and didn't seem well at all.

"See what this Greek has brought, Arima, and decide what you'd like for your marriage," the old man was saying. Melanion had spread a length of fine sueded calfskin on the rugs before him, and he busied himself arranging the chains and pendants, bracelets and earrings, to best advantage. Whatever private dramas were going on here, he'd best ignore them. He came to sell jewelry, make a lot of money, recoup his losses from buying the Cimmerian girl, and then he'd be on his way, off to greater riches with the Persian noblemen come spring.

The girl, with her old serving woman as always at hand, lowered herself gracefully cross-legged opposite Melanion. The move was as effortless as a snake slicing through water and he looked at her admiringly. She truly had the bearing of royalty. Her eyes remained downcast, her long dark lashes moving lightly as she surveyed his wares. He'd sold enough to women; he knew the gasps of excitement, the hands seizing first one thing and then another, the childlike looks on their faces. This girl showed none of it. Her heart was plainly elsewhere. Melanion's stomach sank and he cursed inwardly. All this journey, in the cold of winter, only to be confronted by one of the few women on earth not interested in jewels and trinkets.

"That is nice," she said flatly, pointing to a gold and carnelian Egyptian necklace.

140

"Try it on." Melanion picked it up and held it out to her. Her soft white hands reached out and took it from him. Straightening, she tossed her hair back and held the necklace across from shoulder to shoulder.

"Pretty," the slave woman commented, leaning forward, nodding. "But why not something blue?"

"Yes, Urgimas." The girl returned the necklace to the suede and tried to arrange it as it had been. Melanion reached down to take it from her, and for a brief span their hands collided, jarringly. He was struck by the coolness of her skin.

"Yes, blue," he muttered, looking up at her face. To his surprise, she was staring back at him, and the light in her eyes showed none of the meekness of her manner. They were alert, curious, probing.

Melanion looked down, fumbling with one of his best items, a large pendant of gold and silver set with fine Persian turquoise and done in a Persian style, two winged lions with bearded human heads. Arima's dislike was immediate. "No." She shook her head. The task of selecting her dowry suddenly became more interesting as her manner livened.

"A horse," she declared forthrightly, and Melanion's hopes soared. A commission! An excuse to stay in camp through the winter! He looked at her and she studied his face openly, her blue eyes taking in all his features. "I want a necklace with a Persian horse," she said quietly, "like the one my father just purchased."

Melanion was allowed to use the fine black stallion of Scylas as a model. The sensation it caused the Scyth camp amused him, for while it was indeed a splendid animal, the Persians had many such beasts. In Persia, this would not even be considered the best of their herds. Still, it gave him a chance to get away from the old leatherworker's tent where he stayed, and the oppressive smells of fresh skins and singed hairs and urine-cured leather. The old man's eyes were as keen as a hawk's but his sense of smell must have gone years ago, from the stenches he continually lived with.

It also gave him a chance to see Arima, for she came to visit the stallion and observe his sketching of it nearly every day. Many times Melanion would watch her fondling the horse tenderly, and the fiery animal gentling at her touch, listening for her spoken endearments like a lover.

Melanion pretended to be working, trying to get the horse's head just right with a bit of charcoal on a scrap of deerskin, but in truth he was merely watching Arima. Of all the women he'd known, she had a presence about her that the others had lacked. Not timid and reticent, as most barbarian women were, nor brazen and brash like so many of the prostitutes he'd known. No, she had—how could he put it—a simple complexity to her. She was, quite simply, a complex person, moving in a self-contained manner through her own private world. It intrigued him. Women were simple creatures, that was a fact. Flattery, food, and finery were all that they required. But Arima, she cared little for his golden treasures and did not indulge in idle chatter and silliness. She knew her own mind and kept it, behind that quiet demeanor and those defiant blue eyes.

The thought of being her lover made him ache inside. Oh, he'd been provided a comely enough slave girl by Scylas, along with food and drink and a bed to sleep on. But what was the meaning of it? Another rut, like a hundred others. What would Arima be like in his arms, that fine ivory skin pressed to his own naked body, those silent lips moist against his own, all his skills with women fueling the fires within her that now burned only as rebellion.

"You daydream, foreigner!" Arima's laughing voice roused him. She had left the stallion and stood beside him, the ever-present Urgimas at her heels.

"It is tiring work, sketching when my hands are so cold." He stretched out the deerskin for her inspection. She leaned closer and the long scented waves of her hair nearly brushed his nose.

"Very nice," she said nodding, studying his work, "except I can see that you have little real familiarity with horses." She turned her head and looked at him, her face scarcely a foot from his.

"What do you mean? I thought it was, well . . ."

The girl smiled amusedly at his confusion. Was it his imagination, or was she aware of her effect on him?

"The spirit," she stated simply. "You capture the form, but not the spirit of the creature."

"I don't understand," Melanion answered, suddenly intrigued. Here was that depth of hers, again manifesting itself. She stood and turned to gaze at the stallion, and her eyes took on a faraway look, as if she were seeing beyond him, to other worlds.

"Have you not seen a horse running free and wild?" she breathed. "Have you not felt the wind in its face, the sharp air in its nostrils, the joy of flying like a bird, without wings?"

He stared at her, awed. The girl was not talking a fantasy, a dream. She knew horses, had ridden one.

Arima fell silent, still staring at unseen horizons, and Melanion could almost see the wind in her black hair, flying like the mane of the black stallion. His heart suddenly moved in pity for this blue-eyed raven, as wild and free as the great Persian horse but condemned to be a brood mare. And unlike Sela, there was nothing he could do to help her.

"The wind," she whispered, turning and casting a side-long glance at him. "Sketch the wind, and you will capture the spirit of the horse." Abruptly the girl left the yurt, and Melanion made not to notice the tears that had brimmed her eyes.

Arima lay long into the night, staring at the low hearth fire of Bartatua, listening to his jagged snoring across the tent.

Many times she had wondered about it, when a man takes a woman. She had seen it often enough before—who hadn't? A warrior with his captive, two slaves behind a hayrick. It was as natural as the mating of horses, or a bitch in heat. Even geese, silly things, seemed to have a need for it. But what did it feel like? What would Bartatua do to her? This was the odd part. It wasn't every young woman who stayed in her husband's yurt before her marriage and who had the dubious privilege of seeing, hearing him in bed with his first wife, or with a slave girl who took his fancy. She had listened on many a night to the scarcely human sounds they made, Bartatua and his woman. But she had made herself not look. One day, she knew, the woman would be her.

A tear trickled down her cheek, and she smoothed it away with a forefinger. She could only think of the stallion, so magnificent and free, and the great grey horse of her dreams, so similar in appearance, and of how she never should have tasted riding, for it made her coming captivity all the harder to bear.

And she thought of Melanion the Greek. Of his free-roaming ways, coming and going as he pleased, unencumbered by yurts and herds and wagons and marriages. Of the odd, funny way he spoke her language. Of the look in his eyes whenever they met.

Oh gods! she choked back a sob. The look in his eyes!

She turned away and buried her face in the pillows and cried, silently, so Urgimas would not hear.

The last person she wanted to see the next morning was Lipos, but there he was, entering the yurt unannounced as was his right, sitting cross-legged by the hearth, taking a cup of greasy sheep broth from a slave girl. Bartatua was only just stirring and he sat up lazily, reaching for a heavy felt jacket offered by a slave. "What brings you here so early in the day?" he said, yawning hospitably to the enaree. The half-man was dressed oddly, in riding trousers and a woman's fur cloak. A red leather bag of charms hung about his neck.

"Business." Lipos licked a bit of grease from his mouth. "I must see Arima about the marriage."

Bartatua arched his heavy brows as he swung his legs over the side of the couch and slid his feet into heavy felt boots. "Haven't you already taught her all you must?" he questioned the enaree. "Nothing more remains for you to do till the marriage."

"Yes," Lipos nodded, laughing, "when I must determine if your bride is still a virgin."

Bartatua hooted at the half-man's jest. "Well, my friend," he retorted, squatting by the fire, "under these circumstances," he motioned around his home, "she might not be by the time of the ceremony."

Lipos laughed loudly, joined by Bartatua in high male spirits, and Arima tunneled her head deeper under the cushions, cursing them both. Her ears burned at their words and her heart raced in anger at being treated, yet again, as if she were less than human. She also knew her eyes were red and swollen from a night of crying. Why did Lipos pick now to see her? Why not tomorrow? This evening?

"Arima!" Bartatua barked at her. She moved slowly, sluggishly, trying to seem as if she were rousing from deep sleep. Perhaps Lipos would see this and go away.

"It's alright," she heard the enaree say. Before Arima could feel relief his hand was on her back. "Wake up, Arima," he said quietly. "We must talk."

The girl pulled the cushions from her head and gasped when the icy air hit her warm skin. She was careful to keep her face turned away from him. "What is it?" she muttered.

"Your father, Arima. He is very ill."

The girl tensed at his words. Her heart did not care at the news. If he died, he died. She had little feeling for him anymore. But if he was that ill, her marriage would not be in the spring, festive and warm with neighboring tribes visiting. It would be now, days away. It could not be. It must not be.

"Will you come?" Lipos forced the suggestion into her mind. Arima flung back the heavy blankets and motioned to Urgimas.

"Quickly!" she gasped. "My clothes!"

The yurt of Scylas, for all its size and splendor, was dark and oppressive inside. The old man lay on his bed, his complexion nearly as grey as the snow-heavy sky outside. Arima forced herself to go to him, to kneel beside him, to make herself seem to care.

"Father," she whispered, studying his face. How he had aged, in just a few short months, from the vigorous man he was, to this pallid invalid! Scylas opened his red-rimmed eyes and looked at her.

"Arima," he mumbled. "Bartatua and you must . . ."

"I know, Father. I know." She didn't want to let him finish, didn't want to hear those awful words. Scylas clutched feebly at his chest with one hand.

"Hurts . . ." he breathed.

"What, Father? What hurts?" Arima leaned closer.

"This, here," he replied, so weakly she could barely hear him. "Bartatua, where is he?"

"He is coming, Father. He will be here soon."

"And Rhea?"

Arima's heart froze at the hated name. The Northwoman pushed through the encircling ring of archers and spearmen and servants, wearing only a loose white wool shirt. Arima moved to leave, but Scylas reached for her arm.

"Arima, she is with child," he muttered, smiling. "My child, Arima. Your brother."

Arima stood, horrified. That demon-woman, bearing a child of my father's? In all their years of marriage my mother conceived but once, while this she-devil is already with child? It cannot be!

Backing away in shock, Arima nearly collided with Bartatua. He stood stiffly, grim-faced, as distressed, for his own reasons, at the news as she was. This foreign woman whose coming had brought his chief to death's threshold now carried his child, a child which, if it was a boy, could one day challenge Bartatua's right to the Auchatae leadership. Arima stared at Bartatua openmouthed, unable to speak. The warrior steadied her, his hands on her shoulders, and his first glance at her red eyes surprised him; he did not think she cared that much for old Scylas, to have cried so. But then his eyes fell on the hated foreign woman, sitting solicitously at Scylas's bedside, feeding him some medicine Catoris had handed her. I will kill her, he thought savagely as he watched them. As soon as Scylas is gone I will kill her and solve all our problems.

Arima broke from Bartatua's grasp and stumbled from the Royal Yurt, too numb for speech or action. Her footsteps carried her blindly to the one happy place her life had found, the tent of the black stallion.

The crowds of the past had gone, and in the present crisis, only two grooms remained with Scylas's prize. Arima leaned over the fence and clucked her tongue, and the great black horse pricked its ears and came toward her. He nuzzled her neck affectionately, his nose softer than the finest sueded lambskin. The horse seemed to sense her distress—for it stayed by her as loyally as a pet dog. Bartatua had said they were sensitive creatures.

Mother is dead, Father is dying, my marriage looms closer, and you, my swift black cloud, will only live till spring, for when spring comes and they bury Scylas, you will be strangled to accompany him to the Otherworld, where age never slows the warrior and horses are swift as the wind.

Her heart twisted within her at the thought. Of all the

sorrows she ever had to endure this, she knew, was the worst. Sobbing aloud, she flung her arms around the stallion's neck and cried—for his future, and for hers.

Melanion sought to escape the oppressive atmosphere of the camp by completing his sketches for the girl's necklace. Of course, it might prove to be pointless, for with the old man dying and the marriage hastened, dowries and jewelry might be the last thing on anyone's mind. He cursed his luck. All that money, vanishing like mist. He should have listened to Praxis.

He drew up short at the pitiful sight that met him when he ducked into the Horse Yurt. A disheveled Arima, clothes hastily donned, hair undressed, clung to the neck of the stallion, who stood patiently by like a stalwart old friend while she cried her heart out. Perhaps he should leave, let her cry privately. A quick glance around the tent showed the two grooms who remained off to one side, gambling at knucklebones. With no chief to guide the camp, everything seemed to be falling apart.

The goldsmith decided to stay. Quietly he laid the piece of deerskin and the bit of charcoal on a low stool where he usually sat, and then he stepped over to the crying girl. He wasn't sure what he was going to say or do; he only knew he couldn't leave her there like that, hysterical and alone.

"Arima." He put a hand on her quaking shoulder. He heard her choking back the tears, trying to compose herself in his presence. "I am sorry, Arima," he tried again. His heart always said act! do something! but then it deserted him, and he never knew what he was supposed to do. It had deserted him now. "My father, too, died," he said. "It hurts, but you will heal. In time, you will . . ."

The girl turned her face down, pressing her forehead to the stallion's neck. "He can die, for all I care," she spat out. Melanion drew back in surprise. "He has never loved me, nor I him. Nothing I did ever pleased him, because I was not a son. And then he killed my mother, because of that she-demon he lusts after. Let him die."

"Surely you can't mean that!" Melanion protested. "It is in the natural order of the gods for every child to love his parents. Your tears alone are proof of that!"

She turned her face toward him and the fire in her eyes was gone. "My tears are for this horse. Come spring, he will die a horrifying death to accompany my father on his journey. And I must sit and wait for it to happen. Is that the way of all men, Melanion? To destroy what is good and beautiful in the world? To stamp out laughter and happiness and joy, all because of their own narrow interests? The world must always bend to the whims of men, and the world must always suffer for it."

The old fire flared in her eyes as she spoke, then dimmed and vanished. Bravely she bit her trembling lower lip.

"He cannot die," she whispered. "Melanion—we must save him."

For her anguish and tears he wanted to hold her and comfort her. But her words scared him. Who was he to get dangerously involved in tribal matters? He'd come to work, earn his wages, and leave. He'd do best to remember that fact, especially now with this little raven crying piteously before him.

"I cannot, Arima," he hissed, fearful the two grooms might overhear them. "What you say is insane! How can we save a horse?"

"I don't know! But if he dies, I will die with him! How could I bear to watch the life choked out of him, Melanion? To me he is life, my life, all I have. If he dies, I die."

He could see that she was serious. In her unhappy state of mind, she had come to confuse her own craving for freedom with this beautiful Persian horse, captive, like her, in a tent. Such irrationality was completely alien to a rational Greek like himself. Best sit her down and reason with her.

"Come, Arima," he soothed, disentangling her arms from the horse's neck. "Sit down, dry your tears, and we'll see what we can think of." Woodenly she let herself be guided to the stool. He pushed his drawing equipment to the ground and forced her to sit. Squatting before her, he saw her halfheartedly wiping away the tears, but her eyes never left the stallion.

"What is it that your father suffers from?" he began gently. Perhaps if he could straighten out her thinking she'd drop this horse nonsense and they could all get on with their business . . . such as it was.

Arima shook her head forlornly, dropping her eyes to her hands in her lap. "I don't know. His strength has left him; he has pains."

"Where?"

"Here." She pointed to her chest.

"And how long has he been this way?" Greek physicians were world famous, and while he was no physician himself, perhaps he'd picked up enough that he could find some clue in the girl's halting description of her father's disease.

"Not long," she muttered. "Why do you ask? Why all this questioning about my father, when it is the horse we must save? Scylas is dying. He wore himself out on the Northwoman, Rhea." She spat out the name distastefully.

Melanion's attention roused at her words. Old men often died in the beds of younger women, but it was sudden, not dragged out over months. "Are you saying he was well before she came?" he pressed Arima. She sniffled loudly and looked at him, a slow understanding coming to her eyes.

"Poison." The word slid from her mouth. Melanion nodded. "We must tell someone. Your wise men. Don't they uphold your laws?"

"Yes," the girl whispered.

"The old one, then. What's his name?"

"No." Arima closed her hand over his. "Not Catoris. I have never liked him; he is not to be trusted. Lipos is the one." She nodded, remembering his insistence that she inform him about her father. At the time he had seemed like a traitor. But perhaps he had suspected something all along.

"Lipos, then." Melanion rose to his feet. "You just might have succeeded in saving the stallion after all."

Lipos was at Catoris's side, tending the dying Scylas. Attempting to increase their power and influence over the evil spirits that afflicted their chief, the two enarees had dressed in the symbols of their own totem animals. Lipos's neck was encircled with hawk feathers, and two dried hawk wings ornamented his felt cap. Dried talons and beaks trailed down his right arm—his power arm—in an effort to partake of the swiftness and cunning of the bird. Catoris, too, was dressed as a beast; a wild boar, with a boar's hide hanging down his back, a necklace of gleaming white tusks around his neck. The boar was the most fearsome creature in the forest, and perhaps the evil spirits, too, would be frightened by its power.

Arima entered the Royal Yurt alone. Melanion had not thought it right to appear at such a solemn time. Her heart raced in fear at the unnaturalness of the scene: the hearth fire low, the yurt cloaked in somber shadows, the two enarees hovering over the couch of Scylas like strange subhuman creatures. The feathers adorning Lipos rustled dryly when he moved, and the stiff boarskin on Catoris crackled a reply. Choking clouds of incense and burning oils cloyed the air, making it difficult to breathe. The entire tent seemed to be in the grip of evil.

Catoris held his power-wand over the slumbering Scylas, attempting to summon energies. His efforts seemed in vain, Arima noted, for her father's face was slack, his mouth hanging open, his breathing low and shallow. All their magics were for nothing.

The girl hesitated to intrude, but she knew she must. Pushing through the silent guards who crouched around the bed of Scylas, leaning dejectedly on their spears as they awaited his death, she reached out to Lipos's arm. He was busy tossing hardened drops of frankincense on the fire, muttering as he did so. His concentration was so intense that he flinched when she touched him, as if he had been burned. He turned and looked over his shoulder at her. His face was grey, drawn, scarcely human in the flickering light.

"You must come," Arima whispered urgently.

"I cannot!" Lipos hissed, a rasping sound that seemed almost like the warning cry of a bird.

"You must!" She wanted to obey him, to leave the oppressive tent and return to the free-blown wind outside. But she could not. She must remain and convince him, not for her father's sake, but for the stallion.

The enaree turned away, as if to dismiss her from existence. Angered, Arima closed a hand firmly around his upper arm, squeezing it so tightly she knew he could not ignore her. "Our agreement," she breathed into his ear, stirring the hawk feathers with her words. Lipos did not respond. Tossing a few more drops of incense into the fire, he laid the rest on the carpet, shrugged her hand from his arm, and stood. Silently he left the tent and Arima, relieved, followed him.

Melanion waited in the Horse Yurt, huddled for warmth by one of the two small campfires. He scarcely recognized the young enaree when he entered. His normal soft manner had vanished, replaced by a keen-eyed harshness that was startling. Feathers and talons dangled and floated around him, a look that would have been ludicrous were it not for the perfect blending they made with his own hawklike appearance.

"Go!" Lipos snapped to the Greek, who rose to his feet uncertainly.

"No." Arima stopped him. "He knows, too. He must stay."

"Then you leave!" The enaree jerked one arm toward the

two squatting grooms. Their orders were given by Scylas, but one did not defy a half-man. Scurrying like mice, they fled the tent. "And now, what's to be said?" Lipos turned to the girl. His hawklike demeanor was fading and his features seemed to soften as she looked at him.

"What has been given to my father?" Arima thrust a question at him. "Foods, medicine? Has the she-devil fed him anything?"

Lipos smiled slightly. "Ah, then, so you know!" he mused, shifting his pale eyes from Arima to the Greek and back.

"Arima says his illness began when the slave girl came," Melanion explained, "a circumstance that seemed very odd to me."

"Indeed," Lipos agreed. "I have long known that something was afoot. I asked Arima to observe Scylas, but with the turn events have taken, and she living with Bartatua now, that has become impossible. My suspicions, too, turned to the slave girl. Yes, I believe she gives him something, but how I do not know. I have tried to check his food and drink. She could not be slowly poisoning him without my knowing it. But then how is it done?"

"I can tell you." A voice broke their conspiracy and the three turned to see Tabiti, tiny and swathed in a long fox fur coat, standing inside the door. "It is Catoris," she sighed, as if the disclosure pained her. "They are in league, he and Rhea, for I have seen them, though why I do not know. And the child she carries, Arima, it is not your father's child. It is the child of Catoris!"

Lipos swept into the Royal Yurt, fiercely diving on his unsuspecting prey. Catoris was nearly entranced, his heavy boar ponderousness hovering over Scylas in the darkness, a low guttural chant spilling from his throat. He did not see the approach of his apprentice. He did not see the guards and servants stand and scatter before the hawk-man. He remained oblivious to all until the young enaree did what no enaree had a right to do; his talon-bedecked arm shot out and he seized the power-stick of Catoris, wrenched it from his startled grip, and planted one end of it firmly on the floor, breaking its spell.

Catoris's chant stopped but he remained poised over Scylas's form, his head weaving back and forth slowly, like a boar contemplating attack.

"You have lost, Catoris," Lipos said calmly. "You have been seen, your plot is exposed, and you have lost."

A muffled gasp erupted from the far side of the yurt, and a frightened Rhea slid from her bed. If Catoris had been found out, then she, too, had lost.

"Seize her!" Lipos commanded and immediately two of Scylas's archers took the terrified girl's arms.

"What is the meaning of this?" Catoris suddenly whirled, his disease-ridden eyes red with rage. "I will have you executed for this! Give me back the stick!"

He reached for the power-stick, the heavy boar's tusks around his neck rattling when he lurched forward. But Lipos was swifter and he turned, holding the wooden rod threateningly over the fire. "What manner of enaree willingly loses his source of power?" he retorted. "Admit your defeat. Will I state the charges here, in front of everyone, or do I wait for a proper hearing, a proper trial?"

Catoris stared openmouthed at the wand hovering dangerously close to the flames. "No, don't," he choked, and the mighty figure of a man beneath the boarskin and tusks suddenly seemed shrunken, weak. "A proper hearing, yes, and then we will see who burns, Lipos, you or I. Yes, then we will see."

Melanion had almost become a member of the Auchatae tribe. Through the final span of winter he lived with them, but in his own yurt now, a reward from old Scylas for his part in uncovering the conspiracy against him. He'd seen the hardships the steppe nomads endured through the bitterness of the season. They suffered cold so penetrating even wine in the yurts froze solid. They endlessly cleared away snowfalls that threatened to bury their herds of horses and matted, black-faced sheep. Nearly every morning the frozen carcass of another animal that had perished from the cold, from hunger, from disease or old age had to be dragged away. He saw the gentle side of them, too, sick foals taken into their yurts to be nursed back to health, kittens and puppies sleeping warmly in their owners' beds. Three more tribespeople died during the winter; an old couple, man and wife, who seemed to have chosen to let their hearth fire die—a common thing, Arima explained—and a young girl, barely sixteen, new with child. Their bodies joined that of Opoea on the platform, awaiting burial in the spring. Melanion came to respect these people he had once scorned, to admire their toughness in the face of such adversity. He became loath to call them barbarians.

Scylas ordered a large fire and a steady supply of fuel for Melanion's hearth. He knew the goldsmith could not work in the searing cold, and he wanted a fine dowry for his daughter's spring marriage. Nothing was spared for Melanion's needs and comfort.

This day, with the first hint of spring freshness in the air, Melanion rubbed the final shine onto an elaborate chain dangling with intricate gold medallions, made for Arima to wear across the front of her headdress. He was pleased with how it had turned out. Only a few pieces left to finish for the girl, along with some other commissions he'd picked up in camp, and by spring he'd be on his way to work for the Persians. He smiled to himself at how these people lavished as much gold ornamentation on their favored horses—for that was the bulk of his extra work—as they did on their own family.

A heavy swishing sound and a gust of fresh air made him turn. The young slave boy assigned to serve him rose from the fireside and hurried to the door of the yurt. Arima had entered, alone but for the ever-present shadow of Urgimas. Melanion looked at her, their eyes met in communion, and she smiled.

"How is the work coming?" she said quietly. He had heard her defiant, he had heard her in despair, but when she was calm and happy her voice had a soothing, irresistible musical quality. He held up the chain, outstretched between his hands, and let the gold medallions catch the blazing firelight. Arima drew in her breath in admiration.

"You must be a highly valued goldsmith to the chief of your people," she complimented him. "Why did he let you travel so far, leaving him without your skills and services?"

The slave boy, from habit, drew a low stool to the Greek's side for the girl to sit on. She had visited enough times that he knew what to do. Ladling out a cupful of slushy, half-frozen wine, he set it near the fire to warm.

Melanion laughed at her words and spread the headband over the soft suede that covered his lap. "Oh, we have no chief! No Greek would ever allow himself to be controlled so by another man."

"No chief?" Her blue eyes grew wide with concern. Melanion looked away awkwardly.

"No," he muttered. "I am Ionian and we have our king, but every Greek is his own man, as well."

"I don't understand," she puzzled. "Such a thing is like a herd with no stallion to guide it and see to its safety. A wolf pack with no leader. It is only natural in the world for one to command, and the rest to follow."

He rubbed the curves of a tiny bird in flight. "But we are not animals, Arima. Is it just as natural for a man to lead a woman?" He aimed his words right at the heart of her philosophy and sensed her stiffen uncomfortably. Her femaleness was her vulnerability and her handicap, and he knew it. Try as she might, she could never escape her destiny as a woman. When the girl sat for a long time without answering, he cast a quick glance in her direction. Her face was downcast, staring absently at her slim white hands, the roaring fire dancing splashes of light over her high cheeks and finely chiseled face. Bitterness seized Melanion's heart, and he looked away. Such beauty! Such spirit! And all to be wasted here, among the nomads, bearing babies for Bartatua and dying years before her time. With Sela, he could just buy her and give her her freedom; with Arima there was no such easy solution.

"Cimmerian women are not treated like you are treated, you know." He seized on an idea. Arima lifted her head and looked at him, and this time it was her turn to reflect. Bent over his work, the firelight gleaming off the yellow curls around his face and the golden treasure in his hands, she thought that he must look like Oetosyrus, the god of the sun.

"Tell me about them," she whispered, and her heart shouted gratitude to the gods when he lifted his head and their eyes met once more. In the calm pale blue of his gaze, like the gentle sky of a spring day, dwelt all the peace and comfort her soul had ever known.

Melanion slowly returned to his work. "I knew a Cimmerian woman," he muttered. "She told me their women are treated no differently than the men."

Arima's gasp interrupted him. "That cannot be!" she breathed. "Women who ride and hunt and—"

". . . and fight," he finished her sentence. "Yes, that's what she said. They live just as the men do. From the time they are children they ride horses, gentling and training the young two-year-olds before their real training begins at three years. They hunt with the men; they learn war skills."

He couldn't resist a peek at the awestruck girl. She gazed into the fire, lost in thought.

"In fact," he decided to complete his tale with a flourish, "I may go to visit her when I leave here. Her people live not too far away from yours." Arima's reaction surprised him.

"Yes." She stood suddenly, her voice more choked with ice than the thawing river outside. "Visit this Cimmerian woman, if such a creature could be called woman." Angrily she swept from the yurt. Urgimas sprang to her feet and followed her. The Greek smiled; the tone of her voice left little doubt in his mind. His mention of Sela had consumed her with jealousy. He gave a low laugh at the odd ways of women and returned to his work.

The next morning was almost warm, as if to herald the arrival of the group Lipos had been tensely waiting all winter—a large assembly of enarees, travelling as soon as the weather permitted, to sit in formal judgement of Catoris and his woman.

They made a splendid entourage, gathering from all the nearby camps of allied Scoloti tribes; smaller bands related to the Auchatae, the Catiari, the Traspians, even a contingent of three from Idanthyrsus, Chief of the Pralatae, the Royal Scyths, and High King of all the Scoloti tribes. In a caravan that took several days to arrive, they came to the camp of Scylas. They settled in a clearing by themselves, on a spot deemed auspicious by Lipos's magics. Brightly painted wagons clustered to one side, like so many gaudy beetles against the muddy ground. Slaves and servants scurried to erect their masters' yurts, some as drab as those of the common servants, others more splendid than Scylas's royal quarters. Auchatae boys quarreled for the honor of seeing to their horses and oxen which, like their owners' tents, ran the gamut from breathtaking to decrepit. It didn't matter what condition the animals were in. To do good service to an enaree might mean a high recommendation to a select warrior, the good fortune of a lucky charm in reward, even the rare honor of being approved to become an enaree oneself.

Scylas reclined on a couch in Arima's yurt, for she had returned to the tent of Opoea after the Northwoman's arrest and now claimed it as her own. Lipos eyed him critically when he entered it; restoring him to health had been his main concern in the waning days of winter. "Are they settled yet?" the chief said, sitting and leaning back against the pillows Arima piled for him.

"Almost," Lipos replied. He strode to the fireside where Urgimas was preparing a tea for the old man, took the goblet from her hands, and inspected the brew critically.

"It's what you gave her," Arima announced, rising from her couch and coming to her slave's defense.

"I don't doubt that," the enaree snapped, returning the cup to the Medean woman. "Still, it never hurts to check."

Arima put her hands on her hips and came forward hotly. "Are you suggesting that I am poisoning my own father?" she demanded. Others might fear the enaree, but she didn't. She'd seen dirt muddy their hooves and knew they were as human as everyone else.

"No," Lipos retorted, turning to meet her challenge. "I have just learned to be cautious, to check things on my own."

"Then if you could not trust us with his care, he should have been taken to your tent, where you and your slaves could see to him," the girl snapped.

"That might have been wise, at that," Lipos replied, "where his care would be constant, not as spotty as a spring rain, while you make your forays around camp."

Arima felt her cheeks burn in sudden rage and fear. Did he mean her visits to the black Persian horse, or to see Melanion? And if it was the Greek he referred to, how much did he know, or suspect? Nothing had happened between them, but still, were her feelings all that obvious to Lipos?

"You'd do well to feel shame, and stay hearthside where you belong," Lipos concluded, noting the redness of her face. "Within the moon's passing you'll be Bartatua's wife, and then your roaming days will be at an end." He stared at her deliberately, as if to convey to her that he knew, and that she'd best watch herself before he was forced to take action.

He could see a flicker of fear in her angry blue eyes, but her next move surprised him.

"How dare you!" she spluttered, seizing a carved and painted wood spindle from her bedside and heaving it at him. Lipos ducked, and it hit his shoulder, doing little damage through the padded felt tunic he wore. Still, the act itself was enough. Within the space of a heartbeat Urgimas was gasping in horror, Scylas had leaped to his feet, and Lipos was striding for the door. Let her father see to her, he fumed. Granted, he had been on edge since the approach of Catoris's trial, and yes, he may have provoked the girl, but to physically attack an enaree was not to be borne. When he exited the yurt he was satisfied to hear the sounds of a good thrashing being administered to Arima by her father.

The men had gone to the enarees' ritual, in a clearing far upstream away from women and tents and livestock. Arima rose stiffly from her bed, glad for the silence and the absence of warriors, fathers, and half-men. Her back and shoulders ached unbearably from the beating Scylas had given her, the worst one in her life, since Opoea was no longer alive to protect her. She was the only person who ever successfully stood up to the old chief, and now she was gone.

A sob caught in Arima's throat, half pain, half sorrow. Now, with spring, her whole life would arrive at its goal. If only she'd had the wisdom to step outside and freeze with Opoea; death was the only freedom women knew.

The girl stood and Urgimas leaped to her feet, reaching to steady Arima's tottering gait. "No!" she snapped to her slave. "I want to be alone, Urgimas."

The old woman began to protest, her charge making her way to the door.

"Alone. For just awhile. I will be back before the men return."

"I cannot let you go out by yourself, Arima!" the slave

woman protested futilely. "If your father finds out, he will have me executed!"

"No. I will see that he doesn't. It will be alright, Urgimas. I will go to the bathing place by the river and be back shortly. Now wait here!"

The grass and weeds and rushes streamside were beginning to show green as they pushed up from the rich black mud. Just the buoyant smell of it lifted Arima's spirits; a smell of life awakening. What a welcome relief from the frigid, odorless wind of winter or the stuffy, choking air in the yurts! Spring was the smell of expansion, of change, of freedom.

The word came to her mind again, stabbing her heart like a spear wound. Always, always it came back to that word, that idea. *Freedom.*

She had been careful to remove her felt boots, to keep them from the sticky mud, and she squished her way barefoot, the boots in one hand, her skirts in the other. Nearing the river, she could feel cold radiating from the piles of breaking ice jumbled against the rocks. Far out in the center a channel had opened, and the jubilant rushing of the waters drowned out the sounds of birds and the wind sighing in the hemlocks, everything.

Her favorite rock was sundappled and Arima made her way toward it. Paces away the ice loomed head-high, obscuring her view of the water. It didn't matter. She hadn't come to wade or to fish, to splash in the shallows and collect pebbles and shells as she would in the summer. She'd come to think.

Pulling up a handful of dead grass, she wiped as much mud as she could from her feet then stretched out on the broad, flat rock. How soothing the sun is, she reflected, even on this thin spring morning. How different from the dry, sterile heat of a hearth fire! Inhaling deeply, she gazed overhead, through the tall waving white branches of birch trees, to the milky blue sky above. A pale, gentle blue, like the eyes of a newborn babe.

The river ice split with a thunderous crack and Arima bolted upright, looking around nervously. No need to fear, she calmed herself; the ice always screams like that when it is breaking up and dying.

She reclined again, closing her eyes and letting the warm sun soothe her aches and bruises. The river roared, a constant accompaniment to her thoughts; a floe of ice groaned, screeched against itself and broke free, racing downstream on the current. I could escape on the ice, she teased herself; sit on a floe like an orphaned otter and let the gods take me where they wish.

Another sound nearby whirled her eyes open and she stared overhead, afraid to move. It must have been the churning waters, the unearthly moans of the ice.

She heard it again, closer, and she rose to one elbow. No, she gasped, it cannot be. It is only the mist, stirred by the sun and rising in the chill air. It cannot be.

But it was. Nibbling the sparse new grass, not twenty paces away, was a horse. Not one of the horses of Scylas, shaggy and lean.

The beast lifted its head, looked at her and snorted, shaking its long, matted mane. No, it was a great horse, as large as the black war-horse, thin and in need of grooming, but she recognized it as the horse in her dreams, the one she had ridden so many times before, as grey as the dawning light. Her horse.

Slowly she sat, keeping one eye on the beast. It grazed a bit more, then looked at her again. Arima slid from the rock, leaving her boots behind. If only she could get closer, touch it.

The horse knew people, for when she clucked her tongue, its fine, pointed ears pricked forward. The girl closed the gap between them carefully, keeping her hands low, her body still. Again she clucked her tongue, and again the horse responded. Every fiber of her body yearned for the animal; to touch it, embrace it, as she had done so often in dreams.

She was close enough to see its liquid eyes, and the winter's dirt on its coat, briars and seed heads tangled in its unclipped mane. Come, my beautiful one, she thought fiercely, yearning, a consuming fire. Come.

But dreams are only dreams and will never come to pass. With a loud snort the stallion turned and vanished into the shadows, and Arima's hands fell uselessly to her side. Yes, run, she told it. For even if I caught you, what could I do with you? You would belong to my husband or my father. Run and be free.

Tears stung her eyes in the chill air. She looked at the hoofprints, disappearing into the underbrush. With the noise of the river, she couldn't even listen to the departing echo of the creature's hooves. Nothing but hoofprints in the mud remained to show that it had been real. Placing one cold hand over her face, Arima began to sob.

Melanion picked his way beside the muddy path, trying to keep his leather boots clean as he made his way toward Arima, sitting on a rock, slumped forward over folded knees and crying as if her heart had broken. From the doorway of his tent he'd seen her go off by herself. When she didn't soon return he became worried and, since no other men were around, decided to check on her himself. He put aside the gold cheek pieces he was making for the black horse of Scylas, tucked a Scyth dagger into his belt, and set out. He soon wished there had been another around to do the task.

His home in Greece was on a fine rocky isle, sunwashed most of the time. Even when it did rain, the water soaked into the dry, porous soil or ran off down steep, bare hillsides. In all his travels around the Great Sea he'd never encountered mud like this before. Rich, black, and odiferous, it clung to everything like sticky, overcooked gruel and was nearly as slippery as ice. He'd tried to pick out a way along the edges of the worn path, where dead grass offered drier footing, but when he reached the riverbank and the sobbing young girl, his feet were filthy and the red and blue checked trousers he wore were spattered to the knees. The welcome thought of joining the Persians in the dry, sunny southlands diverted his mind only briefly. Arima weighted down on him, a more pressing concern. Slipping his way across the boulder-strewn clearing, he reached her side and put a hand on her slumped shoulder.

"Arima," he called over the roar of the river. She jumped at his touch and turned, red-rimmed eyes full of terror. Seeing who it was, she relaxed.

"May I sit?" he asked, sweeping a hand toward the rock. The girl nodded, dabbing at her tears with a fold of her skirt and sniffling silently in the din. Melanion leaned toward her and lowered his voice. "What is wrong?" he said, placing an arm solicitously around her back. He felt her body tense at his touch.

"Nothing," she lied, fighting back more tears.

"You don't cry over nothing," the Greek said. "Maybe if we talk, it won't seem so bad." He could easily guess what it was. The impending burial of her mother, her marriage soon to follow, the fact that Scylas and his men now had the beloved black horse and she seldom saw it anymore. So many cares could break even the stoutest heart.

Arima lifted her head and gazed into the empty dark woods, where little tendrils of fog rose among the stark white trunks of the birch trees. Well, Melanion decided, if she doesn't wish to talk I'll just sit here awhile, comfort her, and then convince her to return to camp before she gets in trouble.

"The horse," he heard her blurt into the still air. He looked at her in surprise.

"Scylas rode it upriver to the—" he began, thinking she meant the Persian stallion.

She shook her head and turned her sad eyes up to him. "No, here! Another horse, my horse."

He wasn't sure he had heard the last part right, but he let it pass. A horse here? Why should that upset her so? "Was it injured, Arima?" he tried to guess. "Sick and dying?"

"No. Come, I'll show you." She slid from the rock, took his hand, and pulled him behind her through the mud and brush and dead grass. Beneath the birch trees she stopped and pointed. "There," she said, a small light of triumph in her eyes. Melanion looked at the ground and saw, large and clear, the hoof marks of a horse. Arima suddenly turned, seized the sleeves of his padded wool tunic, and gripped them frantically. "I have dreamed of this horse, Melanion!" she said, her voice choking. "Since the autumn, I have dreamed of it many times. It is always my horse, a big grey horse, like the Persian stallion. I am riding it and we are free. We are free, Melanion, a feeling like no other. And today, here, he came. My horse . . ." Her voice died away like a forlorn child's and she stood in her mud-spattered clothes, her face buried in her hands, and cried.

"Come now." The goldsmith put his arm around her awkwardly. He wasn't quite sure he believed her tale of the dream horse, or understood its importance to her. "Perhaps it will come back."

Arima turned her face away and shook her head and the gold ornaments on her cap swung and sparkled. "He must go, must be free," she said, so low he had to put his face by hers to hear her over the roar of the river. When the girl suddenly lifted her head, he found himself so close that their faces nearly touched. She stared at him awkwardly, both of them aware that they were alone together, for the first time. No guards, no slaves, no servants.

He wanted to kiss her, to grab her in his arms, pull the cap from her head, and tangle his fingers in her thick hair, feel that full young body pressed against him.

"Melanion, I . . ." he heard her mutter awkwardly. A

moon's passing and she would be Bartatua's, and he would never see her again. She would be in Bartatua's yurt, in Bartatua's bed, in Bartatua's arms.

He raised a hand and slid the back of it, trembling with fear, down one soft, flushed cheek. Her breath caught, and she closed her eyes at the feel of it. Her mouth moved silently, speaking without words.

Arima, he thought, cherishing the feel of her skin. Instinctively his other hand slid behind her neck, crept into her hair, and he pulled her closer.

"No!" Her mouth tried to form the word through the roar of the river. She opened her eyes and looked at him in alarm. Melanion lowered his face, pressed his lips to hers, and silenced her protests. He felt her hands flutter lightly, helplessly up and down his arms, as if she could not resist her own self's desires.

One kiss, light, almost chaste, but it held all the sweetness of wild honey. Awkwardly they pulled apart. He swept a glance filled with longing and shame over her and without a good-bye he made his way back through the mud to the campsite.

The trial day of Catoris dawned warm and clear. Above the river bottom, far out across the steppes, spring flowers bloomed—white whitlow and the red and yellow of wild tulips. The herds were turned out onto the plains, fattening and regaining strength on the young grass before the first of many migrations began, following the northward greening like a slowly advancing tide. On such a day of beauty the trial of Catoris commenced.

In the clearing of the enarees all the assembled half-men gathered, sitting cross-legged and stern faced around a carved and painted pole hung with their various sacred charms and totems. Here they focused their powers, brought strength and wisdom to the solemn task of judging one of their own.

Arima and the other women were allowed to watch from between two yurts, but were forbidden to speak or interrupt the proceedings. Melanion, a stranger, was also barred from the trial and so he sat, with a knot of curious slaves and servants, across the clearing from the women. Before them all the half-men waited, Scylas and his warriors waited, Lipos waited, squatting nervously at the edge of the group, going over the evidence in his mind while one hand toyed absently with the red charm bag around his neck.

Finally Catoris appeared, his arms bound behind him at the elbow, wearing a simple wool shift that reached to his knees. All badges of rank and wealth were gone from his person; his long grey hair hung loose and thin around his face, which was both haggard from his long confinement and defiant of his fate. Behind him Rhea was escorted by two spearmen. Arima could almost feel sorry for the girl, if her hatred was not so strong. The Northwoman's seductive beauty had fled, replaced by a translucent paleness of skin. Her splendid yellow-white hair hung corded and dirty, and beneath her plain white shift Arima could see the swelling of the girl's belly. Rhea was thrust roughly to one side, forced to her knees, and held there.

An old, withered man, the chief enaree of the Royal Scoloti rose immediately, his power-stick in hand. Tassels of red squirrel tails dangled around his shoulders and across his chest, his totem the cleverest animal of the forest. "Lipos, bring your charges," he instructed the young enaree. Lipos rose to his feet, his own hawk wings pinned across his chest, and stepped toward the squirrel-man.

"I charge that the enaree Catoris plotted to kill the chief of the Auchatae, Scylas by name, by slow poisoning; that he used this foreign girl to aid in his plan; that he was responsible for the death of the Chief Wife Opoea; and that he is no half-man at all, but an imposter who used the foreign woman as his mistress and got her with child," he said.

A shocked murmur rose from all quarters at his words. From the tribesmen, who had lived with such wicked deception in their midst; from the enarees, who were now faced with precisely the kind of thing their rank had worked generations to prevent—infiltration by an outsider, who used the power and privilege of the half-men for his own gain. Such a thing was strictly against their code. An enaree worked for the will of the gods, through the forces of nature, to the benefit of the tribe—never for his own ends.

"He lies," Catoris blurted. Lipos stiffened at the denial. "He is envious of my power. Everyone knows he seeks that power for himself. Who has not seen how he tried to ingratiate himself with the chief's only child, Arima, seeking to win her over, and through her influence, her father."

"You seek to save yourself by slandering another," Lipos spat, his grey eyes growing heated.

"As you yourself do," the old enaree sneered back. "Everyone knows of your journey to teach her things, as you put it; a journey usually reserved for young boys. They have seen you speaking to her privately, she in your tent, you in hers."

Arima's ears burned at his words, and she shifted uncomfortably, aware of the women staring at her. Rarely was a woman ever brought into such weighty matters as a trial. Against such calumny Lipos was her only defense; she was allowed to say nothing herself.

"Well?" the squirrel-man turned to Lipos. The young enaree stood stiffly, rage livid on his face.

"The girl is the only child of our chief, his only heir," he retorted. "Anyone in camp can tell you of her rebellious nature. I knew, for her sake and the sake of the Auchatae people, she must learn the error of her ways. Scylas had many times tried to beat it into her; I tried to reason, to teach, to make her understand. That is no crime—it is doing the task of an enaree."

Scylas, seated on a low stool and surrounded by his men,

nodded agreement at the words of Lipos. The Royal enaree saw this and was satisfied. "No more!" he barked, drawing his stick upright across the air, side to side, as if to cut off the argument. "To the task at hand. What is your evidence against Catoris?" He looked at Lipos, and the young enaree turned to Scylas.

"Our chief was a hearty, robust man until the foreign woman came. She possessed him as a woman seldom possesses a man, body, mind, and spirit. And from that day, bad luck plagued his people as he neglected his duties."

Scylas sat stone-faced, staring ahead as if refusing to hear the half-man's words.

"His own daughter, the only child of his loins, nearly died because of it, and his chief wife, the noblewoman Opoea, did die. And day by day Scylas weakened with only the foreign woman feeding him, caring for him, ministering to his needs. Catoris saw to him daily as his health failed, and between the two of them they would let no one else assist. Not me, not his daughter, not his old blind slave of thirty years. No one cared for him but these two."

"But still that is no proof," a brown-haired enaree, a large gold and turquoise earring dangling by his cheek, spoke up. "Their concern could have been genuine."

"I agree," the squirrel-man said. "That alone is no evidence of crime." Catoris rocked back on his heels, a slight smile crossing his face. Arima looked at Rhea. The girl still knelt upright but her body was sagging against the grip of the two warriors, obviously tired from the strain. The proceedings didn't even seem to interest her. Perhaps they would, Arima mused, if she knew the outcome of a guilty verdict. The foreign woman plainly had been told nothing.

"There is this." Lipos's voice broke through her thoughts, and she saw the enaree presenting a blue leather bag to the gathering. At the sight of it Catoris's cheeks paled. Lipos slowly pulled open the drawstring and dumped a pile of dried, crushed leaves into the palm of his hand. "Have you seen these before?" he said, thrusting them at Scylas. The old chief recognized the leaves as well as the bag that held them.

"Yes," he nodded gruffly. "An herb Catoris gave me. He said it would strengthen me, restore my health."

"And did you take it?" Lipos asked. Again Scylas nodded. "Yes. It was mixed in my wine. To cover the taste, Catoris said."

Lipos swung around and slowly walked before the seated half-men. As he passed them, like a tide rising in his wake, an agitated murmur arose as each identified the herb. At the end he presented it to the Royal enaree, who crushed a pinch of it between thumb and forefinger and sniffed it cautiously.

"Datura," he announced. "With this, you were poisoning Scylas's heart."

Catoris tried to maintain his defiance, glancing around the assembly arrogantly.

"And the foreign woman?" a bony old enaree piped up. "Was she his accomplice, or just used by him? And what of the child she carries?"

"It is not mine," Catoris snarled. "To even accuse me of lying with a woman is to insult me beyond all measure. I will not—"

"Silence!" the squirrel-man thundered. "Such a trial as this is not entered into lightly. Lipos must have had good evidence, or he would not have summoned us. What is your reply, Lipos?" He studied the young half-man. A slight smile of triumph pulled at the corners of Lipos's mouth.

"You were seen," he said quietly, as if he discussed the weather. "Tabiti, wife of Bartatua, has seen Catoris creeping into Rhea's tent, the tent of Opoea, after Scylas had returned to his own. She said he went behind the yurt and Bartatua found a piece of padding there where the stitching was pulled free, allowing him to enter almost directly onto Rhea's couch." He turned to Bartatua, standing at Scylas's side, and the chief warrior nodded in affirmation.

"And what of her slaves?" the squirrel-man pressed, the annoyance in his old voice evident at such a sordid tale involving another enaree. "Did they see nothing? Were their tongues cut out? Could they tell no one?"

At this Rhea lifted her sagging head, and Arima saw sudden fear in her pale blue eyes.

"Most saw nothing. They were asleep. But a few admitted to it," Lipos said curtly. "To the nights Catoris slept with Rhea, to their talks and intrigue."

"And where are these ones now?" the squirrel-man asked.

"Dead. They were tortured, and a swift sword stroke ended their suffering."

Rhea sobbed aloud at his words, the awareness of her fate dawning.

"Then the child could be Catoris's?" the Royal enaree concluded, his brown eyes firing hatred at the disgraced half-man. How could he have fooled so many for so long, hidden his true nature, shamed his sacred calling?

Scylas suddenly stood, and for the first time in her life Arima saw pain on the old man's face. "The child must be Catoris's," he blurted. "The gods only granted me one offspring; the Northwoman's child could not be mine." The crowd noises died away, the tribesmen waiting for further explanation. None came. "Just tell me, Catoris." Scylas stood numbly, his shoulders sagging, a humiliated man. "Why did you do it? What did you hope to gain?"

Catoris knew he'd just as well tell them. His fate was sealed anyway. "The Persians," he announced. "They pay well, do they not, little Rhea?"

The Northwoman lowered her face and turned away, attempting to hide behind her tangled hair.

"Oh, you are not allowed to tell them, so I will," he went on. "It was all set up, planned for months. The swarthy Arab merchant was really a Persian, sent to spy. The Persians have spies all over your lands. Rhea was planted here to help me."

The instincts of the warriors rose, and Scylas's stomach turned in dread at the direction Catoris's confession was taking. He'd seen enough wars, enough intrigues. He knew all the signs, and so did his men. Their jaws set, and their eyes hardened, their hands tapping reflexively the gorytas and dagger sheaths strapped to their thighs.

"You ignorant fools!" Catoris's voice rose. "Our aim was to bring chaos to the Auchatae Scyth, and we nearly succeeded. Kill your leader, confuse your people. You are the southernmost of the Scoloti people, you see."

"What does that matter?" Lipos broke in. "What interest have the Persians in us?"

"Little man," Catoris laughed mockingly, his grey hair lifting in the breeze, "the Persians are very thorough. Conquest is what they seek, and come summer they will have you."

The day descended into a nightmare, mocking the beauty of the spring. At the meeting of the enarees, Melanion, who had made no secret of his coming employment by the Persians, was put under guard and hurried away. Arima thought her heart would break, seeing those fine skilled hands bound with a leather thong, and the tall, muscular body pushed away between two angry warriors. What will happen to him? she wondered, aching for him. Will our meetings be at an end, our quiet talks, our one stolen kiss? Surely he won't be executed!

Her breath came labored, thick as gruel, at the thought of it. No! I will plead with Father, threaten my own life, before I would let him die! To live on this earth and know that he has perished, I would sooner perish myself.

A sobbing scream from the foreign woman pressed into Arima's lungs, nearly choking the life from her, as if the scream were a terror from her own soul.

"No," Rhea gasped, struggling against her two captors, trying to flee. Catoris stood immobile. He knew the next words to be spoken; he'd pronounced them himself on rare occasions.

"For the disgrace you have brought to your profession," the Royal enaree proclaimed, "and for the attempted murder of a lawful chief, I order you to die by fire, to cleanse the earth of the stain of your existence and your memory from the minds of men."

No mighty burial, no proper rituals, no grave goods to carry him into the next life. Simply burnt to ashes, as if he had never lived. And without time for reflection, for delay, for fear.

The wagon was already prepared, pushed forward by a handful of slaves. It was piled with brushwood, and Arima felt nausea at the sight. Women were not told such things, and she had never herself seen the way to death of a disgraced enaree.

Guards were pushing Catoris toward the wagon, his arms still bound behind him. As he passed Lipos, he glanced at him with a final defiant sneer. "Practice your arts well, young man," he laughed, "for in the coming year you will need them." Awkwardly he climbed into the wagon and settled himself onto the brush while his knees and ankles were bound. Then Rhea was dragged up, struggling against her captors.

"No!" she choked, terror in her eyes. "Some other way! Not that! Behead me, please. Scylas! Arima! I appeal to you, save me." She found Arima in the crowd of women and collapsed to her knees. "I am not an enaree. Behead me instead! Please . . ."

A guard bent and tied her feet, then tossed her atop the wagon as if she were a sheaf of straw. Catoris sat stonily, ignoring her hysterical screaming. Face lowered, his lips moved silently. Arima knew he was chanting himself into a trance. When the fire came, he would scarcely be aware of dying, while poor foolish Rhea . . .

The wagon rolled forward, pushed away from the tents

and paddocks and hayricks and up a narrow path to the steppes above. Arima grabbed Urgimas's arm and pushed through the milling women, ducked behind the yurts of the enarees, and ran to where her father stood with his men, watching the impending execution. By the time she arrived, the wagon had reached the bluff overlooking the camp and the wails of Rhea wafted through the air to them like smoke.

"You must do something!" she appealed to Scylas, kneeling in front of him and Bartatua and lowering her face. "You see what Catoris is doing! It won't be fair! You must do something!" She did not look up, but she saw their booted feet shifting as they consulted with one another. Then Bartatua stepped away.

"Go!" Scylas barked, jerking Arima to her feet and pushing her away. After his earlier humiliation, he didn't now need to look as if he were taking direction from a girl. Her face still lowered, Arima hurried away to see what Bartatua would do.

She and Urgimas had barely rounded the yurts when the sound of rapid hoofbeats approached, and she saw Bartatua racing a small swift gelding up the path toward the wagon. Riding with no hands, he pulled his bow and an arrow from his gorytas, pressing the animal forward with his knees. When he drew alongside the wagon, he let fly the arrow. Catoris bellowed and clenched the arrow, protruding from his upper arm. The pain was too great, ripping into the muscle as it did. Bartatua had succeeded in stopping the half-man's chanting, and thus his trance.

Arima hated the subservience of women, and she hated the thought of marriage, but she couldn't help but feel a surge of pride as she observed the fine, skillful warrior who would be her husband, the father of her children. Still with no hands, Bartatua raced his horse in tight circles around the wagon, keeping an eye on Catoris. He had another arrow fitted to his bowstring, waiting. Atop the hill, against the clear blue spring sky, the slaves filed away from the wagon and two enarees approached it. Suddenly the cart burst into flames, front and back, and the roar of the fire mingled with the inhuman screams of Rhea. Bartatua slowed his horse and paused to watch the immolation. The horse moved again, turned, and Bartatua urged it into a gallop. Catoris must be up to some new trick, for when she saw the warrior's form clear against the sky, his bow was raised to his cheek, ready to shoot. The fire leaped higher, and Bartatua disappeared behind the wagon. The terrified cries of Rhea abruptly ceased.

Bartatua emerged from behind the wagon, the bow replaced in his gorytas. He circled the pyre one last time and trotted the gelding down the slope to camp. Catoris had made no other sound.

Next morning the camp prepared to move. The gathered half-men decided that it was time for the burial of Opoea and the other victims of the winter. The Auchatae would travel north, taking their herds and belongings with them, following the tall human-shaped stone pillars that marked the way across the trackless steppes until their burial grounds were reached. Then, after ceremonies of interment and the covering of the earth mound of the chief wife, they would continue on, following the greening of the steppes throughout the spring and into the summer, feeding their horses and livestock. It was the cycle of their lives, like the cycle of the seasons, as immutable as time.

The horses had gone ahead as had the sheep and cattle. Arima supervised the packing of her wagons, with Urgimas and a few slaves flying to do her bidding. The yurt, the matting and tent poles went on one wagon; for herself, she now had use of Opoea's covered carriage, lighter and more comfortable. Arima didn't mind the concealment its padded sides gave her. In fact, she welcomed the privacy. Since the trial of Catoris, his execution, and the arrest of Melanion, something had fled from her life. Hope, her will to fight—she wasn't sure. She only knew that she suddenly felt resigned to her marriage, which was to be immediately after her mother's funeral. It was her lot, decreed by the tribe, and there was no escaping it, just as for Rhea and Catoris there had been no escaping their fate. Unchanging laws ruled the ways of men and no one, no one, could evade them.

The spring air was buoyant with smells when Arima climbed into the stillness of her carriage. But they were lonely smells, reflecting lonely times for her. Rich loam churned up by departing animals, and the sweetness of the hemlocks cloaking the riverbank; dry dust from yurts being dismantled and the cold ashes of empty hearths. She settled to her couch, took a grey cat onto her lap, and watched the enarees reverently take down the swaddled bodies of the dead. They laid them out, each on its own flat wagon, each corpse surrounded by grave goods given by grieving family and friends. Arima had seen well to Opoea's comfort in the next world, having dressed her in a brilliant scarlet shift, a necklace of gold plaques, her best cap lavished with gold atop her head, her arms and fingers adorned with gold bracelets and rings. Around her the family piled her dearest possessions; pots and ladles and sewing needles, a small loom, spindles and whorls, a bronze mirror, clay jars of perfumed oils and incense, a small bronze dagger. Arima reserved some of their best felt coverlets for her, folding them at the foot of the corpse, to cover Opoea's body in the tomb.

That is all I can do for her now, Arima thought as she watched the half-men waft incense over the bodies to protect them from evil on this, their final journey. A few days' time and the tribe would set up camp, and the final mourning ritual would begin. A few days' time and Opoea would be gone.

Arima blinked back tears and turned to face the opening at the rear of the wagon. Such an eventful winter camp this has been! she reflected as the wagon began to roll away. The arrival of Melanion, the death of Opoea, the trial and execution of Catoris. It was more than had happened in years.

The wagon climbed the rutted track to the steppes above, and the looming dark trees along the riverbank receded. Arima watched idly, holding onto the high curved ends of her couch to keep from sliding off while the carriage lurched and swayed. Between the dark evergreens and budding birch trees she could see the rushing river, sparkling in the early sun.

And there, from the depths of the shadows, Arima glimpsed a dappled coat of grey. She pushed the cat from her lap and slid to the end of the wagon, scarcely believing her eyes. The great grey horse stood, as pale as the morning mist, watching them go. Lifting his head, he called out to the departing horses, tossed his mane, and walked into the forest.

The Auchatae set up their yurts a day's walk from the burial grounds.

"What of him?" Bartatua snapped to Scylas, and Arima poked her head from her carriage. The chief warrior stood by his own wagon, Tabiti secreted away inside it, and motioned across the clearing to Melanion, bound loosely hand and foot and leaning against a loaded cart. Melanion! She studied him carefully; he hadn't shaved, and his eyes looked grey, as if he hadn't eaten or slept. He was nothing like the handsome Greek with the devilish twinkle in his eyes that she had known before. Fearful, she jumped from the wagon and walked toward Scylas, keeping her manner suitably meek and submissive. She'd learned the lesson well; to get what you want from a man, let him think he has won your battles.

"Father," she spoke quietly, "my marriage will be soon. After so much work and time has gone into preparing my dowry, one might think it wasteful not to have it completed to your satisfaction."

Scylas squatted by a large chest, examining his bridles and horse fittings. He barely glanced at the girl to check on her demeanor, then returned to his inspections. "True," he muttered. "Have a tent set up for the Greek to finish his work—under close guard."

Bartatua cut his eyes to Arima with sudden suspicion, his bearded face dark, and left to see to his chief's orders. Relieved, the girl returned to her carriage, glancing at Melanion as she went. Through the rising dust and the passing figures she could see him looking at her, and the expression on his haggard face was one of gratitude.

Arima saw the goldsmith no more for days, so busy was she with the funeral preparations. A framework was erected over Opoea's bier, hung with herbs and flowers and gaily colored tassels, and each corner was protected by a sacred wand of an enaree. Special tents were set up for the men and women to cleanse themselves. After purification with a paste of herbs and frankincense, the women dressed in their finest clothes, donned their best jewelry, and prepared to set out.

Melanion watched the brightly decked funeral carts lined up across the central clearing, attended by enarees and guards from his yurt's doorway. Of course he was not allowed to go, but their odd customs still intrigued him. If he ever got out of this mess alive, he would have much new material to use in his goldwork. Soon Scylas appeared, on foot, surrounded by his chief horsemen. All were finely dressed, in loose patterned trousers as bright as a rainbow, long wool tunics belted at the waist, the customary gold earrings in their left ears and wearing the ever-present dagger and gorytas. They seemed almost drugged, wide-eyed and swaggering as they walked, and Melanion assumed they had ingested some sort of potion in their cleansing tents. Scylas advanced to his wife's bier, stumbled, and caught himself against the dried herbs and flowers. A sudden cry erupted from his throat, wild and forlorn like a starving wolf, and his men murmured loud sympathies. To his surprise, the old man pulled off his tunic, withdrew his knife, and gashed himself across the arm, sobbing loudly as he did so. Melanion gulped down rising nausea at the blood spilling from Scylas's wound. Bartatua and the other men also drew their daggers, keening their sorrow at the loss of their chief's wife, and cut their hands and foreheads and earlobes as a sign of respect. Blood seemed to be everywhere, trickling down fingers and snaking through beards, and Melanion looked away shakily. The enarees were chanting louder and louder, their singsong rising above the moans of old Scylas. The chief took his knife and pierced an earlobe, then sliced it across his chest, as if he could feel no pain; as if his grief were genuine. Then the women appeared, clothed as fine as if for a wedding, silent and controlled except for their crying. Arima led them, her long dark hair undressed and tumbling down her back, her skin shining with a soft glow. A goddess must look like that, he mused, studying her with an artist's eye. Serene in her grief, only the presence of tears trickling down her cheeks showed that she mourned. She passed by him, only a few paces away, and he longed to go to her, speak to her, touch her. But she advanced to her mother's bier as if she hadn't seen him. The wagon began to move, escorted by the grieving husband, the bleeding warriors. Behind Arima and the women came two horses, splendid young geldings as fine as the two mares that pulled the bier. Melanion knew their fate, and the fate of the two faithful slave women who followed Arima; they would accompany Opoea on her journey into the afterlife. He watched until the procession was gone, then reentered his yurt, his bound ankles shuffling annoyingly, to finish his work on Arima's dowry.

* * *

Arima had been up all night, listening to the drunken, drugged cries of the men around camp. They had returned from the burials by sundown, but still the mourning continued, driven to a frenzy by the genuine sorrow of Scylas. Through the night gangs of slaves would work to complete the huge earthen mound that was the grave of Opoea. Not until she was gone did the old chief realize what a fine woman she had been. And so he mourned, unceasing, putting to shame the lesser energies of Bartàtua and Oricus and the rest of his men. Seldom had anyone seen a man grieve so for a woman.

Returning to her own sparsely furnished yurt, Arima washed the dust from her hands and face, drank some wine, and lay down tiredly on her couch. How she longed for a little boiled mutton, or a fresh hot bit of bread, but eating was forbidden until dawn. Turning on her side, she played with one of the cats and watched the small hearth fire burn. How many hours till dawn? she wondered. How long till the keening and moaning and drunken shouts and stuporous cries stop echoing in the night, as if the camp were one vast city of the dead? Urgimas and the women servants curled up on their sleeping mats and dozed, waiting, like Arima, for the men to fall asleep, for the night to end. There were no guards, no husbands, no brothers; all the men were gone, partaking of the intoxicating herbs and free-flowing wine. Only one shaggy brown dog guarded the yurt of Arima.

She rose, when the night was not yet over, and drew a dark blue blanket around her shoulders. The camp had settled down, but still did not sleep. Occasional shouts and cries cut the stillness, echoing across the vast black grasslands, muffled by the thick wool padding of the yurts, as eerie and forlorn as the lone wolf howl that suddenly answered.

Fear gripped Arima's stomach at the unnaturalness of it. She had never experienced a royal funeral before, and all the necessary ritual it involved. And to have it continue so, into the night when all should be still and quiet save for the low talk of the posted guards, the peaceful murmur of the horses, an occasional sharp bark of warning from the dogs. Such sounds were comforting, familiar, and they marked the boundaries of her life.

It might be her only chance to see Melanion. Within days she would be married, and her seclusion would be worse than it was now. And he? Who could say what his fate would be.

Urgimas and the women slept soundly. The dog stretched out by the hearth, twitching in a dream. On silent bare feet Arima left the tent.

Melanion sat cross-legged by his hearth fire, still awake and working despite the late hour. His ankles were bound tightly, his wrists less so, and he was able to tap a fine chased design on a horse collar for Bartatua. Arima had seen no guards outside his yurt, and when she poked her head past the heavy felt door flap, looking carefully to either side, she saw none within, either. Scarcely believing her luck, she entered.

The goldsmith looked up when a gust of air stirred the fire before him, and his face crossed in a slight smile. "What are you doing here?" he whispered, moving his manacled hands in an invitation to sit on the carpeting at his side. Arima moved hesitantly across the floor. To be alone with a man in his own yurt violated every taboo she had ever learned. What if the guards returned? Bartatua and her father would take turns having her thrashed for such an act. Perhaps she should leave quickly, she thought.

One look at his dirty, bearded face, and the sparkle in his eyes at seeing her again, extinguished her doubts like a swift summer storm. Resolute, she crossed the yurt. "How have you been treated?" she asked quietly, noticing the pallor to his skin, the leanness of his face and hands. "Are you fed? Do you sleep?"

Melanion's face saddened, and he returned self-consciously to his work. Arima waited, knowing he was **a** man of few words. The words he did speak were carefully chosen. "There is little point in food and sleep," he said. Arima blinked at him, puzzled. Lifting his eyes, he studied her face. "You've given no thought to it, then?" he muttered. "I might be a Persian spy. They could not prove or disprove it, so why take chances? When your wedding is over and my work here done, they will kill me."

Arima gasped, and the color drained from her face.

"It's true." He looked down at the horse collar. "By whatever method you people use to kill foreigners, I will be one less worry for them. And who will miss me? My mother? Praxis? All the whores in Olbia?" He snorted and leaned closer to his work.

"But why don't you escape?" Arima said, her voice choked, trying to still the wild pounding of her heart. "There are no guards here. Let me cut your bindings and you can escape."

"Do you really think I could?" he asked cynically. "I, on foot, in an unfamiliar land, chased by a hundred skilled horsemen? Arima, open your eyes!" He lay his hands lightly across the thin gold foil and looked at her. "We are both doomed, you to your fate and I to mine."

"No." The girl shook her head defiantly, desperately searching his face, refusing to see his head severed by a sword blow, bloodied and staked atop a pole. A tightness in her chest threatened to squeeze the breath from her. He could not die! She would not let him! "I will find a way, Melanion. I will save you."

How could he help but be attracted to her, to her spirit and her intelligence, her innocence? She was of a fierce nomadic people, with so little knowledge of the world, ruled by fires and passions rather than rational thinking. He raised his bound hands stiffly and lightly touched her chin. Arima did not flinch or withdraw; she stared at him openly, forcing herself to a path she knew led to disaster.

"Go," he said in resignation, lowering his hands. "My goldwork will be my gift to you; think of me when you wear it."

Arima glanced over her shoulder toward the doorway, leaned forward, and kissed him gently on his stubbled cheek. "I will save you," she breathed into his ear. "Trust me. I will not let you die." She quickly rose and left; Melanion gave a silent half-laugh of doubt and returned to his work.

Lipos ministered to a steady stream of mourners the next day, men with headaches, stomachaches, and festering self-inflicted wounds. He normally kept an ample stock of potions on hand, to which he had added the goods of Catoris, but he feared his herbs would run out before his patients did. He did not expect to see Arima, so pale she seemed ghostlike, with a thin blue shawl draped over her head and clutched beneath her chin.

"Lipos," she muttered, plopping herself on his couch in exhaustion. Urgimas hovered over the girl, anxiously rubbing her limp hands and gazing at her face.

The enaree was ladling out another wooden cup of headache remedy for another stumbling warrior and could only glance at the girl while he worked. "What's wrong with her?" he snapped to Urgimas.

"I'm not sure," the slave woman answered. "She woke up ill this morning, said she had barely slept and her stomach hurt."

Lipos laughed and hurried the warrior on his way. "Very few of us slept last night!" He came to Arima; the girl did look ill, her fine skin dull and ashen, the light in her eyes gone when she looked up at him.

"Leave us," she directed her slave. Urgimas rose hesitantly and looked at the half-man. He, too, looked drawn and tired.

"Go," Arima repeated, and Urgimas left the tent. "I

cannot sleep," the girl blurted to Lipos. "For days, ever since we left our winter camp."

The enaree nodded. "It is no surprise, Arima. You have been through much lately, and there is much yet to come."

"Yes," she agreed. "I am afraid I will be ill by the time of my marriage. So ill that I will not look beautiful, as a royal bride should, and I will be too ill to ride a horse."

Lipos looked at her sharply. "Do you still hope to outride Bartatua?"

Arima looked down sheepishly. "No, not really. But I want to try. What will people say if I don't at least try? That Arima, who all her life has been too headstrong, was tamed by betrothal to Bartatua?" She smiled slightly and looked at him. "I cannot let them think that, Lipos! You are my friend; you must help me!"

"Is sleep all you want?" he asked, pulling down a leather sack that hung from the yurt's cluttered framework. Without waiting for her answer, the enaree withdrew a soft suede pouch and handed it to her. "Have Urgimas mix a little of this in wine before you retire at night," he instructed, "but not too much—just a pinch or two. There should be more than enough in here to help you through the remaining days till your marriage."

Arima took it and stood, weakly supporting herself against the couch. "Thank you, Lipos, thank you," she breathed, and her gratitude was deep and genuine.

Arima let two days pass, two maddening days of unceasing preparation for her wedding, endlessly trying on the skirt Urgimas was embroidering, and the jacket Tabiti insisted on making for her. The skirt was of deep blue wool, embroidered with red griffons, and the jacket was of red felt sewn in gold thread. She knew she would look breathtaking in the finery, with the lavish gold jewelry of Melanion to set it off; she almost looked forward to the wedding. It would be so easy to go through with it, three days hence. To appear in her best, to be swept off her horse by Bartatua, carried to the marriage yurt, undressed by him, held in his arms, kissed and caressed and made love to by him, Bartatua, Chief Warrior of the Auchatae. So easy.

Arima rose resolutely from the late evening hearth fire of her yurt. She had deliberately stayed up late, keeping the slave women working till their eyes were falling shut. "Urgimas, I will fix my sleeping wine," she said. The slave glanced up, seemed to debate the idea, and relented. She had sewn and sewn on Arima's new skirt until her back felt like a broken sapling. The girl stood with her hands on her hips and studied the weary servants gathered around the firelight. "You have all worked so hard," she announced, "I think you deserve a treat. A bit of my good wine will cheer you and help you sleep more restfully." The women looked up in surprise. Some of the good wine of Arima, rich and sweet and heady, instead of the sour vinegar they usually drank? This was a fortunate night indeed!

Arima passed around smooth wooden cups, dark and burnished from years of use. She took her own golden goblet and stretched out on her couch. "Good night to you all." She raised the cup to them. "With Lipos's magical herb, I will soon be asleep. Enjoy your drink, and I'll see you tomorrow."

She gulped her wine hastily, as she always did. The finely powdered herb would be nearly tasteless in the thick, unwatered wine she had poured but she made a great show of being eager for sleep though her own cup was pure. She lay down wearily, sighed, and closed her eyes.

Not a sound stirred the tent when Arima rose. The slaves were sprawled across the carpets, deep in drugged sleep, their needleworks dropped carelessly. Urgimas slumped forward, her plump face resting on the skirt she had been making. The girl flew around the room, slipping on a heavy coat of spotted goatskin and boots of oiled leather, stuffing several flat bread loaves and dried meat in a sack, along with a change of clothes and her own small dagger. Filling a skin bag with wine, she added a few pinches of Lipos's sleeping herb. Perhaps it would not be enough. She dropped in a bit more, just to be sure. Tucking her parcels under her coat, she gave her grey cat a farewell kiss atop its head, crept round the sleeping dog, and slipped out into the night.

Melanion's two guards sat inside the door, tiredly tossing knucklebones and betting ridiculous wagers on the outcome. Arima lay her travelling pack behind a nearby yurt and approached them, wineskin in hand. "I need to question the Greek about this," she smiled, holding out the black felt headpiece she would wear at her wedding. "Will you come in to guard me while I speak to him, and for your trouble I brought you this." She produced the bag of drink. Their drowsy faces brightened at the sight and they stood, picked up their spears, and escorted her in.

Melanion lay on a padding of sheep's wool in a dark corner of the tiny yurt. He sat up in surprise when Arima entered, his guards at her heels. The girl looked at him calmly, and when their eyes met she conveyed a message to him, a message he had trouble believing.

"Here." She thrust the wineskin at the guards. "Sit by the fire and warm yourselves. I won't take long." Headpiece in hand, she approached Melanion. With a swift motion to silence, she crouched in front of him. "Are you well?" she hissed, pretending to show him the cap. He nodded. "Is there food here? Clothing?" Again he nodded. She could hear the men talking low behind her, and she waited. She knew it would not take long, but the suddenness of their silence startled her. Melanion looked over her shoulder and his mouth dropped open in surprise.

"Come!" She withdrew her knife and cut his leather bindings. "We must hurry!" Jerking him to his feet, he stumbled as he turned toward the unconscious guards.

"What did you . . ." he began.

"They are asleep. Now hurry!" She searched the tent for a

leather sack and thrust it into his hands. "Melanion!" She seized his arms. "Time is short! We must go. Find some clothes and food and a water bag. Quickly!"

The goldsmith roused from his surprise and rushed away. Arima turned to the guards. They would need more weapons than her one small woman's knife. Bending, she pushed one of the heavy men onto his back and eyed the long dagger strapped to his leg. He smelled of dirt and sweat and horses, and she didn't even want to touch him. Probing gingerly at the leg, she unbuckled the leather straps that held his knife sheath in place. "Take the other one," she hissed when Melanion stepped to her side.

"And the gorytas?"

She shook her head. "We don't know how to use a bow. Leave it."

Ever the rational Greek, Melanion ignored her instructions and took the man's gorytas anyway. One never knew when it might come in handy. He strapped the weapons on, Scyth style; but not until he saw Arima buckle the other knife belt around her waist did he realize that she intended to come with him.

"You're not coming, too, are you?" he asked in disbelief. She looked up from buckling the knife belt, surprise on her face.

"I must. There is no way I could save you without implicating myself. Either we both flee, or we both stay and meet our fates." Her face was open, honest, her argument too logical to dispute.

"But you cannot ride a horse!" the Greek protested. "How are we then to escape?"

Arima smiled slightly at him. "I can ride a horse," she said proudly, "but it will not be necessary. A horse is too noisy. We will escape on foot."

"On foot! Arima, that is madness!"

"I have a plan. Find a coat and come. We must leave."

BOOK 4

SELA

Often enough God gives a man a glimpse of happiness,
and then utterly ruins him.

—*Solon*

MEGAPHERNES WHEELED HIS HORSE AROUND, SQUINTING WHEN HE faced the sun. The fine bay stallion pranced sideways, scenting excitement in the air and eager for the lion hunt to begin.

"Ho, my friend! Why the unhappy look?" It was Artapas, his friend, his cousin, his fellow "table companion" in the retinue of Darius, the great King of Kings, ruler of the Persians, the Egyptians, the Medes, Lydians, Elamites, Assyrians, Kushites, and other peoples too numerous to mention.

"It is not sadness," Megaphernes replied, dropping the tassled reins to his felt saddle pad and lowering the ear coverings of his leather cap. "It is the sun, too warm today for springtime."

Artapas nodded and turned his mount into the stiff breeze blowing from the blue mountains rimming the high Persian plateau. "At least we are blessed with wind here," he commented, scanning the horizon. "Wait until the campaign begins, then you will have deserts and unrelieved heat to contend with." He straightened, thinking he saw movement in the heat-shimmered distance. Megaphernes turned his horse and waited. Any moment now the beaters and guards would appear, in fierce pursuit of a lion and chasing it off to the southwest, toward the waiting entourage of the king. It was not his idea of sport, but Megaphernes didn't complain. It got everyone into the sun and wind and out of the palace, away from the endless, boring rituals of state.

"Do you think he will come?" Megaphernes asked over his shoulder.

"The Greek?" Artapas shrugged and tied his riding cap across his chin. He was sure he saw dust rising in the distance; it wouldn't be long now. "I expect he will. There is little Greeks crave more than eating and making money."

Megaphernes laughed and walked his horse out onto the broad, dusty plain. The hunters were definitely coming, and if he and Artapas let the lion escape, they'd pay for it with their heads. The sound of horses' hooves came to them like the far rumble of thunder, and the dust cloud grew thick and sulphurous. Megaphernes lifted his spear from across his lap and waited. Ah, wonderful life! he mused, feeling a heady rush of excitement welling within him. The life that, in the past, made our people strong and cunning and able to conquer empires. He shifted, enjoying the comfort of the traditional Persian leather breeches against his skin. "Soft lands breed soft men," the great King Cyrus had said, and it was true. And this concerned many of the nobles at court, who saw the increasingly opulent lifestyle of the king threatening the very fabric that had made them great. So far the empires of old had bowed down before Persian might like stalks of grass in the wind. But one day it would end. Like so many nations, their own softness would destroy them.

The deep bark of the great Assyrian mastiffs boomed in

his ears, and he knew the time was at hand. From the advancing dustcloud figures emerged: galloping horsemen, their bright clothes and horse trappings blooming like flowers in the barren desert; slavering dogs, nearly as yellow as the dust; and before them a huge reddish lion, racing futilely for its life. With a cry Megaphernes and Artapas joined the chase. Veering toward rocks jumbled across its path, the lion attempted to escape, but Artapas cut it off. With a deft rush from his highly trained horse, he turned the beast and chased it back. Megaphernes deflected its efforts to run the other way. The lion leaped through the pass, its long tongue nearly dragging on the ground, and the two cousins took off in pursuit. The creature's next opponent would be the king.

Artapas saw the king's pavilion a short distance ahead, with gold-embroidered pennants streaming stiffly against the cloudless blue sky. Darius saw them coming and raced out in his chariot, the golden sides of the vehicle nearly blinding when they caught the sunlight. He was in his midthirties, a little older than Megaphernes and Artapas, but despite the years of easy living still fit and athletic. Artapas could see the king's driver racing the four white chariot horses over the stony desert, the chariot bouncing wildly with each bump. Darius held on gamely, one hand at the grip inside the chariot, the other rising into the air, spear in hand, when the lion approached. They were on a direct course for each other, lion of the desert and King of Kings, and the cousins slowed their horses to watch. The lion, his savagery intact, saw the king's team of horses and sprang into the air with a bellow of rage. The driver turned the team at the last instant, and Artapas could see the liquid fear spilling from the horses' eyes at the sudden appearance of this ancestral enemy. But they were well-trained animals and did not bolt. Functioning like a single entity, they turned under the experienced hand of the driver, and the spear flew skillfully from the hand of Darius. The lion stood as little chance against Persian might as had the Lydians. The king's spear pierced its body, and the great-maned creature fell dead.

"Splendid! Splendid!" they heard Darius shouting against the wind. The king sprang from the still-moving chariot and ran to his prize, wary guards on his heels. Sometimes a lion only seemed dead; a swipe from a huge paw, a dying gesture of defiance, could still kill a man. But the king had few doubts. Bending over, he pulled the massive head up for all to see. His beaters had done a good job, selected an especially fine specimen. There would be ample rewards for all, and a feast of celebration tonight.

"An exciting hunt, eh?" Megaphernes muttered caustically. Artapas half-laughed at the jest. "What more would a king be allowed to do?" he questioned. "He surely could not endanger himself." But he knew what his cousin meant. Such a poor excuse for a hunt was no match for the real thing. He remembered the boar hunt the two of them had had on their return from scouting the Greek trading colonies. Ah, now there was excitement to get a man's blood flowing!

"Perhaps Darius will send us on another spying mission." Megaphernes seemed to read his thoughts. They removed their leather riding caps, and the wind felt good, cooling their hot, sweaty heads.

"I don't think there will be time," Artapas answered, walking his horse toward the king and his cluster of admirers. "I expect any day now Darius will tell us of his plans to conquer more nations."

The shade beneath the pavilions was a welcome relief from the glaring desert sun. Canopies of dyed goatskin covered enough area to shelter a hundred men dining in comfort, seated before small round tables of precious woods, ivory, and gold. It was a feast away from the close confines of the palace and court, and Darius was still

Persian enough at heart to enjoy it. Egyptian musicians wandered between the tables, playing reedy flutes and jangling sistra and plucking delicate harps that were barely loud enough to be heard above the gusting wind, the sharp retort of a windscreen erected upwind of the pavilion, and the din of the feasting men.

Megaphernes stretched his booted feet, sipped the good Egyptian beer the king had provided, and listened to an animated conversation going on behind him. Two old generals were arguing the merits of bows, the large Egyptian bow against the smaller Scythian one. He thought their squabbles pointless, for each bow had its purpose; the larger Egyptian bow was meant to be used by soldiers on foot, or in chariots. Such a thing would be useless on horseback, where the smaller Scyth bow was as lethal as any. And for speed he'd match a Scythian warrior and his horse against an Egyptian or Persian chariot any day. He supposed when men got too old to fight they resorted to arguments about fighting, but it seemed plain to him that neither of the two generals had much experience with the nomads to the north.

"You've not seen the Scyth, then?" He impulsively turned on his camp stool and broke into their conversation. The generals looked at the polished young man, annoyed by the interruption.

"We've seen enough," snapped one of them. A common sort, Megaphernes noted wryly, his grizzled beard cropped short and his hair uncurled, undressed.

"But you've not seen the Scyth," the nobleman corrected him.

"And what of it?" the other general interjected. "We've been on campaigns for twenty years, enough time to know the merits of weaponry. What is your experience, that so exceeds ours?"

Megaphernes could see the two men eyeing his fashionably styled hair and gold necklet and fine, colorful greatcoat. He read the scorn on their faces. "I have been among them, my friends, and that's how I know. You cannot judge foreign warriors by your theories if you have not seen them for yourselves."

"Bah!" One general spat a wad of grape seed directly beside Megaphernes' feet. "If that was so we could never attack an unknown people, and we would not have the vast empire we now control. You speak nonsense, boy."

Megaphernes' ears burned, and his eyes grew dark. He would not take such insults from a common soldier whose every word revealed his ignorance. "I have seen them, fool," he shot back, trying to keep his voice low and level so as not to intrude on Darius's feast. "Seen them ride with no reins, turning to shoot over their horses' rumps, knocking the head off a dead sparrow at forty paces, at full gallop. They time the release of their arrows to the beat of the horse's hooves, and their mounts are so well-trained that they will lie concealed in the tall grass, leaping up to surprise their prey when they are commanded. The Scyth would make lion-bait of an unwieldly chariot corps."

The young nobleman paused, catching his breath and suddenly aware of a hush falling over the gathering. Straightening, he cast a nervous glance around the pavilion. Nearly everyone was turned toward him, listening to his heated words. Darius himself, seated at one end of the tent and picking at a roasted suckling pig with greasy fingers, lifted his gaze from his meal and cast a level stare at Megaphernes over the heads of his people.

"Is this so?" he commented idly. Megaphernes bowed low from the waist and looked at him.

"It is, my lord," he answered.

"And what else can you tell us of these nomads?" Darius continued, chewing on a long strand of meat while his towel-bearer wiped his fingers for him.

"They are wedded to their horses, Sire, more so than to their women. The women are only there to breed more warriors, who are put on horseback almost before they can walk. And their horses are the best, selectively bred, well-trained, cared for better than they care for their own children. As horsemen, no nation can exceed them, my lord."

Darius smiled faintly and allowed the dripping grease to be wiped from his beard. "We will see," he chuckled, lifting a gold drinking horn to his lips.

Artapas tried to soothe his cousin's anger as Megaphernes paced back and forth before the long line of parked chariots, his cheeks flushed red with rage above his dark beard. "You were not made a fool of!" he reassured Megaphernes. "The king asked you a direct question, before all those men. Consider it an honor!"

"Yes," his cousin whirled, his long embroidered Persian coat twisting against his legs, "and then he dismissed my words. Publicly, as if I were some half-wit or a teller of tales."

"It is no tale, Megaphernes. The king knows that. He just meant to say that—"

"You also know it is no tale, Artapas!" Megaphernes stopped, glaring at his cousin through the brief evening gloom of the desert. "I know it is no tale! We have seen it for ourselves. The Scyth are rich, skilled, and savage. And do you know what Darius intends to do about it?"

Artapas's shoulders sagged and he looked down at the rocky yellow soil. "I'm afraid I do," he muttered.

"Yes, he is thinking about invading them! We already know this season's march takes us north, across the Bosporus and on to Greece. It is a small step beyond to the most fertile plains of the Scyth. To their grain and gold and horses. It will never work." He shook his head bitterly and looked up at the winking stars.

"It might." Artapas looked up as well. "Don't underestimate the king or the skill of his army."

Megaphernes felt only fear and foreboding in his heart and gave no reply to his cousin's cheery words.

In late spring the army of Darius set out, seven-hundred-thousand men from across the vast Persian empire, the greatest empire the world had yet seen. Foot soldiers from Nubia and Greece; charioteers from Egypt and Assyria; skilled horsemen from Parthia and Armenia. North to south, east or west, they marched with their master, Darius the Great, accompanied by a vast retinue of supply wagons, servants, craftsmen, camp followers, oxen and mules. The lure of Greece had beckoned the king, an irresistible siren's call. The bickering city-states would be easy prey, he the hawk swooping down on these unsuspecting lambs and picking them off, one by one. So sure was he of his Greek victory that Darius allowed a side trip, once he had crossed the straits on a network of bridges built on pontoon boats. Another bridge, across the Ister River, and the Persians would head north. Sixty days, the king told the Greek allies he left behind to guard his bridges. I will have the Scyth nomads conquered and return here within sixty days.

Three of Scylas's men returned to the campsite, their horses heaving and slick with sweat. The old chief stood, but he knew from the looks on their faces that they had not found the runaways.

"Nothing." The leader leaned over his horse's slumped neck and looked at him. Scylas shook his head, perplexed.

"No trace at all? A footprint, a broken twig? They have flown into the air, then?" the chief growled at the man. The warrior drew his lips back tightly, annoyed by the mockery in the old man's voice.

"We searched the trackway we came on, all the way back to the river. They did not flee that way or we would have seen it," the warrior retorted. "A she-boar, heavy with young, several great wild oxen, a small herd of steppe antelope, but your daughter and the Greek did not go that way." He straightened up, satisfied he'd done his job well, and without waiting for a reply from Scylas walked his exhausted mount to the paddock.

Scylas swung around, looking for Bartatua. The chief warrior had been nearly more furious than he when one of the serving women stumbled groggily from her yurt, screaming incoherent words about Arima. A hasty search had turned up the bitter evidence—all seven of the girl's woman servants had been drugged, and the two guards of the Greek as well. The women were rousing when they were found, but the men were beyond help. Overdrugged and slowly dying, two quick spear thrusts ended their plight. Scylas felt the men would have understood his decision. Every Scyth knew the value of speed and mobility, and the herds had to be moved away to more fertile pastures. Two dying men would have slowed them considerably. The burial fields were close at hand; the men were sent to the next world in a manner befitting their status as warriors.

But the women! They had been dragged in front of the yurts, bound hand and foot and numb with shock. Six young female slaves and the old Mede, her round face grey, her fine silver hair hanging loose down her back. His men had roughly forced them to their knees, their heads hanging low in shame.

"Why did this happen?" Scylas had shouted, pacing before them like a stalking cat. The women's answers had been brief and muffled, the slaves choking on their terror at the fate that awaited them. No matter. No answer they could give would have satisfied him.

"And you!" he demanded, motioning a guard to pull the old Mede's head upright so he could see her face. Her eyes were dull and hollow, but her wrinkled old mouth was firmly set. Scylas found it admirable, a contrast to the groveling pleas from the younger women. "Why did you allow this to happen?" he snapped.

"It should not have happened," the old woman muttered woodenly. "I neglected my duty to her."

Scylas approved of the old slave's answer. He would reward her bravery and honesty. He would allow her to be the first to die. He nodded to the warrior who held a fistful of her hair. Seizing her bound arms, the man pulled her heavy body to her feet and forced her forward, in front of the other slaves, and back to her knees. The old woman, grunting at the unaccustomed exertion, made no sound, no plea for her life. But suddenly, to the chief's surprise, a huddled mass of fox fur materialized at his feet, as if from the air.

"Please, my lord and chief," Tabiti begged, gripping his dusty booted feet in her small hands, "spare the Mede. She was drugged. Like a man with wine or kumiss, who can resist the sleeping powers of a drug? Let me take her, my lord, and teach her the proper behavior for a slave. My husband will beat her if need be. But remember, my chief, she was loved by your wife and loved by your child and she has been a good and loyal servant for many years."

The words tumbled from the lips of Tabiti in a rushed cascade, as if she hoped to wash him away with their urgency. Indeed, she almost convinced him. But when he looked up from the huddled woman at his feet to the slave woman Urgimas, he saw her looking in their direction and then quickly look away. His anger rose. These two, like all women, were deceitful and in league together, not to be trusted. The Mede, at her age, could never be made a proper slave. He nodded slightly to his warrior, and, before the old woman realized it was coming, a sword flashed, slicing her head from its body. The other women screamed and wailed in panic, fighting when their turn came to die or quietly collapsing in terror. Let them die. Scylas bitterly chewed his lip as he watched. Women are weak creatures anyway. I'd sooner trust my horse or my hunting dog. He left before the last two slaves were executed, returning to his yurt and a fortifying drink of kumiss to get the taste of dust and blood from his mouth. The silent form of Tabiti still huddled on the ground in empty supplication. She did not rise and leave till the warriors finished their task and the bodies of the slaves had been thrown from camp, to feed the wolves.

Scylas angrily shook off the memory. They had failed in their duty, every one of them. Who else would want such wastrels as slaves? They could never be trusted again; for all he knew, one of them was a Persian spy, too, sent to aid in the Greek's escape. Especially the Medean woman Bartatua's wife pleaded so piteously for. The Medes were allies of the Persians. It was just as well.

The old chief snorted and returned to his stool by the fire. Bartatua appeared at his side when another rider galloped into camp. This man's face held more promise and Scylas leaned forward, eager for some good news. "Well?" Bartatua shouted before the horse's hoofbeats had died away. The warrior reined his mount to face Scylas and nodded in triumph.

"North, Sire," he gasped. "We found their trail heading north."

Bartatua cocked his head in disbelief while one hand toyed with the leather ties of his riding cap. "Are you sure?" he asked, his eyes narrowing. "Why wouldn't they head downriver, to the Greek settlements? There is nothing to the north but—"

"The burials," Scylas finished, musing, trying to see the sense in it. They must have some plan, some scheme they were carrying out, and it must be the Greek's doing. Women were incapable of such cleverness. "Go," he said simply, looking at Bartatua. The warrior had anticipated the command and had tied his riding cap in place. He was dressed in plain leather breeches and tunic, and the only Scyth finery he allowed himself was a single gold earring. Scylas was pleased; the man obviously meant business. "Track them, find them, and bring them to me," the old chief concluded, looking up at the cloudless sky.

The only escape was to the north, Arima decided. The vast Scyth burial fields were sacred, a place not visited by casual travellers or passing merchants. There would be more places to hide among the mounds and grave trappings than on the flat, open steppes. And the tracks into and through the burials were old and well-worn from generations of use. Who would notice two more sets of footprints? Beyond this, all she could do was cast her fate to the gods and forge ahead, hoping that somehow their folly would succeed.

The path they followed narrowed, going through a sea of dancing spring flowers. To her dismay Arima saw that the broken plants in the cart tracks from the passing of Opoea's funeral wagon had already sprung back, growing so vigorously in places that they would have trouble passing by undetected. She heard Melanion stop behind her and exhale slowly.

"Well," he whispered, "this will be a challenge!"

Arima studied the tracks, chewing her lower lip pensively. Her feet ached, her head hurt, and her back was stiff from the bundle she carried. What she really wanted was to lie down, curl up, and sleep.

"If we step to that side," she pointed to her right, "and go a few paces, then back this way, you see, the flowers end soon and the dirt track resumes."

Melanion nodded. Soon, he knew, they would have to stop, rest a moment, eat a bit. Then he would ask her exactly what her plans were and where they were headed. For now, there was no time. Every passing breath weighed down on him, the terror of hearing approaching horsemen, of meeting death far sooner than he'd expected always with him.

"Hurry!" Arima took a delicate leap to the side and landed, as lightly as a Greek acrobat, on a patch of crushed grass. Another leap, gazellelike, and another, till she had cleared the narrow, flower-strewn path. Shifting his heavy sack of goldworking tools to the center of his back, Melanion summed up his boyhood memories, of skipping from rock to rock along the shore of the island where he grew up. Setting his jaw, he sprang.

He didn't see how she did it. Melanion could see Arima was tired by the weary droop of her shoulders, the monotonous tread of her feet, but the young heiress refused to stop for a rest. Even though she was just a woman, she was a tough one, and her endurance and resolve exceeded his own. I have lived too long in easy towns, the Greek mused, studying the ground and placing his feet exactly where Arima had stepped. Too much wine, too many days sitting at my work and nights at old Medusa's house of pleasures. And now I am shown up by a mere girl.

Arima paused, tilting her head to the evening breeze. "Listen," she whispered.

Melanion stopped behind her, his heart racing in sudden fear. He could hear only the wind, incessant and maddening, sighing through the young grasses and bright flowers. He shook his head and looked at her. She seemed to be concentrating on something.

"There!" She looked at him. "Can't you hear it?"

He listened again, trying to listen like Arima, not a city dweller but a wild thing. When he no longer focused on what he thought was there, but instead let his hearing roam unbound, he heard a different sound. A groaning, moaning below the whistle of the wind. "What is it?" he began, looking into Arima's wide blue eyes.

"The dead," she whispered. "It is the sound of the dead." Turning, she led the way, through the blue dusk, through twilight gleaming with stars, the noise growing louder in his ears till Melanion thought it would drown out the very winds. The sounds of the dead? The idea sent ice down his spine. Were they entering some Hades, off-limits to the living, a place from which they would never return? The creaking and groaning grew louder, and Arima halted, pointing to the left. Melanion threw down his pack and crouched in the grass at the sight of many horsemen, dark against the far evening sky. Arima looked down at him and smiled at the terror on his face.

"No, no, Melanion!" She reached for his arm and pulled him to his feet. He didn't understand it. If there were so many horsemen, then surely they would be discovered. And if they were discovered, he shuddered at the thought.

"See?" The girl pointed westward. The horsemen still cluttered the red horizon, but Melanion noticed they hadn't moved. "Come," Arima said, squeezing his hand. She took a path directly toward the warriors. The army grew larger, closer over the grass and hillocks, till the two fugitives emerged onto a wide, open plain, and Melanion gaped at what lay before him.

Mounds and hills, as far as the eye could see. Great ones and small ones, like an odd chain of mountains, some grassy and unadorned, some edged and crowned with stone, and some, the largest, topped with ghostly armies, spread out before them. Dead, straw-stuffed horses were ridden by the bodies of young men, mounted high on poles and halved wagon wheels, encircling the graves of their chiefs and riding on endless patrol in the endless wind of the steppes.

So that is the sound, he exhaled in slow relief, studying the black forms through the gathering night. The creaking and moaning of hides tanned by sun and wind, the rubbing of wood on wood, the dry rattle of dangling bones. This was the voice of the dead.

He followed Arima's measured tread as she circled the

nearest mound, steep and grassy and crowned with a single stone spire. The girl seemed to have a destination in mind, and he could guess what it was. His guess proved true—a smaller grave edged with rough-cut upright stones, the fresh earth of its summit covered with carefully laid sod. The tomb of her mother, Opoea.

"We will be safe here for the night," Arima said, lowering her sack to the grasses, still crushed from the recent funeral. Melanion, looking around nervously, jumped at a brief high shriek when a sudden gust of wind twisted a dead warrior on the tomb behind them. The corpses and their eerie voices didn't seem to bother the girl. Well, he realized, she was used to heads staked out in her campsite, enemy scalps dangling from horse trappings, and burnings and be-headings every year of her life. Silently she spread her fur coat on the ground by her mother's grave and curled up on it, facing the path they'd just travelled.

"Shouldn't one of us keep watch?" he suggested, spreading his fur apart from hers, by the retaining walls of Opoea's tomb. The stones' solidity somehow reassured him, a time-less permanence amidst all the reminders of death and the impermanence of life. Melanion swallowed dryly and shifted his gaze from the hypnotic sway of a shriveled horse's hoof nearby. Arima's eyes were on him, as blue as the indigo evening.

"I will watch first," she agreed. "Get some rest while you can. We must set out again before daybreak."

Melanion stood by his makeshift bed and wondered at her gaze. She was there, and they were alone. Abruptly he turned and lay down. He could hear her shifting her position, and he closed his eyes, exhausted. Around him the night did not sleep. It was alive with the sounds of dead warriors and night creatures, they haunted his dreams and taunted his awakening too short a time later.

Arima lightly shook his shoulder. Melanion awoke to her

face shrouded in shadow, so close he could feel the warmth of her breath. "It is time to take the watch," she whispered. Her wide eyes flickered over his face, caught his gaze uncomfortably, and looked down.

Stiffly the Greek sat, his muscles still aching from their long, hurried journey. "Arima, I . . ." he began, as awkward as a schoolboy. With prostitutes he had no problems; a witty remark, an exchange of money, and the deed was done. But what should he do with a nice girl, well brought up, intelligent and sensitive, and plainly attracted to him?

"Am I plainer than Greek girls?" she whispered shyly. She sat back on her heels, her hands in her lap, and he half-smiled at her innocent remark. "I, I have waited so long to be with you." She tentatively touched the back of his hand. Turning it, he closed his fingers around hers.

"Yes," he said simply, stating the obvious. She wanted him, and he wanted her. Life was brief enough, and tragic enough; love was all the sweetness it held. One could not afford too much caution and still have memories to look back on. Without a word, he drew her to him.

The touch of his lips on her neck, the feel of his face so close and warm, shocked Arima. It was not eagerness, but fear that gripped her. Seventeen years of seclusion and taboos screamed stop! but she could not stop. The first kiss, brushed lightly, led to the next kiss, and the next, each harder, more frantic, till he was biting at her flesh and his hands groping against her clothes. Embracing her on his fur cloak, he shifted his chest over her and let his mouth explore her jawline, her cheeks, her eyes, his stubbled cheek rough against her skin. Arima lifted her hands and buried them in the tangled curls behind his neck. The strength, the warmth and tenderness of a man overwhelmed her. There could be no wrongness to it. Melting her will to his, she cast her life and her heart to wherever the fates might take them. She never dreamed life could be so exquisite.

Melanion fumbled at her felt jacket. "Take this off," he whispered hoarsely. Arima unhooked it, gasping when she felt his hand warm over one breast. He was enveloping her beneath his body. She had not known a man could be so insensate with lust. He was no longer rational but was driven by wild animal need.

"Arima," he sobbed, his tongue caressing her bare shoulder. Abandonment, that is the key, she realized. I have violated every law, deserted my people, and now I must abandon myself to this moment like Melanion is doing, and let the future deal with itself. Lifting her face, her mouth found his, and they rolled over. Doubts gave way to enjoyment, and enjoyment gave way to fire, raging upward like a burning torch. Smothering a cry as wild as an eagle's, she pressed her face to the reassuring warmth of his shoulder.

Melanion made no sound, spoke no word. Rising on one elbow, he fumbled to untie his breeches and pulled them down. His head was whirling, full of the noise of his own rushing blood and the soft sobs of Arima and the unceasing groans of the dead warriors. Such lust was more than a man could take. Pushing her legs apart with one knee, he readied himself. Surely she knew there would be pain. Surely she would brace herself for it. He knew she must be a virgin, and it was he, not Bartatua, who would change it. Lifting her body to him, he took her with one hard thrust. Arima gasped violently and pressed her fist to her mouth. "No," he heard her whimper weakly. Lying down, he comforted her with his body and rode her quickly, briefly, and it was done.

Arima snuggled childlike against him, and he wrapped one arm around her. His passion cooled as the night breeze rose, chilling the sweat that dampened his hair. The winds sighed around the tomb of Opoea and rattled the silent armies overhead. I have taken another man's woman, he thought, suddenly grim, lowering his face to his pallet to shut out the sounds of them. "Is there any future in this thing that we have done?" It bothered him but a short while. Exhausted, he fell asleep.

Arima awoke to the sharp morning whistle of a marmot nearby, her heart so full of love and joy that she thought it would burst. No matter that they were probably being hunted; no matter that she had thrown away her life with Bartatua, or that they could die at any moment. For the first time in her life she felt happy. For the first time a dawning day brought not despair and sorrow, but the hope of new dreams, new adventures. For the first time she felt truly alive.

Melanion stirred beside her. Arima rose on one elbow and looked into his sleepy blue eyes, thrilling when they crinkled at her in a smile, for in that look dwelt her entire existence. "Greetings," he murmured, kissing the tip of her nose. "The sun is up," he observed, pressing her forehead to his lips. "You said we should travel by darkness; we must be up and on our way."

She didn't want to move, to stir from the exquisite comfort of his body, but she knew he was right. Sighing, she sat up and stretched the knots from her back. It looked to be a clear day, the milky morning haze already burning off; a good day for walking. She sucked in the fresh air greedily. The harsh life the gods had so long condemned her to seemed finally at an end. Her fortunes had changed, and with Melanion at her side, she felt they could conquer the world.

There was no way to cover their tracks. Vibrant early grasses, blue sage, and pink and white wildflowers stretched to the horizon like a tapestried carpet. "Well," Arima sighed, lifting her pack, "I suppose the best we can hope for is some animal track we can follow to hide our footprints." She cast a glance at Melanion. He'd brought his goldsmithing tools and much of his jewelry, as well as food and water, and he knelt at the base of Opoea's burial mound, trying to fit everything back into his pack. "You brought too much," she observed somberly. He looked up, worry on his face.

"These tools are my life. I had to bring them. Without them I'd be nothing." Gingerly he tied the bag shut so as not to crush anything. He stood and strapped the gorytas and dagger to his legs, tossed his fur coat over one shoulder and the heavy pack over the other. "Where to?" he grunted.

"To the west, I think. There are mountains that way, but before we reach them we will turn southward. Perhaps some other tribe will find us and help us; the Neuri, or the red-haired Budini, or the Melanchlaeni, who wear cloaks of black."

"And they might help us?"

"We must hope so; they are our only chance." She paused, searching his eyes. The wind had not yet risen, and the smells of fresh loam and warming flowers and the dry dustiness of the desiccated bodies around them filled her nose. Surely he must know the seriousness of our situation, she brooded, watching him.

"Well," Melanion blurted, breaking the silence between them as he gazed at the dangling hooves and shrunken flesh of the nearest horse and rider, "I suppose I'll never see the likes of this again."

"Few strangers have and lived to tell of it," Arima muttered. The light and happiness left her face. "Come," she said, and walked off through the flowers.

It wasn't long before they found a broad winding animal track following a rise of land. "Steppe antelope," Arima observed, pointing to the elfin scrapes and hoofprints in the soil. Mixed among them were a few large hoofprints of what looked to be cows. "Wild oxen," the girl explained. Melanion was astounded at their size.

"Oxen, you say?" he marvelled, picking out occasional clear prints as they walked. "They seem to be much bigger than the oxen in Greece."

Arima laughed and watched a flock of buntings rise, wheel, and disappear before them. "They are not man's oxen!" She smiled. "They are giant wild oxen, so fierce no one can tame them and so huge a man can scarcely reach their shoulders. The span of their horns is wider than a warrior's reach."

Melanion felt a twinge of fear. Even domestic oxen could be powerful beasts. But giant wild oxen? "What do we do if we see any?" he asked apprehensively. Arima cast a somber glance at him.

"Pray," she jested.

Midday they caught up with the herd of steppe antelope. The sight of a dust cloud rising in the distant haze, the clear thunder of hooves that they felt as much as heard, made Melanion worry that they were coming on some of the fearsome giant oxen. Surely tiny antelope could not make such noise! To his relief, when they crested a hill he saw a vast herd of creatures spread away before them. Red-brown as the soil, they galloped with leisurely purpose toward a distant riverbank to drink. Their sheer number astounded him; he'd do just as well to try to count the stars overhead.

When the herd had passed, the two travellers descended the hill and followed the rutted trail. By dusk they saw the treeline of the river and Arima, tired though she was, pressed on.

"We'll never reach it," Melanion grumbled. He hated to admit Arima was right, but his pack *was* too heavy. He feared he would never be able to walk upright again. "We could rest here," he suggested, motioning toward a small rise of land. Arima glanced over her shoulder at him, her blue eyes intense in the pale light.

"We must reach the trees before we stop," she stated. "There is no shelter out here. If Bartatua doesn't find us, a wolf pack or great cat might. We will be safer in the trees along the riverbank."

She turned and marched on. The girl seems made for walking, Melanion mumbled to himself. Despite the fact that she was a well-brought-up woman he was dismayed to see that her stamina outpaced his. Too much wine, too many women, he repeated, forcing his legs to follow her. When I get back to Olbia, it is time to visit the gymnasia.

Even Arima was exhausted by the time they reached the cover of the trees clustered along a small, shallow stream. It was not the powerful river she had hoped for—it was barely twenty paces wide—but it was, at least, a haven for the night. Drawing in a long breath of air that burned her weary lungs, she stumbled toward a dense thicket of budding white dog rose and dropped her pack. Melanion slumped to a protruding tree root and let his heavy parcel slide from his shoulder. "I don't know how much longer I can do this," he sighed. "This is just the second day, and already I feel like a beaten donkey."

"The thought of dying at the point of Bartatua's knife will spur you on," Arima remarked. She savoured the descending silence of the night and listened to a large flock of birds settling into the trees overhead. Unplugging her small skin bag of kumiss, she took a brief gulp. It was all one needed to restore energy quickly. Another swallow and she offered it to Melanion.

"No." He shook his head. Not to be impolite, but he found their fermented mare's milk brew to be unpalatable. "I'll just have some water." Shrugging, Arima replaced the wooden plug and sat the bag beside her pack.

"I'll wash off the dust and then we can sleep here, where the rose thicket affords a little protection," she said. Melanion had located a dry, stale crust of bread in his pack and he chewed it pensively, staring into the dark tree shadows. The sudden sound of splashing roused him, and he followed Arima's trail through a tall patch of rushes and to the stream. The girl waded in the pebbled shallows, her heavy wool skirt held up with one hand while she splashed her face and arms with the other. Melanion grinned wryly and shook his head.

"Here," he announced, stepping from the rushes, "I'll show you how a Greek bathes." Arima looked at him and smiled through the rising moonlight; a smile that sagged into openmouthed astonishment when the goldsmith stripped and splashed naked into the stream. "See?" he said, lowering himself into the dark water and clenching his teeth against the cold. "It is so much better this way!"

Arima continued to stare at him. His skin looked faintly bluish in the moonlight, delineating the muscles of his arms and chest in stark light and dark. Such a thing was unheard of among the Scoloti—for a man to strip naked in front of a woman not his wife. But in some small corner of her memory, whispering like the trees, she recalled another time when she waded in another stream and wished she could fling off all her heavy clothes, and swim and dive with the joy and freedom of the fish and otters.

Melanion sat waist-deep in the water, grinning at her, and extended an arm in her direction. The water rolled along his arm and dripped silverlike back into the stream. Arima watched, feeling the old Arima clash with the different, new, free person she was just beginning to explore.

Sheepishly she unfastened the bodice of her felt jacket and tossed it into the dry rushes. Dragging her skirt down and into the water, she threw it ashore. Last came her fine white wool undershift. She pulled it off over her head and discarded it, then stood foolishly naked before him, as he had never seen her before.

Melanion knelt in the water, took her hand, and pulled her into the stream beside him. Arima gasped when the chill water slid over her warm body and reflexively rose up on her knees, her teeth chattering. The Greek broke into laughter.

"Be still and you'll get used to it," he said grinning. "See?" He lifted a handful of water to his shoulder and let it slide in silver trickles through the thick yellow hair on his chest. Arima lowered herself gingerly back to the stream. Melanion put an arm around her and pulled her close, and even through the cold water the touch of his skin felt warming.

"Now," he said, cupping his free hand in the water and splashing it over her shoulder. Arima tensed, resisting the impulse to flinch. Lowering his hand into the water again, he wetted her other shoulder. And a third time, but now the water slid from the base of her throat, downward, sluicing between her breasts. She watched it, entranced, and his hand lingered lightly against her skin. A heat was rising within her such as she had never felt before, and she found herself wanting Melanion, yearning for him, his body, his touch, his being, to meld with him till she no longer existed as a single entity. He was the half that made her whole.

He dipped his hand into the stream a last time and poured the water over her breast. Silent, transfixed, she watched it slide away, and his hand smoothly follow it down the curve of her flesh. He pulled her close against him and she looked into his eyes.

By the gods, I do love you, she thought desperately as his mouth clamped hungrily to hers.

They slept half the night, a deep sleep of exhaustion, and before morning they were awake, stretching their aching muscles, dreading the day's long journey. They would head downstream, they agreed; if they followed it far enough, the stream would reach a river and the river would find the sea, and along the shores of the sea were the Greek settlements that Melanion called home. It was the best plan they could devise. Beyond that, their future rested with the spinning thread of the Fates.

* * *

The army of the dead sighed their secrets as Lipos stared into a still, silver bowl of water. Stared and stared until his senses ebbed and the glaze of a trance filled his eyes. Bartatua shifted impatiently on his haunches, squatting like the rest of his men around the silent enaree.

"Well?" Oricus hissed at Bartatua's shoulder.

"Shhh . . ." Several of the warriors glared at him. A trance such as Lipos was attempting was a difficult task, one that could not be interrupted by foolish comments. It seemed to Bartatua that Lipos flinched at the intrusion, and he hoped it did not leave the half-man open to evil influences from this evil place.

The enaree settled back to his reverie. "I see," he said, his voice breaking the heavy silence of the burial mounds and their hollow-eyed armies. Bartatua tensed in expectation. "Water, there is water—a river," Lipos muttered blankly. Bartatua looked up, his eyes narrowing, and waited for more words from the half-man. It seemed as if the enaree were seeing many things.

"An otter slips through the water," his voice droned on. "The river is not wide. Hemlocks. Yes, hemlocks, and many boulders. A vast herd of saiga antelope come to drink."

Bartatua didn't wait for any more revelations. Standing abruptly, he strode from the circle. A rocky stream and a stand of hemlock where saiga come to drink—the description couldn't be clearer. He knew their direction now; to find the waters and follow them to the sea, to the colonies where the foreigners dwelt. Another plan of the goldsmith, no doubt. His hands itched to find them, to run his dagger through the Greek spy and reclaim his foolish woman. Turning to the grooms and waiting men, his resolve hardened within him like a stone festering in a horse's hoof. He had done kind things for Arima far beyond what most men did for their women, hoping to soften her heart, and this was how she repaid him. With humiliation and shame. He had to find her and set matters right. He knew a place such as

Lipos had described. That was where he would look for them.

Arima would not rest. Day and night, haunted by some inner prompting, she forced Melanion to walk. Sometimes the way was easy, snaking through dense silent forests; other times the stream narrowed, jumbling between rocky embankments they had to struggle to climb over. By the rising and setting of the sun they determined their direction; all seemed well, but her sense of unease would not go.

"If they haven't found us yet," Melanion observed over a hurried morning meal, "perhaps they never will. It has been seven days. Perhaps they didn't even search for us."

Arima looked at him, his face so ragged with a new yellow beard that he reminded her of a shaggy winter pony. "It is plain you do not know my people well," she remarked, studying the dirt and filth on her hands. "Neither my father nor Bartatua would allow such a crime to go unpunished."

"We might have eluded them," he offered hopefully. "If they lost our trail, they would turn back and we would be safe."

Wiping a hand across her skirt in a futile attempt to clean it, Arima slid a last morsel of soft white cheese around in her mouth and stared at the Greek. "A Scoloti warrior can follow a trail more carefully hidden than ours. A man scouting for an enemy, a stalking lion, an escaped stallion. When he is seven, the young warrior is taken by his teacher and left far out on the steppes; he must follow his own trail to return to camp. No, our tracks would be simpler than those they use to train little boys." She stood, swallowing the cheese and abandoning the attempt to clean herself. Melanion stretched his aching legs and groaned. He knew it was time to march again.

"A few more days and then we will rest for a time," she encouraged him. He was a man, true, but he was also a foreigner. Everyone knew the gods had not cut them from the same tough hide as the Scoloti. She wondered how much longer he could go on. Taking a last gulp of water from his goatskin bag, Melanion stood and lifted his heavy pack.

"The day will come," Arima observed, "when you will abandon some of your precious goods." He shook his head in determination. Arima shrugged and began walking. "The choice might come down to them or you," she jested. Closing his ears to the truth of her words, Melanion fell in step behind her.

Lipos was troubled. Even in his trance he had kept his wits about him. Like most with the ability to prophesy, he kept much of what he saw to himself, and what he'd seen hadn't been encouraging. The Greek was barely his concern, but the stupidity of Arima's actions, and her subsequent fate, disturbed him. He had liked the girl and tried to help her. Now she had condemned herself to her tribe, her father, her husband. Nothing could turn that back. What future did she have?

He ran a hand through his fine yellow hair and stared into his campfire, turning his thoughts like stones in a field, looking for answers. Around him stretched steppes and solitude such as he craved; after scrying with the water bowl he'd made excuses to return to camp. Bartatua and his men went one way; he went another. Tomorrow he would reach the camp of Scylas and would have to report to the old man on what he'd seen. Tonight he must make some hard decisions while he still could.

The unnatural stillness of the air allowed the campfire to burn as it wished. The Persians considered fire to be a living thing, holy and pure. Was it? In the orange and yellow flickering before his face he saw another face, Arima, as he had seen her in the water's surface.

Laughing, happy, a light in her eyes such as he had never seen before. Such radiance in a woman could only mean one thing; she was in love.

Hard indeed was the soul who could not identify with that, when the heart has found its calling. He had felt it once himself, long ago, and could share Arima's feelings. Shrugging off his pensiveness, Lipos stretched out on his side, ready for sleep. He'd made his decision; tomorrow at sunrise he would act.

The warm smell of his skin was all the world Arima could desire and she hated to rouse herself, to be up and dressed and on the march once more. She snuggled close to Melanion, enjoying the comfort of his presence, and marvelled that the world could be such a beautiful place. Once, she never could have dreamed it, but here it was, contentment, belonging, joy.

Melanion stretched and opened his eyes, looking at the tangled white birch limbs overhead. The fragrances of spring had soothed him like the finest myrrh or cedarwood and gave him the kind of deep, restful sleep he'd needed. "Time to go!" He smiled at Arima, kissing her cheek lightly. This time it was she who protested, yawning and grumbling good-naturedly. "Come now," he urged as he sat up, pulling on his dirty wool tunic, "the river is widening. We are making good progress. If we only knew where we were, we could judge how soon we would reach the sea, the trading posts."

"Many, many days, I'd guess," she responded, sitting up beside him, looking down at her naked body. She liked the feel of being without clothes, of her skin against his, of making love. Why did everything have to be so rushed all the time? Why couldn't their life together be a normal one? When would this incessant flight end?

Melanion looked at her downcast face. "Go and wash," he suggested. "It will lift your spirits." Arima nodded and kissed his bearded cheek.

It was too chilly to bathe, or she'd have dived into the water like an otter. Here the river was wide enough and deep enough to swim like they couldn't before. This morning she merely knelt on a mossy slope and splashed water over her face and body. The high-pitched cry of a hawk shattered the morning stillness and Arima looked up, startled. It sounded nearby, but in the heavy shade of the surrounding forest she could not see it. Shrugging, she returned to her bathing. There were many hawks on the steppes and along the riverbanks; to hear one was no surprise.

Again it cried and Arima looked overhead, at the tall hemlock branches patterning the sky. She spied it, its small sleek body dark against the milky morning haze, perched on a branch. The bird ruffled its feathers, shifted its wings and cried again, its sharp hooked beak opening wide. With a drop it took off, wings opening wide as it soared out over the river, circling and calling, then returning to the branch above her. Puzzled, Arima stood, ignoring Melanion when he carried her clothes to her. The hawk preened a moment and flew off again, swooping low across the water, crying as if calling to her. It reached a spot in the forest opposite and vanished.

"A hawk?" the Greek questioned, handing her the clothes. A fine bird, symbol of kings, messenger of gods, but what matter was that to them? They must be on their way.

Arima dressed in silence. Melanion noticed how her gaze kept returning to the spot in the forest where the bird had vanished. "You must like hawks," he commented as they shouldered their packs. The girl threw him an odd look.

"Our course has changed," she stated abruptly.

"What?" he protested. "We are making good progress following the river. Why should we change it now?"

"I don't know, but we must. Follow me." She had decided and there was nothing to do but follow. Snorting in baffled derision, Melanion began walking.

My lovemaking must be too much for her, the Greek jested to himself, for her change of course appeared to be the same way they had been marching for days. Downstream

Arima went, still taking care to hide their trail as much as possible. She walked till the morning was half spent when suddenly, in a sloping grassy meadow, she veered to the left, toward a narrow sandy beach by the water. "Whatever you do, don't stop," she directed him over her shoulder. "It is critical. Follow me and do as I do."

Shaking his head at the odd ways of women, Melanion followed. Through broken rushes, crushed and muddy from recent floods, through the sand, their booted feet leaving a trail an infant could follow. And into the water . . .

"Arima!" Melanion barked. Surely she has lost her senses.

"Don't stop!" she called back. The water was to her waist and she kicked off, swimming for the middle of the river. Cursing to himself, the Greek followed her. His heavy pack and wet wool clothes turned what would have been an effortless swim into a nightmare, and he labored against the swift pull of the current midstream. Arima was also having difficulty, and as she struggled he nearly caught up to her. The opposite bank was not far away. If he could just draw a last burst of strength from his exhausted muscles, he could reach it.

A soggy dark mass floated past his face and he rose up from the water, watching it. Like some laden cargo ship it floated downstream on the current—Arima's heavy fur cloak. He looked at her and saw that she seemed unconcerned by its loss. She was still swimming, but this time upstream. Upstream?

"Arima! Wait!" he called over the rush of the water. She didn't seem to hear him. On she swam, pulling away from him with the weight of the fur gone. Melanion's legs were beginning to feel like stones, dragging him down to the bottom, and he toyed with the idea of dropping his heavy pack into the river. No, he wouldn't give her the satisfaction of having been right. Gritting his teeth, he forced himself to follow her.

Arima emerged, gasping, onto a flat boulder. She crawled

from the water and collapsed facedown on the stone. Melanion joined her, his dripping pack clattering loudly when he flung it down. "I congratulate you," Arima gulped, rolling onto her back and wiping ropes of wet black hair from her face.

"On what?" The Greek sat beside her, slumped forward on his arms. Arima pointed to the pack.

"You kept it." She grinned, and Melanion burst into laughter.

"Is this another attempt to make me abandon my worldly goods?" Melanion grumbled when Arima informed him that they must resume their swim. "Over half the day has passed and we are going backward, toward the Scyth lands, not away from them. You must tell me what it is we are up to!"

Arima looked at him, her blue eyes dark and worried. "I'm not sure," she muttered.

"Arima, this is insane!" he spluttered. "Is it time for your monthly curse? Is that what has struck your brain?"

The girl stood tall and eyed him icily. "If you have faith in nothing but yourself, your brain, and your logic, then stay, Greek," she retorted. "If not, come with me." She squared her shoulders with all the resolution of a man and walked away, slipped into the water, and began swimming. Angrily flinging a pebble into the underbrush, Melanion rose and followed her.

This leg of the swim was the last. As if she had been looking for something, Arima suddenly turned in the water and emerged on a jumble of rocks, nearly hidden by low-swept branches of pine and cedar. Melanion was astounded. It was the mouth of a dry gully, a channel of boulders that cut its way through the riverbank and back into the forest, choked with ferns and mosses and heavy with cool, sweet dampness. Now he saw the logic of her plan.

Following the river downstream they would throw any pursuer onto the wrong course; then, changing direction by swimming upriver, they could escape up this rocky defile and leave little or no trace of their passing on the clutter of stones. "This is brilliant!" he complimented her, peering through the forest at the pathway vanishing into the green shadows. "How did you know of it?"

She shrugged and smiled slyly at him. "The hawk showed me. This is the spot where he disappeared."

Bartatua soon picked up their trail, heading for a nearby stream, as Lipos had seen. He could tell they were trying to cover their trail by following the vast tracks of an antelope herd and as futile as their attempts were, he was surprised at the cleverness of their tactics. Squatting, he touched a crushed blade of feather grass and read by its wilt and browning the time since the two fugitives had passed by. A day or more, it was plain. Rising, he squinted through the afternoon haze yellowing the horizon and watched the great tracking dogs casting about for a scent. Their grass-colored coats blended into the landscape as they raced away, noses to the ground, on a good trail.

"Come on!" the chief warrior shouted to his waiting men. Vaulting atop his black and white gelding, Bartatua yanked the reins around and galloped up a hillock after the vanishing dogs.

No matter how clever that Greek thinks he is at hiding his trail, Bartatua vowed, he will not escape me. He will not get away alive with my woman.

Arima thought the night had been one of the most uncomfortable in her life, curled amidst rocks and boulders in the narrow gully. There wasn't a soft spot of earth or moss anywhere, and the dry stream cut was so close they had no hope of stretching out their weary bodies. They had slept apart, curled like cats between the stones in whatever comfort they could manage. She heard Melanion groan stiffly through the heavy dripping of the morning-wet trees.

"Mother Hera, I may never walk normally again!" he grumbled. Arima sat up and swung her legs down over the damp rocks, trying to regain some feeling in them. Melanion slowly rolled onto all fours, like a turtle righting itself, and she couldn't help but laugh at him.

"Amusing, is it?" he muttered in good-natured anger. "Consider your future if I am permanently stuck in this position." He looked over his shoulder and wagged his eyebrows at her.

"Oh, let me help you, then!" Arima grinned, slipping down the cut toward him. "The future for both of us will be brief if you are waddling around with all the agility of a pregnant sow!" He had straightened by the time she reached him and she balled up a fist, dug her knuckles into his back, and worked the knots loose.

"Ah, that's good," he sighed. "Is that an old Scyth trick?"

"Riding in a cramped wagon all day can ruin a person's back," she replied. "We have our ways of dealing with it."

A deep, distant bark shattered the morning, and the words died on her lips. "Dogs," she breathed, looking up at Melanion. A pallor of fear replaced the merriment on his face. His blue eyes shifted downward, probing hers.

"Bartatua," he guessed.

She could think of no words to shape a reply. Fear had risen like a knot in her throat, threatening to choke her. Her eyes flew over his face swiftly, lightly. Every dirty curl of yellow hair, the small creases around his eyes, the beard sprouting on his chin, all dearer to her than her own soul. She could not see him suffer and die.

The dog bayed again, joined by another, and Arima thought she would collapse from the terror that gripped her. "Come!" she choked, grabbing his hand. They would leave no trail in the stony little gorge. If the warriors couldn't track them across the river, they would be safe. But the dogs seemed to have picked up a scent and their voices rose, an eager chorus that brought tears to her eyes.

"Hurry," she sobbed, to herself as much as to Melanion.

Bartatua waved the riders back. He could see the dogs galloping to the water's edge, panting and slathering in their eagerness. Beyond the rushes were footprints, clearly visible across the open sand. As clear, he mused, as the tall stone figures that marked the trade routes through the empty steppes. The feet of his gelding thudded hard into the earth as he pulled it to a halt. His men drew around him, and he chewed a corner of his beard in thought.

Years of training as a warrior and hunter had taught him one valuable lesson; to think like your quarry. He shifted his eyes through the forest gloom and to the water. The beach there was narrow, but long. Why would they choose to cross the surging river at just that spot? Narrowing his eyes, Bartatua searched the dappled shadows. A wall of forest loomed across the water, dark and featureless. Downstream the sand gave way to tangled tree roots. The dogs were insistent; Arima and the Greek had entered the water at that spot. But why? Another trick of the Greek's, no doubt.

He motioned to four of his best men. "Cross it," he snapped. The horses could swim, the dogs could swim. Pulling out his dagger, he rose up on his horse and swiftly hacked a large double blaze on the streamside trunk of an old tree.

"Find a shallow, cross over, take half the dogs with you, and search the far bank from this spot." He motioned to the marked tree as he replaced his knife. "We will continue looking on this side. Somewhere they have left a trail, and we will find it."

Their flight over the stones was painfully slow. Stumbling, slipping, scrabbling on all fours, they progressed up the cut, always pursued by the sound of the Scoloti dogs. They didn't sound closer nor farther, but always there, as steady an accompaniment as the pounding of their hearts in their ears, the mournful dripping of the trees.

We cannot escape them, Arima thought, swallowing the terror in her throat. As fast as we flee, they follow. One knee was swelling where she'd fallen on a rock and with the bruise and stiffness she had trouble moving the leg.

"Come on." Melanion crawled back for her. He put an arm around her and she groped at his hand in desperation.

"We're going to die, aren't we?" She began to cry, looking into his face for some sign of hope. Melanion could see her resolve breaking and despite his own fear he tried to calm her. Panic would be the worst thing for them now.

"We'll get out somehow," he said as he pulled her to his chest. "If we two have such difficulty in this steep, narrow gorge imagine mounted horsemen and a pack of dogs more used to the open plains." Her shoulders quaked with sobs and he cursed himself roundly. "I'm sorry I brought you to this, Arima," he whispered, embracing her and stroking her dark tangled hair. Truly, he was. A trusting young girl with no knowledge of the ways of the world, and now she faced ruin and death because of his rash, impulsive actions. Pressing his cheek to her head, he closed his eyes sadly and held her.

Arima ran as best she could, even though her body ached and the will to live had nearly left her. Only for Melanion did she go on. For herself, she would just as soon sit down, resigned, and await her death. After all, resignation to the will of men was all she had known, all her life. It would be simple, quick, and then it would be over. But for Melanion, she ran. Late in the day an odd silence fell, the sounds of the dogs vanishing like a summer's mist. Melanion dragged Arima to a halt, a look of disbelief on his face.

224

"Listen," he hissed, squeezing her hand. Arima cocked her head. Gusts of dry afternoon wind swayed the treetops. A distant bird chattered and was answered by another. Speechless, she looked at him. The dogs were silent.

"Can it be?" Melanion straightened, ear cocked to the breeze. Arima sagged against him. She felt like crying, screaming, dancing from rock to rock like a flitting dragon-fly from the sheer joy of relief. With such a love, such a warmth, such a strength, how could anything ever happen to them?

Then a dog yelped, wild and eager, and Arima fell to dry sobs. No! she choked into Melanion's sweaty tunic. This sound of doom, of creatures from the afterworld, would pursue them to the grave. "We'll never get away!" she cried, tears streaking her dirty face. "They're going to catch us, Melanion! I cannot let you die."

"Come on," he snapped, jerking her behind him. He couldn't afford the luxury of fear or hysteria, though he thought it would be a welcome relief. He just had to escape.

He could not believe his eyes when he looked ahead. The boulders ended abruptly, as if cleared away by some giant hand. The cut rose into a slope of black loam, and then stopped. Beyond it stretched the vast, flat, empty steppes and grasslands.

The yelping of the dogs wavered into an unceasing monotony, blending with the breeze that rose as the sun went down. Arima and Melanion huddled near the last big boulder they could find, awaiting their fate.

"We will flee, once the sun is down," he murmured into her ear. Purple evening shadows splotched and spread from the protruding rocks above them. Apparently Bartatua wasn't going to stop for the night; fresh on their trail, he intended to capture them as soon as he could. Arima looked at Melanion's face, ruddy in the setting sun.

"What good will that do?" she whispered. "On the steppes they can chase us down easily. We have no hope now."

"Then let them," he said bitterly. "A spear to the back while running, it will be quicker that way." He gazed off into the sunset. What regrets could he now see in his life, now that it was ending? The home he'd never had, children hanging from his knees while he told them a tale, sunwarmed figs from a tree in his own courtyard. Little things, unimportant in themselves, that fit together like stones, building the edifice of a man's life, these were his regrets.

Melanion's hopeless words tore at Arima like talons. "I cannot watch you die." Her voice wavered. "I would sooner attack them, make them kill me first, so I wouldn't have to see you . . ."

Melanion gazed up at the treetops, uncomfortable with the depth of her feelings. Feelings were another thing he had always avoided. "We had a little time," he muttered. "I am glad for that." He turned and tried to smile at her. "We'd better go now. We can leave our packs here and return for them, later."

Arima could see fear in his eyes, a tight intensity to his gaze as it caught the last of the setting sun, and she ran a hand tenderly down his cheek. How could such terror and hopelessness exist amidst such love and joy. A thousand-thousand sunsets had happened in the past, and a thousand-thousand more would come, yet here they sat beneath their final one, as insignificant before the majesty of the sun as two bugs beneath a wagon wheel. How could it be?

Arima fought the tears when Melanion kissed her forehead, the tip of her nose, her mouth. To find him, and then lose him, she cried silently; by the gods, may every last one of you never find peace for such cruelty.

Too soon, it was over. His lips left hers, and he pulled her to her feet as the black night fell, thick and absolute, around them. The dogs wavered on, their baying echoing on the wind. "Run," he said quietly, "and if they find us, split up. That way," he paused awkwardly, "that way you won't have to see it."

Arima nodded, embraced him fiercely, and together they climbed to the grasslands.

Arima couldn't help stumbling on her swollen knee. She felt she should tell Melanion to run, to save himself, but she wasn't that brave. She wanted him with her as long as possible, just to feel his nearness, his large hand enclosing hers, to let her heart absorb the sight of him. She sacrificed all for a last few moments with him. When he went, she knew, one way or another her life would be over.

Over too soon. Arima's heart cried out at the sound of hoofbeats in the distance, a scream of such outrage that she felt it must tear the fabric of heaven and topple the pillars of the world.

On they came, not one horse but many, and she looked aside at Melanion. By the grim set to his mouth, the empty way he stared, she knew he heard it, too. "Melanion!" Her voice choked against rising panic and the helplessness and the night air that burned her lungs. Did he not hear her? Did he not care? Without a parting glance he squeezed her hand tightly, broke free of her desperate grasp, and ran off into the darkness. They had agreed to it, she knew. But when the moment came she would sooner have welcomed the death that awaited her.

"Melanion!" she screamed, and her heart shattered. She fell to the ground, defeated.

Hooves drew closer, but she did not care. Huddled on the cold ground, she awaited her capture and death. What use to flee now, with her only joy vanished into the night? She had thrown away her life to save his; she could only beg the gods of the earth to help him now, when she no longer could.

Horses were nearly atop her, and she could feel the pounding of their feet through the hard soil below. Distract them, yes! She suddenly saw a course open to her. Their pursuers might gallop about the steppes till dawn, looking for the two of them, or thunder off after Melanion, who would be a larger and more visible quarry, with his fair hair gleaming like a beacon in the night. Small as she was, Arima might be able to crawl into a clump of grasses and hide, but then what would her life be worth?

Rising to her feet, she peered one last time at the trail where Melanion had fled. With every beat of its blood her heart cried out against what it knew. He was gone.

She ran off at an angle from his path, making no effort to conceal herself. Let it sound out, she cried, tears rolling to her chin; wild wind and wide grass and me, alone and free on this final night I live. Let the world cry and moan and tear at my skirts and pull on my hair. Life no longer matters.

Relief came swiftly, an end to her waiting. Three horsemen galloped from the night, slowing to a trot around her as one would circle a wounded antelope. Blindly, Arima kept floundering through the grass.

Kill me, she chanted inwardly; quickly, do it, kill me.

Were they toying with her? A cat worrying a mouse? Glancing to the side, she could see a horseman sitting easy on his mount, his figure faint against the night sky. He seemed unconcerned, unhurried. Was this the action of a Scoloti warrior, retrieving a woman who'd violated tribal law, disobeyed her chief, dishonored her future husband? On impulse, Arima turned and lunged at the man, trying to bring on a confrontation. The warrior said nothing, did nothing, merely wheeled his horse a few steps sideways and paused.

Again Arima threw herself at the horse. Again the warrior

eluded her. Her terror was giving way to rage, to impatience to be done with the game. "Kill me!" she screamed and ran at the horseman with what little strength remained in her weary legs. In the name of all the gods, be done with it!

The warrior moved out of her way and Arima fell to the broken grasses, her heart pounding wildly.

"No one wishes to die," a calm voice drifted through the night. A soft, low, kindly voice—a woman's voice? Arima lifted her head and spat grass and dust from her mouth. Squinting through the darkness, she saw the warrior pull back his leather riding cap and a cascade of hair spill down. The warrior was a woman.

"What's to be done with you?" the woman continued, as if lecturing a naughty child. "Surely there must be some tale behind this—a Scoloti woman wandering our lands alone, without horse or wagon, and begging for death."

Arima rose to her knees, forcing her weary body erect. To die groveling and crying at the hands of one's own people was one thing, but before a foreign tribe? Never!

Another warrior sprang to the ground and jerked her to her feet, and she could tell by his hands and his strength that this one was a man. Binding her hands before her, he remounted and held the end of her rope, leading her behind him like a tethered calf.

"We will let my father decide your fate," the woman concluded, and Arima limped silently behind them as the three warriors slowly rode into the night.

They allowed Arima to rest several times and fed her kumiss to revive her failing strength. One by one five other horsemen joined them while they travelled back to their camp. Arima guessed that several of them were women, by their figures and the way they held themselves. Whoever they were, there was one fact she was sure of and it gave her enough hope to go on. They had not found Melanion.

Their camp turned out to be small, temporary, and open to the stars, without a single yurt for shelter. Arima could not understand such mysteries; women who rode as men, who carried weapons, who slept on the ground as men did, unsecluded in tents and wagons. Perhaps she had died, after all, and this was some strange unreal afterlife.

The woman warrior who'd captured her seemed to hold some high rank, for when they reached camp and she dismounted, she did not see to Arima but left it to two other horsemen, a man and a woman.

"Sit!" her woman guard demanded, pushing down on Arima's shoulder with surprising strength. The girl was forced to obey. The man took the lead rope tied to her hands and bound her ankles, then fastened it to a wooden horse stake driven in the ground. Accepting of whatever fate was to come, Arima waited.

"Well, girl, what is your name?"

A male voice jerked Arima awake, and she lifted her sagging head. Blocking out a low morning sun was the stocky figure of an older man, with the woman warrior at his side. In a decision as swift as an eye blink, she determined not to tell him.

"Can't speak, eh?" She heard him smiling at her. Before she had seen it, the woman drew a heavy iron knife and used the point to lift her chin.

"She doesn't look common," the woman observed, studying her face. The man nodded agreement. "Bring some food," he barked, and Arima's defiance softened at the thought of ale and fresh roasted meat. "You'd best talk, girl." The man squatted in front of her. "Who knows, we might decide to return you to your people or make a good slave out of you if you don't cross us."

The prospect of either did not gladden Arima's heart, and she swallowed hard against the knife point below her chin.

"What's your name?" the woman repeated, lowering the

dagger. Her eyes were odd, almond shaped, and they seemed to dig right through the defenses Arima had tried to erect.

"Arima," she muttered. The man and woman burst into loud laughter, and Arima's cheeks stung red with shame. Her name had always been a loathsome thing to her, but she had learned to live with it.

"So you still don't wish to tell us, eh?" The old man nearly choked on his merriment. "'One?' That is your name? 'One?' One what, girl? One goose girl who lost her flock? One outcast slave, or one spy perhaps? One what?"

"'One' because I was my father's only child," she said, fighting tears, seventeen years of hurt and humiliation she'd suffered because her father had named her One. A number. Not named for a goddess, nor a flower, nor a revered ancestor. A number, he had said, so she could never forget her worthlessness in his eyes. Arima sat silently, wept silently, letting the boil of long suffering, lanced, drain away.

"So that is your name, then?" the woman said, squatting down by the man. Arima nodded. The woman chewed her lower lip, lost in thought, and then abruptly leaned toward the old man. "Father," she said quietly, "I think I know of this one. She is the child of Scylas."

Arima's head jerked up at the name.

"And her mother was Opoea, your sister."

"Sister?" Arima breathed the word. "But you are not Scoloti. No Scoloti man would ever allow his woman to . . ." She cast a fearful glance up and down the frightening figure of the woman, male-clad in trousers and tunic, gorytas and dagger. The woman laughed again.

"But did you not know?" She cut the bonds on Arima's wrists and ankles. "Your mother was not Scoloti. She was of us, Cimmerian."

A windbreak of decorated felts had been erected for Arima to wash behind, protecting her from male eyes, but it still afforded nothing like the privacy she was used to in a woman's cleansing tent. She suppressed a shiver when the chill open air breezed against her wet skin. Odd, she mused, the men didn't even seem to try to look at her. Dipping a wad of wool into the basin of tepid water, Arima sluiced it hurriedly over her bare shoulders. Drying briskly, she looked at her old clothes. They were torn and dirty but the Cimmerian women had no other skirts and jackets to give her, and she could not bring herself to wear the men's things they generously offered, so she cleaned them as best she could and put them on again.

A woman guard, squatting by the windbreak, rose when Arima emerged and the girl thought she eyed her womanish clothes with slight amusement. "I am Api," she informed her. "I am to help you, teach you, show you our ways. A meal has been prepared, and they are waiting for you now."

Arima followed her through the camp and to the campfire, where she was shown a place beside the woman warrior who'd captured her. Nervously she glanced around the circle of faces. Here, there was no separate place for women. Here men and women, warriors of both sexes, mingled freely, talking and drinking and eating together as if the gods had made them all the same. Sleek, fast hunting hounds roamed the gathering, snapping up scraps tossed to them, and a few of the men had hooded falcons perched on their shoulders.

"Sit," Api instructed, puzzled by the young girl's stillness. Surely she must be hungry! Reluctantly Arima lowered herself to a dyed wool carpet spread on the ground.

"We all await your tale!" the older man boomed jovially at her as he fed a scrap of raw meat to his falcon. Arima looked at him, his weathered face open and honest, and her heart froze. To address a gathering, to speak familiarly with men, how could she do such a thing, when all her life she had been trained to keep silent? She swallowed hard and looked aside, and when a slab of boar meat, dripping fat and steaming fragrantly, was presented to her, even the gnawing hunger in her stomach turned to sand.

"Some kumiss will loosen your tongue," the man suggested, and at his directing a young slave boy thrust a drinking horn of the thick liquid into her hand. Arima's stomach churned at the pungent smell of it.

"I don't think I can," she whispered, gazing at the polished horn self-consciously as she spoke, "you see, I . . ."

The woman warrior patted Arima's folded knee kindly. "I understand," she replied, smiling. "Eat, and the two of us will talk later. Father!" she barked good-naturedly at the man, "let her be. She is tired, and she is a Scoloti. Her tongue has been beaten into submission."

Arima winced and turned away. She did not want to see the blow come to the woman, for speaking so to a man. It did not come. "Yes." The father's voice grew subdued. "I know how it is with the Scoloti. I heard of the life my sister led. Take your ease, child; we will give you no worries."

Arima looked up at the man, directly, into his dark brown eyes—unafraid, without cringing or shame—and felt like hugging him. Her hunger returned, and she tore into the meat like a starving wolf.

Arima could speak openly to the woman warrior once the two of them were apart from the others. "We are cousins." She had smiled, showing Arima to a thick horsehide pad where she could sleep. Together they sat on it and watched the camp go about its business.

"How did a Scoloti heiress come to be wandering our lands?" The woman repeated the vital question.

"I was to wed," Arima explained slowly. "After the burial of my mother, I was to wed my father's chief warrior. He would then be his heir."

"Why didn't you?" The woman leaned forward, fixing a piercing, almond-eyed stare on Arima.

"I did not want to live that way," the girl said. She must

choose her facts carefully. If Melanion could escape the
Cimmerians, too, all the better. As a foreigner, his fate at
their hands might be no better than at Scylas's. "I fled," she
concluded, "and when I heard hoofbeats I thought it was my
people, coming to capture me."

"And you preferred death to marriage?" The woman
straightened and drew in a sharp breath admiringly. "You
are indeed the daughter of a Cimmerian."

Arima looked up and studied the woman warrior. She was
a few years older than Arima, and her face was unusually
lovely, odd, exotic, and with a hardness not seen in Scoloti
women. "You say this is your land," Arima blurted, "but
that cannot be. The lands of the Scoloti are vast. I did not
walk them all. What are you doing here? I see no grandmothers, no children, no cattle and sheep and geese. Where
are the rest of your people?"

The woman laughed lightly and clasped Arima's hand.
"Oh, there is some dispute about the borders of our lands.
We own a tiny portion, a remnant of what we once did. You
say it is yours, we say it is ours. At times we try to cease the
bickering, as when Opoea was wedded to your father. Have
the gods drawn lines across the land, as the Greeks do? Shall
we erect fences and all live like sheep? No, Number One,
who can say whose lands these are? At least it was we who
found you. That is one thing the gods did decree, that you
live like a slave no longer. Wasn't that your wish?"

Her grey almond eyes narrowed and she pierced Arima
with a stare again. "Didn't you dream it, with every bit of
your flesh and every shadow in your soul? Didn't you
whisper it into the very winds?"

The words were too accurate, wounding her like arrows.
Fighting for self-control, tears filled Arima's eyes and the
camp wavered and swam before her. "Many times," she
breathed, hiding her face in one hand. If only this woman
could know how many times she had dreamed it, cried it,

prayed it. Thoughts flew to her vividly; of yurts smokey and stifled while outside springtime quickened the land; of lurching wagons within which women hid away like squirrels; the beauty of the old mare, galloping like the wind, and nights spent under the stars. Freedom.

"There you are!" the woman warrior said triumphantly. "You know wishes whispered to the wind travel to the ears of the gods. They heard you, Arima. Don't you see? And now you must not insult them by refusing their gift to you. You must stay here with us and learn all the things you couldn't before. To ride, to hunt, to fight."

Arima would just as soon have heard that she must learn to fly. Riding was a joy she would welcome, but the rest?

"You will learn." The woman stood, straightening the gorytas at her side. "Tomorrow we are moving again, searching for wild horses to enlarge our herds. You will ride with us."

"Wait!" Arima called when the woman began to walk away. "Your names, what are your names?"

"My father is Creusa, a Cimmerian king. I am his daughter Sela. Good night, Number One; sleep well."

Was it excitement, or fear, that kept her blood racing? Arima sat alone on the horsehide mat, watching riders leave the camp and return; warriors walking by, laughing and jesting, men and women together; a young wild horse, in a cloud of dust, being broken, a rider draped across its back to accustom it to the feel. Sleep? How could she sleep when the violet dusk fell, and silence came, and the stars emerged, glittering through the gentle wind?

Melanion, she thought. I can only hope you are alive and making your way to safety, for your existence must remain hidden from these people who have adopted me. I cannot try to find you, or follow you. We are forever apart, until the gods decide otherwise.

What was it that Sela had said about the wind? That it

carried wishes to the ears of the gods? Arima inhaled deeply, crossed her legs on the mat, smoothed her heavy skirt, and closed her eyes.

Melanion, she whispered into the night breezes. Melanion, Melanion.

She could only pray that, somehow, her words would find him.

A sick man does not forget how to walk. Neither did Arima forget how to ride. When they brought out a young dun mare the next morning, Arima eyed it as eagerly as a child with a new toy. "She is gentle," Sela remarked, "a good horse for you to learn on."

Arima smiled inwardly. What a fine surprise it would be, when Sela saw that she already knew how to ride! She, a Scoloti woman.

"She is a smart horse, not willful, and will soon understand what you want from her. By the time we reach our settlement, the two of you will be as one," Api predicted. She hoped the chore of teaching a flighty Scoloti heiress to ride wouldn't be too difficult; she had her own family's horses to see to.

This horse was young and healthy, not old and decrepit like the mare Arima had once ridden. Its eyes burned with a fine, keen intelligence. She took the reins and stroked the mare's shaggy neck while they grew accustomed to each other. The Cimmerians had clipped the mare's mane, fitted the leather bridle with red horsehair tassels, and put down a fine silk saddle cloth for Arima to sit on. Altogether it made a splendid sight and her blood cried out to be riding.

"Can you mount?" Sela questioned her. Arima pretended not to know, hoisting herself up on the horse as awkwardly as she had the first time. Wiggling around and swinging one leg over, she pulled her skirts back in a most unwomanly fashion and several of the male warriors lounging nearby hooted appreciation at the bare leg she revealed above her boot tops. Sela shot them a withering glance and looked at Arima's legs disapprovingly.

"We'll have to do something about that," she remarked. "We cannot have you riding about like the camp harlot. Now, give Api the reins to walk her."

Arima straightened herself and held the reins. "No, let me try just once," she pleaded, almost childlike. "I'll go slow and be careful, I promise."

"Arima, I can't." Sela reached for the reins. "You have never ridden before. It is not as easy as it looks. You could get killed if you do the wrong thing. A horse is not a toy."

Arima pressed her heels to the mare's sides and the horse sprang away from Sela and Api. Oh, the feel of it once more, skimming over the ground, the wind in her hair, made her almost forget the ache in her heart.

"Arima!" she heard Sela screaming. The girl galloped the mare in a wide circle beyond the campsite and trotted back to her openmouthed cousin and the warriors who were scrambling for their horses to pursue her.

"Arima is 'The One' alright," one of the startled warriors called out, his brown eyes gleaming admiration. "The One Trickster; she already knows how to ride!" The men broke into loud laughter.

Sela had her hands on her hips. "What else do you know how to do, trickster?" She pretended anger. "I suppose you can hunt with the best of them, and shoot the head off a dead bird at full gallop."

"No." Arima pulled the mare to a halt. "Riding is my only secret."

"Good." Sela motioned for her horse to be brought up. Api and the male warriors joined them. "Then there are still some things I can teach you. Come."

Thin smoke clouds promised rain on a morning when Arima awoke, two days into their journey. She cursed the luck of it, for as they travelled toward the Cimmerian settlement, she knew that day by day they distanced themselves from the river she and Melanion had fled across, and the rocky gorge, and the packs they left behind before their attempted escape. The flat steppes the horsemen traversed had given way to undulating grasslands, and treelines of distant rivers seemed always at hand. And as they travelled, Arima grew increasingly frantic, determined to go back to the gorge, retrieve her few belongings, and see if Melanion's pack still remained. She felt this day, rain or no, must be the day.

She sat up quickly on her horse pad, her mind churning with plans. She had tried to keep watch as they journeyed, noting conspicuous hillocks and prominent trees. Could she retrace their route by herself? Living the sheltered life she had, her tracking skill was almost nonexistent. A trail through the grasslands and following the stars—what did she know of such things? Squatting, Arima picked grass and dirt from her horse's pad and folded it, lifting it as she stood and whistled for her mare. The horse wandered nearby, picking at the sweet summer grasses, and she came forward slowly on hobbled feet at the sound of Arima's call. Cimmerian horses seemed to be as well-trained as Scoloti, which wasn't odd, Arima mused as she tied the saddle pad on the mare's back, since many Cimmerian horses seemed to have once belonged to the Scoloti.

"Number One!" Sela strode toward her, bright eyed despite the earliness of the day. "Why are you up? With all the horses to tend, we will not be leaving for some time." The young woman was braiding her long hair behind her neck, preparing for a hard day's riding.

Arima shrugged and squatted to remove the hobbles from her mare. "I have some business to see to," she said casually. *They are not going to approve,* she warned herself. *Old Creusa will forbid it, and then what will I do?*

Sela took the hobbles from her cousin and tossed them

over her shoulder. "Business?" she questioned. "What business could you have besides riding with us, Arima?"

She may as well say it, get the argument over with. Arima stood and faced Sela squarely. "I need to go back to the river, near where you found me."

She broke off when Sela shifted her booted feet in abrupt irritation and emphatically shook her head.

"I want to retrieve my pack. I left it there when I knew I would have to run to escape Bartatua. It was too awkward to take with me, Sela." She grabbed her cousin's arms as if to force her logic into her. "I must! In that pack is all I still own in this world. I have thought about it many times as we travelled, and I know I cannot leave it behind. I must go back for it, Sela, I must!"

Sela lifted her head and glared at Arima. "You cannot, girl!" she snapped. "You don't know what it is you ask. It is too far and too dangerous. You cannot."

They fell silent, staring at each other; two tall women-warriors whose minds were made up.

"I must," Arima stated again, dropping her hands from her cousin's arms. Pointedly she tied the lower strap of her new gorytas around her leg.

"You will not," Sela retorted, watching her. "Cousin, you are the stubbornest woman I have ever seen. No wonder you fled your tribe, your father, and your marriage. You are like a horse with a burr under its saddle pad. The Scoloti are probably enjoying the peace you left behind! It is too dangerous, Arima. You have lived your life in seclusion, always guarded by warriors and slaves. Our world is not like that! Out here are many dangers. A woman does not ride off alone on an adventure. Whatever you have lost, I will replace. But you will not go, Arima, for I will not let you."

Sela broke off abruptly and looked at Arima, a puzzling sorrow in her eyes. She reached almost helplessly to touch the girl's arm. Arima did not understand. She looked away, uncomfortable with her cousin's words. Pulling the impatient mare closer, she pretended to straighten her bridle. The horse snorted, and its feet thudded heavily against the dry soil. She was eager to be off. Sela's threats and pleadings had meant little to Arima. She had weapons now, and a good horse; she could take care of herself.

"Slave traders, Arima," Sela suddenly blurted. "You don't want to get caught by slave traders, do you? Think of your fate then."

Arima had heard enough. She sprang onto the mare and turned it. "I will ask Creusa," she said, and walked away through the awakening camp.

The warrior Ariantes easily kept pace with Arima, his peaked leather riding cap tied in place, his gelding hardly winded by the mare's leisurely gallop. Arima hadn't wanted an escort, but Creusa had insisted; it was the only way he would approve her request. And Ariantes, of course, had volunteered.

She cast a quick glance in his direction. He was gazing elsewhere, studying the horizon, looking for game or danger. She couldn't tell which; she only knew that warriors and hunters were like that. Like a great cat, their eyes were never still.

"Can we ride into nightfall?" she called to him. He turned abruptly and grinned, his teeth white and fine in his bearded face. "Can you manage it?" he jested. Arima smiled back blandly. For two days the rain had held off, though the sky was heavy with moisture. Travel had been good. They were so close now, a ride by night would surely bring them to the river.

"Yes," she answered. To be so close to an answer; how could she stop and sleep? "I am as tough as you!" she retorted. Ariantes laughed loudly, said "I hope not!" and returned his searching gaze to the horizon.

The skills of men! Arima marvelled. After so many days,

Ariantes found what remained of the trail she and Melanion had crushed through the grass and wildflowers. Like a dog with its nose to the ground, the warrior retraced it, back to the rocky cut, as easily as if he were finding the door to his own yurt. Arima followed, leading the two horses, wondering how he could even see in the starless night. It crossed her mind that Bartatua had also been as skilled. When she had foolishly decided to escape from him, only luck and the hawk's guidance had saved her. But saved she had been, and now here she stood, male clad, with her own horse, and weapons at her side, looking at the sudden dark pit of the cut before her, where the grasslands dropped away to blackness.

Ariantes straightened and jerked the leather riding cap from his head, letting it hang down his back. He scratched his sweaty hair and stared down the rocky slope as Arima stepped to his side.

"What is it?" she whispered, trying to read a clue on his face. The night was still and silent and scarcely a rustle of leaves came from the trees before them.

"I don't like this," he muttered. "You can't see a thing down there. We could blunder right on top of a wild boar, asleep in the bushes." He turned and looked at her. "We have to wait until dawn. You sleep, I'll keep watch, but we must wait."

Arima nearly argued with him, but stopped. His words did have a logic to them, and dawn could not be too far off. "I cannot sleep anyway, Ariantes. You sleep first and I'll sit guard."

Ariantes seemed glad to hear her words. He pulled the horse hobbles from his belt as he led his gelding from the cut. Arima cast a final longing glance into the darkness and followed him. So close to an answer, so close.

Men sleep like dogs, Arima mused as she sat watch and waited for the dawn. Ariantes snored softly on his back, as gone to the world as a hunting dog by the hearthside. Stretching her legs, she chuckled to herself. In these few days she had lived with the Cimmerians, she had come to know men as she never had before. Men as people, not men as remote as if they were some different form of animal life. Fierce old Creusa, his horse's bridle heavy with enemy scalps, yet his heart so full of love for Sela, his daughter, that it spilled from his eyes every time she came to speak to him. The male warriors, sharing tasks with the women who rode with them. She hadn't known men could be so . . . human. And Ariantes!

She laughed again and rose to check the horses when she heard them moving restlessly. *I think Ariantes has wanted me since the time I first joined the Cimmerians. If only he knew my heart is not mine to give away. Melanion has it.*

The horses were fine, just startled by some shadow in the dying night. Yes, soon it would be over. She checked the horses a final time, broke a few dry twigs to feed the campfire, and slipped away toward the gorge.

She could remember little of it, returning in the predawn darkness, climbing down the rocks and back in time, to another night, a night of terror and loss and heartbreak. The slippery boulders were unfamiliar, the trees above her strange. Stooped over nearly on hands and knees, Arima felt her way forward. At last, when it seemed she must have gone too far, she touched the damp edge of her leather sack, wedged between two rocks. Drawing her knees up, she squatted awkwardly, propping herself against a tree trunk. She could see nearly nothing in the gloom, only vague shapes and masses, dim light and shadow. No matter. Eagerly she slipped her hands over the sack. It was as she had left it.

A wail split the night, like the tortured cry of a demon, and Arima looked up in horror, her hands halfway risen to her face. On a high branch, nearly overhead, was the long, dark mass of a panther. It cried again, looking down at her, and its teeth shone white in the night.

"Don't move," Ariantes hissed from the top of the gorge. "By the gods, move a muscle and he'll leap."

Arima knew little about wild things, but his words rang true. How often had she seen her cat toy with a mouse that tried to flee, and ignore one that huddled in terror? A soft scrape came as Ariantes withdrew his bow and arrow. The great cat, too, heard it and rose slightly on its legs, looking toward the sound.

"Lower your face," the warrior whispered. Slowly Arima turned her face down into her hands, every muscle of her body knotted with fear. She tensed her back against the strike of the great cat and waited. The cat cried out again, a call that chilled her blood, and the branches overhead rustled. A quick snap from Ariantes' bow and the cat fell heavily beside her, dead before it left the trees. In two bounds Ariantes was at her side, bow in hand, and jerked her roughly to her feet.

"Curses, woman," he snapped, "I hope whatever was in that pack was worth nearly dying for!" Anger and relief crowded his face as he glared at her, but his words flew harmlessly past the girl. In silence Arima looked down at the leather pack in the grey dawn and felt like crying with relief. Stones had been placed around it, weighting down the edges. She had not done this before they left. And next to it, oh joy of the gods, was nothing! Melanion had escaped! He was alive!

The journey to the Cimmerian settlement took six days, and by the time they reached it Arima was so sore from riding that she could hardly walk. She had thought riding was fun, exhilarating; it was also hard work. The wool trousers helped, when she had finally donned them at Sela's insistence, but every night Sela had to doctor raw blisters on Arima's behind with crushed coriander seed and honey.

Her archery lessons began, too, and that led to sore

shoulders, arms burned by the bow string, and fingers nearly as blistered as her backsides.

"You will learn," Api remarked, twisting a new bow string onto Arima's small curved bow. "We begin by playing with toy bows when we can barely walk. You are starting late; be patient." She noticed the girl rubbing a mutton-fat salve onto her red forearm. "You could wear a leather guard for that, but real warriors would laugh at you." Looking into Arima's eyes to judge her response, Api was pleased to see defiance there. "In time you will hold the bow better, so it will stop skinning you, and your fingers will harden to the string." She passed the restrung bow to the girl and watched her test its pull. She has natural ability, Api observed, and a determination that is admirable. Truly, she is one of us.

The Cimmerian camp sprawled along a ridge with a broad swift river to one side and rich pasturelands on the other. This was different from the wandering camp of the Auchatae people, for here small patches of grain and vegetables were grown, secured by woven wicker fences to keep out roaming livestock. This meant that most of the tribe stayed here till autumn, a settled existence that Arima found puzzling.

"What happens when all the grass here is eaten by your herds?" she asked Sela as they walked their horses along the ridge, through the outermost fringes of camp.

"Oh, the horses are herded where it is necessary for them to go. The sheep and cattle remain here, to feed on what they can. They are not our wealth, as the horses are."

Arima mulled this over, watching the excited faces of children who ran out, laughing with joy, to greet them. Most of them carried toy weapons and seemed healthy and well cared for. She also noticed they all seemed happy.

"Did you catch a horse for me?" asked one young boy who had several teeth missing and wore a tunic too large for him. He ran beside Sela's horse, leaping like a gambolling lamb. The woman grinned and looked down at him.

"I brought you something better." She motioned her head toward Arima. "A new cousin."

The boy's feet touched the dusty soil, and he stared at Arima as she rode past him, his eyes wide and solemn.

"Another cousin," Sela explained. "The youngest child of your mother's youngest brother. Oh, you will find many new kinfolk here in camp!" She cast a quick sidelong glance at Arima and wondered at her perplexed, almost gloomy expression. "Don't worry about the lad!" she tried to jest with Arima. "I think we have just the horse for him, a young one he can break himself. Let us change and rest in my yurt, and then I'll show you the horses we captured."

Arima wondered how many of them she would recognize as from her father's herds.

Everyone knew Sela, and she seemed well loved by all. Walking at her side through the bustling camp, Arima felt as awkwardly conspicuous as if she'd been strolling about naked. She was used to slipping furtively from tent to tent, guards and slaves around her, seeing few women and ignored by the men she passed.

"You will learn who everyone is." Sela laughed at her cousin's frown. They had washed off the dust of travel, downed a hasty meal, and now walked through the camp of Creusa, going to view the newly acquired horses. "Many we found along the river bottoms, strays from passing caravans," Sela explained. Ahead of them a low haze of dust hung in the air above the penned and milling animals.

"How many did you capture?" Arima asked.

"Thirty or so. Some very young, some good for little but the stew pot, and a few very fine ones that appear to be crossed with Persian horses."

Arima's curiosity roused. She recalled the fine black

Persian stallion of Scylas, and how she had loved it. Through the sapling fence ahead she could see the horses' bodies, patches of dusty color, and hear the cries of their fear.

"See?" Sela climbed the fence. Arima followed and saw from the top a vast sea of horse backs, surging and turning like a wild river. Sela inhaled deeply and smiled.

"Ahh, nothing smells better than a horse," she commented. "See them all, big and little, beautiful and ungainly. We got a very good . . . ." She looked at Arima and her words stopped at the expression on the girl's face; shock, disbelief, recognition. Arima's lips moved, but Sela could not hear her over the din.

"Arima?" She leaned forward to look into the girl's face and saw tears brimming her eyes. "What is it, Arima?" She shook her arm.

Arima could not answer. Speech had been struck from her. In the middle of the paddock, its head tossing grandly, its mane still matted and torn, stood her great grey horse.

"I must have it!" Arima pleaded to her cousin. The young women had climbed from the fence and Sela seized Arima's hand, dragging her back to her yurt, annoyance plain on her face.

"You cannot," Sela snapped. "That horse is meant for one of the men."

"No!" Arima resisted, pulling against Sela's grip. All the longing she felt for Melanion, the emptiness of her childhood, the bewilderment over the Cimmerian way of life, found their release in the great grey stallion. In him there was the familiar, the sense of belonging, fulfillment of all her dreams. She must have him, the last thing in her life that mattered to her. "You don't understand." Arima whirled around in front of Sela, halting the woman's angry strides. "It is my horse."

Sela's loud laugh of disbelief cut her words. "Your horse? It is a stray, escaped from some trader or horse thief. A fine Nicean stallion, Arima. You, a woman who barely knows how to ride, are not worthy of such a beast. It will go to a man, to one who can handle it. Keep your dun mare, Cousin, and be a bit more grateful for the hospitality we have shown you."

The anger in Sela's voice was real. Arima appeared to submit, a lesson she'd learned all too well in her life. But she knew the defiance she nurtured in her heart. She'd lost Opoea. She'd lost Melanion. She would not lose the horse. It was hers, and she would have it.

Arima pitied the horses singled out for slaughter the next morning; old mares, one-eyed stallions who'd seen too many fights, horses physically unfit for warfare or long riding or breeding. Herded off by men and dogs, that left eighteen good mounts in the paddock, including her Nicean stallion. He stood above the horses of the steppes like a king; taller, sleeker, more regal of bearing despite his dirty coat. Not for him the mindless milling of his companions. Aloof, he stood his ground, tossing his head, nipping at a fellow captive who got too close.

"A bad sign," a voice startled Arima's reverie. She looked down from the fence and saw the brown eyes of Ariantes smiling up at her. Tall and well muscled, he climbed the fence in two strides and leaned his arms over the top.

"The grey one bites too much. That is not good," he observed.

"He wants to be left alone, that is all," Arima retorted.

"Ah yes, and in the midst of battle, when your life depends on him, what if he decides he wants to be left alone then, too, eh?" The young man studied Arima. "You'd do well to consider some other horse."

She refused to return his gaze. Was it so obvious, her love

for this animal? Deceptions and game playing were alien to her. How should she go about getting it? Bluntness, trickery, how? "It is my horse," she intoned. "I must have it."

Ariantes laughed broadly. "Your horse, girl? Your horse? And how is that so?"

"I dreamed of it. And I saw it many times, long before you did. It is my horse, Ariantes. Mine."

At her words all expression left the young warrior's face. He turned and leaped down, the arrows in his gorytas rattling when he hit the ground. "Come," he snapped, reaching up for her arm. "You must see the mother of my grandmother and tell her about your dream."

The old woman's yurt was so encrusted with age and memories they were almost palpable. She sat on a three-legged stool by the hearth; thin, doubled over, moving as slowly as the seasons. Awkward and awed, Arima stood close to Ariantes' side.

"Grandmother," Ariantes spoke slowly, allowing the woman's one good eye to follow his lips. The other eye was wide and white and useless. "This is Arima, cousin to Sela, niece of Creusa. Her mother was Opoea." With an elbow he nudged Arima forward.

"A fine girl," the old woman chuckled, and Arima was at first unsure of who she meant—herself, or her mother? "I remember her well. Bright little child, with hair like a waterfall and the spirit of a wild bull. Should have been a man, that one." The old lady tilted her head and squinted aside at Arima. "So you want the horse, eh?"

Arima drew back in fear. How could she have known that? Ariantes had only now brought her in to see the woman.

"Oh." The woman grinned toothlessly, delighted with Arima's astonishment. "I know many things. Many things. Give me your hand."

Arima hesitated. Something about the old woman was

odd. Perhaps she was a witch, one who could read souls and cast spells.

"Give me your hand!" the grandmother ordered, as if commanding a dog. Without thinking, Arima thrust her hand at the old lady. The woman's fingers twisted, clawlike, and she turned the girl's hand, feeling it, studying it. "She is not the one," she blurted, and Ariantes looked away, embarrassed. "Her fate lies elsewhere."

Arima's doubts gave way to intrigue. "Elsewhere?" she whispered, her eyes on the hand the grandmother held.

"Elsewhere, far away," the grandmother repeated, "but tell me of your dreams."

Arima's jaw dropped. How did she know? Deception would be useless, so she told the woman everything: the horse, the hoofprints in the snow, the stallion by the riverbank. The grandmother nodded understanding. When the girl had finished, the old woman looked up at Ariantes.

"Go and fetch Creusa," she ordered. "I must speak with him."

As soon as the young warrior left the smokey tent, the old woman peered at Arima. "While the men are gone, I must warn you, dear," she hissed furtively. "All that you strive for, a man will destroy. Beware of men, girl; they will ruin you. That is your destiny. Now go." She waved a gnarled hand impatiently at her.

Arima was almost too numb to comprehend the words. But she knew that, like an enaree when a prophecy had come and gone, when it was over, it was over. Pursuing it was useless; questions would be futile.

Arima stood at the wicker gate to the horse paddock, alone but for the warrior who untied the leather closure and swung the gate open just enough to admit her. Swallowing her fear, Arima slipped past the shaven cedar gateposts and into the pen. The fence above her was ringed with faces, watching. Creusa and Ariantes, Sela and Api, all her new-found kinsmen and friends. The gate scraped shut behind her, and her heart suddenly throbbed with fear. Before her were horses, wild and dangerous. The smells of sweat and heat and manure and dust assailed her nose, and the smell of fear from the horses, almost stronger than the rest. She looked down at her hand and felt like giving up her dream; all she carried was a braided leather bridle.

The grandmother had sought this opportunity and, surprisingly, Creusa had agreed. The old woman had seen the sign of a horse's hoof in Arima's hand and knew that horses were the girl's future. If the dreamworld had directed horse and girl to be together, then no earth-dwelling Cimmerian man should interfere. Arima must have her chance.

So now she stood, trying to quell the doubts raging in her breast. Horses could sense fear, she knew; she suspected that was why war-horses did not like women. She must calm herself, and she must approach her Nicean stallion with confidence. He must know her and submit to her, as their spirits had found each other in their dreams. Keeping her hands low, Arima began to back around the edge of the paddock.

Nervous, the horses whirled and whinnied and shied away from her, milling at first, then trotting to the far side of the fence. In all the dust and confusion Arima could not see her stallion, but her heart cried out to it like a lost child to its mother. Onward she crept.

A brown stallion lunged at her, guarding the mares, his lips drawn back and his teeth snapping the air in front of her face. Arima instinctively threw up an arm to protect herself and the horse retreated. Uncertainty assailed her. Was this madness, to claim a half-wild stallion as her own because she had dreamed of a similar horse? She would only get herself killed. Yet she could not back down. Everyone was watching. The shame of it would be worse than death.

The brown horse seemed to have taken a dislike to her.

Doggedly he followed her steps, his head low, eyeing her. Calmness was best, she decided; to chase it away would only provoke a confrontation. She was halfway around the paddock when she saw him, his silver-grey head above the surrounding horses, looking at her as if he knew she was coming. Arima's heart leaped with gladness at the sight, and all the old feelings of happiness and freedom rushed back to her. She feared a human voice might startle the stallion so she whistled low, the way Bartatua had, and saw the grey ears prick forward at the sound. She whistled again and took an unthinking step forward. The brown stallion saw this as a challenge and, screaming rage, he charged.

Arima turned at the sound of pounding hooves, horror on her face. The sky was suddenly filled with a huge brown head, eyes wide, teeth bearing down on her. She could hear cries, screams from the watching tribesmen. The paddock turned into a swirling sea of panicked animals, trying to flee but having nowhere to go. Dropping the bridle, Arima scrambled for the fence.

By the gods, she gasped as her blistered fingers and booted feet scrabbled frantically at the wicker. Arms and hands extended down to help her. Desperately she reached for them when a blinding blow knocked the air from her lungs, the reaching fingers slipped away, and she sagged to the ground. What will this death be like, she wondered, closing her eyes and scraping her fingers helplessly into the pounded dust and straw.

Another scream tore the madness, louder and fiercer. The stallion, attacking her. Arima dared not look. Futilely she pulled her arms up over her head.

Ariantes had reached the top of the fence, bow and arrow drawn, and was ready to kill the brown stallion to save Arima. At a sudden fierce scream he halted. The grey Nicean horse charged through the frightened herd, fire in its eyes. What the beast did next stunned the onlookers. Rising up only partway, the grey horse jabbed out with its front hooves repeatedly, as it had been trained to do by some skilled former master. He had heard of such horses among the Persians, war-horses taught not just to carry warriors but to fight themselves, but he had never before seen one. It was an awesome sight.

The brown stallion was thrown off completely by the strange attack of the challenger and nearly lost its footing. Snorting rage, it lashed out at the grey horse, only to be met with stunning blows to the shoulder, the ribs. He knew when he was beaten. Dancing sideways and crying a parting defiance, the brown stallion retreated.

Arima heard the screams, the hooves, but not till a whiskered nose breathed against her cheek did she dare to look. Above her the milky blue sky spread out, and circled around were the figures of people, peering down. And in her face, close and warm, the vibrant grey mass of a horse head.

Her horse.

She sat up and reached out a tentative hand to it. The stallion did not shy away. It waited patiently for her touch, a touch so similar to one it had known long ago, of a Persian horsewoman who had loved it, trained it, and lost it. So long wandering, alone and bewildered, the great horse, at Arima's touch, bonded to her, as if what it had lost had finally been regained.

Arima shakily pulled herself to her feet, catching her breath against the pain in her bruised back. The stallion stood patiently while she began to rub his broad cheek and pick burrs from his mane, and she found tears filling her eyes. Can it be that dreams do come true? That the great grey horse lived, and was hers?

Ariantes sprang to the ground beside her, his bow still in hand. "Come," he touched her shoulder. Arima turned at the interruption, and the warrior saw past her, to the head of the great Persian horse. Strange, he thought, looking into the creature's liquid eye; now that Arima has claimed him, he seems completely tame. Perhaps he was, as she said, waiting for her.

"We must go," he urged the girl, taking the bridle from the ground and putting it on the stallion. "You can begin to teach him now, to be like a Cimmerian horse." He looked up at Creusa, and the old man's face broke into a grin.

"Yes," he called down, "like the horse of a Cimmerian warrior! Lead it out, Arima!"

She had not understood, but now she did. Horses of steppe warriors were not tugged about like sheep. In herds, they were gently led from behind, with only an occasional light switch on the rump to guide them. But for a warrior's individual mount, even this was not done. Stepping away from Ariantes, she held out a hand and whistled low to the stallion. His ears pricked and he came toward her a few paces. She spoke encouraging words and whistled again, urging it toward the gate. Ariantes stepped back, crossed his arms over his chest, and nodded. The grandmother was right; Arima was a natural horsewoman.

"I cannot get her off the beast," Sela complained to Creusa over their evening meal. "She rides, she shoots, as if she were born to it. And rather than Api teaching her, as you directed, Ariantes has appointed himself to the task."

The old king chewed a piece of tough horse meat and grunted. "The old grandmother says she is born to it. That it is her fate. Not husbands and babies, but horses. Let her be, Sela. Could it be that you are jealous of her horse, and the attentions Ariantes pays to her? She must learn. It may be that one day soon she will have a chance to test these skills she practices so well."

Sela sat cross-legged on a carpet near the fire, and like the other warriors gathered for the meal her curiosity roused at Creusa's veiled hint of something afoot.

"Does this chance you speak of have anything to do with the Scoloti warriors who visited yesterday?" Api asked. The woman was holding one of the chief's favorite hunting falcons, feeding it bits of raw meat. When the three grim warriors had ridden into camp, like everyone else she assumed they were looking for Arima. She had been glad the girl was out riding her new stallion. The men disappeared into the yurt of Creusa and remained there till nightfall. Spurning an offer of a meal and a place to sleep, they left as abruptly as they came, riding back to their people by starlight.

"It has," said the old king. He swallowed the meat and downed a mouthful of kumiss, then looked around the campfire. Except for Arima and Ariantes, all his chief warriors and elder nobles were there, as well as his own ranking kin. It was as good a time as any to tell them.

"The warriors were from the king of the Royal Scoloti, the Paralatae," he said loudly, the authority in his voice attracting the attention of the assembled warriors. Lowering drinking horns and skull cups, they waited. "He speaks for all of the Scoloti tribes. They told us what we already knew." He paused while a slave boy cut another chunk of boiled horse meat and served it to him.

"The Persians march to Greece," Creusa continued, "but along the way they have set their covetous eyes on the rich lands and gold of the Scoloti. It is a small detour for them. Their Great King plans to conquer them by midsummer and be into Greece before autumn." The old man chuckled knowingly. "I suspect the task will not be so easy as they imagine."

As one the warriors exhaled and cast uneasy glances at each other. A royal cousin, a young man with a reworked Greek helmet at his side, asked the question all of them were wondering. "But what has that to do with us?" he snapped, leaning forward. "We are not Scoloti. Our lands are small;

we are not in the line of Persian march. We are as much a friend of the Persians as we are of the Scoloti—maybe more so. Why did the three Scoloti visit us?"

"They seek our help." Creusa roamed his dark eyes around the gathering. "They feel that if we all unite, we will be sure to defeat the Persians."

Voices of dissent rose. "But we have no quarrel with the Persians!" Api spat. "The Scoloti are fools, to think we will bring warfare down on ourselves, just to aid them!"

Agreement with her words seemed unanimous. Creusa smiled, pleased. In the fading light his skin looked like aged leather, but the anger lighting his eyes was plain. "That is just what I told them. Their only reply was bitter silence."

The voices died away, and the warriors shifted uncomfortably. Sela put down her wooden platter and wiped her greasy fingers against her leather boots. Looking to the left, she caught her father's hardened gaze. "And what of Arima?" she said tightly. Creusa knew what she meant.

"Go and speak with her," he directed. "Tell her what is in the wind. Let her decide for herself what she will do—stay with us, or return and fight for her people."

Arima sat on a high bluff overlooking the river, watching tendrils of evening mist gather among the treetops. The Nicean stallion grazed behind her, as content with its life as an animal could be. Sela saw them from a distance, as still as a wood carving, and hated to intrude on so peaceful a scene.

"Number One!" she called out, slowly riding her red gelding to Arima's side. The girl looked up, startled from her reverie. "We must talk." Sela slid to the ground, looking around for Ariantes. She was surprised that he was not there. "And then you'd better get back to camp for some food while there is still some to be had." Without waiting for an invitation, Sela folded her legs beneath her and settled on the grass beside her cousin. Arima returned her gaze to the gathering fog and shadows around the tall birches below. A flock of crows flew over, raucously settling into the trees for the night.

"Ariantes is not here?" Sela asked in a friendly tone. Arima shrugged.

"He was, but he left," she answered. "One of his father's horses has been sick."

Sela nodded silent understanding. She decided to get right to the matter at hand. "My father says he received an envoy two days ago," the woman began.

"I know. Ariantes told me of it," Arima interrupted. Sela studied her cousin's profile against the horizon. Her freedom had done her well; her pale alabaster skin now glowed golden, her cheeks bloomed with good health, and her deep blue eyes shone even brighter against her new complexion.

"You heard of the Scoloti envoy?" Sela prodded. Arima had become a girl of few words, as if part of herself was always off in another place.

"Yes," Arima replied, not shifting her gaze. "From their descriptions, I can even guess who they were. Two are distant kinsmen, one with a scar across his chin. They both are known for their fine speaking. The third is a younger brother of Idanthyrsus, King of the Royal Scoloti, though I do not know his name." Her voice died away, and she drew a deep, weary breath.

"But do you know why they came here?" Sela said.

Arima shrugged and looked down. "Looking for me? Why else? Father went to Idanthyrsus himself to get help in finding me."

Sela grinned and wrapped an affectionate arm around Arima's shoulders. "Oh, Number One, be at ease about that. Your name was never mentioned. They came on business, concerning the Persians." She felt Arima's body grow tense in her embrace.

"What about them?" Arima hissed, turning to look at Sela. To her, the very name was an abomination, and anything to do with them meant trouble. The spying of Catoris, the death of her mother, the loss of Melanion—all were linked to that hated name.

"They wanted us to join with them and other tribes of the steppes, to resist a coming invasion by the Persians."

"I heard of it," Arima said bitterly. "They had spies in our tribe."

"Ah, then you know their Great King wishes to conquer the Scoloti and their lands and herds and gold."

Arima nodded.

"And that their march has already begun?"

Arima drew back and stared into Sela's grey almond eyes. So soon? Yes, she had known of the invasion, but it had been a distant thing. Now? Tears filled her eyes, against her wishes. "Why do you tell me this, Sela?" she asked. In the dusk her cousin's face looked tired, and she tightened her embrace of Arima.

"Because Creusa refused to aid them," Sela said. "Many tribes have also refused. Relations between my people and yours have often been bad; it is the luck of it that now, when the Persians come, my father is still angry over the death of his sister Opoea. He blames Scylas for that. We have no quarrel with the Persians. It is not us they hope to conquer. We will not fight them, Arima. Now you must decide what to do."

Arima looked down, weariness clinging to her shoulders. The freshness and mystery of the evening had fled, leaving behind it only the cold dark foreboding of a tomb. "What can I do?" she muttered. "They are my people, but if I return I will be executed or wed to Bartatua. They will not let me remain as I now am. My heart will suffer for them, and I will pray to our war god for their victory. But . . . I cannot return to them." She looked up, and tears were trickling down her cheeks. "Blood is strong, Sela," she said fiercely. "To sit by while your people struggle and die is a terrible burden to bear. But I will not go back to them, to

257

their slavery. The gods may curse me for it, but I cannot."
She wiped angrily at the tears with the back of one hand and
returned her gaze to the birch trees. Sela straightened.

"I understand, Arima." She nodded. "Don't forget, you
are half Cimmerian as well. Stay with us here; it will be best
that way."

"I will never see how Mother did it, either," Arima
whispered.

"Did what?"

"Survived such a transformation, from free Cimmerian to
enslaved Scoloti wife. It is as if a butterfly were forced to
return to the cocoon." Arima's voice was low and sad. Sela
sat in silence, not knowing what to say, until the evening had
gathered thick around them. A small spotted owl hooted
somewhere near the river bottom.

"Come." Sela roused and stretched out her legs to stand.
"The sun is nearly down. Let's return for some food.
Ariantes says you have been practicing your bow from
horseback." She thought the talk of horses and weapons
would cheer the girl, but Arima's sad expression never
changed. Sela settled back to her cousin's side. "Arima,
what is bothering you?" she asked. The girl inhaled deeply
and looked off down the embankment.

"Sela, what do you know of love?" she said tentatively.

"Love?" Sela slumped back on one elbow. "What does
anyone know of love? It comes, it goes, and no one can
capture or control it."

"Warm one minute, demanding the next," Arima said
quietly. "Giving you a headache or gladdening your heart.
As unpredictable as an infant. When it cries, you must
answer; when you beg it to respond, it chooses not to. It lives
by its own whim; it disrupts your life. Perhaps that is why
the Greeks call it Cupid and portray it as a baby. And I
suppose," she added as an afterthought, "that while all
babies may look alike, a mother responds to and wants only

258

her own special child." She looked at her cousin, and her young face was drawn with some unspoken strain.

"Ariantes wants me," Arima blurted. "He tries to control himself but many times he begins to teach me things, warrior's things, and then he tries to make me submit to him."

"Why don't you?" Sela asked, jealous but puzzled. "He is a handsome warrior, intelligent and strong. Everyone knows he likes you. Let him take you, Arima; one day he could be your husband!"

The girl shook her head emphatically. "I have tried, Sela, but I just can't. I try to force myself, to abandon myself to him. We kiss, and I feel nothing. Once he grew more insistent, and I went along. He began to undress me, and I still felt nothing."

"Nothing?" Sela sat up, incredulous. She could well imagine herself in Ariantes' powerful arms, and what she would be feeling at the time. Arima shook her head sadly.

"I wanted to, but I could not love another. I pushed him from me, got on my horse, and rode away."

Sela knew she was speaking of someone in particular. Just to be talking of him, remembering him, made Arima's voice soften and her eyes gleam with love. "Who is he?" She seized the girl's hand eagerly. "Someone in our tribe? A Scoloti? A trader?"

A slight smile etched Arima's mouth and then faded. "He is no one," she said bitterly. "He was here, and now he is gone. He is no one."

"No one? Arima, don't talk nonsense! How could no one put such light in your eyes? He must be a trader. A foreigner?"

"He is a Greek."

Sela's heart chilled at the word. A Greek! "But how did you come to know a Greek, Arima?" she pressed, truly curious.

"He came to the camp of Scylas. He was a goldsmith."

Sela felt as if her heart had withered within her. Surely there must be many Greek goldsmiths wandering the land! How many nights had she remembered their parting, outside the gates of Olbia, and her sad, grateful embrace for the man who had saved her from a terrible fate. And how she had admitted it only to herself, that small bit of love that had grown for him during their times together. What manner of man was this Greek if her cousin, too, had succumbed to his charms? Melanion, slayer of women's hearts.

"What happened to him?" Sela asked gently, knowing how love could hurt. Suffering was plain all over Arima's face, and loss, and the bitterness of sweet memories such as any woman could understand and feel sympathy for. Arima merely shook her head.

"He is gone," she said simply, finally. "But I know we will be together again. I know he is well, and that somehow I will find him in this vast world, or he will find me." A sad defiance shone in her eyes, and Sela's heart moved in pity.

"Arima," she said, smiling kindly, "sometimes it is best to let the past die. It is over. Look to the future. Ariantes is here, he cares for you. Loyalty is an admirable thing, but give yourself a chance with another man. Perhaps in Ariantes' arms you will forget this man, what was his name?"

"Melanion."

The conversation stuck in Sela's throat. The same Greek goldsmith! And poor Arima, sheltered and innocent, could not know what manner of man he was. Nice and kind and decent, true, but never the type to stay for long with one woman. For him, there would always be more. More women, more wine, more adventure.

"Don't waste yourself on him, Arima," she forced the words out. "Find another and get on with your life. It will hurt, but you will heal. One day you will remember this

Greek and laugh; you will never understand what you saw in him. Few things are funnier than looking back on a love that has died."

Arima angrily pulled her hand free of Sela's grasp. "I will not," she snapped. "My life began when I met him. Without him I am half a person, an empty shell. I will never give him up."

Sela did not argue. She knew the futility of it. Standing, she whistled for her red gelding and returned to camp.

BOOK 5

WIND CHILD

I have never been afraid of defeat by the Scythians;
The danger is that we should fail to find them.
—*King Darius the Great of Persia*

WHEN IDANTHYRSUS, KING OF THE ROYAL SCOLOTI, SUM-
moned, one did not refuse to answer. One did not even delay
a response. This was custom, it was law, and not even crusty
old Scylas dared to defy it.

He had been without a woman for many days, his
daughter was still missing, his mood was sour to begin with,
and now this. The Royal messenger stood inside the yurt of
Scylas, shifting impatiently from foot to foot, waiting for an
answer. Scylas looked at him with a mixture of scorn and
envy. The man's tunic was of a brilliant saffron color,
liberally spangled with gold ornaments. A large gold earring
of Egyptian design hung from one ear. His boots were of fine
black calfskin; altogether an admirable figure. One lone
brown scalp, reddened from age and exposure to the ele-
ments, dangled at his right hip.

"Twenty, is it?" Scylas reconfirmed what the man had just
said. The messenger nodded curtly. Scylas knew by law and

custom he should offer the man hospitality, but he decided against it. He wanted the man gone, and as soon as possible. Twenty of his best warriors, archers and spearmen and himself as well? To go and fight the Persian armies, as he'd feared. Idanthyrsus had tried to summon help—the Cimmerians, the Tauri, the Neuri and Sauromatians, and others. Out of all the steppe tribes, only the Sauromatians, the powerful Budini and their allies, the Geloni, had responded with offers of aid. Scylas grunted and glanced at Bartatua and Oricus. They had been waiting for it to come to this.

"Very well." The old chief looked into the messenger's eyes as calmly as he could. "Twenty it will be. When are we to arrive?"

"Within six days. Any who exceed that time will be sacrificed to the God of War. Such untrustworthy men must not go into battle. The king has said it."

"Don't question the trustworthiness of the Auchatae," Scylas snapped. "When do we fight?"

"The seventh day. The enemy is nearing our lands. The great wooden city of the Budini has been evacuated and will soon be destroyed by the Persians if their present line of march continues. We must act at once if we are to defeat them."

"And what is the plan of Idanthyrsus?" Bartatua narrowed his eyes at the man. He wondered how such an overdressed warrior would measure up in battle. The dangling scalp attested to his prowess, but fighting was for hard men.

"It will be told to all of you when you have assembled. Till then, only the king and his closest advisors know it. And one other thing."

The Auchatae warriors looked at the man expectantly.

"The king says to pack up your women, your tents and wagons and herds, and all else you value, and send them north, away from the Persian advance."

Scylas's jaw clenched and veins bulged at his forehead. Six days to prepare not only himself and his warriors and their mounts, but the families and all their goods as well? It was unheard of! There would scarcely be time to sleep!

"It will be done," he muttered angrily. The Royal messenger turned. It was plain he'd be receiving no kumiss or food or a woman slave from this petty chieftain. He'd just as well be on his way, and sleep under the stars this night.

It was Bartatua who stepped before Scylas, fuming, after the man departed. "Six days!" he said and spat to the carpeted floor. "To take our best warriors, I must call back the six who still hunt for Arima. With the camp breaking up and the women leaving, all hope of finding her will be gone." He fingered his inlaid knife handle in an instinctive motion and glared at Scylas. "Can't you send other men? The tracker is needed to find her trail where we lost it at the river. With him sent to war, how can we continue?"

"Accept it, Bartatua," the chief muttered. "That is the hardest lesson a good warrior must learn—when he can do no more, and his best efforts have failed, and he must retreat. Arima is gone. Accept it."

Bartatua raged across the yurt, pressing his men back to the walls like a storm dividing the grasses. "I will not!" he shouted. "She could not vanish from the earth. She is out there somewhere, and she will be found. I will not be made a fool of by some girl with no brains and less self-discipline. She is a poor example of a Scoloti woman and she will not get off so easily."

"Enough!" Scylas lurched to his feet. "She is a fool, and too headstrong, but she is my daughter. I say she is gone. Leave her to her fate. Recall your men, Bartatua, or I'll have Oricus made my chief warrior and your head turned into my drinking cup."

The assembled warriors watched the dark defiant face of Bartatua, the stolid grey storm of Scylas. The chief warrior glared at the old man, his fingers flexing rage around his knife handle.

"I will send for them," he muttered, and strode from the tent.

Twenty picked warriors made a sizeable assemblage, with a slave each and five spare war-horses per man. Their supplies were few; knives, daggers, and gorytas, and for those adept with them, long iron-tipped spears. In their saddle bags the men carried yoghurt and millet and dried meat strips, and a leather bag of kumiss to drink. That was ample supply for a long, hurried ride. When their pace slowed there would always be fresh game, wild greens, and clean stream water to drink. Speed and mobility were what made the Scoloti warrior a success, and for this he had learned to travel light.

For four days Scylas and his men rode, eating and sleeping astride their mounts, exchanging horses when one became tired and needed to rest and feed. They knew they were nearing the great camp of the Royal Scoloti when a band of warriors stopped them. The men were all as lavishly attired as the king's messenger had been. Gold spangled from tunics and the tops of boots; gold earrings glinted next to bearded cheeks. Their cloaks were of the finest spotted cat or sable, and dyed horsehair tassles and dried human scalps dangled from their horses' elaborate felt fittings.

"Scylas, chief of the Auchatae tribe," Bartatua leaned forward on his horse and announced to the glaring men. His manner was easy, the reins slack in one hand, refusing to be awed by them.

The warriors studied the arrivals in silence, face by face, returning several times to the impassive countenance of the old chief. He stared off to the far horizon, his long grey hair held down by the riding cap hanging behind his neck. "What is your mission here?" the Paralatae guard growled at Scylas. It was not the place of a chief to address another chief's warrior. Scylas cut his eyes menacingly to the man, spat once on the ground, and returned his gaze to the horizon.

The Paralatae guard seemed satisfied. The old man was indeed a chief, no Persian imposter. He pulled his horse around and spoke to the dark-haired chief warrior of the Auchatae. "Come," he announced, "we will lead you to our camp."

Each Scoloti tribe had been assigned its own area, surrounding the vast central settlement of the Royal Scyth like piglets around a sow. Bartatua thought he had never seen such splendor, and his blood raced with the excitement he always felt at the start of a new adventure. He and his men rode through the fringes of the camp of the Catiari Scyth, watching their warriors groom the fine red war geldings they were famous for. At the first clearing he wondered if they were to stop, but it was set aside for the Traspies, who had not yet arrived. They were the tallest of the Scoloti, and many had hair the color of autumn leaves; he was anxious to see them. They skirted the central settlement of the Paralatae, the Royal Scyth, who were descended from Colaxais, chief son of their first divine king. Envy mixed with scorn at the sight of their wealth. Yurts dazzled with gold ornaments flashing in the sun. Brightly painted wagons, three times the number the Auchatae possessed, lined the far side of a spacious sheepfold. It seemed every man of the tribe, high or low, wore an abundance of gold neck-chains and earrings and bracelets over brightly dyed trousers and tunics. Even their soft leather boots sported gold trinkets. Bartatua had never seen such a wealth of gold and furs and lavish weapons, but their horses, ah, their horses!

All were large, and part Persian by the looks of them. After all, the Scoloti had ruled the Medes of the southlands for twenty-eight years, ample time for their large, powerful horses to be interbred with the Scoloti war-horses until they became a new breed in themselves. The coloring, too, had changed, from the reds and browns and dead-grass coats of the Scyth horse to fine greys, a cream-colored mare nearly the shade of new gold, white horses with a sheen of grey smoke over them, even a few solid black geldings like the Persian horse of Scylas. It was enough to feed a man's dreams for a lifetime. Somehow, he must find time to negotiate for the mating of one of these stallions with a mare from his herd, but what did he have of value to pay for the seed of so splendid an animal?

The procession drew to a halt on the far side of camp, on a rise of ground that gave a good view of the whole encampment, a generous-seeming gesture until Bartatua noted that the highest point of land was occupied by an outpost of Paralatae guards. In their seemingly privileged position, the Auchatae men were right under their noses. Any move they made would be easily observed. It must be a bad situation indeed with the Persian invasion, for the Paralatae not even to trust their own kinsmen.

Camp was quickly set up, the horses staked, and their meager baggage piled round a campfire fed by the bones of butchered animals. The Auchatae warriors stretched tired muscles, listened to two of their companions play merry tunes on reed flutes, and awaited the evening meal.

An altar to the Scyth war god was set up outside the great camp. Throughout the night slaves gathered brush and piled it in a great heap that by dawn stood twice the height of a man and was many arm-spans wide. With the first rays of morning sun, a few senior enarees purified the area around it, marching slow circles as they burned incense and chanted their rituals. By the time day arrived, hundreds of warriors were assembled, sleepy-eyed and hungry for their morning meal. But food must wait, they knew; the final ritual before battle must be performed, the sacrifice of the last Scoloti to arrive.

Bartatua milled about with his men, wondering who the unfortunates would be. When they were led out at a summons from the enarees, he was not too surprised; three old men, plainly clothed and bound, heads of families of the Catiari, and six of their warriors. He knew their lands had suffered much flooding recently. It was likely that some of their men should have been delayed in their trip to Idanthyrsus's camp. Well, he mused, it was the war god's will; he had chosen these to die.

The young warriors would be a loss, Bartatua observed. They were vigorous and well muscled, an asset in the coming battles. The victims said nothing, did nothing. They knew their fate was determined. When an enaree carried out a great and ancient iron sword, reverently, with both hands, and was helped up a makeshift ladder to the top of the brush pile, one of the older men seemed to sway with sudden fear. But he righted himself in manly fashion, and stared blankly ahead while the enaree on the ladder fastened the sacred sword, handle down and tip skyward, atop the brush pile. Such was the altar to the Scoloti war god, a fitting altar for a wandering people. Nothing fancier was needed.

Without ceremony the nine bound men were led forward and made to kneel. Obediently they lowered their heads as their wool tunics were torn down on their shoulders. The chief warrior of King Idanthyrsus, decked in his finest gold ornaments, drew his sword and stepped forward. The warrior knew he must perform the sacrifice swiftly and flawlessly; if anything went wrong, it would be a bad omen for the coming war. With an abrupt blow the youngest man's head thudded to the ground and his body fell forward. The warrior stepped behind the next victim. And the next. Bartatua paid little attention, the falling bodies only dimly sounding in his ears. He'd seen it enough times, before nearly every battle he'd fought in. One day, he knew, the victim could be him. A horse pulls up lame, a stream is in flood—it was the will of the war god, King Idanthyrsus, and the enarees. The last men always died.

Bartatua's eyes roamed around the faces of the assembled men. Surely someone would want to dicker over horses, or a stud fee. He'd have to start inquiring as soon as the sacrifice was over. The thought had scarcely left his mind when a collective sigh rustled the gathering, and he looked to the foot of the altar. The victims all lay dead, cleanly so. Bartatua grinned and fingered his beard. The omens for the great Persian war were good.

The Paralatae king was young; too young, Bartatua thought, eyeing him through the smoke of a roaring campfire over which several dismembered cattle boiled in the skin of their own hides. He must be not much over twenty years, but, despite his youth, his face held a hardness that came only from experience. Bartatua knew he had been king for six years; a lad that young does not succeed his father and keep his title without cunning and hardness of character.

All the Scoloti were gathered in the Paralatae camp, sitting cross-legged on sheepskin mats and feasting on fresh meats, gruel, and kumiss and Greek wine in great abundance. The noise of their voices, boasting and laughing and bargaining for horses, nearly drowned out the great campfire over which their meal cooked. They were the prime of Scyth manhood, their most skilled warriors, young and vigorous and eager to fight, to win their war trophies, scalps and skulls, horses and gold.

When the boiled cattle had been eaten and the dripping hides removed, when the men lounged contentedly around him, their bellies full and their spirits at ease, Idanthyrsus the Royal King gave a nod to his chief warrior. The man stood, clanking a spear loudly against his oak and leather shield to get everyone's attention. The warriors shifted, sat up, leaned almost as one toward their chief king. Idanthyrsus remained seated and spoke conversationally, as if meeting with kinsmen in his yurt.

"Persian spies are everywhere," he launched into his subject. "Be warned that anyone acting at all suspiciously will be put to death at once, without trial or defense or appeal to the enarees. They have agreed to this." He glanced to his left, to his own chief enaree. The roughly dressed old man gave a slow nod of assent. The gathered warriors grew more wary. It seemed every word, every bit of information about this Persian invasion was more alarming than the last.

"We face a crisis," the king continued. Feed them all his news like he fed them all his food, and then let each warrior digest it as he will. "Of all our neighboring tribes, only the Sauromatians, the Budini, and the Geloni will join us to fight the Persians. Count the others who have refused to help us. To the south the Tauri by the sea, and the Cimmerians; north the Agathynsi, the Neuri, the black-cloaked Melanchlaeni and the Androphagi, who eat the flesh of men. Many of these we once called friend. Others we have helped, when times demanded it. Now we ask for aid, like brothers, and silence is their reply."

The warriors muttered darkly about such a foul betrayal. Tribes often fought with one another; it had been that way since the time of the gods. Except for the warfare between the Scoloti and the Cimmerians long ago, it was never serious: a little bloodshed, stolen livestock and women, a few new slaves. But whenever strangers threatened from the outside world, without fail the steppe tribes rode together. What were they to make of such cowardice, such deception as this?

"Tonight," Idanthyrsus went on, "each chief is to send for the rest of his able-bodied warriors. My Chief Warrior Scopasis will lead them and the Sauromatians. As for you, the best of the Scoloti fighters, you will be under my command. We will fight with the Budini and the Geloni. Listen well, for it has already been decided by myself and the kings of these tribes."

Idanthyrsus paused, for when he spoke a thing he only spoke it once; every man must hear his words now.

"We leave at dawn. Already the Persian army, as numberless as a plague of locusts, is two days' march over the river and into our territories. We must race out to meet them."

Old Scylas stood up, crusty and brusque and used to doing as he pleased. Idanthyrsus paused, humoring him.

"But I've heard it said the army of the Persian king numbers many times our own," Scylas growled. "If that is so, it makes no sense to divide our forces. Even if we were all united, we would still be greatly outnumbered by them."

The Royal King saw many men nod agreement with the old chief. Idanthyrsus looked at Scylas and smiled. "Let me ask you a question, my friend," the king addressed him. "When the wolf hunts, what is his easiest prey?"

"Those encumbered in some way . . ." The old man stopped and suddenly grinned then sat down on his wool mat, satisfied. Bartatua, too, understood. What man among them didn't? When the wolf hunted, the swift, young, vigorous pack members prowled. And the easiest prey? Those encumbered, as Scylas said. The mare, heavy with foal. The old boar, held back by disease. A great wild oxen, crippled by a winter's fall. Always it would be this way; the swift attack the sluggards.

And an army of so many men, with wagons and supplies and followers, must be very sluggish, indeed.

Scoloti horsemen saw the Persians on the third day after they had crossed the great river Ister on a bridge of boats. Bartatua thought their army was so vast that its end must still be at the river while its head was before him. The men waited in silence, watching like great striped cats as their prey spread slowly along the horizon. The wind brought to them the distant sounds of rumbling wagon wheels and plodding hooves, like a low summer thunder, and the flash of metal in sunlight carried to them a warning of weapons, and gold. Idanthyrsus was brief. "Now!" he said, and his party of warriors pounded toward the Persians.

The Persian cavalrymen raced out to meet the nomads; they thundered forward in scaled armor on powerful horses, carrying large bows, short swords, and heavy battle-axes. Behind them rattled chariots pulled by four horses, with cutting scythes on the wheels mowing down the steppe grasses as they spun. Idanthyrsus led his men to within bow shot of the invaders. A whine cut the air and an arrow landed beside Bartatua. He whirled his horse aside with his knees. The black gelding's nostrils were flaring, and his eyes gleamed excitement. He knew what to do, as he and his master, through long years of practice, had become one. He knew the smells of his own herd, his own people. These Persians, man and beast alike, were alien. Blood racing, the horse cut in toward the advancing mob and wheeled at a slight touch from Bartatua. The warrior let fly and a Thracian cavalryman fell to the ground, an arrow through his throat.

Turning, the army of Idanthyrsus raced away, pursued by jolting Persian chariots and winded Persian war-horses. The Scoloti and their allies vanished ghostlike over the horizon and the weary invaders returned to their waiting column.

"They seem to have escaped us," Megaphernes groused over a tasty meal of fresh-caught wild duck in a berry sauce, crusty bread, and good ale. His fellow companions grunted agreement. For days they had followed the small Scyth army, over empty grasslands and across another wide river and into a forested land where Darius burned a great abandoned city of wood and destroyed crops and home-steads. On the banks of another river the king halted and ordered a line of forts to be built. This was half done when the Scyth they had been pursuing turned back and disappeared. Heartened by their retreat, Darius abandoned his forts and took off in pursuit, marching toward the west. Megaphernes could not believe what the king believed, that the war was over so simply. He'd seen the Scythians dicker and trade, and he knew they were craftier than that. Still, tonight's camp was comfortable and secure, the food was good. He'd wait and see what the morrow brought before he did too much worrying about it. Perhaps Darius had been right. Perhaps the Scythian War was already over.

Idanthyrsus emptied his gilded skull cup of wine and leaned forward toward the chiefs and captains of his men. In the darkness, by the low campfire, their bearded faces were barely visible. Only the gold of their earrings glinted as they moved.

"Now, a new tactic," the king said, his teeth white in the night. The men listened eagerly. This battle had been more exhilarating than most. Racing, eluding, outsmarting like cunning foxes, always a day ahead of the ponderous Great Army of Persia. It was a joy to be here, to take part in the humiliation of the mighty Persian king.

"We are now out of the forested lands of the Budini and Geloni and back on our own steppes. The army of Scopasis is a day away. Tomorrow we will join them, and as we lead the Persians through our lands we will leave them nothing on which to survive. We will burn the fields and pastures and poison the wells. They are so far into enemy territory that it will do them grave harm to have no food or water for themselves and their livestock. Even a retreat will be difficult."

The warriors laughed low into the night wind and their eyes sparked eagerness at the plan.

All night the encamped Persians smelled smoke, and on the horizon saw a low orange glow reflecting beneath thick clouds. They could only guess at what it was. Grass fires were common on the plains. Their wagons were drawn in and an extra guard was put on the tent of Darius. The men on duty fingered their spears nervously, watching the orange glow rise and fall, shrink and spread in the black night. The nomads were as unpredictable as wild animals—was this some strange plot of theirs? No one knew what to expect next.

Dawn brought answers soon enough. A pack of Scyth warriors, with some of their tall, red-haired allies whooping wildly, thundered down on the tense Persian camp like stampeding cattle. The chariots were ready, the cavalrymen were waiting. Everyone had slept fully armed, anticipating some morning trick. The Persians and their allies raced out to meet the nomads, the Scythians wheeled and fired a few parting shots over the rumps of their horses, and the enraged Persians swept after them.

Darius remained behind, standing in his chariot, his four white horses shifting restlessly, their backs streaked with steppe dirt and fine ash. He fingered his curled beard absently, but his eyes were not on the pursuit by his men. The Great King had ridden to the edge of camp, and he shook his head in dismay. Horizon to horizon, the land was black and burned, the grass they'd need for their return trip totally destroyed. This action by the Scyth left him little choice. He'd have to go on, deeper into their territory, and defeat them quickly in order to have food for his army and fodder for his horses, and to stop their depredations. Turning, he gave his steward the order to march.

Idanthyrsus reclined wearily against his padded saddle, his eyes closed, the gilded skull cup resting on his stomach. His clothes were grimy and stank, his long hair and beard were stiff with sweat. Ten days now he had led the Persians on, deeper and deeper into Scoloti lands, burning pastures and poisoning wells as they went, and still the fools kept following him. Like a chase for a stag that has gone on too long, his men wearied of the same tired game. Something new must spark their interest until the Persian king decided to give up the hunt.

With a soft sound of crushing grass two tall Budini guards emerged from the darkness, leading three Persians, their arms bound behind them at the elbow. A stir circled the tiny campfire, and the weary men roused from their exhausted drowsiness. Idanthyrsus stood and handed the skull cup to his groom. "What is this?" he asked the Budini.

"Messengers." One of the men spoke the Scoloti word carefully.

"Messengers?" Idanthyrsus played on. It was plain who had sent them. One was elderly, the other two younger, but they all wore the same unmistakable Persian greatcoat, brightly dyed and embroidered, and their curled hair and beards and lightly reddened cheeks gave them the look of hairy women. "Who sent you?" Idanthyrsus addressed the eldest of the three men. The old man understood their tongue, for he stood erect and unfrightened and answered calmly.

"The King of Kings, Great King of the Persians, the Assyrians, the Medes, the—"

Idanthyrsus cut the man's litany off irritably, withdrawing the long knife at his thigh and pressing the point into the soft, wrinkled skin near the man's right eye. "The name," he growled. "Say the name."

The two younger envoys tried to pull away from the bloody spectacle they thought they were about to witness, but the shackles binding their arms held them fast. "Darius," the old man said, closing his eye in a futile attempt to protect it from the knife point.

"And your message?" Idanthyrsus pressed the point tighter into the flesh below the man's eye. The envoy swallowed hard and muttered the memorized words over the dryness of his tongue.

"The king asks why you keep flying before him? Why you

do not stand and fight or . . ." He seemed reluctant to utter the last words.

"Or what?" Idanthyrsus's knife point broke the skin and the man flinched at the pain. Blood spilled in a slow trickle down his pale cheek and into the oily curls of his beard.

"Or surrender to him." The words came out as fearful as a child's. The old man calculated his life was finished. Instead, the Scyth king removed the knife and with a loud laugh walked away. The shadowy warriors sitting around the firelight chuckled low at the idea.

"Feed them," the king snapped. "Tomorrow you shall return with my answer."

Darius could not believe the insolence of these nomads. In good faith he'd sent an envoy, offered them terms of surrender, and this was their answer?

He stopped pacing the carpeted floor of his tent and glared at the blanched face of the old man, and the bloody hole where his right eye had been. "Cover it, man!" he snapped. The oozing wound turned his stomach, and he did not want to lose his morning meal. The envoy seemed ready to swoon from pain and the loss of blood, and a servant stepped forward, draping a white linen towel over half the man's head.

One of his messengers half-blinded, and the other two? "Beheaded." Darius fumed. The old man placed his fingertips respectfully to his lips and bowed as low as he dared without fainting.

"Yes, Lord. It is their custom to keep the severed heads of their enemies." How he wished this interview would be at an end, so he could go and visit a physician! The gaudiness of the Royal Tent, the cloying reek of incense, the smothering carpeted silence, all reeled in his pounding head.

"And their reply?" Darius whirled suddenly and stood as stolid as a great Assyrian bull, his face showing no pity or concern for his mutilated messenger.

"A simple one, Lord." The man bowed his head again. "To you, the Scyth king said, 'Go weep.'"

Megaphernes and the other noblemen were offered some relief, a relief only too welcome after the endless days of chasing Scyth ghosts across the grasslands. A small herd of steppe antelope had been spotted, displaced by the burned forage Idanthyrsus had left behind him. To the weary Persians they were a happy sight: food! With his warriors on constant duty, Darius allowed his nobles the pleasure of the hunt. Beaters and footmen were sent to surround the wandering herd, and the king hoped to have as much fresh meat as possible by nightfall.

Megaphernes breathed deeply and trotted his horse toward the haze of dust and ash obscuring the horizon. After so many days of hunger and nights of fear, the wide, open freedom of a hunt was balm to his soul. He caught his cousin's eye, several paces away, and they grinned at each other. With a companionable wave Artapas held his bow high and galloped away, eager to be first at the hunt. Megaphernes put heel to his horse and followed.

The tiny antelope were barely visible beneath the dust cloud, and Megaphernes heard them before he saw them, thousands of small hooves pounding the hard soil as they raced toward him. His first glimpse of the creatures was disappointing. Tiny compared to the graceful antelope of Persia or Egypt, they were stocky in build, drab, with long faces, and oddly humped noses. Not much of a trophy, he mused as he fitted an arrow to his bow. It will take many of these to feed the great army of Darius. Even their speed could not match their desert kin; it was almost too easy, Megaphernes thought as he felled one. Well, it is food we need, and not trophies. In minutes he had killed eight.

Half the herd was down when the survivors suddenly wheeled, seeking an escape. They rushed toward Megaphernes and his companions, throwing the Persian horses into a panic. Lithe, long-legged antelope they were used to, but not this small, determined army of brown creatures bearing down on them. Megaphernes' stallion reared and turned, crying shrilly, and the nobleman fought to control it. The antelope were everywhere, surrounding him like a surging tide, and his horse leaped crazily to avoid them. Through the din he could hear other horses, also terrified. He had nearly calmed his stallion when a knot of eager hunters raced in on the rear of the fleeing herd. Their bows were drawn, their arrows ready. The steppe antelope thinned, straggled out, and were gone, galloping away to freedom. Megaphernes turned his panting horse just as a hunter raised his bow. He heard the bowstring, saw the arrow, but could not avoid it. It hit him in the side, exploding in a blaze of pain, and Megaphernes fell forward onto his horse's neck, gasping numbly, trying to call out his cousin's name.

Since the Persians continued to follow him like obedient children, Idanthyrsus thought he may as well put it to good use. After ravaging the Scoloti steppes, his army led the invaders into new territories; to the lands of their former brothers, those who had refused to aid them in their fight. If they thought idleness and cowardice would exempt them from this war, he would give them a second thinking on the matter.

The black-cloaked Melanchlaeni were first. They sat by as the two armies approached, disbelieving at first, then stunned. In terror they packed their families and livestock and fled the destruction, offering no resistance to either the Scoloti or the Persians. Idanthyrsus's opinion of them as cowards was confirmed. The Scyth army descended on them like a summer storm. They ravaged at will through empty settlements, butchering any forgotten livestock that might give food to the army of Darius. Yurts and small cabins stood abandoned; the Scoloti took from them what they wished and burned the rest. They loaded captured horses with booty and fresh meat and rode on. Next came the Androphagi, and the Neuri. Like the Melanchlaeni, they fled before the invaders while Scoloti and Persians alike devastated their lands at will. When he led the Persians next to the borders of the Agathyrsi people, their king sent out a warning. If they invaded their territories, they would be resisted with force of arms. Not wanting a war on two fronts, Idanthyrsus withdrew, heading back to his own steppes. But along the way he had one more visit to pay; to the small holdings of the once-mighty Cimmerians; enemies, friends, and now enemies again.

"Turn, Arima! Turn around!"

The girl grinned at Ariantes as she galloped past him, her thick black hair bound behind her neck, a bow and arrow in hand. Ariantes leaned against his dun gelding and shook his head. Arima could ride well, she could shoot well, but she had trouble combining the two, especially the rump shot that was so vital to steppe warfare.

He watched her turn in the distance, both hands on her bow, and he was pleased that she was using her knees to guide the horse. The great stallion raced forward, and he could feel the pounding of its mighty hooves coming through the soil. They ride as one, he thought admiringly as she galloped past.

"Turn around!" he called again. To his surprise, this time Arima did it, firing an arrow behind her and into the small bag of straw that dangled from a post. Ariantes laughed loudly, jerked his grazing horse's head up, and sprang onto its back. He raced away, after the retreating dark-haired figure.

"Congratulations!" he shouted, pulling up beside her. They slowed their horses to a walk and Arima turned, her jaw dropping when she saw her arrow in the target.

"I did it?" She seemed surprised by her own skill and looked at the young man. "I did it?" she repeated, breaking into a slow smile.

"You did it." He nodded. Her face was flushed from the exertion and sweat glistened across her forehead, moistening stray tendrils of dark hair. He found her to be infinitely desirable. "See, once you get the paces right, it's easy!" Ariantes said. How he wanted to reach out and touch that reddened cheek, press his mouth to those sweet, dusty lips.

Arima broke his reverie, turning and walking the stallion to retrieve her arrow. Ariantes halted his horse and watched her go, and his heart ached with a vague unease. How he admired her, and wanted her! But this, this Parthian rump shot, had been the final hurdle in her training. And now she understood it. More practice, as every warrior needs, but her basic teachings were over. The great Persian army advanced, and Arima, his Arima, was ready enough to fight them. The grey horse broke into a spirited gallop and pounded away. She had pulled her arrow and intended to try the shot again. Ariantes sighed, squared his shoulders, and watched her advance, sadness engulfing him.

Any day now, the Persians would be here; any day now, he and Arima would join the war.

Ariantes could not get the words of his old grandmother from his mind. Many going into battle avoided the soothsayers for fear their messages would weaken their bow arm or put cowardice into their hearts. But Ariantes could not resist it. He had slipped into her painted wagon just before the old ones and women and children had fled, and asked her to read his future. It was not for himself that he feared, really, but for Arima.

He looked at the girl now, cutting back the mane on her big grey horse so it would not interfere with her weapons in battle. It was a common thing, an act he'd seen done countless times before, yet in her hands it was graceful, sensual. She loved her horse the way he wished she could love him.

He turned and fitted the cheek pieces of his gelding's bridle into place. What would she say to him, after this war, when he asked her to be his wife? He'd thought of it long and often, comparing her to other girls he knew, wondering at Creusa's reaction, and Sela's.

He paused, and his callused fingertips ran absently down the thick, sun-warmed coat of his horse's neck. Once he would have wed Sela, but when she returned from her enslavement in the Greek trading post she was a different woman. Marriage no longer seemed to interest her. He had ached in silence, bewildered and alone, until Arima came, and then he knew why the gods had intervened. Now here he stood, and the world seemed so right, so normal, the sun hot on his back, the familiar war smells of horses and padded wool tunics and boiled leather armor in his nose. Everything was as it always had been.

And yet, what was it the grandmother had said? "The battle will change your life." Change it? How? The woman would not say, only to hint that after the Scoloti came, his world would be far different than it was before. And Arima?

The crone looked at him with her odd, one-eyed stare and shook her head. Ariantes would always remember that, in the stuffy confines of her wagon, with the musty smells of old felt and dried herbs and the light nearly as dim as twilight. She had shaken her head at him with neither joy nor regret, and she had said the awful words: "She will no longer be Cimmerian."

Ariantes didn't want to believe that. Her mother, Opoea, was Cimmerian. How could she not be Cimmerian unless, unless she was dead?

The warrior turned and looked over his shoulder at Arima. She had mounted the Nicean horse and walked him in easy circles, using only her knees, checking her weapons as expertly as a man born to ride. Fate was not immutable. A man could change it if he tried hard enough, and even old grandmothers could be wrong. He would stay near her in battle, to protect her from harm. They would survive it, and then they would be wed.

The Nicean stallion cantered away, and Ariantes watched till the girl was lost to the milling throng of horses and warriors, preparing for the coming fight. On impulse, he mounted his horse, threaded his way through the crowds, and followed her.

Arima rode to a rise of land away from the bustling Cimmerians. Her heart felt heavy as a stone, as if it had ceased to beat. Was it fear, regret? She sat on the stallion and stared blankly at the silver horizon. Seventeen short years she had lived, and now, was she about to die? Enough there to fear, but what was there to regret?

Melanion, she whispered into the gentle winds. If my wish finally reaches the ears of the gods, it may be too late. Would it matter to you if I was killed? My heart feels that you are alive and well, for no one ever captured you, and the hunting dogs found no body, not even blood or bones. When Ariantes and I went back to the gully, only my pack remained where we had left them; you must have taken yours. Somehow, you escaped. Where are you?

She lowered her eyes from the horizon and blinked back tears as she stared at the horse's cropped mane. How cruel a place the world is, she mused; to let me be so short a while with the man I love, and then never to see him again.

"Arima?"

She didn't look up; she knew the voice was that of Ariantes. He walked his horse to her side and seemed concerned by the tears rimming her lashes. "Come," he suggested, "I've brought a little kumiss. I know this is your first battle; let's sit down and talk."

She had no reason to refuse him, nothing else she should be doing. Nodding silently, she slid from her horse and lowered herself to the ground by its feet. Ariantes joined her, sitting so close she could feel the warmth of his body. It disturbed her.

"Here." He offered her a kidskin bag of the pungent drink. Arima took it and downed a hefty gulp. It warmed her arms and settled her stomach, and she looked at the warrior with gratitude when she returned the bag to him.

"When you are in battle, you won't have time to fear," he offered, guessing at the cause of her tears. "Even a wound, should the gods will it, seems as if it belongs to someone else."

His words addressed the very real fear she had, lying awake these last nights under the clouds and the stars, knowing the Persians and the Scoloti were fast approaching. "What of death?" she whispered, reaching to take the kumiss back from him.

"No one thinks of it," he said. "To do so would drive you mad. If it comes, time enough to face it; if not, why worry?"

"But I have lived so little, Ariantes, and so many regrets, so much left to do." Her lower lip was trembling, and her words somehow gladdened his heart. To a woman, "so much to do" could mean only one thing; marriage, babies. Touched by her candor, he reached for her and was surprised when she slumped willingly against his chest. Oh, the joy of the moment! He held her as tenderly as a frightened child, with her tears spilling onto the front of his leather armor, a stain he would wear proudly into battle. "Arima," he whispered, "don't fear. Your future will be a bright one, I feel sure of that."

She looked up at him, her blue eyes wide. "Don't say that," she said softly. "You cannot know what it is you say. Don't crush my heart with false hopes, Ariantes."

False hopes? How could she, nestled in his arms, call them false hopes? What more could he say or do to show her the truth of his feelings? Raising his hands, he cupped them around the delicate small curves of her chin. He had tried before, but she had always rebuffed him. Was it the looming threat of death that finally softened her, the knowledge that one of them might be killed? This time she sat still, blinking up at him trustingly. He ran his fingers over the fine smoothness of her skin, studying her. Such a precious thing, yet perhaps to fight, to bleed, to die. Perhaps the Scoloti were right, to keep their women at home.

She did not move when he untied the front of her leather armor, when he pulled up her boiled wool tunic, when he saw her naked from the waist up and groped eagerly for her breasts. By the gods, she threw back her head and sighed and seemed to have no fight left in her. She let him do anything he wished, and he scarcely could believe his good fortune. Hurrying before anyone approached, he unbuckled her belt, and his; he pulled down her breeches, and his. The creaminess of her body spread out on the grass before him was almost more than he could stand and he ran his fingers over it, exploring her. No matter that she didn't respond; no matter that she made no move toward him. After so long, she was finally his. His excitement was so great that he feared he would spill himself too soon as he tried to move between her legs. Arima suddenly gasped as if awakening from a dream, pushed him backward and sat up, pulling her clothes down to cover herself. She gave him a stricken look, pulled up her breeches, whistled to her stallion, and rode away. Puzzled and angry, Ariantes sat in the grass and watched her go.

With her eyes closed, she had tried to do as Sela said. She had tried to give herself to Ariantes, so fiercely that she almost succeeded. So long without Melanion, she could admit that the feel of a man's mouth and arms and hands excited her. But the voice was not Melanion's. The hands and the eyes and the smell of his skin were not Melanion's. In the end, she could not go through with it. Ariantes was not Melanion.

Three horsemen came thundering toward her, from the

direction of the setting sun. Briefly she wondered if she had put her clothes back on properly, but their words sent all such thoughts fleeing from her head.

"They come!" they shouted as they raced past, toward the campsite, and her heart began pounding as violently as their horses' hoofbeats. Straightening on her stallion, she scanned the horizon. Rising before the summer's haze came another cloud, lower, darker, hugging the ground and roiling like a dust storm. An unseen mass of horsemen, pounding into Cimmerian lands.

In the name of Papaeus, she gulped, fighting a sudden panic and ignoring Ariantes' stony gaze when he galloped wordlessly past her. Jerking the reins she turned her horse toward camp, and as she left she whispered one last, heartfelt plea into the ears of the gods . . . Melanion.

"Arima!"

Sela trotted to her cousin's side. She had seen the young girl's blanched face, the nervous wetting of her parched lips, and she knew the signs of fear. It was only natural, the first battle of one who had led such a sheltered and safe life till now. Yet the fear must be controlled or, like a war-horse gone mad, it could destroy her. Arima turned her head at the sound of her name, but stiffly, as if only reflex responded to the call. The wind pulled at her long black hair, streaming it from the band that tied it behind her neck.

"I know what you are feeling," Sela said, reaching out a comforting hand to her cousin's shoulder. Even through the leather and felt of her body armor, she could feel the girl's anxiety. "The only humans who do not know such fear are those who are mad. But you must fight it. Discipline your mind the way you discipline a horse."

Arima looked into Sela's face, her eyes almost unseeing, and waited for her next words.

"Recite your weapons lessons. Count the paces to shooting your bow between the horse's strides. Go over and over the slashing strokes of your sword."

"I cannot do it," Arima mouthed the words.

Sela would not hear of it. She shook her head resolutely to ward off the idea. "You can do it, and you will. All your life you have fought for this moment, to be a person on equal footing with a man. Will you toss it aside now?"

"I cannot," Arima repeated, turning her face into the wind, toward the far horizon and the antlike shapes of the approaching enemy. A tendril of hair blew across her mouth and she pulled it away. "My father is there, Sela," she whispered. "Bartatua, Oricus, men of my tribe, people I grew up with. Can I fight them, kill them?"

Sela seized the Nicean horse's bridle and jerked the animal and its rider toward her in annoyance. "You made a decision, and you will live with it!" she barked at Arima. "All your life you have drifted, chasing elusive clouds, never satisfied. Well, this is your life now, Arima. You have chosen it and you are here. This is what you must act on, respond to. Stop always living in a world other than the one you now inhabit. For the love of the gods, girl, grow up!"

Arima's eyes flashed, and her eyes stared stonily at Sela. The young woman sat regally on her dark gelding, her almond eyes returning the defiance, and for a moment Arima saw in them an oldness, an experience, a pain that she had not imagined in her highborn kinswoman. It stilled the words of reply on her tongue.

"Live one life at a time," Sela stated flatly. "It is sufficient for anyone." Turning, she walked her horse away. Ariantes was waiting for her and together they disappeared into the silent throng of warriors.

"One life is sufficient," Arima repeated as she waited for the enemy mass to reach them. Lipos said it was not a woman's nature to kill; today I will find out the truth of his words. She ignored the rapid pounding of her heart, the dryness of her mouth. She checked her three-edged arrows, the dagger at her thigh, her seat on the stallion.

One life is sufficient.

No more did she smell the buoyancy of the wind, or see the red peonies blooming across the grassland. Withdrawing her bow from the gorytas at her hip, she rechecked the string, replaced it, absently recounted her arrows. The enemy was near enough now to see the light and dark of faces and beards, to hear their cries if they had been shouting. But they came on silently, swiftly, like a deadly plague.

One life is sufficient, Arima told herself.

The birds grew silent, or did she just not hear them? Her horse shifted beneath her, nervous, eager, scenting the coming battle. Arima fitted an arrow to her bow and looked at old Creusa, his white hair fringed from beneath a battered Greek helmet. His arm was raised high, a painted standard tassled with dyed horsehair pointing skyward. She licked her lips and swallowed hard.

One life is sufficient. The standard fell, and the Cimmerian army thundered out to meet the invaders.

As planned, the Cimmerians divided into thirds, one racing to the left, one to the right, and one dancing and wheeling in front of the Scoloti and Budini and Geloni. A day's march behind them, they knew, were the pursuing armies of the Persian king. They were not their concern. Let them come, and let them go, and be but a memory in the minds of old men. It was these fellow steppe-dwellers who were the problem. Traitors who would not give them the peace they asked for, who had taken their lands generations ago yet now forced them into a war they wanted no part of. The Scoloti must be repulsed, turned away before they came any farther into Cimmerian lands, and with them would go their shadowing Persian army.

Arima put her knees to her horse and wheeled him toward

the right flank of advancing horsemen. They came out to meet the Cimmerians, circling just as skillfully to counter their movements. It was a dance of two hornets, swooping, jabbing, neither having an advantage over the other.

She looked desperately for an opening, trying to distinguish between Cimmerian and enemy in the swirling throng. Sela and Ariantes were right. All fear had left her. There was no time for fear in the midst of battle.

Her fellow horsemen cut away and she saw before her a tall, red-haired man, naked except for breeches and weapons and a thin gold necklet. His bow was raised, looking for a target, and when he saw Arima he turned sideways on his horse, taking aim. Arima's speed surprised her. There was no time for reflection or doubts. It was kill or be killed. Thundering past the man, she let fly her arrow and the warrior tumbled to the ground. It happened so fast she didn't even see where her arrow struck. In an eye blink she was gone, and the body of her first slain enemy was crushed beneath a mass of pounding hooves.

Cutting free of the melee, Arima raced across the grasses, exhilaration in her eyes. She was now a warrior, as real as Sela or Creusa, or even Bartatua. Her one regret was that she had not been able to take the man's fine red scalp, to hang from her horse's bridle, as Sela had on hers. In a movement as reflexive as breathing, she had another arrow fitted and ready by the time she turned her horse and dove in for a second strike. She could not have felt more complete if she had been a great black eagle, slicing through the sunlight above, or a lion chasing down its prey.

Whooping exuberantly, an instinct like a wild animal's, she raced after a Geloni who had just felled a Cimmerian. It appeared he intended to turn back and claim the head or scalp. A surprise attack by Arima, a quick arrow, and his plans were ended. Grinning, she raced away again, her confidence soaring. Two enemy already slain! From the corner of her eye she saw thick fighting to the left and veered toward it, bow at the ready. Something of value must be holding so many warriors in so tight a knot. Creusa?

She cast a quick glance over the fighting as she neared it and didn't see the old king's standard. Had he fallen elsewhere, or retreated, or was this his body, being fought over as a grand war prize? She put heel to her stallion and raced forward.

In the madness that met her she could scarcely tell friend from foe. Dust obscured clothes, horses, faces. Warriors were soaked and spattered with blood. A man turned, his horse nearly colliding with hers, his dagger drawn and gored with blood, and she barely recognized him as a fellow Cimmerian. "Go!" he hissed to her before his horse carried him away.

Go? Was Creusa already dead?

Another warrior pursued the man, not Cimmerian but Scoloti. Or was he fleeing? She did not recognize him. In the gap that opened behind the departing warrior she could see many Cimmerians, fighting savagely from horseback with Scoloti, dust rising till vision was nearly impossible. Only a king could bring about so fierce a struggle. Thrusting her bow in its case, she withdrew her dagger and forced her way into the opening left by the departing Scyth. Shrieks of horses, wounded and terrified, pierced her ears, and she fought a rising nausea at the stench of fresh blood in the close-packed mob. They seemed to be circling something, like wolves closing in for a kill. Lashing out at a passing Scoloti warrior, Arima's eyes fell on a bloodied figure, the object of all the fighting, still valiantly astride his horse, but weaving and swaying as if at any moment he might fall. It was her father, she saw with a shock, Scylas.

Arima's knife arm froze in the air at the sight, at the white face, and all the blood that matted his greying beard and fine tunic. A savage lunge swept by and pain ripped up her arm. The knife fell, useless, from her numb fingers and disappeared into the dust and milling hooves below.

Father, she gasped. Oblivious to the blood soaking her arm, Arima's gaze shifted and her eyes fell on Bartatua, his leather armor slashed, fighting bravely in defense of his chief. The Cimmerians seemed to be outnumbered but were nevertheless savage in their desire to kill the old man. Scylas's men fought back with fury, faces grimaced with rage as they swung and slashed. She could only admire their bravery, for a sad truth had suddenly awakened in her.

When the mighty foreigners invaded, it was not the Cimmerians who dared to resist them, nor most of the other steppe tribes. It was the Scoloti, her own people.

Behind Bartatua a youthful Cimmerian prince appeared through the thick dust, his rank evident from the splendid felt headpiece on his horse and the bronze-plaque tunic he wore. Scylas sagged forward, and one of his men reached to support him with one arm. The pain from her wound was burning in Arima's head, and she blinked against the mists rising in her eyes, not daring to believe what she saw. The Cimmerian prince lifted a spear and rose on his horse, ready to thrust it into Scylas's slumped back.

Arima was silent, cunning, fierce. Forcing strength into her throbbing right arm, she withdrew her bow and fitted it with an arrow. Driving her stallion forward with her knees, she clenched her teeth, raised the bow and drew it, pulling against the ripping pain of her wound. Gasping, she let fly. Before he could lunge his spear, the face of the Cimmerian prince split open beneath her arrow.

His death broke the war-fury of the Cimmerians. Time seemed to freeze as the prince toppled from view behind Bartatua and faces turned and stared at her. Hostile faces, once friendly, disbelieving what they saw. One of their own, the child of Opoea, had killed a Cimmerian prince, a kinsman. Scoloti faces, too, were frozen, mouths agape. Faces she once knew, faces of her people. Or were they? Who, now, were her people? Was there a tribe she could call her own?

Screaming rage, the Scoloti took off after the departing Cimmerians, leaving Arima alone with Scylas, and Bartatua, and a handful of Scyth warriors.

"Father!" she choked, sliding from her horse. His guard had dismounted, and the old chief was lowered to the bloody ground. Arima fell to her knees beside him, and Scylas looked up at her, his eyes sunken and grey.

"Arima?" he said, but so softly she could barely hear him. She bent low brushing his long grey hair, matted with blood and sweat, from his face.

"Yes, Father," she said, her voice choked, "it is Arima."

On the other side of his body she saw the dusty booted feet of Bartatua stop, and he lowered himself to one knee by his chief.

"So you are Cimmerian now," the old man whispered, looking at her warrior's clothes. "Like your mother." He tried to laugh, but the laughter died away into a choking cough. Arima stroked her fingers down his leathery face in impotent desperation, trying to halt his dying.

"Father, no." She began to cry. "You are all I have left."

Scylas looked at her and spoke sternly. "Don't cry, girl," he rasped. "A warrior does not cry."

Arima lifted her eyes and stared at him. A warrior? Had he called her a warrior?

"You could have been my son," Scylas whispered, "but Papaeus chose to make you a woman. Even so, Arima, I have been proud of you." Blindly he groped for her hand, and she clasped it tightly. "Today you proved yourself. My spirit is within you." He shifted his gaze to Bartatua. "We have ridden together as father and son; I name you as my heir. Let those here be witness to it. I leave to you my gold and herds and slaves. I give you my black Persian stallion and rulership of the Auchatae people. But by your honor as a warrior, you must let Arima go. She is no longer yours."

Bartatua looked over the old man's blood-soaked tunic, and his dark eyes met Arima's. He did not speak as he studied her. True, she dressed as a man, rode like a man, killed like a man, but somehow it made her even more female, more desirable than she had been as timid Arima. Her face was tanned and healthy, her body was firm and strong. He wanted her fiercely. He made a move to stand but Scylas seemed to read his thoughts.

"Go." The old chief squeezed Arima's hand. She looked down at him, tears brimming her eyes, and shook her head.

"Girl, do as I say." He smiled weakly. "For once in your life, do as I say. While I live, I am still chief, and Bartatua cannot pursue you. I will cling to my life as long as I can, to give you time to escape. It is my parting gift to you, Arima, your freedom."

Arima bit her lip and slowly laid her cheek on his bloody tunic, feeling the final beats of his heart, the fading warmth and strength of his body, a closeness she had never known in childhood. A warrior could not profess love to another warrior. She understood now why he had shown so little love to her. Not that he did not feel it, but that long years of training forbade its expression. Lifting her head, she gazed into his dimming brown eyes. A warrior could not profess love, and a warrior could not cry.

She touched his cheek fondly.

"Good-bye, Father," she whispered, and read in his gaze all the feeling he had never been able to show her.

There was no time to linger. Reluctantly she slid her hand from his and stood. Oricus was leading her stallion to her.

"A fine animal," Bartatua muttered, standing and taking the horse. "Where did you get it?" When Arima took the reins from him he seized her hand and stared at her, trying to force his will into her eyes as if she were another beast in his herd. Angrily she jerked free of him.

"A gift," she said icily, mounting as expertly as she could to impress him. Oricus held up a bloody brown scalp on his knife point; the hair of the Cimmerian prince, her first battle trophy. Bitterly she shook her head, refusing it. Cradling her wounded arm, she turned the great stallion with her knees and looked down at Bartatua's dirty, bearded face.

"Rule well," she muttered. Taking the reins in her good hand, the horse sprang away across the bloody grasslands.

It was a summer rain such as often swept the steppes, heavy, unceasing, turning the black soil sodden and feeding the rapid growth of tall grasses and swollen streams. A torrent sent by Api the Earth Mother to cleanse her world of the spilled blood of foolish humans.

Arima walked the grey stallion along a rise of land, visible to any pursuer but also more able to see them herself. Her leather riding cap shed the rain into her draggled hair and cascaded it down the stiff leather bodice of her armor. She shuddered at the dampness soaking into the neck of her wool tunic and spreading the blood on her sleeve like a colorful red dye. Alone, betrayed and betraying, her mind was too numb to feel any pain.

She knew if she followed the rise, eventually she would reach a rivulet or stream, and from there a larger river, drinking water, and the shelter of trees. If only she could reach it.

She had her doubts. Going into battle, she had not carried with her any of the necessities of travel; no kumiss, no saddlebag of millet and dried meat. Only one large drinking horn from the great wild ox, slung under her left arm, filled with water and fortifying herbal infusions, and a pouch of ground coriander seed at her waist, to apply to wounds. She had her bow and arrows, and had retrieved a dagger from the battlefield. She could try to hunt, but in the rain, any game she caught would have to be eaten raw.

The stallion walked on, as tired and dispirited as its rider, and without stopping Arima pulled the drinking horn forward, opened it, and took a gulp of the brew the enaree had prepared. Slowly she washed it through her mouth, over her tongue, around her teeth, cleansing the dust and dryness of battle away. It refreshed her, alerted her mind, and she plugged the horn, saving what remained for later.

But perhaps she did not want her mind alert, for with it came doubts and fears. She had no people now. No Scoloti, no Cimmerians, no one. Where was she to go? What would her future be? She snorted, and with her good hand wiped the rain from her face. Why concern myself with the future? Sela was right. One life at a time is enough for anyone to live, and right now my life is not tomorrow, it is today. Today, drawing to a close of greyness and rain that has seen my whole world rent apart, the betrayal of my mother's people, and the death of my father. Now I have no one.

She lifted her face into the downpour and closed her eyes. A warrior does not cry, she warned herself, but despite her resolve she could not help but add her tears to the weeping of the heavens.

"Well," Creusa said, lowering his weary body to a log end and smiling with unfamiliar savagery to the assembled warriors huddled under the rain. "Sixteen of our people dead, including the lastborn son of my own brother." He shot an angry glance at Sela, her face streaked with dirt, squatting on her haunches out of the mud. The young woman did not look away; instead, the gaze she returned to her father was as angry as his own.

"What is to be done?" he continued. "The Scoloti are gone, driven from our lands. Because of the rain our crops were spared from burning, but many of our wells were poisoned by them as they left."

"Where are the Persians?" a warrior interrupted. They had no quarrel with the Persians, it was true, but who knew what damage an army that size, thirsty and half-starved, could do?

"Following behind Idanthyrsus, like good and faithful dogs," Creusa snapped, lowering his war standard across his lap. The dyed horsehair tufts dangled forlornly into the mud at his feet. "A few of our people who did not flee in time have been taken captive, a small part of our croplands was stripped, but when their foragers came riding nearby they were repulsed with ease. Idanthyrsus's plan is working; the armies of the Persian king are weakening and their spirits sag. Who can say how much longer their cat-and-mouse game will continue?"

"So they are no threat to us?" Ariantes asked. He squatted by Sela, his spear propped upright to support him.

"Not today," Creusa muttered, "but who knows where Idanthyrsus will lead them next? Back into our lands, as revenge for his losses? We have scouts keeping a close eye on his every move."

"Then shall we return to our settlement and take the dead to the enaree for burial?" another asked.

Creusa nodded and looked at his daughter. "For you," he directed, "I have another task. Track down your cousin and bring her back to us for trial at the hands of the half-men. If you feel you cannot do the job, I will send another."

Sela rose to her feet, her jaw set firmly, and pulled the wet hair from her face. "I can do it, Father," she muttered. "I will do it." Receiving his dismissal, she strode away into the storm.

Arima found a stand of trees, their dappled foliage hanging heavy to the ground. Dismounting stiffly, she led the horse under them and was relieved to find the rain less intense in their shelter. What a stroke of good fortune that she saw them, clustered around a jumble of rocks by a wide swollen stream. Here she could rest, treat her wounded arm, find some food, and plan her next move.

She sank to a protruding rock with an audible sigh. The hunger of a day without food was beginning to affect her, as well as the weakness and pain from her arm. She wanted to sleep, to curl up on her side and forget everything; wars, weapons, bloodshed. To sink into oblivion, to remember only the warmth of Melanion's arms, the gentle sound of his voice, the smell of his body, as if that were the only world she needed, the world where she belonged . . .

She drew her dagger angrily and cut the stiff, bloodied cloth from her arm. Rain seared into the exposed wound and she hung her head, biting her lip against the pain. A woman can endure childbirth, she told herself; a woman can endure this.

Fumbling with her left hand, she took the pouch of coriander seed from around her waist. Pulling it open with her teeth, she extracted a fingerful of the seed, pounded with sheep's fat and honey. It kept a wound clean and able to heal. Setting her jaw, she patted the ointment across the gash. It would need binding, she knew, for the fibers to mend together. Sliding up the stiff leather of her body armor, she cut a strip of dry cloth from the bottom of her wool tunic and tied it as best she could around the injured arm. Allowing herself to feel relief, she succumbed to exhaustion and lowered her body to the rock. Raindrops plopped brokenly through the trees and onto her side, puddling on her cheek, prodding through her wet clothes like fingers. Arima did not care. She whistled for the stallion and he plodded forward, hanging his head in tired protection over her. Gingerly cradling the wounded arm, her eyes fell shut, and she dreamed of the only real happiness she had ever known—the warm summer nights spent safe and happy in the arms of the man who ruled her heart.

Sela lost Arima's trail soon after setting out. As if to cover her escape, the rain had washed out all trace of Arima's passing, the hoofprints in the soil, the crushed grass blades. The young woman was forced to return to camp to fetch a black-faced Assyrian mastiff to follow the trail, and in doing so lost nearly a whole day's travel. It was dawn of the next day before she finally set out, the great war-dog pacing eagerly before her.

She led the dog a wide circle around the corpse-strewn battlefield, black with vultures and ravens and crows. No need to waste time stopping to go over it; all gold and heads and scalps and weapons had been retrieved the previous day. The only thing that remained was food for the scavengers. It was best to avoid the area entirely, and the danger of lions and wolves and the great striped cat, fiercest of all.

Sela looked for the last place she'd seen Arima's tracks, by a hillock of sedges, their ripening tops crushed by the big grey stallion. In the hazy morning light the landmarks looked different than they had the day before, and she had trouble remembering the spot. When she thought she had found it she let the dog run for a moment, encouraging it to investigate the grass thoroughly and get a good mark on the stallion's scent. The mastiff paced back and forth, nose to the ground, its excitement growing.

"Good boy," Sela urged. "Good boy. Go get it!"

Abruptly the dog broke away on a trail, following an unerring course south.

Sela wanted to go faster, to catch Arima quickly, but she had to match her pace to that of the dog. It frustrated her to be plodding behind the eager beast. At least it seemed to have a good scent; only occasionally, at a pool of water or a slick, mud-washed hillside, did the dog falter. But with midday, approaching a rise that dropped away to a meandering stream, the dog halted, gazed down the slope, and the hackles on its back rose.

This is not right, Sela cautioned herself. Had the dog found Arima and her horse it would not react in this manner. Something else is disturbing it.

A low growl arose in the mastiff's throat and it crept forward, stiff-legged and alert. Sela swiftly drew her bow and fitted an arrow. In the aftermath of battle, who could say what might be lurking about. She was determined not to be caught unawares a second time, captured and enslaved.

The dog's growl rose to a snarl, the snarl to a fierce barking. "Go!" Sela shouted, putting knee to her war-gelding. The dog sprang forward, heading for a clump of wild almond trees. Sela saw the underbrush rustle. A wild boar? Abruptly the quarry broke and ran for the stream below, and the safety of the water. It was a young clean-shaven man, Parthian, one baggy-trousered leg soaked in blood and barely able to support him as he tried to outrun the attacking dog.

"Down! Stop!" Sela bellowed at the mastiff. She could not let the dog kill the man. It would be swift, but perhaps he had tales to tell. What were the Persians, his masters, up to? Had he seen a lone Cimmerian warrior on a grey horse pass by?

The mastiff reluctantly slowed its attack, pacing warily around the Parthian horseman, who cowered in near-helplessness by an ancient chestnut tree, his arms raised protectively to his chest. Sela trotted her horse closer and raised her bow to fire. "Throw down your weapons," she commanded. The man rose stiffly on his good knee, keeping the injured leg extended stiffly to his side. Pulling an iron dagger and a battle-ax from his belt, he tossed them to the wet grass.

"Why are you here?" Sela snapped. She spoke in Scoloti, the language most tribes knew. The young man seemed to understand her.

"Escape," he mumbled low, never taking his eyes from the dog.

"Escape? Why?" Sela doubted him. A spy, perhaps, who'd angered his Persian keepers. "You are wounded. Why didn't you stay with your armies? They have physicians—Greek, Egyptian, Mesopotamian."

"The army has gone," he sighed, sagging to the ground. "Darius has given up."

The words came like the morning song of the buntings

after a fierce night storm. Given up? Retreating? "Tell me, Parthian," Sela snapped, "and I will let you go. Why has the Great King given up?"

"No food. No water. The troops are starving and terrified. They say they are fighting demons, ghosts of the steppes. The Scoloti will not fight, they will not surrender, they will not be captured. Like the wind, they move on."

"But why did you not go with them on their retreat?" Sela still found his story to be shaky.

"Darius had deceived us." The man grimaced hatred. "I heard his plans and decided to seek my own escape."

"Plans?"

"He will leave the wounded behind, with tents and weapons and campfires, and enough booty to trick the Scyth warriors. They will be bait, to occupy the wolves on horseback. While the Scyth make sport of them, Darius and all his able-bodied men will have time to make good their escape."

Sela's ears had suddenly stoppered, as if they did not want to hear his words. At any other time this would be such good news that she would return at once to tell Creusa, but not now. She thought back to a Neuri envoy who'd come, warning the Cimmerians of the Scoloti deceit, of the Persians being led through their lands, and of the riches to be had if the great Persian train should fall. The splendor of the Great King himself, his vast treasure-laden wagons, chariots decked with gold, noblemen aplenty who even brought their own goldsmiths along. She had smiled when she heard it. Somehow she knew Melanion, her old friend and lover, would be one of them. He had an eye for opportunity. He'd told her of the visiting Persian noblemen and their offer. How could he miss such a chance? She had smiled at the envoy's words, but had not pursued it. Arima was in love with the Greek. It would only bring her pain to know where he was. Dear, sweet Melanion! she had thought, and let the matter drop.

Sela gazed at the cowering warrior with sudden fire in her eyes and drew back her bowstring. "Search your mind well, coward," she snarled through clenched teeth, "for if you give me a bad answer to my next question, you will die."

The man swallowed hard and nodded.

"What goldsmiths travel with the Persians? Are any of them Greek?"

The warrior stared at her, and she could see him trying to think. Doubts welled up within her. What if he knew nothing? What would a common horseman know of the goldsmiths of the nobility? To her relief, a sudden light came to the man's dark eyes.

"I know of one," he offered. "He would often go out with the soldiers, drinking and wenching."

"And his name?"

"I don't remember, but he was tall. His hair was yellow, and they say he was a very skilled fellow."

Sela lowered the bow. Melanion! It had to be him! "Where is he now? Do you know?"

"In camp, I suppose," the man said. "I know he was wounded, days ago. A spear raked his back. He could hardly move, they say, for he no longer joined us when we drank. He would not be able to flee with the king."

Sela returned the bow and arrow to the gorytas at her hip. "Remain where you are till the dog leaves with me," she directed. "Then you are free to go." Turning her gelding, she whistled and the mastiff reluctantly left its quarry. She made no effort to get the dog back on Arima's trail. Melanion was wounded and faced certain death at the hands of the Scoloti. Worse, he didn't even know it. He had saved her life once; surely Father would understand if she disobeyed his orders to retrieve Arima and went to Melanion's aid instead. But Arima had murdered a Cimmerian nobleman. Should such a crime go unpunished?

Sela turned suddenly on her horse. The young man still crouched where she'd left him, peaked Parthian cap in hand, awaiting the departure of the dog. "Have you seen another Cimmerian pass by?" she called to him. "A warrior on a grey horse?"

"Only this morning," he cried out. "She was following the stream, heading southwest."

"And when will King Darius begin this retreat you spoke of?"

"Tonight."

His answers decided her. Calling to the mastiff, she urged her horse into a gallop, following the southwest course of the stream.

The clouds were gathering, promising more rain by nightfall. Arima had taken advantage of the day's brief sun and had scouted for food to make a filling meal; fish caught with her hands from among streamside tree roots, and wild mustard greens and onion tops, baked on a flat rock by a small campfire. It was no feast, no roasting game or rich stew of millet and boiled mutton, but it revived her and gave her enough hope and strength to go on with her journey. The only plan she had devised was to turn back toward the rising sun and travel north. It would take her away from the Northern Sea, away from the lands of the Auchatae and the Cimmerians, and into the territories of the Royal Scyth. Traveling by night to avoid detection, she could cross their lands in a few days and continue on to the distant range of mountains. At the foot of these dwelt the Argippaei, a race of men so blond the Greeks thought them all to be bald. They carried no arms, settled disputes among neighboring tribes and lived off the fruit of their trees. With them, anyone who sought shelter was safe from pursuit. If only she could reach them!

She hacked down a few scrubby bushes to make a dry seat and stretched out her legs, watching the blooming garden of the steppes dance before her in the wind. Her stallion grazed nearby, as refreshed as Arima was with food and rest and clean water. A lone sparrow chirped musically, near the stream behind her, and she focused on the sound. How sweet and pure it was! How peaceful, after the chaos of war and battle. Arima found herself nodding, drowsed by the warm sun and the bird song and a stomach full of food.

A heavy thud of horse hooves whirled her awake and the girl tensed, snatching her dagger from her left leg. Cautiously she glanced over her shoulder, toward the sound. A rider approached, on a dusty brown war-horse, a massive war-dog plodding beside them. Arima narrowed her eyes into the sun, studying the figure. As it drew closer, she recognized the rich brown hair and the high cheekbones. It was Sela.

There could be only one reason for her coming. Jumping to her feet, Arima whistled as she raced for her horse, desperate to be on it and gone. Sela kneed her gelding into a run. Arima knew it was useless. The dog was already beside her, bounding and barking a warning.

Gasping, she and her stallion met and she whirled, her bow and arrow ready to fire, her back to the horse's neck. She would never be captured by her cousin, she vowed, nor taken back alive to face execution. She would fight here, and die like a warrior.

Sela recalled the dog and slowed her horse to a walk. Oddly, she approached Arima with no weapons drawn.

"Kill me," Arima hissed, a fire of defiance in the blue depths of her eyes. She moved her bow menacingly, like a snake waiting to strike.

"I will not kill you, Cousin," Sela stated, and her voice seemed sad rather than angry. Arima swallowed against her fear and studied her cousin more closely. The young woman's face showed concern, hurt, but not the keenness of a hunter after prey.

"Why are you here?" Arima questioned, lowering the bow slightly. "Surely you did not track me down just to talk."

"I will be direct, Arima. There is little time to waste. I tracked you on order from Creusa; to take you back for trial and execution for what you did."

Arima raised her bow again and pointed it at Sela's heart. Her draw arm quivered against the pain of her wound, but she fought it. Unless the dog attacked too swiftly, she could kill her cousin before Sela could make a move. Sela saw Arima's intent and straightened on her horse, daring her to shoot. "The gods have changed my plan, Arima," she said. "Melanion is in great danger."

Arima's bow sagged. Melanion? "What do you know of Melanion?" she croaked.

Sela sighed and leaned forward on her horse. "Put away your weapons, Arima," she said. "I am going to dismount, and we must talk. His life is in danger, and you must save him."

Arima replaced her bow and arrow blindly, moved by instinct, her mind awhirl with her cousin's words. Save Melanion? She? In the name of Papaeus, she would die for him.

Sela slid to the ground and approached the grey warhorse. It turned to protect Arima, eyeing her suspiciously. "Father will understand when I tell him I let you go," she told Arima. "We owe the Greek a great debt, and if this is the only way to pay it, so be it."

Arima was as confused as a blinded bird. All she could do was remain silent and listen.

"I knew him once," Sela explained. "A year ago, I was captured by passing traders when, like a fool, I went out to hunt alone. They sold me to a brothel." A sharp intake of air from Arima interrupted her words, and Sela looked down at her muddy horsehide boots, ashamed and pained by the telling.

"It was in the Greek trading port of Olbia. Melanion, you see, saved me when I was about to be sold off to a Thracian seaman. He saved my life, Arima."

The girl was staring at her, openmouthed, as speechless as if her tongue had been cut out. Not Melanion the Hero did she think of; Melanion the good-hearted who saved her cousin from a terrible fate. Her mind raged with nightmares of Melanion in a brothel with other women, naked in his arms as he had once held her, even Sela.

"You and he . . ." she stammered, fighting against a searing wound in her soul that burned more fiercely than her arm. Sela nodded awkwardly.

Arima had loved Sela, admired her, owed her her freedom, her life, her new existence as a warrior. All that she now was, she owed to Sela. The trousers on her legs, the weapons in her hand, the horse she sagged against, numb with shock. And now she hated her. Thrusting her bow and arrow angrily into the gorytas at her hip, she turned away from her cousin, buried her face against the horse's felt saddle pad, and began to cry.

Melanion and Sela.

Sela touched her shoulder and she jerked away angrily, trying to cradle her aching arm against the stallion.

"Arima, we were only friends. Don't you think if I loved him, I would go for him myself? I give you that chance, girl. As he once gave me my freedom, so I give you yours. I know you love him. Go and save him, Arima. Quickly, or he will die."

Sela's words had the clear ring of truth. He was a man; Arima knew that. Surely she did not believe that she was the first woman he'd had. She must try to put the awful visions from her mind. "Where is he?" she mumbled, wiping the tears away before turning to her cousin.

"I learned from a fleeing Parthian that he is with the Persians. Darius is going to retreat, but to divert the Scoloti army he is leaving behind the sick and wounded. Melanion will be there, at the Persian camp, because he was injured by a spear. Darius leaves tonight; your people are camped a day's march away. You must fly like the wind, girl, to reach him before tomorrow. If you do not reach the camp before the Scoloti, there will be nothing left but carrion for you to find."

Arima understood. She strode away from the horse and picked up the nearly dry leather body armor she'd laid out in the sun and quickly put it on. Sela helped her tie the sides in place.

"Is your wound bad?" she asked, seeing the clumsy bandage on Arima's arm. The girl shook her head.

"It hurts but I can manage. I will be lucky if this is the worst that happens to me in my lifetime." Arima paused, her eyes locking awkwardly with Sela's. "A warrior must not cry," she choked on the words. Fiercely the two cousins embraced.

"Find him," Sela said, fighting back her own tears, her face buried in Arima's black hair. She knew, deep in her soul, that she would never see her cousin again. "Find him and be happy."

Arima nodded against Sela's dusty shoulder and pulled away. "I will tell him you send greetings." She tried to smile.

"Yes," Sela said. "Tell him I am to wed."

"Who?"

"Ariantes."

"He is a good man," Arima nodded, and felt a pang at the name. Once, she could have been his; now he and Sela were one. "I must go!" Arima turned away, pulling herself wearily astride her stallion. Sela returned to her gelding and untied a saddlebag full of food and kumiss.

"Here!" she said, tossing it up to Arima. The girl caught it and smiled wistfully. "My life has been full of good-byes lately," she said sadly. "May your life be a good one, Sela."

"And yours," her cousin said, smiling. She watched the great Nicean horse stride away, its tail tossing. "Ride like the wind, Arima," she thought to herself as they vanished over a rise of land. "Hurry and save Melanion."

* * *

Melanion!

Arima's heart sang at the thought of seeing him again, its song sweeter than the trilling of a streamside sparrow. In a day she would be with him, hear the voice and feel the touch that brought life to her soul. Exhilaration rose and rampaged, and she felt not fear, but joy.

In the name of Papaeus! she cried, tears streaking her dirty cheeks; let it rain, let it storm, let the grounds tremble and the sun burn the grasses and the wind blow all before it! What is that to me? Soon I will be with the man I love, and with that blessing nothing else matters.

Leaning low over the horse's cropped mane, she urged him on. Her love for the Greek could not be contained. The grey horse raced on under a grey sky as Arima threw her head back and sang an old Scoloti love song.

The stallion could not keep the pace. Arima knew that. Sweat streaked his sides and foam dropped from his mouth, and she slowed him to a walk, frantic at the delay. When the weary horse cooled she halted, jumping stiffly to the ground and leading him to a marshy lakeside to rest. If only she had three horses, like a travelling warrior, then there would be no need to stop.

Reclining against a fallen log, she took a swallow of the fortifying herbal drink in the ox-horn at her side. How much longer might it take? she wondered. Yet the horse must rest; we cannot keep going all day. Leaning sideways on the log, she kept an eye on the stallion while her thoughts danced with anticipation.

They walked through the night, a dark clouded night spattered with light showers. Without the stars she had trouble keeping her direction, but with the sound of the wide river always to her left, she knew her course would be steady enough till dawn came. She did not dare stop to wait for sunup. Even now the final, fatal Persian camp had been set up, no doubt by the same brooding river she was following. Even now the unsuspecting victims slept, Melanion among them, tossing from their wounds and fevers, digesting their last meals, while the Scoloti warriors dozed on horseback, a day away or less, unaware of the victory they had won against the Great King. While all the world slept and awaited the fate of tomorrow, she did not dare.

Dawn broke with a sliver of creamy sky beneath the clouds and Arima knew the day would clear. Through the night her course had remained steady; with a slight adjustment to the west, she continued her way through the wet, drooping grasses.

Had Sela been mistaken? The sun was nearing midheaven, blazing hot and burning off the moisture from the rain, and Arima still saw no sign of the great Persian camp. The stallion plodded on, a steady, even pace all steppe nomads and their mounts knew and could keep up almost indefinitely. Arima straightened her weary back, and her eyes scanned the endless horizon. An army like that of the Persian king would not hide its camp; there would be no need. Displaying itself was half its terror. She should see smoke from campfires, tall tent tops, waving banners. She saw nothing.

Desperately she rechecked the sun's position, the treeline of the distant river. She was still on course, as Sela had directed. Had the Parthian lied when he told Sela where the army was? Or had she passed it in the night, unaware in the blackness and drizzle that it was there? Shifting uneasily on the felt saddle pad, she fought the panic churning in her stomach. Time was running out. By now the Scoloti would know the Persians were retreating, and they would be racing to plunder the abandoned camp. If she did not reach it soon, Melanion would die.

A glint to the left caught her eye and she pulled the horse to a halt. Searching the horizon, she waited. There! Again it flashed in the sunlight, far out beyond the grasses. Was it the camp, or the departing Persians, or the advancing Scoloti? She couldn't tell, but she determined to find out. Frantically she kneed the weary stallion into a trot.

It was midafternoon when she saw it clearly from a swell of land, drowsing under the hot summer sun on the banks of a small stream that fed into the great river; the Persian camp, sprawled in so careless a fashion that any warrior would have laughed to see it. With this Darius hoped to fool the Scoloti and their allies? Banners flew, campfires smoked, hauling wagons sat scattered about.

Arima approached slowly, her dagger drawn. The outlying grass had been trampled by the departing armies, and cast-off packs and weapons littered the landscape. In their haste to flee the army of ghosts, the Persians had taken nothing with them that was not necessary. Lying in the weeds, a fine, odd sword of foreign make caught her eye. She was tempted to stop and retrieve it, but she did not. The day was already old, and Melanion awaited. At any moment, she feared, she would hear the pounding hooves of approaching Scoloti warriors. She rode on.

The Persian tents loomed closer, still and quiet and of a curious construction. Poles stood outside the tents, and a single layer of skins or thick brown felt covered them. Had they never seen a yurt? Such a dwelling as this seemed awkward and would not remain standing for long in a harsh steppe winter. Bright cloth banners streamed before the entrances of some, and Arima passed them warily. The tent flaps were drawn up, and she leaned low over the stallion's neck, peering inside. They were dark and empty. No hearth fires, no possessions, no food. The Scoloti ghost army was about to conquer a camp of nothing . . .

The wind mourned balefully between the deserted tents, catching their fabric and breaking the silence with loud retorts like great sails flapping at sea. The silly tent poles rattled dryly against the gusts. There were no horses, no camp dogs, no livestock for rations. Only silence as heavy as the grave. Arima replaced the dagger and slid her bow and arrow from the gorytas, readying them to fire.

The hair on Arima's neck prickled at the eerie, empty camp. She wanted to race through it, find Melanion, and be gone, but she dared not try. Stealth and cunning must be maintained. A weak moan tensed her and she walked on, her bow drawn, turning the horse with her knees. She passed a large square tent—square! Didn't the Persians know that corners provided hiding places for demons?—and emerged on a broad open area. Circled around a central fire, lambs for the sacrifice, lay hundreds of wounded men. Her heart leaped in her breast, and she replaced her weapons with quaking hands. Melanion!

The stallion walked forward, skirting men lying on litters, men sitting by their packs, men talking and men barely alive. Men bandaged and bloody; a head swathed in so much cloth that the poor fellow could not see. Another was beyond hope, lying on his back, a fly-infested bandage draped over his open abdomen. He was still alive, still aware, one arm resting over his eyes to shield them from the sun. The men scarcely noticed her when she passed, as silent as the breeze.

Horror rose in Arima, and pity. She could not look away, for everywhere she looked was suffering. These were the hated enemy, the Persians and Parthians, Assyrians and Medes, husbands, sons, and fathers, all men like any other —hurting, bleeding, dying. What transforms a man so, she wondered, holding her breath against the awful smell of old blood and festering wounds; to leave his home and children and march off to kill and be killed?

A Persian man, his bandaged side soaked in blood, rose on one elbow and raised an arm to her as she passed. Her eyes could not avoid his dark gaze. He seemed well-bred, his beard still oiled and curled stylishly, his clothes expensively done. He called up to her, a question so it seemed, but she

312

could not understand his language. Only one word, the name of his Great King, and she shook her head in reply. The nobleman collapsed back to his pallet and closed his eyes.

"No," she muttered, looking away bitterly. No, Darius had not returned. Darius would never return. Her joy at finding Melanion had crumbled to a ruin.

A harsh animal cry startled her and she halted the horse. Before her stood twenty tethered . . . horses? No; they were odd creatures, such as she had never seen before. Almost horses, yet the ears were far too large, the faces too coarse, as if an inexperienced craftsman had put them together. White ringed their eyes and tipped their noses. Her presence seemed to concern them, for another one cried out, a call like that of two cats mating, and then several more. Shaken by this apparition of nonhorses, Arima quickly trotted away.

The wounded seemed unending; moaning, sobbing, or silent, waiting for a return that would never come. There was no panic or fear. They were oblivious to their fate, and with rising anger she understood the Great King's deception. They believed the armies had ridden off to battle and would soon come back for their comrades.

"Help me!" a voice suddenly cried in Greek and Arima would have gasped with joy if she hadn't realized it was not Melanion's. On the far side of camp sat a man who must have once been handsome. Now disease ate at his flesh, and a cloud of flies noisily tormented him.

"Please," he begged her, his brown eyes shining intelligence. Arima broke into dry sobs and could not answer. She had to get away from this nightmare; find Melanion and flee. She galloped ahead carelessly, leaping over bodies, dodging abandoned wagons and cold campfires. A realization came to her as she raced by the blur of bloody faces, pleading faces, dying faces.

Lipos had been right. This was the reality of men; greed

and destruction, warfare and death, conquering and being conquered. It was not a woman's reality, a reality of life and caring. There was no joy of warfare here, no exhilaration at the killing of an enemy. These were the enemy. They were people who suffered and feared just as she did, and it broke her heart to see them. Like a spider caught on a web of its own making, every man made by the gods was trapped by his own maleness. To dare to be otherwise would make him less a man in the eyes of his fellows. By this measure, no man was ever free; they were always held in bondage to one another.

A voice suddenly called her name and she halted. There, nearly beneath the front hooves of her stallion, lay Melanion.

She doubted she would have recognized him. He rested on an old saddle pad; his face was heavily bearded and smeared with dirt and sweat, his eyes were sunken, but when they looked up at her their old bright sparkle of welcome stabbed her heart. Springing to the ground, Arima fell to her knees at his side, her hands gently touching his face, his hair, his neck, as if to be sure that he was real. What wonder love brings, when at the mere sight of him all death, all suffering around her vanished. Her mind whirled with memories, her heart swelled with emotion, but there was only one word she could think to utter. "Melanion," she cried. His name, so long cherished, remembered, whispered to the ears of the gods. Only his name.

"What are you doing here?" he rasped, surprise on his bony face. "I thought you were dead. I went back and, but no matter. You must leave; the Persians will catch you."

She shook her head and rested her fingers against his beard. How could she tell him, get him to flee with her, without tormenting everyone around them with the knowledge of their approaching doom? "Can you travel?" she whispered. "How badly are you wounded?"

"My back," the Greek replied. "The wound will not kill

me, the physicians say, but the pain comes near to it every time I move."

Arima's keen warrior's eye flitted around him and took in the remains of a meal at his side, a half-full goatskin of water. "But if you cannot move, then where did all this come from?" she motioned.

He grinned and looked toward the central campfire. Approaching was a slim, dark girl with hair like the black mane of the stallion of Scylas and eyes as large and brown as a doe's.

"Who is she?" Arima snapped.

"Angel." Melanion chuckled. "I don't know her name. That's all I call her, angel."

"Who is she? Your woman?" Arima's teeth clenched against the rage she was feeling.

"No," Melanion sighed, returning his sunken gaze to Arima. "She's a loan from one of the Persian noblemen. She cares for me."

Arima didn't pursue his statement. She didn't care to know. When the doe-eyed girl squatted by Melanion she angrily rose to her feet. I should leave you here, she thought bitterly, watching the girl lift his head and trickle some water into his mouth. You and your little slave girl. But no, I'll carry him away from the little Persian vixen and he'll need no other woman but me.

"We have to go," she snapped, leaning down and pushing the girl's arm away from Melanion. The slave girl looked up at her in surprise.

"Go? I'm not going anywhere, Arima," Melanion retorted, rasping his voice as forcefully as he could. "I have a good position here, my sack is full of gold; I will stay with the Persians."

Arima bent lower and thrust her face into the Greek's. She had not come so far and sacrificed so much for nothing. "The Persians have gone, Melanion," she hissed. He gazed back at her skeptically. "Why else would I ride openly into an enemy camp?" she said. "I came to rescue you. The Persians have fled and left all of you as bait. Don't you see?"

The doubt in his eyes left and he grimaced, struggling to sit. The Persian girl, alarmed, tried to help but Arima thrust her backward into the dirt. The Greek didn't seem to notice. "Then we must go!" he said loudly. "Help me up!"

"Quiet!" Arima motioned him angrily. Those closest to Melanion turned at the outburst, shuffling and moving uneasily against their own sufferings. The slumbering tranquility of the drowsing camp had been disturbed, but for what reason?

"If you alert the others they will mob us in their panic," she told the goldsmith. "We must leave quietly and quickly."

"But my friends are here!" he protested, easing his throbbing back. "The Lydian armorer who crushed his foot. Two of the finest horsemasters I have ever seen; even Megaphernes, the nobleman who hired me, was wounded in the side a few days ago." He looked at Arima, disbelieving what he knew her answer would be. "There is no hope for them?" His voice died.

She motioned over her shoulder to the great grey stallion standing patiently behind her. "That is all I have, Melanion. There are no other horses in camp. Can he carry six people? Their only hope will be that their deaths are swift."

Melanion looked at the stallion blankly. His brain seemed to want to refuse the words he'd just heard.

"Come; there is no time for delay," Arima pressed him. She knew how strong the bonds of men's friendships could be. She knew that leaving his friends would be a hard thing for him to bear. She slipped an arm behind his back, over a bulky bandage, and eased him to his feet. He tottered weakly and she guided him to her horse, pushing the slave girl away when she tried to help.

"No!" Melanion muttered, seeing the bewildered look on

the young Persian girl's face. "What of her? Will she die, too?"

Arima snorted and looked the slim girl up and down. She had plainly been well raised and well cared for. Her long skirt tumbled with a colorful flower pattern and it did not escape Arima's notice how her full breasts strained at the blue fabric of her bodice. No, she would not die. Some Scoloti chief would find much pleasure in her. Maybe Bartatua.

"Tell her to mount one of those odd half-horses yonder and flee," Arima answered. "That is the best I can do for her."

Melanion spoke rapidly to the girl. Her eyes grew wide with understanding, and in the pleading expression that suddenly filled them Arima felt pity. Another heart fallen to Melanion. The slave reached forlornly for the Greek, saw Arima glowering at her, and stopped, dropping her arms helplessly to her sides. She retreated a few steps and halted, still gazing at Melanion. He spoke a few more stern words and the girl turned and ran away, sobbing openly.

"Come." Arima helped him mount the horse. Melanion, breaker of women's hearts.

They galloped back the way she'd come, past the strange horse-beasts, through sagging, empty tents, with Melanion clinging tightly to her waist and sagging his head against her shoulder. Perhaps, if there's time, she mused, I can stop on the way out and retrieve that fine foreign sword I saw. Emerging from camp she pulled the stallion to a halt at the trampled edge of the grasslands. The beast tossed his head, scenting the air nervously. She could hear them even before she saw them, the far-off rumble of advancing horsemen.

"Dear Mother Hera," Melanion whispered in her ear, raising his head and looking around. Death coming, so soon, for all his friends.

"Can't we go back—kill them ourselves, quickly?" he

asked. What manner of man would he be to abandon them to torture and pain, when there was something he could do to help them?

Arima put heel to the horse and they sprang away, hugging the fringes of the camp, racing from the approaching Scoloti. "Answer me!" Melanion snapped, jerking her body with one arm.

"I just did," she called back with the rushing wind. "Pray they have a kind death. That is all you can do now."

She rode the war-horse as well as any man, dodging an abandoned sheep, leaping a broken supply wagon. The Greek clung to her tightly, his forehead pressed to her shoulder, his heart heavy with grief. He had always enjoyed life, lived it to the fullest, savored it like good wine, and evaded it as skillfully as Arima's stallion evaded obstacles in its path. But now there was no evasion. Life had caught up to him. A wound tore his back, his friends were soon to perish, his slave girl was cast away, even his gold and smithing tools were forgotten in the rush to flee. All he had was Arima, who had risked her life to save him.

"The stream." He freed one hand and pointed in front of her. The girl understood and drove the horse harder. Behind them, the low thunder of the advancing nomads had resolved into the neighing of horses and shouting men. Soon they would be on the camp, and he didn't want to hear the sounds that would arise then.

The cover of the streamside forest beckoned them like friends. The stallion was gasping, and Arima leaned forward, speaking into the animal's ear. Melanion lay low against her back. Like a swooping hawk the three dove into the concealing shadows.

Was Arima's heart that hard, or had she just learned to control her emotions as part of her warrior's training? Melanion was no warrior; he was a good-natured soul whose heart tore with every scream and piteous cry that drifted over the grasslands to them. Arima walked the horse on, as stoic as any Spartan general, plodding by the tiny brook, pausing to rest the stallion, and plodding on again. Sela was Cimmerian, and a warrior, too, but Sela had still been very much a woman. But what of Arima? What had happened to her?

A low wavering scream snaked through the blue twilight, almost animal in its suffering, and Melanion shuddered. "Arima, we must stop," he gasped. "I need water, rest." Tears of pain and pity rimmed his eyes, and he clenched them shut. He had lain immobile for five days since his wounding by a barbarian, and all this riding seemed to have torn him open again.

"There is kumiss in the bag," the girl spoke low. "We cannot stop."

"Kumiss?" He loathed the thick, sour drink, but he supposed it was better than nothing. With any grace from the gods, it would get him drunk and he'd forget this horrible journey. Reaching an arm forward, he took the goatskin bag, opened it, and tried not to gag at the smell. Arima rode on, stony and silent.

They stopped when a cat's claw moon hung low in the sky and the stars were so abundant they seemed about to crush the bowl of heaven above them. Arima slid to the ground, scarcely winded by the long ride, and helped Melanion dismount. He could feel the linen bandages clinging to his back, sticky with new blood. Hobbling like a bent old man, he made his way to a carpet of thick mosses and lay down, curled gingerly on his side. Arima took the saddle pad and bags from her horse, rubbed the sweat from its heated body, and hobbled it to feed and drink. Carrying the saddlebag with her, she squatted by the Greek's side.

"Are you alright?" she asked gently, reaching out a dirty hand to his cheek. He turned his head and looked at her through the darkness, his vision bleary from pain and the kumiss. Her form stood out black against the starry sky, wavering when he blinked. "What do you warriors use for wounds?" he said with a grimace, pressing his cheek back to the cool moss. Arima pulled a pouch from inside her tunic and sat down.

"Let's get your shirt off and see how the wound is," she said, as kindly as any mother. Moving his arms weakly, Melanion helped her remove it and rolled onto his stomach. It was almost a relief when she pulled the crusted linen strips from his back and the fresh night air soothed the cut. With water from the stream she cleaned the wound and dabbed her warrior's ointment onto it. Melanion closed his eyes wearily, feeling the pain ebb and exhaustion take its place. Snuggling against the mosses, he slept.

Arima remained at his side, watching him till sunrise. She cradled her wounded arm while the fingers of her good hand gently stroked his shoulders, slid down across his waist and back again, over and over, till her starving soul could fill itself on the wonderful feel of his body. The image she had carried with her in her heart, the man that gave her life, slept on, his weary face turned toward her, peaceful in the dappled night.

What are you, Melanion? she mused. I thought you loved me, yet you show little joy at seeing me. I could have no one but you, yet I find you with a concubine and scarcely concerned if I was alive or dead. Your gold, your women and wine, but what of love, Melanion? What of devotion?

She ran her fingers lightly through the damp matted curls of his hair. It is caring that ennobles a soul and sets us above the beasts. Would you ever have sacrificed for me, as I have sacrificed for you? Was Sela right? Should I have forgotten you?

She rested her hand on his shoulder. The touch of his skin filled her like the warm glow of wine on a cold night. I could not have forgotten you, my love, she reflected. If I had, you would now be dead, your fine scalp dangling from some

320

Scoloti chief's belt. Perhaps Bartatua's; he would have paid well for it. In this, the calling of my heart was right. She lowered her cheek to the warmth of his shoulder and let it rest there, closing her eyes, savouring him, fighting away the question that rose demonlike in her mind. She did not wish to face it.

Melanion, do you even want a love like mine?

They followed the river to the thick black forests fringing the great Northern Sea. Then they headed north, to Melanion's home, the trading city of Olbia.

The six days of their journey were hard on the goldsmith. His strength barely grew, and his spirits flagged with each leg of the trip. But when they came closer to the city, with horsemen trotting past them and laden wagons from the far north, men of every shading and nationality, Melanion began to smile once more. He seemed to draw life from the bustling city, as a hawk does from the open air.

Arima's spirits, in turn, sank as his rose. She had never imagined so many types of people existed, people who multiplied and tangled like honeysuckle vines the closer they got to the city. Their presence forced out the trees, the wild creatures, the grasses and flowers underfoot. She had once seen a migration of frogs, unnatural, numberless, and faceless, and all the people surrounding her reminded her of that. There were dark men from the south, their eyes darting and keen; giant men from the north, as pale as Rhea had been, with hair as fine and white as a spider's threads and muscles that strained against armbands and wristlets; tall, fierce Kelts, their hair brushed back with lime, herding lines of bound, fur-clad slaves. Goods passed by such as the girl had never dreamed of. Wagonloads of furs, rich and dark, or piled with grain from the lands of the Scoloti. Salt and ores, boxes and chests, great clay jars and bound bales. Pack-horses of all sizes and the strange half-horses she'd seen in the Persian camp. The noise, too, grew till the beauty of her horse's hooves solid against the earth was lost in the din of shouts and babble, curses and cries. Arima's heart sank.

The busy wealth flowing into the city was only a precursor. The city itself was the nightmare. Arima fought terror when she first saw it, rounding a bend in the dusty road and coming upon it, past the thinning trees and down a gentle incline. Perched on a low shoreline, Olbia presented to her a vast wall of cut and trimmed tree trunks, and beyond it the tall tops of dwellings, covered not in felts but in greying slices of wood. Such houses were not meant to be moved about. No one living in them could travel, unless they left their goods behind. It was unnatural, an abomination against the world as Papaeus had made it.

"See the gate?" Melanion's voice had a note of joy in it. Arima looked down the rutted path sloping away in front of her. The masses of people, wagons, horses seemed to be directing themselves toward one opening in the great log wall, as neatly as fish being driven through the trap of a streamside weir. She nodded stiffly to Melanion.

"Go through it, and I will guide you to Praxis's house," he directed. What manner of place is this, she wondered uneasily, when one could not approach it and enter it from whatever direction one chose, as free as the wind? Instead, the people were herded in, like sheep in a pen.

Nearing the gate, the crowd compressed, and the grey stallion shied at the commotion, unused to the feel of men and horses and wagons so near. Arima, too, would shy if she could, but she patted the horse's neck reassuringly and spoke into its ear. The stallion calmed, but she could still feel its muscles tense against her legs, as the old mare's had been when wolves prowled nearby.

Four men who she took to be soldiers stood outside the gate, studying every face that entered or left the town. Like nearly everyone else they wore brown tunics and long, baggy Parthian trousers, but their heads sported helmets of gleaming bronze with high crests of dyed horsehair. Long red capes were thrown behind their shoulders. They held round painted shields nearly as tall as they were, with spears almost twice the length of Scyth spears at their sides. Arima tried to wet her dry lips when her turn came to enter the town. Urging the war-horse forward, she fell in behind an old wagon groaning under the weight of orange iron-ore and lumps of black tin and tried to keep her gaze to the front, to hide her fear. The soldiers barely glanced at her and she walked on, beneath a massive overhanging portal, and into the town of Olbia.

Arima rode blindly, like a child following its parents, turning this way and that to Melanion's voice in her ear; past long lines of parked wagons, past bronzesmiths and woodworkers, by shops piled high with furs and cloth and shops where the stench of old wine burned her nostrils. Men stumbled by them, arm in arm and obviously drunk, and Arima frowned in disgust. Drunk at midday, and not even a feast or funeral to excuse it. No Scoloti man would ever, she stopped herself and they continued on. It was no longer her concern what Scoloti men did. Long-legged pigs rooted in the swill thrown from windows and doors and scrawny dogs seemed to be everywhere yet belong to no one.

To her relief Melanion finally directed her to a quieter part of the town, and to a small wooden house squeezed between two others. It was two rooms high, and she could see a man's breeches draped over the upper window ledge, drying in the late summer sun.

"Praxis!" Melanion bellowed with surprising vigor from behind her. They waited in silence and in a few moments a man's face appeared in the upper window. He looked down at them, and a great smile split his face.

"Melanion, you son of the satyrs, what are you doing here?" he shouted to them. Melanion raised one arm and motioned tiredly. The man's face froze when he realized the goldsmith was wounded, and the head vanished back into the house. He soon emerged from the doorway and helped Melanion to the ground. "Stay here with your horse, or someone will steal it," he instructed Arima. "I will be back and show you a safe place to keep it." Arima nodded and slid from the stallion. Standing by its head, she held the bridle and watched the men enter the dwelling, peering beyond them in an effort to see what the interior of the place looked like. It was too dark to see much beyond a few plain-looking stools and bare, undecorated walls. Taking a deep breath of the dank city air, she rubbed the stallion's nose and waited.

Arima left her war-horse in a tiny fenced yard behind the row of houses and followed Melanion's friend through a narrow back door and into his home. She could scarcely believe it when she entered. The room was square, the log walls covered inside with dried mud. The earthen floor was bare except for a few mats of reeding. The only bit of color in the place was a painting along the front wall of figures dancing and playing musical instruments; she guessed the Greek had done it himself. Arima looked up. There was no smoke hole, no posts supporting the roof, only low heavy beams upon which the second level of the house rested. Shifting nervously on her feet, she looked around for Melanion.

His friend saw her bewildered expression and smiled kindly. "I am Praxis. And you are?"

Arima studied him solemnly. He seemed nice. His face was thin, but pleasant and open, and his pale grey eyes shone intelligence. His lanky body lacked muscle, though; he was obviously no warrior. "I am Arima. I am Melanion's woman," she added boldly, to make it clear to this man and all else in this odd city just what her status was. The Greek seemed to suppress a laugh and motioned her to a table of rough boards.

"You must be hungry," he said, pulling a round loaf of half-eaten bread from a shelf and taking warm beans from a small clay oven. "Eat and rest, and then we'll see about feeding Melanion. And tell me, if you will, what has happened to him." The man sat down hospitably across the table and poured them each a wooden cup of ale. Leaning forward, he folded his arms and waited to hear her tale.

Arima spent that night in the air, high above the ground on the second level of the house of Praxis. Like a bird in a tree, she thought, sleeping little and shifting uncomfortably on the hard cot the Greek had given her. She longed for her spacious bed and a soft pile of deer-hair pillows, or the embrace of a bed of sweet dried grass on the open steppes. Even a simple horse pad of felt. On the narrow cot she feared she would fall off every time she turned over. When she lay still on her back, rather than sleep she listened to the unfamiliar night sounds; the troubled, weary sleep of Melanion, on the other side of the room; the never-ending babble of the city, worse than the pointless gaggling of geese; the disturbed snorts and shufflings of her great grey stallion, penned below the tiny back window. The breeze wafted through timidly, from one window to the other, seeking its freedom. No starlight shone upon her, nor moonlight. Above her all she could see was the black, empty ceiling of the house of Praxis. Closing her eyes, she tried to force herself to sleep. Finally, peace came, and she slept.

The evening air was full and buoyant, and Arima too felt expansive, galloping as she had so often done through the scattered trees above the seaport. She would stay out longer, through the abrupt blue twilight and into the night, except that Praxis had warned her of the dangers. Only ride in daylight, he had said, and never go far. She recalled the fate of Sela, too, when the townsmen, rough and dirty, eyed her as she rode through the city. Her weapons and man-clothes seemed to unnerve them, though. Other than shouted comments, no one had bothered her.

How she wished she could stay out, away from Olbia! The sun was slipping behind the dark western treeline, and Arima paused above the city, looking at the lights beginning to twinkle in the dusk. One last long draught of clean air, sitting upright to fill her lungs, and she reluctantly walked the stallion down the sloping roadway.

Soon, she knew, Melanion would rouse from his pained slumber. Then they would be together. That was all she lived for, in this alien, fetid town. To hear his voice, clasp his hand, gaze into his loving eyes. To stroll with him through the forest and make love again by a star-shrouded stream. He had slept for two days, rousing only for food and wine and one visit by the town's Greek physician. After the examination, Melanion, Praxis, and the doctor had conversed seriously in their tongue, and Arima had not understood a word. The physician had treated her arm, said not a word to her, and left.

On this evening when she entered the back door of the house of Praxis she heard laughter coming from the upper window, and the thin song of a flute. Curiosity flaring, she trotted across the dark lower room. Praxis was not at his workplace as he usually was, shaping and polishing his gemstones. Arima bounded up the narrow wooden stairway by the wall and stopped abruptly.

Melanion was awake and sitting up on his cot. Praxis lounged by the window, ale cup in hand. A large man with red hair and two buxom young women perched around the room, at the foot of Melanion's bed, on her own cot. A third woman danced in the center of the floor while one of the girls played a tiny double flute. They laughed loudly every time the dancer missed a step. Melanion looked across the room, spied Arima at the stairs, and motioned her forward.

"Come, meet Arima!" he said in her tongue, so she would

326

understand. "I'm afraid they only understand Greek, Arima, so I'll have to translate for you." His face, newly shaven, was still thin but his eyes were bright and happy. He spoke to his visitors, and they grew silent, turning to study the new arrival. Arima felt like a slave being examined for purchase.

"Who are they?" she blurted to Melanion. For days she had patiently waited for him to rouse, to speak to her, to kiss her. He had always been too ill. Now, feeling better, he awakens to this.

"Ars," he motioned to the burly man, "is a guard and the three ladies are, ah . . . friends." He nodded toward the dark-haired young woman sitting at the foot of his bed, and she flirted back openly. Arima's fists clenched. Such a one as these were not called ladies in Scoloti lands.

"Have some ale." The goldsmith extended his cup toward Arima. "You saved my life; I owe you a great debt. Come, meet my friends."

"It is not old debts I came for," she muttered, backing toward the steps and shaking her head numbly. "I have to . . . feed my horse."

The giant man must have known a few words of her tongue. "Horse!" he bellowed and broke into loud laughter. Her face burning, Arima turned and ran down the steps.

She had no comb or brushes for the stallion, so she fashioned a curry from a handful of twisted and bent grasses. Frantically she groomed the horse, fighting tears and trying not to hear the merriment above her. Over the broad grey flanks, up the stallion's side, down and down and up again, brushing till his coat gleamed and her arms ached with weariness.

"Arima," a voice called gently.

She brushed harder, reaching the stallion's shoulder, not wishing to see Praxis or anyone else.

"Melanion means you no harm." The gem cutter stepped to her side and watched her deft hands at work, as skilled in her way as he was in his. "It is just his way. I know he thinks very highly of you, but he, well . . ."

Arima paused, resting her hands against the horse's neck. "He doesn't love me, does he?" she whispered. Praxis shifted his feet in the straw.

"I think he does, Arima, as much as he is able to love anyone. You couldn't ask for a better friend than Melanion; he would give you his last drachma. But to settle down with one woman is just not his way."

Tears rose unbidden to the girl's eyes at the harsh sting of truth she knew was in his words, a truth she had long known but had refused to see. "Then why doesn't he tell me?" she choked. "Why doesn't he tell me himself?"

"He runs from truth, Arima. He has all his life. It endears him to others, but it is also his downfall, again and again. The truth that he was without a roof over his head after he bought the Cimmerian girl's freedom. The truth that it was a dangerous idea to run off after two Persian noblemen into unknown lands in early winter. The truth that he was leading your heart astray, and one day he would have to face up to it. Those women up there, Arima, he never has to worry about what their hearts are doing, for they have none. And the final truth, that he is mortal and will grow old and die. As long as he has a few obols with which to buy ale and a woman, he thinks he will never have to face that, either. His life is one long adventure of avoiding the truth."

"But, Praxis, I would love him even if he was poor and old and riddled with infirmities. That is one beauty of love. Why can't he see that, and believe it? I have given up everything for him. Does someone do so for a whim, a passing fancy?"

The Greek took a deep breath and patted the stallion's neck absently. "He knows that, Arima. I truly believe he does. But he is afraid of you."

Arima lifted her head and turned her red-rimmed eyes to his. "Afraid?" she whispered.

Praxis nodded. "Is a wild horse afraid of another horse? A

sparrow? A hare? Of course not, for such things are no threat to it. He is afraid of what he has a reason to fear; he is afraid of something which is able to capture him and end his freedom."

Arima looked down at the potter's straw she had cast about the yard. Suddenly she understood. Melanion's coldness to her was not because of a lack of feeling—it was because of an abundance of it. Praxis put a comforting hand on her shoulder.

"There is nothing you can do, Arima. He is one stallion you can never tame. The harder you try, the faster he will run. The gods can crumble mountains, but they cannot change one single human heart." He squeezed her shoulder lightly and left her.

Truth is a wicked thing. No wonder Melanion feared it and spent his life avoiding it. This truth of Arima's had pierced her heart, demolished her dreams, and now the knife turned yet again at a burst of feminine laughter from above. Burying her face in the sleek grey coat of the war-horse, Arima cried.

She crept upstairs in the darkness of night, after the visitors had gone and Praxis slept. She would tell Melanion of her feelings, inform him of all she had gone through because of him, demand at least the courtesy of some answers. Stars glittered like jeweled wall hangings through the windows at each end of the upper room, and she could hear the rhythm of Melanion's breathing while he slept. Arima slipped across the rough wood floor and stood by his cot, staring down at his shadowed face. He slept deeply, wearily, surrounded by an aura of ale as if it were a shield that would keep out the ills of the world. Kneeling by the bed, she studied his features and knew that to awaken him, to talk with him, would be futile.

"I would have loved you," she whispered to his sleeping face. "Wherever you went, I'd have gone. All your adventures and your pains, your successes and your failures I would have shared. When the young women shunned you because age had taken its toll, I would still have cherished the merest touch of your hand. When all laughed because you were poor, I would have given my last crust to you. You would always be beautiful in my eyes."

His image swam, and she blinked back the tears, shaking her head numbly.

"Perhaps we are too alike," she went on. "Perhaps, like two hawks on one tether, we both love our freedom so much we would have pounded each other to death in our desperation to escape. But know this, my dear one. My heart is like a vessel which had been filled, but with chunks of ice; cold and jagged, they left many empty spaces. But the fire of my love has melted them so that now my heart is so full of love, clear and pure, it has no empty place for anyone else."

She gently pressed her lips to his sagging cheek. *If only you could take me in your arms one last time, kiss me and hold me and love me.*

The stallion snorted below the window, and Arima closed her eyes tightly. *One last smell of your body, one last touch of your skin, you, who are my heart, my love, and my life.*

She rose. The horse was saddled, fitted and ready. A new adventure awaited, in the land of the Argippaei. The great war-horse did not belong in this city, nor did she. It was Melanion's world.

"Good-bye . . ." she whispered, touching his hand, and silently crept away.

The guard above the gate heard the massive joints below him creak, and the heavy thud of horse hooves echoing through the pristine night. Curious, he looked down. One lone horseman walked out on the road and stopped, hung his head, and listened to the gate groan shut behind him. With the final solid boom that sealed the town away, the rider suddenly put heels to the horse, and the splendid beast broke into a run up the center of the path. The guard watched them ascend the hill, ghostlike in the darkness, to where the roadway split. Unerring, the rider turned to the right, the northlands, and rode along the clifftops of the sea. The hoofbeats echoed long after the horse and rider had disappeared, as regular as a heartbeat on the sweet summer night, as free and unfettered as the wind.

> After despair comes wisdom,
> Through the awful grace of god.
> —*Aeschylus*

AFTERWORD

DARIUS THE GREAT OF PERSIA ASCENDED THE THRONE IN
522 B.C. at the age of twenty-eight. After quelling revolts
throughout the Persian Empire and restoring stability to the
throne, he began a plan of conquest, expanding first into
India. In 514 B.C., en route to an invasion of Greece, Darius
crossed the Danube River on a bridge of pontoon boats and
invaded Scythia, in the modern Ukraine area between the
Don and Danube Rivers. Not only were the Scyth wealthy,
they provided much of the grain and shipbuilding timber
used by his Greek adversaries. He assumed it would be an
easy conquest, but the Scyth engaged in guerilla warfare. He
chased them futilely over the steppes for two months.
Finally, with his army starving and dispirited, Darius
withdrew, leaving behind his wounded to occupy the nomads while he made good his escape. The king returned to
Persia, but his troops went on to conquer Thrace and
Macedonia. A few years later, the Persians on land and sea

were defeated by the Athenian Greeks at the Battle of Marathon, ending the myth of Persian invincibility. After ruling for thirty-six years, Darius died at age sixty-four, and within forty years of his death the vast Persian Empire was crumbling.

Scyth power lasted a bit longer. After the collapse of Persia the still-vigorous nomads spread to Macedonia, and by the time of Alexander the Great, in 336 B.C., they had set up outposts in the Balkans. But by then they were being conquered by a more insidious foe than weaponry; the civilizing and sedentary allures of Greek culture, the foreigners they had once so despised. Within one hundred years of Arima's story, the Scyth were being pushed from the steppes by more vigorous nomads. In another two hundred years, the Scyth were no more.

GLOSSARY

1. Agathyrsi—a tribe of the steppes of Russia, said to hold all their wives in common
2. Androphagi—cannibalistic tribe of the steppes
3. Api—Scythian earth goddess
4. Argimpasa—Scythian goddess of love
5. Argippaei—a race of bald men who lived at the edge of the steppes, shunned warfare, and were able to give asylum to refugees
6. Ariantes—Cimmerian horseman
7. Arima—Scyth girl, 16–17 years old, daughter of the Auchatae chief Scylas
8. Arpoaxis—one of three sons of Targitaus, the divine founder of the Scyth; he was the ancestor of the Catiari and Traspian Scyth tribes
9. Ars—northern guard at the brothel in Olbia
10. Artapas—a Persian nobleman, "Table Companion" of King Darius, who spied on the Scythians

11. Auchatae—one of four Scyth tribes, they were descended from the divine son Lipoaxis

12. Bartatua—chief warrior of Scylas, he was to wed Arima; age about 27

13. Borysthenes—the Dnieper River in Russia

14. Budini—a red-haired, blue-eyed tribe living in forested lands near the steppes; allies of the Scyth, their wooden city was burned by Darius in 514 B.C.

15. Catiari—one of the four Scyth tribes, descended from divine son Arpoaxis

16. Catoris—chief enaree of Auchatae chief Scylas

17. Cimmerians—a tribe of the southern steppes, they were powerful 200 years earlier but by the time of the story, following wars with the Scyth, only a remnant remained

18. Colaxis—youngest son of the divine founder of the Scyth, he sired the Royal Scyth, the Paralatae

19. Creusa—King of the Cimmerians, father of Sela, uncle of Arima

20. Darius, King—King of the Persian Empire, 522 to 486 B.C., at the time of the invasion of Scythia, 514 B.C., he was about 37 years old

21. Drachma—common coin of the time, they could be of various metals and in various denominations; one drachma, double drachma, or a four-drachma piece; pay for a Greek foot soldier was 25 drachmas a month

22. Enaree—"half-men," the holy men or shamans of the Scyth, evidently homosexual

23. Geloni—kin of the Budini, they allied with the Scyth to drive out the Persians

24. Idanthyrsus—King of the Royal Scyth, chief king of all the Scyth tribes, he led the resistance to the Persian invasion

25. Ister—the Danube River

26. Lipoaxis—son of the divine founder of Scythia, he was the ancestor of the Auchatae Scyth

27. Lipos—second enaree of Scylas, an ally of Arima, age about 30

28. Medes—people of northern Persia, their empire was conquered by Persia
29. Medusa—old-woman brothel-keeper in Olbia
30. Megaphernes—Persian nobleman and "Table Companion" of King Darius, he spied on the Scyth and died in the Persian retreat; age midtwenties
31. Melanchlaeni—steppe tribe said to wear black cloaks; otherwise similar to the Scyth
32. Melanion—Greek goldsmith in Olbia, Arima's lover, age about 24
33. Neuri—steppe tribe similar to the Scyth
34. Northern Sea—the Black Sea
35. Obol—small coin denomination, six obol made a drachma
36. Oetosyrus—Scyth sun god
37. Olbia—Ionian Greek trading colony located where the Dnieper River empties into the Black Sea, in present day Ukraine
38. Opoea—wife of Scylas, mother of Arima
39. Oricus—friend of Bartatua, warrior of Scylas
40. Ox, wild—giant breed of European wild ox later called auroch, they became extinct about 300 years ago
41. Papaeus—Scyth supreme or father god
42. Paralatae—the Royal Scyth, chief Scythian tribe, their king ruled all the Scythians; descended from Colaxis, youngest son of the divine founder of the Scyth
43. Parthians—tribe of skilled horsemen who lived southeast of the Caspian Sea; allies of Persia
44. Praxis—Greek gem cutter in Olbia, friend of Melanion
45. Rhea—northern slave girl, concubine of Scylas
46. Sauromatians—steppe tribe north of the Caspian Sea, allies of the Scyth against the Persians
47. Scoloti—name the Scythians used for themselves
48. Scopasis—commander under Idanthyrsus, he led a second army against the Persians
49. Scylas—chief of the Auchatae Scyth, father of Arima
50. Scythians—Greek name for the fierce nomadic horse-

men who lived on the steppes of Russia, in the present Ukraine area, about 600–400 B.C.; King Darius of Persia attempted to conquer them in 514 B.C.

51. Sela—daughter of Cimmerian king Creusa, cousin of Arima; age about twenty

52. Steppe antelope—small antelope of central Asia, today called saiga

53. Tabiti—Scyth goddess of the hearth; also the first wife of Bartatua

54. Tanais—the Don River in Central Russia

55. Targitaus—divine founder of the Scyth, his three sons began the four Scyth tribes

56. Tauri—"gloomy" tribe who lived near the sea and worshipped a sea goddess

57. Thrace—land north of Greece and below Scythia

58. Traspians—one of four Scyth tribes, descended from divine son Arpoaxis

59. Urgimas—Mede slave woman of Arima, age about fifty

60. Yurt—a circular, dome-roofed tent dwelling of central Asian steppe dwellers, from the Scyth of the Ukraine to present day Mongolia; a wicker framework was thickly covered inside and out with heavy felts, carpets, wall hangings, etc. and floored with wool rugs; a yurt could be completely erected in about two hours